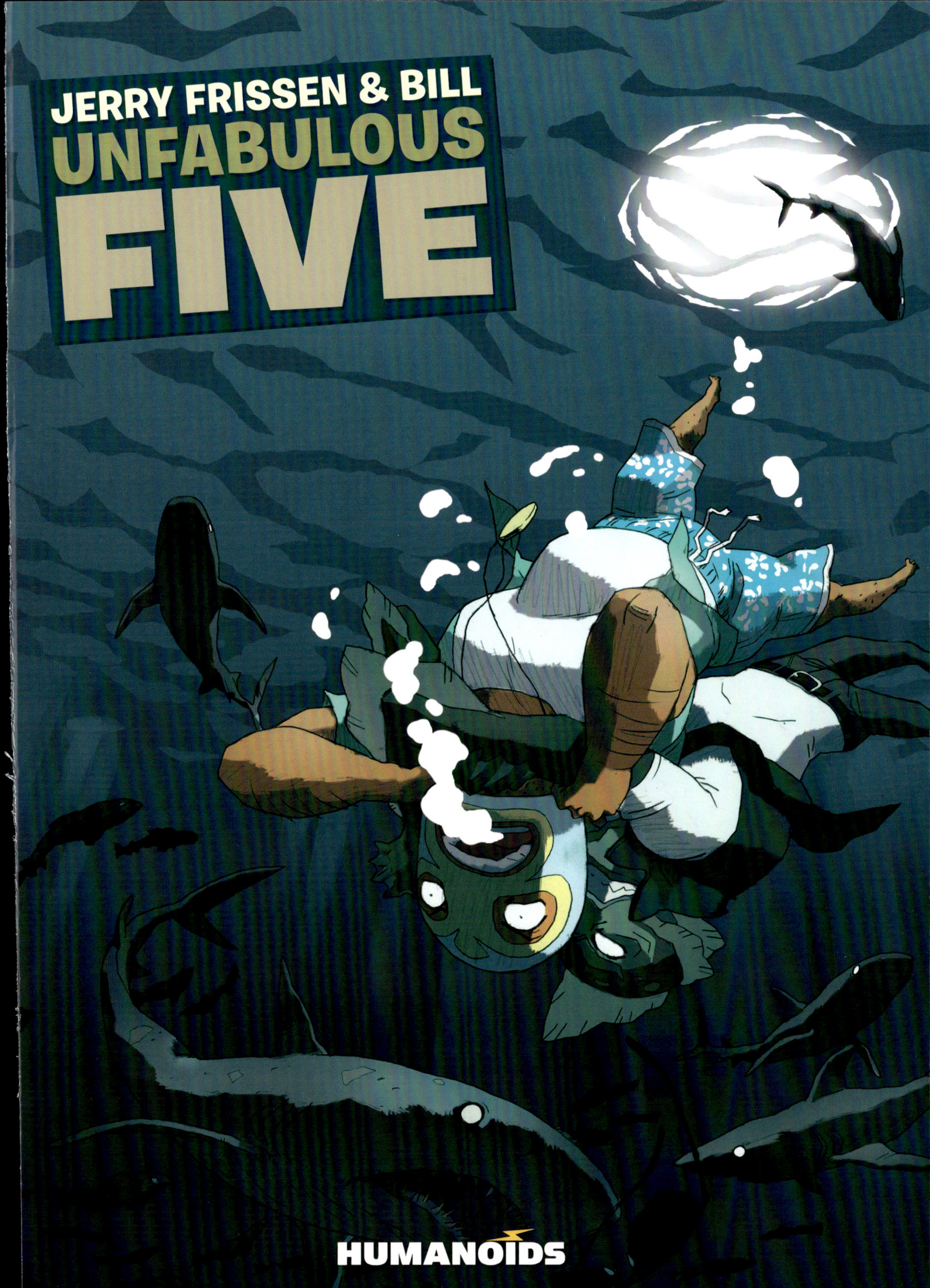
JERRY FRISSEN & BILL
UNFABULOUS
FIVE
HUMANOIDS

JERRY FRISSEN
Writer

BILL
Artist

BILL & LUCIE FIROUD
Colorists

HICHAM BENKIRANE
and **NATACHA RUCK**
& **KEN GROBE**
Translators

ALEX DONOGHUE
U.S. Edition Editor

JERRY FRISSEN
Book Designer

Fabrice Giger, Publisher

Rights & Licensing - licensing@humanoids.com
Press and Social Media - pr@humanoids.com

UNFABULOUS FIVE
THIS TITLE IS A PUBLICATION OF HUMANOIDS, INC. 8033 SUNSET BLVD. #628, LOS ANGELES, CA 90046.
COPYRIGHT © 2014 HUMANOIDS, INC., LOS ANGELES (USA). ALL RIGHTS RESERVED.
HUMANOIDS AND ITS LOGOS ARE ® AND © 2014 HUMANOIDS, INC.

CHAPTER ONE

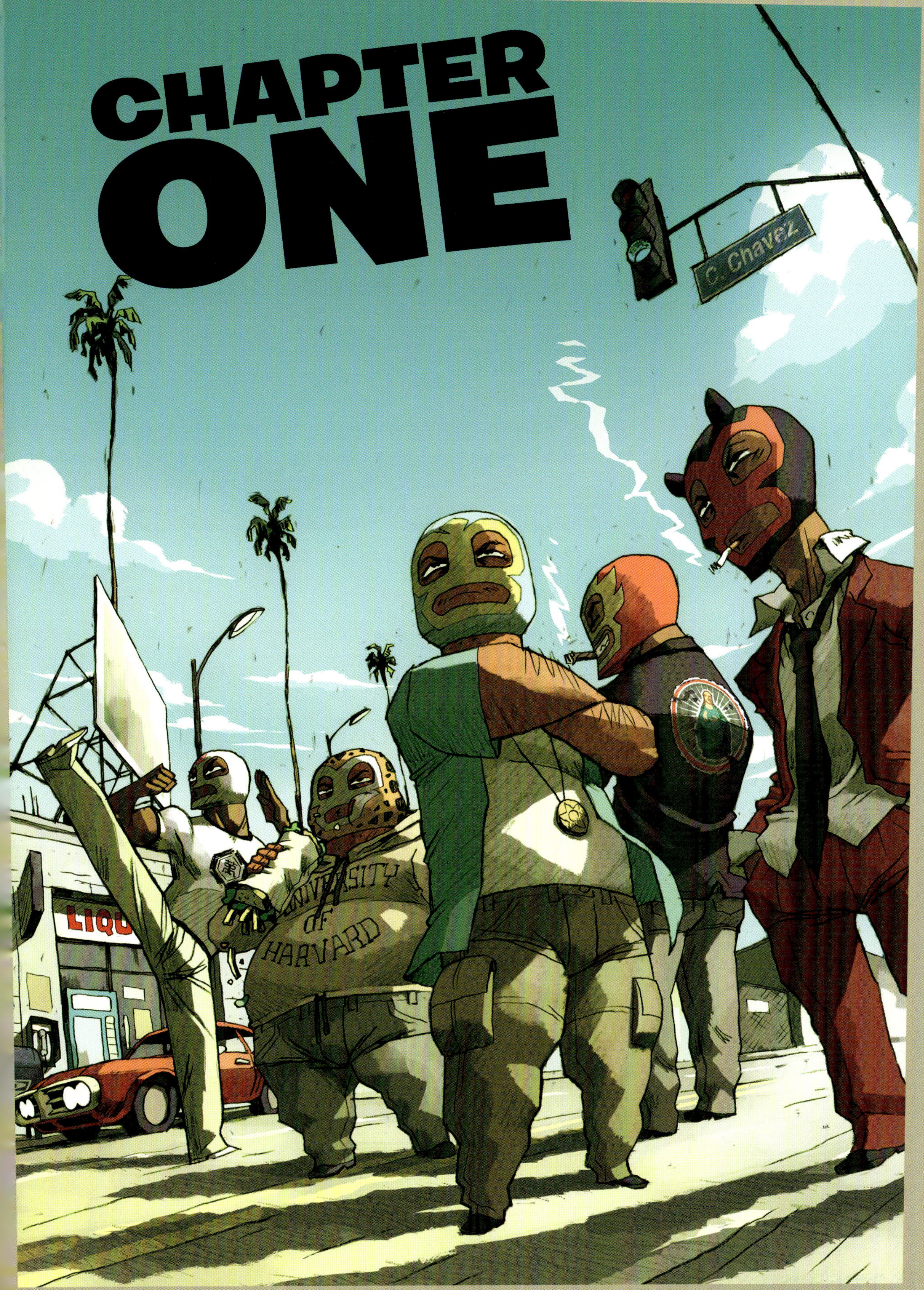
C. Chavez
UNIVERSITY OF HARVARD

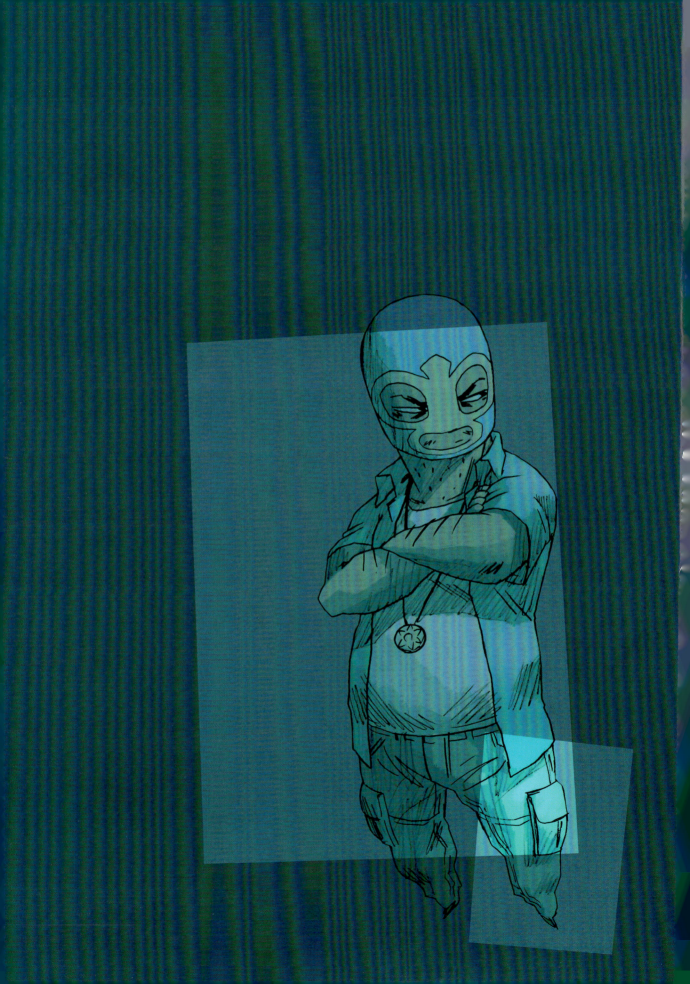

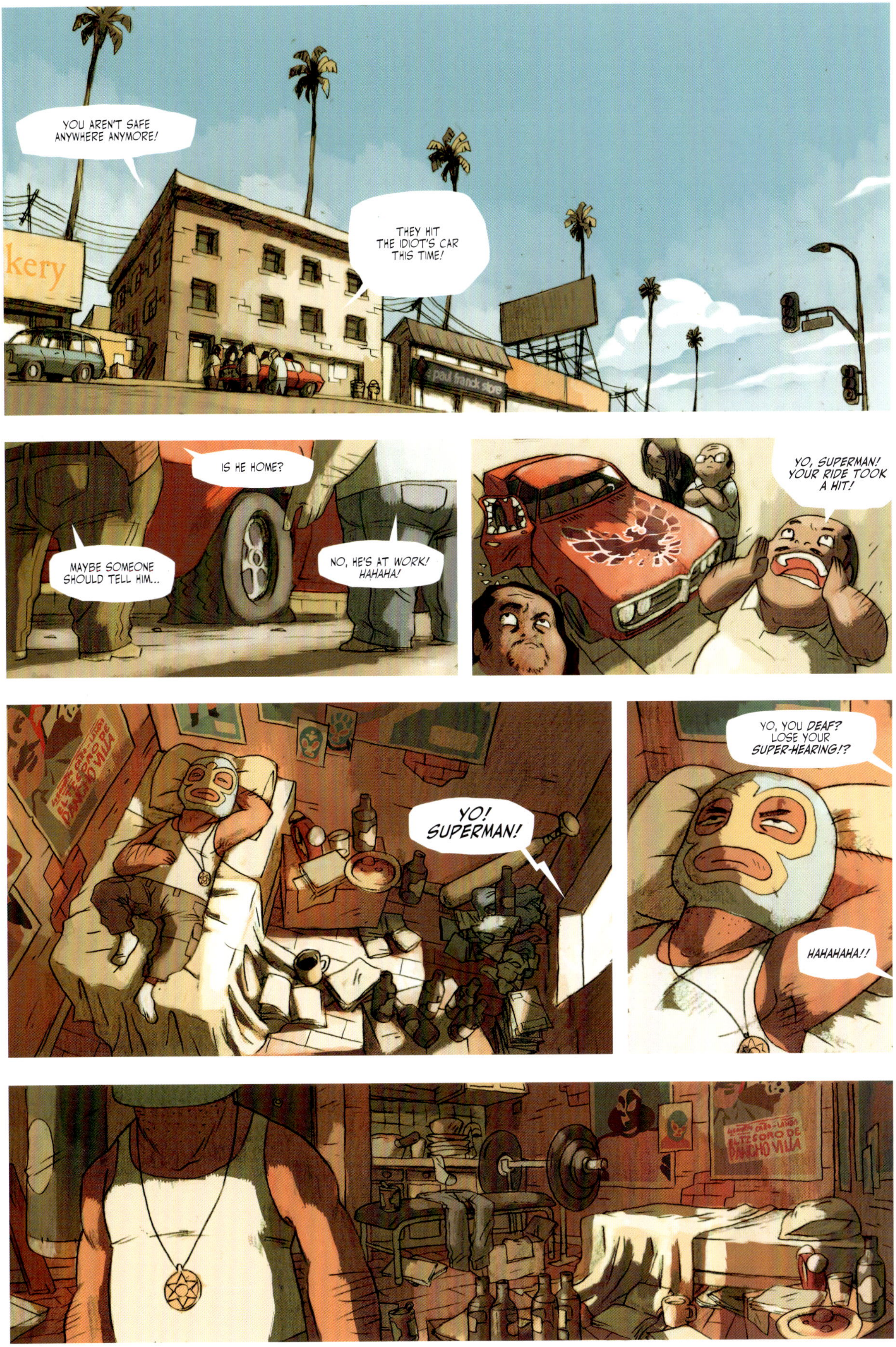
kery
YOU AREN'T SAFE ANYWHERE ANYMORE!
THEY HIT THE IDIOT'S CAR THIS TIME!
paul franck store
IS HE HOME?
MAYBE SOMEONE SHOULD TELL HIM...
NO, HE'S AT WORK! HAHAHA!
YO, SUPERMAN! YOUR RIDE TOOK A HIT!
YO! SUPERMAN!
YO, YOU DEAF? LOSE YOUR SUPER-HEARING!?
HAHAHAHA!!

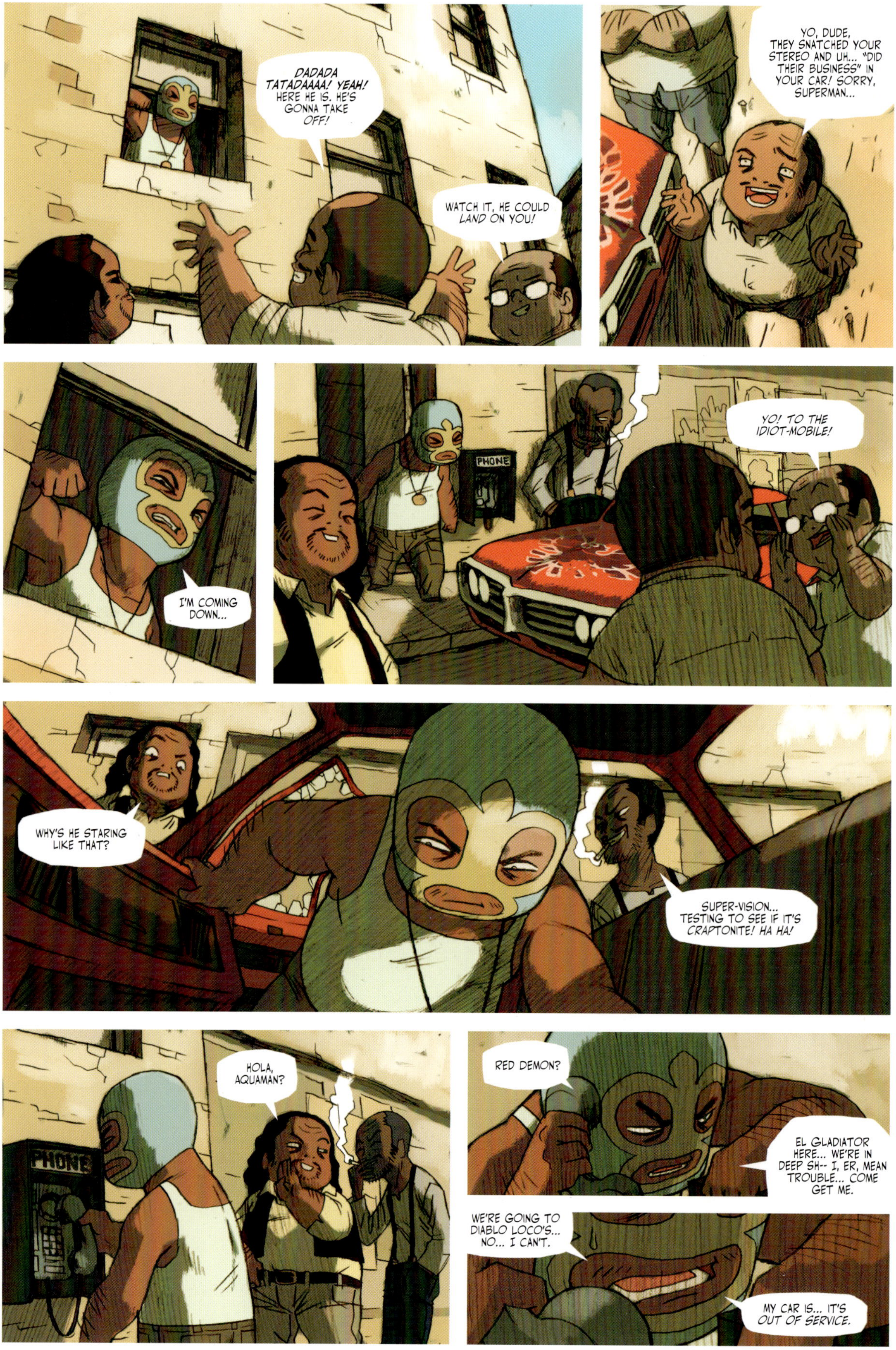
DADADA TATADAAAA! YEAH! HERE HE IS. HE'S GONNA TAKE OFF!
WATCH IT, HE COULD LAND ON YOU!
YO, DUDE, THEY SNATCHED YOUR STEREO AND UH... "DID THEIR BUSINESS" IN YOUR CAR! SORRY, SUPERMAN...
I'M COMING DOWN...
YO! TO THE IDIOT-MOBILE!
PHONE
WHY'S HE STARING LIKE THAT?
SUPER-VISION... TESTING TO SEE IF IT'S CRAPTONITE! HA HA!
HOLA, AQUAMAN?
PHONE
RED DEMON?
EL GLADIATOR HERE... WE'RE IN DEEP SH-- I, ER, MEAN TROUBLE... COME GET ME.
WE'RE GOING TO DIABLO LOCO'S... NO... I CAN'T.
MY CAR IS... IT'S OUT OF SERVICE.

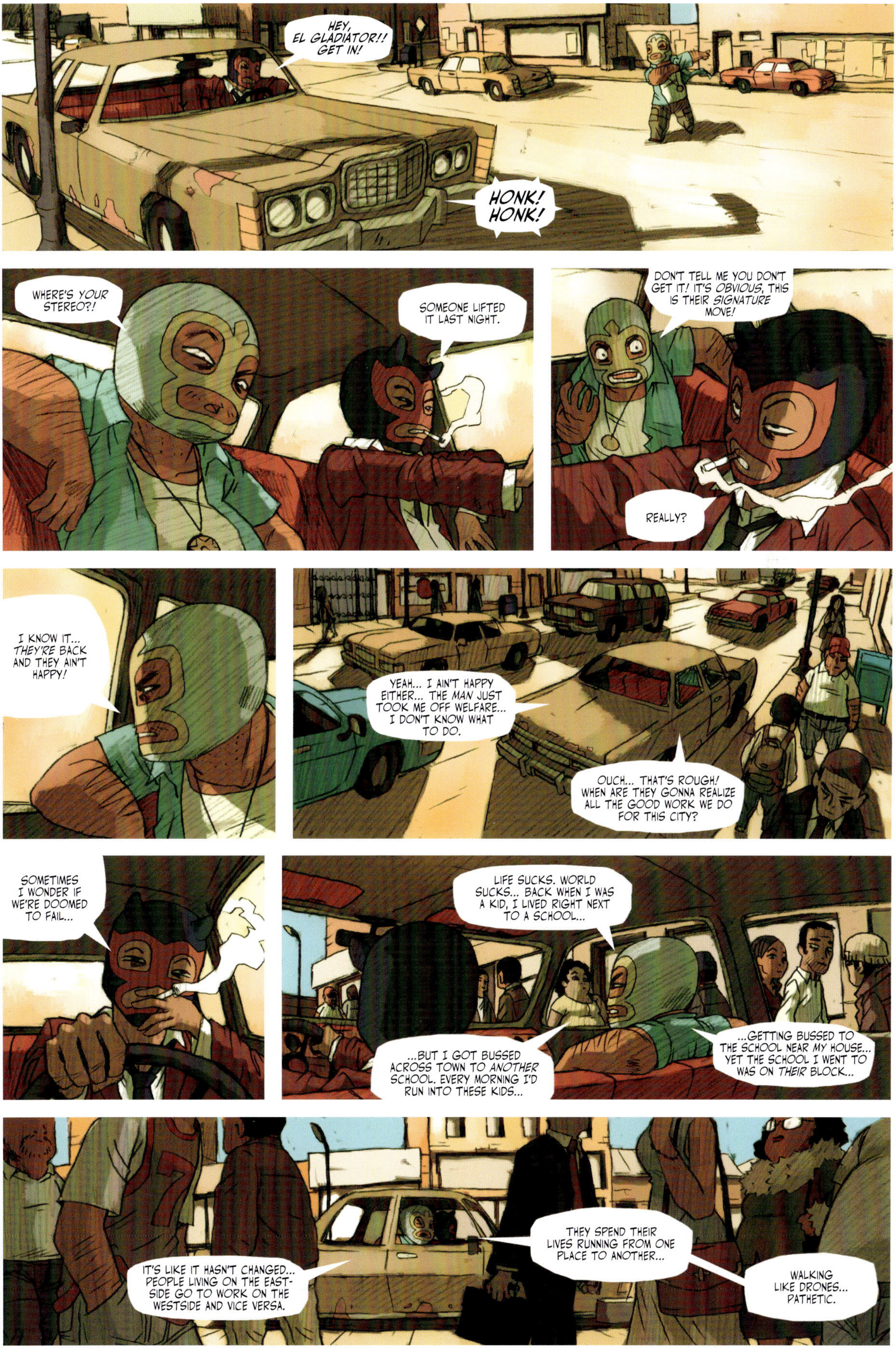
HEY, EL GLADIATOR!! GET IN!
HONK! HONK!
WHERE'S YOUR STEREO?!
SOMEONE LIFTED IT LAST NIGHT.
DON'T TELL ME YOU DON'T GET IT! IT'S OBVIOUS, THIS IS THEIR SIGNATURE MOVE!
REALLY?
I KNOW IT... THEY'RE BACK AND THEY AIN'T HAPPY!
YEAH... I AIN'T HAPPY EITHER... THE MAN JUST TOOK ME OFF WELFARE... I DON'T KNOW WHAT TO DO.
OUCH... THAT'S ROUGH! WHEN ARE THEY GONNA REALIZE ALL THE GOOD WORK WE DO FOR THIS CITY?
SOMETIMES I WONDER IF WE'RE DOOMED TO FAIL...
LIFE SUCKS. WORLD SUCKS... BACK WHEN I WAS A KID, I LIVED RIGHT NEXT TO A SCHOOL...
...BUT I GOT BUSSED ACROSS TOWN TO ANOTHER SCHOOL. EVERY MORNING I'D RUN INTO THESE KIDS...
...GETTING BUSSED TO THE SCHOOL NEAR MY HOUSE... YET THE SCHOOL I WENT TO WAS ON THEIR BLOCK...
IT'S LIKE IT HASN'T CHANGED... PEOPLE LIVING ON THE EAST-SIDE GO TO WORK ON THE WESTSIDE AND VICE VERSA.
THEY SPEND THEIR LIVES RUNNING FROM ONE PLACE TO ANOTHER...
WALKING LIKE DRONES... PATHETIC.

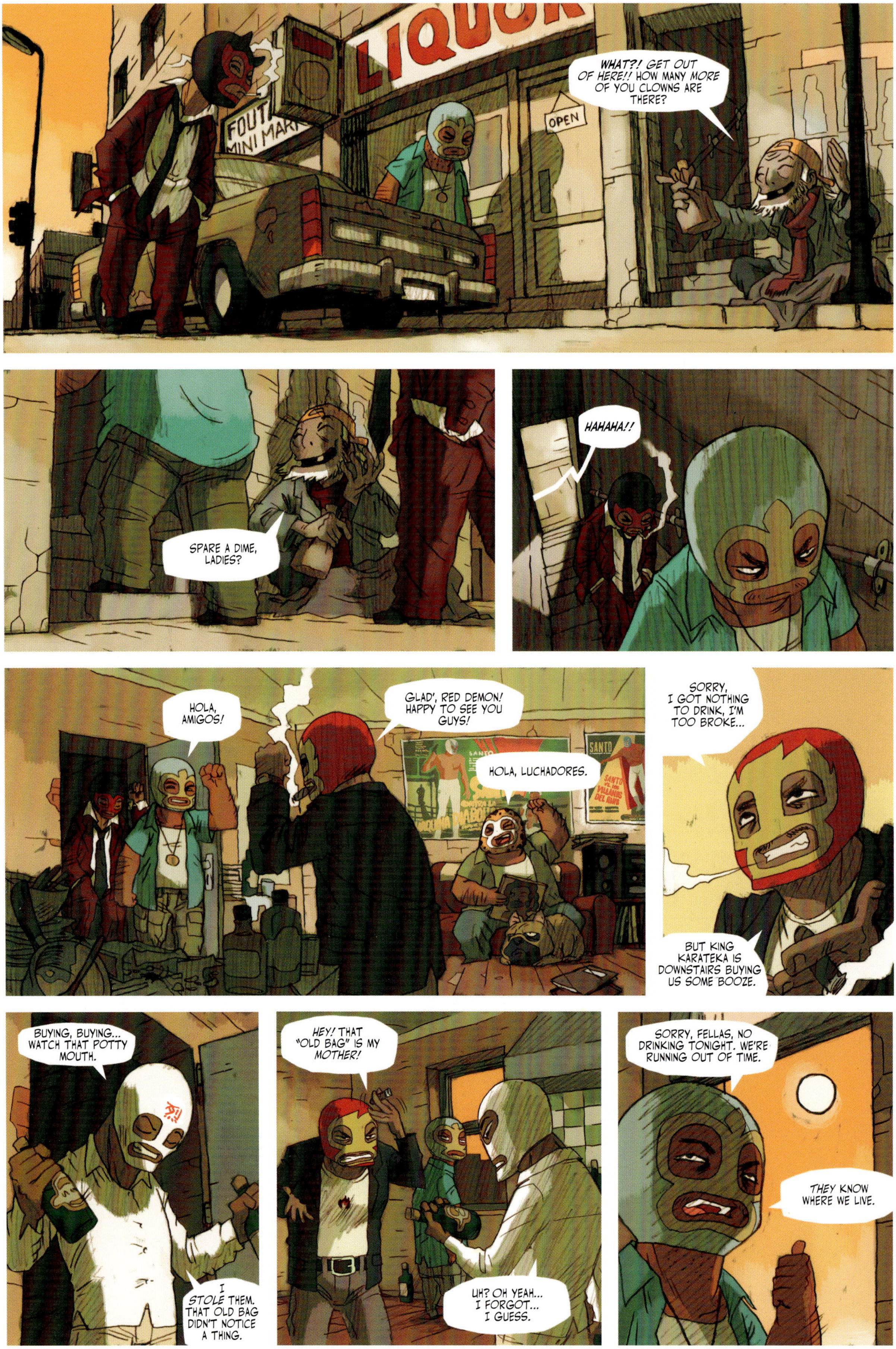

LIQUOR
FOUT MINI MART
OPEN
WHAT?! GET OUT OF HERE!! HOW MANY MORE OF YOU CLOWNS ARE THERE?
SPARE A DIME, LADIES?
HAHAHA!!
HOLA, AMIGOS!
GLAD', RED DEMON! HAPPY TO SEE YOU GUYS!
HOLA, LUCHADORES.
SANTO
SORRY, I GOT NOTHING TO DRINK, I'M TOO BROKE...
BUT KING KARATEKA IS DOWNSTAIRS BUYING US SOME BOOZE.
BUYING, BUYING... WATCH THAT POTTY MOUTH.
I STOLE THEM. THAT OLD BAG DIDN'T NOTICE A THING.
HEY! THAT "OLD BAG" IS MY MOTHER!
UH? OH YEAH... I FORGOT... I GUESS.
SORRY, FELLAS, NO DRINKING TONIGHT. WE'RE RUNNING OUT OF TIME.
THEY KNOW WHERE WE LIVE.

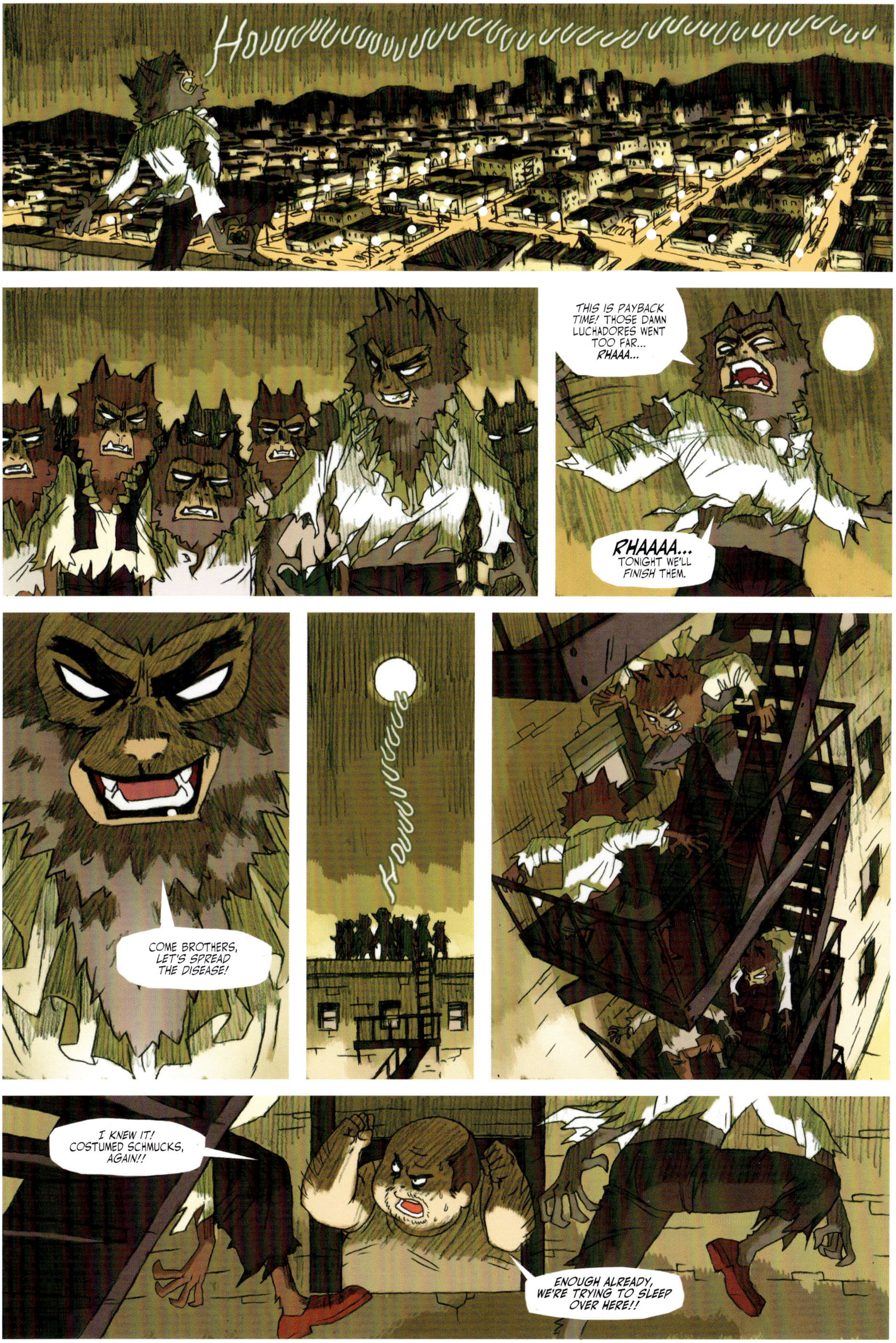
THIS IS PAYBACK TIME! THOSE DAMN LUCHADORES WENT TOO FAR... RHAAA...
RHAAAA... TONIGHT WE'LL FINISH THEM.
COME BROTHERS, LET'S SPREAD THE DISEASE!
I KNEW IT! COSTUMED SCHMUCKS, AGAIN!!
ENOUGH ALREADY, WE'RE TRYING TO SLEEP OVER HERE!!

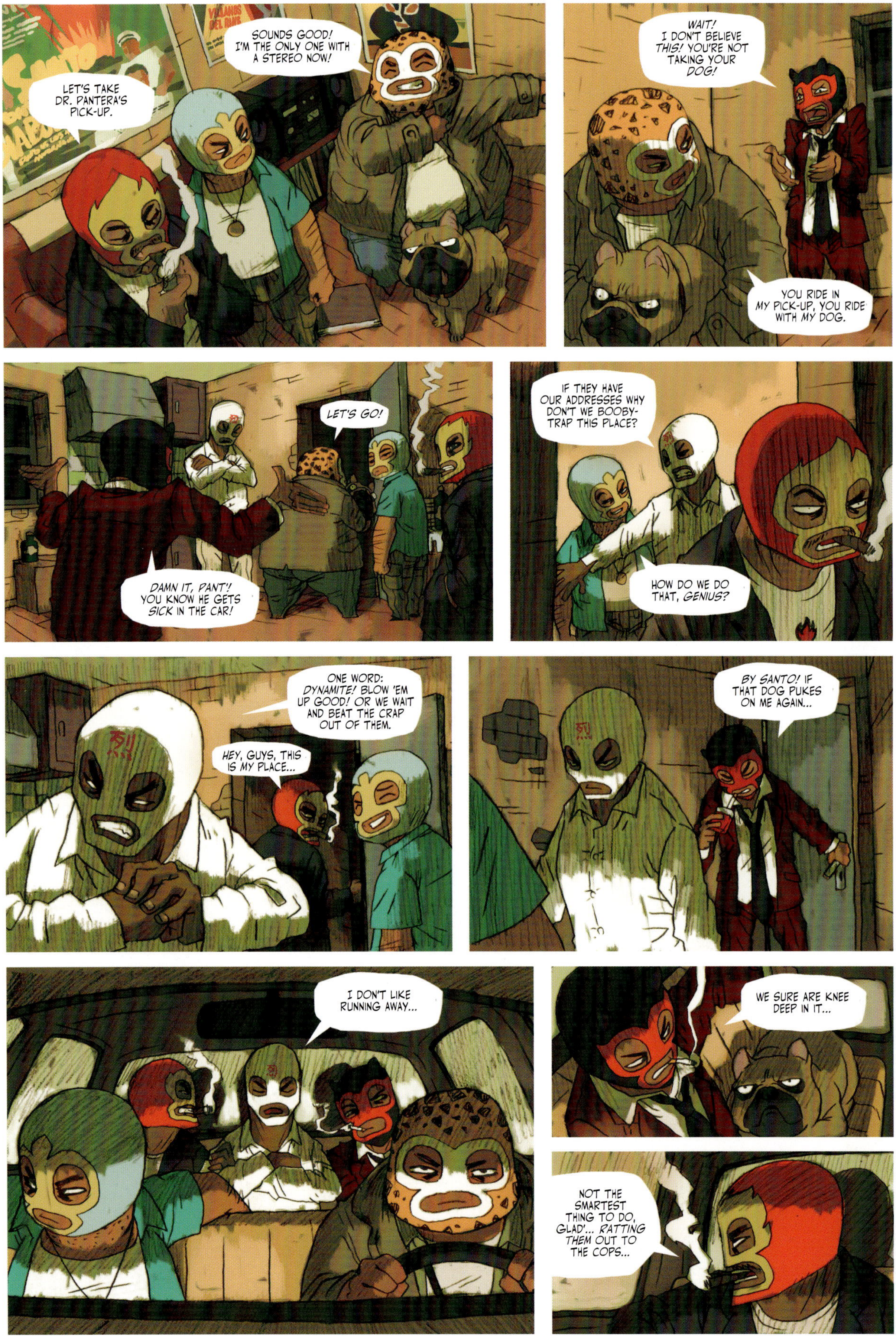
LET'S TAKE DR. PANTERA'S PICK-UP.
SOUNDS GOOD! I'M THE ONLY ONE WITH A STEREO NOW!
WAIT! I DON'T BELIEVE THIS! YOU'RE NOT TAKING YOUR DOG!
YOU RIDE IN MY PICK-UP, YOU RIDE WITH MY DOG.
LET'S GO!
DAMN IT, PANT'! YOU KNOW HE GETS SICK IN THE CAR!
IF THEY HAVE OUR ADDRESSES WHY DON'T WE BOOBY-TRAP THIS PLACE?
HOW DO WE DO THAT, GENIUS?
ONE WORD: DYNAMITE! BLOW 'EM UP GOOD! OR WE WAIT AND BEAT THE CRAP OUT OF THEM.
HEY, GUYS, THIS IS MY PLACE...
BY SANTO! IF THAT DOG PUKES ON ME AGAIN...
I DON'T LIKE RUNNING AWAY...
WE SURE ARE KNEE DEEP IN IT...
NOT THE SMARTEST THING TO DO, GLAD'... RATTING THEM OUT TO THE COPS...

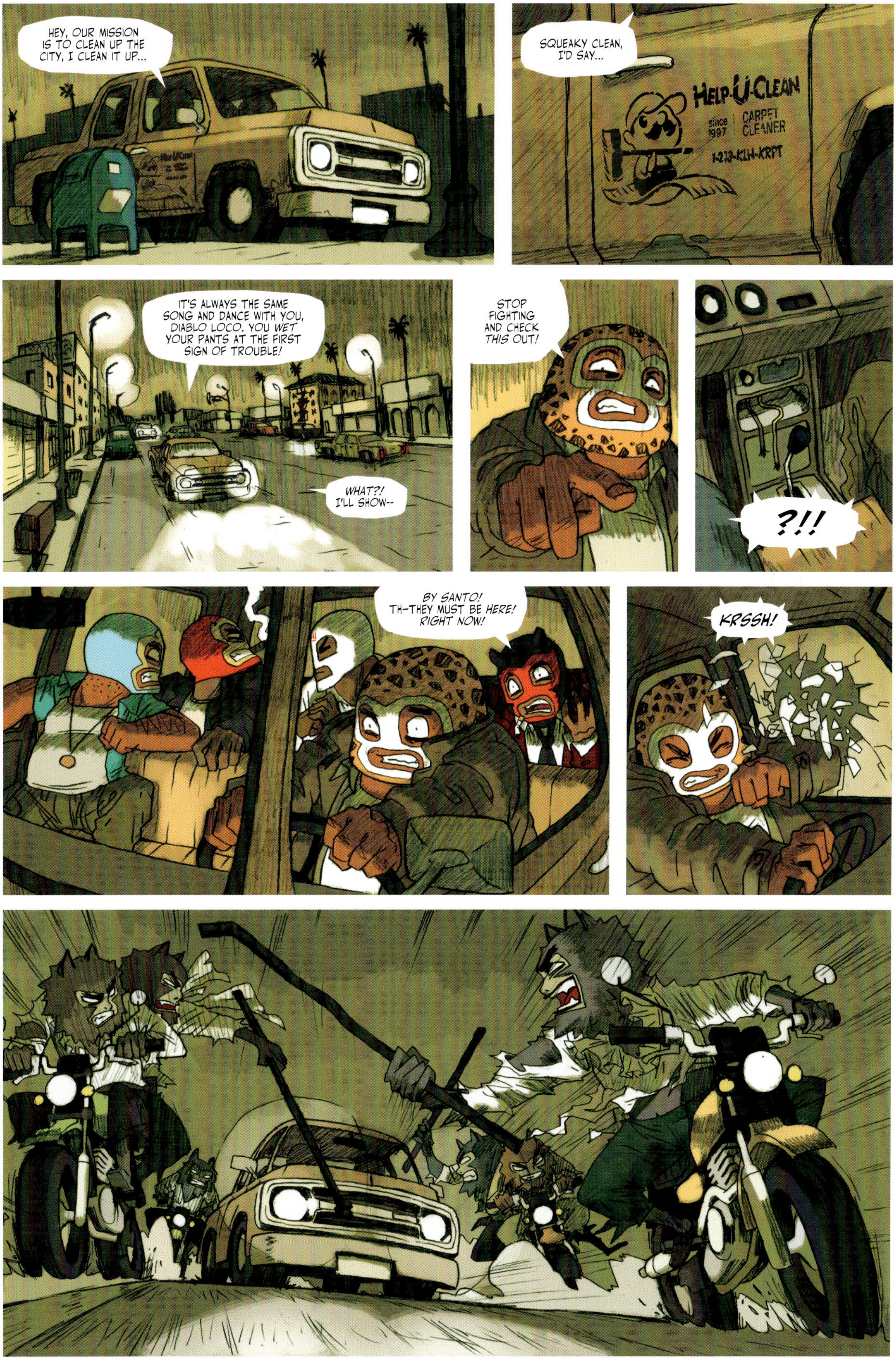
HEY, OUR MISSION IS TO CLEAN UP THE CITY, I CLEAN IT UP...
SQUEAKY CLEAN, I'D SAY...
HELP-U-CLEAN
since 1997
CARPET CLEANER
1-213-KLN-KRPT
IT'S ALWAYS THE SAME SONG AND DANCE WITH YOU, DIABLO LOCO. YOU WET YOUR PANTS AT THE FIRST SIGN OF TROUBLE!
WHAT?! I'LL SHOW--
STOP FIGHTING AND CHECK THIS OUT!
?!!
BY SANTO! TH-THEY MUST BE HERE! RIGHT NOW!
KRSSH!

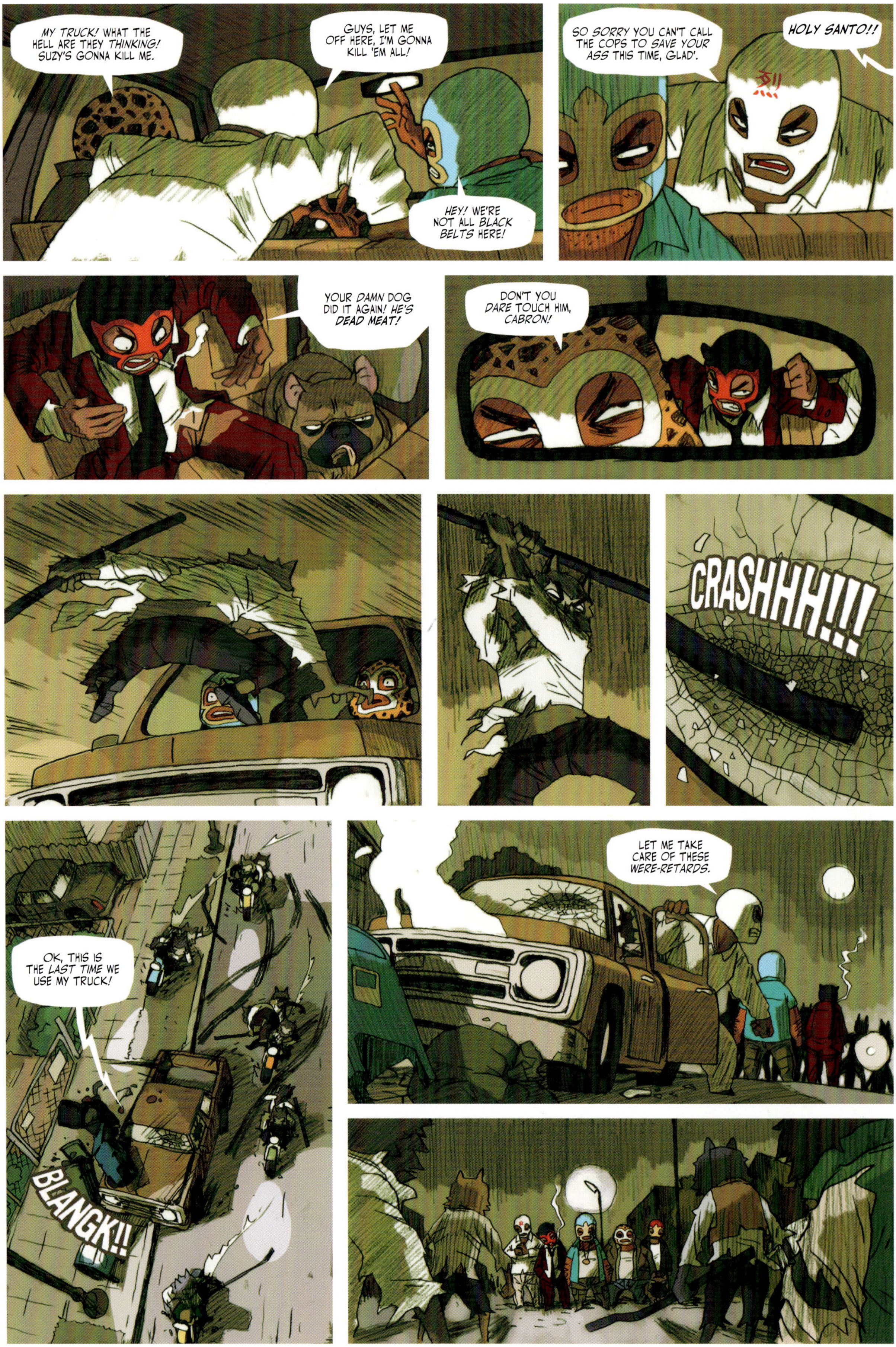
MY TRUCK! WHAT THE HELL ARE THEY THINKING! SUZY'S GONNA KILL ME.
GUYS, LET ME OFF HERE, I'M GONNA KILL 'EM ALL!
HEY! WE'RE NOT ALL BLACK BELTS HERE!
SO SORRY YOU CAN'T CALL THE COPS TO SAVE YOUR ASS THIS TIME, GLAD'.
HOLY SANTO!!
YOUR DAMN DOG DID IT AGAIN! HE'S DEAD MEAT!
DON'T YOU DARE TOUCH HIM, CABRON!
CRASHHH!!!
OK, THIS IS THE LAST TIME WE USE MY TRUCK!
BLANGK!!
LET ME TAKE CARE OF THESE WERE-RETARDS.

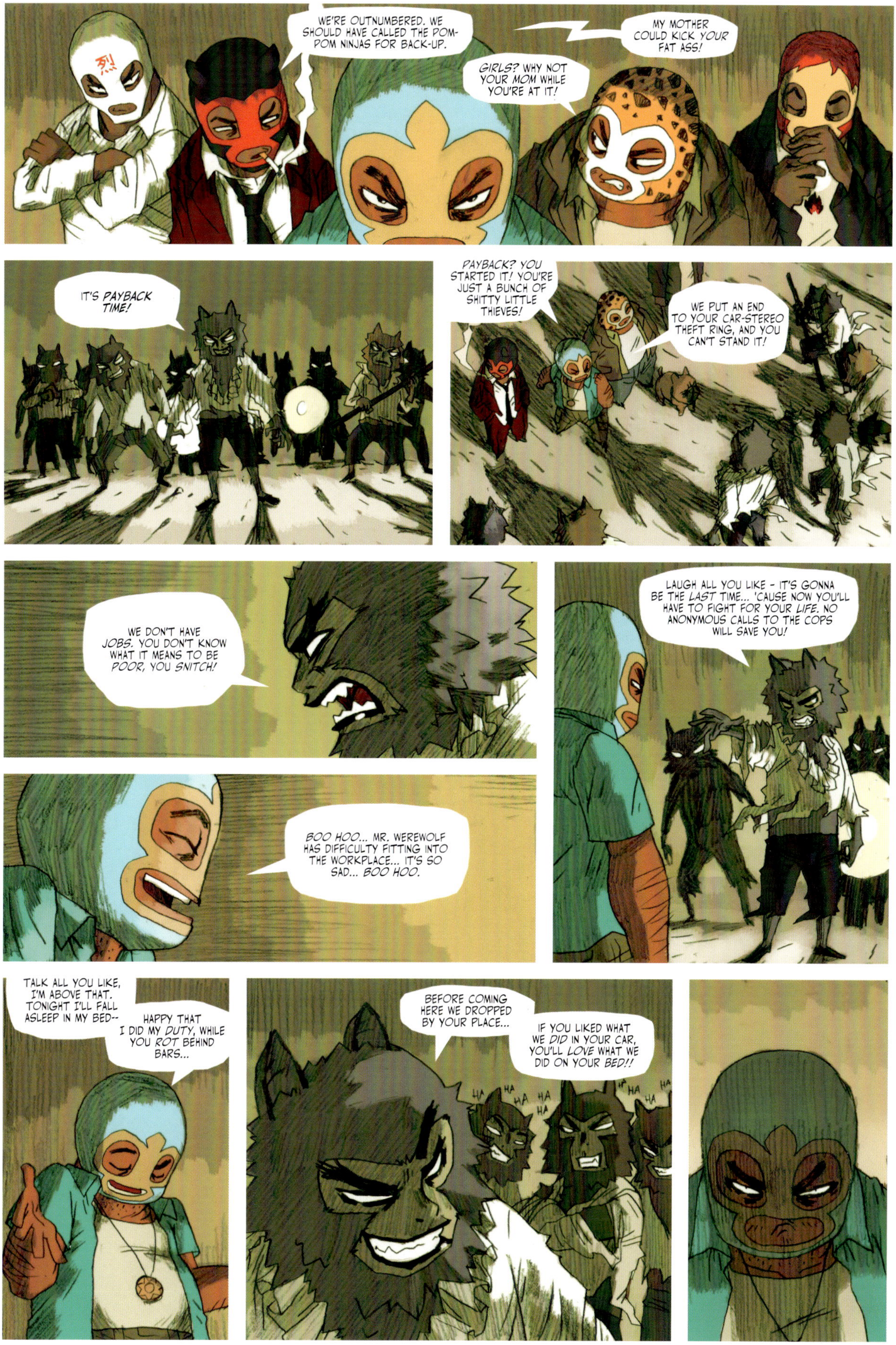
WE'RE OUTNUMBERED. WE SHOULD HAVE CALLED THE POM-POM NINJAS FOR BACK-UP.
GIRLS? WHY NOT YOUR MOM WHILE YOU'RE AT IT!
MY MOTHER COULD KICK YOUR FAT ASS!
IT'S PAYBACK TIME!
PAYBACK? YOU STARTED IT! YOU'RE JUST A BUNCH OF SHITTY LITTLE THIEVES!
WE PUT AN END TO YOUR CAR-STEREO THEFT RING, AND YOU CAN'T STAND IT!
WE DON'T HAVE JOBS. YOU DON'T KNOW WHAT IT MEANS TO BE POOR, YOU SNITCH!
BOO HOO... MR. WEREWOLF HAS DIFFICULTY FITTING INTO THE WORKPLACE... IT'S SO SAD... BOO HOO.
LAUGH ALL YOU LIKE - IT'S GONNA BE THE LAST TIME... 'CAUSE NOW YOU'LL HAVE TO FIGHT FOR YOUR LIFE. NO ANONYMOUS CALLS TO THE COPS WILL SAVE YOU!
TALK ALL YOU LIKE, I'M ABOVE THAT. TONIGHT I'LL FALL ASLEEP IN MY BED--
HAPPY THAT I DID MY DUTY, WHILE YOU ROT BEHIND BARS...
BEFORE COMING HERE WE DROPPED BY YOUR PLACE...
IF YOU LIKED WHAT WE DID IN YOUR CAR, YOU'LL LOVE WHAT WE DID ON YOUR BED!!
HA HA HA HA HA HA HA HA HA

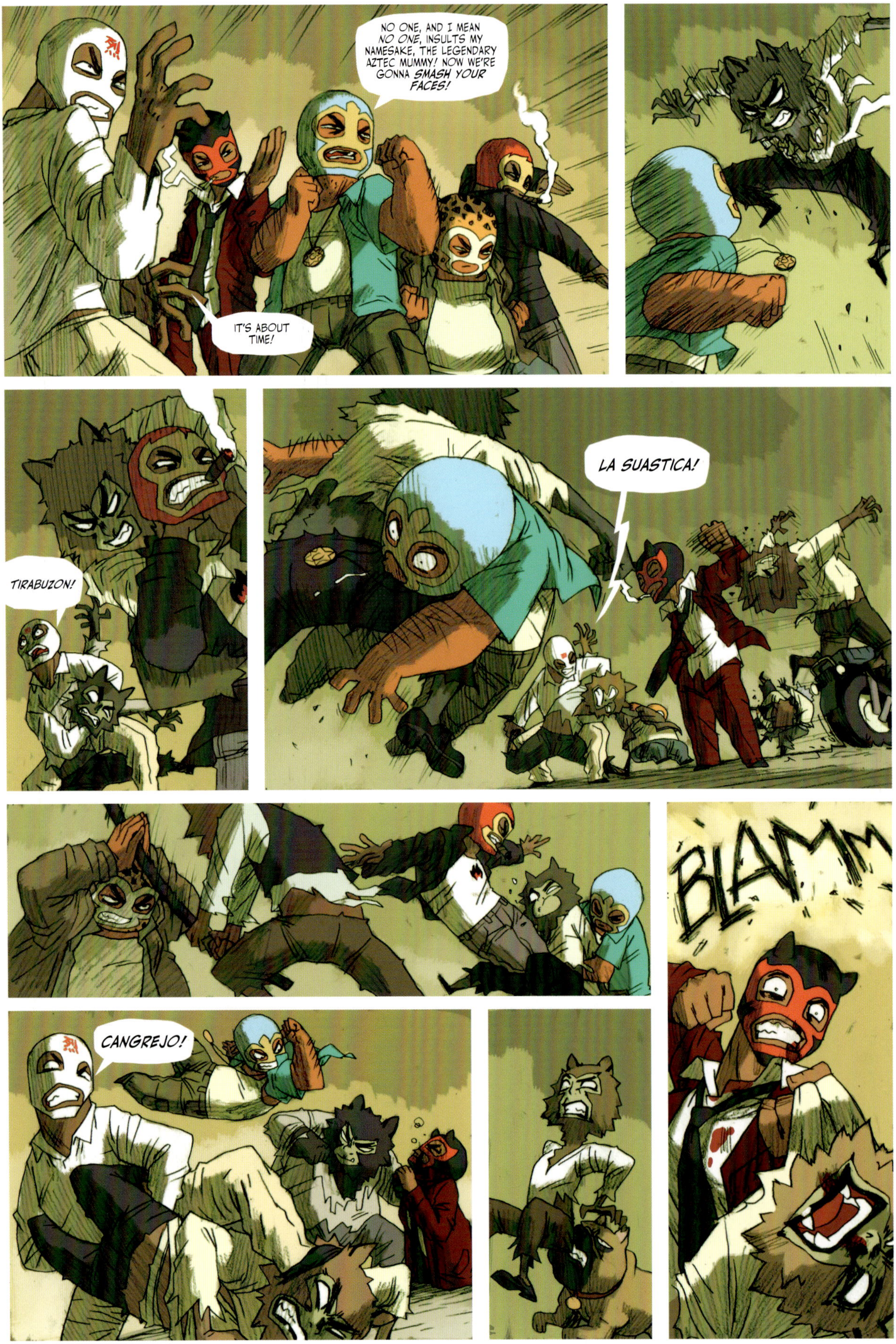
NO ONE, AND I MEAN NO ONE, INSULTS MY NAMESAKE, THE LEGENDARY AZTEC MUMMY! NOW WE'RE GONNA SMASH YOUR FACES!
IT'S ABOUT TIME!
TIRABUZON!
LA SUASTICA!
CANGREJO!
BLAMM

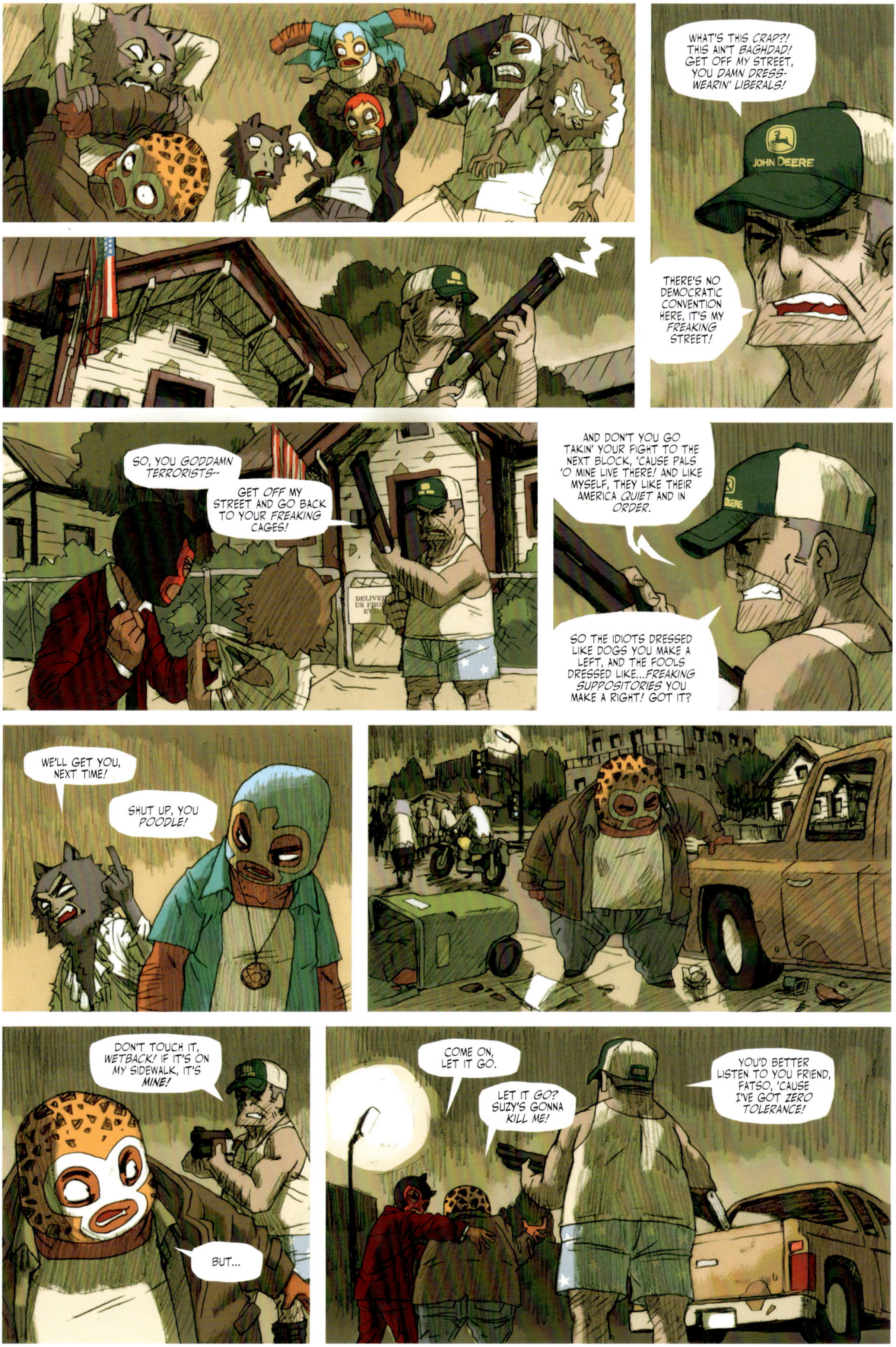
WHAT'S THIS CRAP?! THIS AIN'T BAGHDAD! GET OFF MY STREET, YOU DAMN DRESS-WEARIN' LIBERALS!
JOHN DEERE
THERE'S NO DEMOCRATIC CONVENTION HERE, IT'S MY FREAKING STREET!
SO, YOU GODDAMN TERRORISTS--
GET OFF MY STREET AND GO BACK TO YOUR FREAKING CAGES!
AND DON'T YOU GO TAKIN' YOUR FIGHT TO THE NEXT BLOCK, 'CAUSE PALS 'O MINE LIVE THERE! AND LIKE MYSELF, THEY LIKE THEIR AMERICA QUIET AND IN ORDER.
SO THE IDIOTS DRESSED LIKE DOGS YOU MAKE A LEFT, AND THE FOOLS DRESSED LIKE...FREAKING SUPPOSITORIES YOU MAKE A RIGHT! GOT IT?
WE'LL GET YOU, NEXT TIME!
SHUT UP, YOU POODLE!
DON'T TOUCH IT, WETBACK! IF IT'S ON MY SIDEWALK, IT'S MINE!
BUT...
COME ON, LET IT GO.
LET IT GO? SUZY'S GONNA KILL ME!
YOU'D BETTER LISTEN TO YOU FRIEND, FATSO, 'CAUSE I'VE GOT ZERO TOLERANCE!

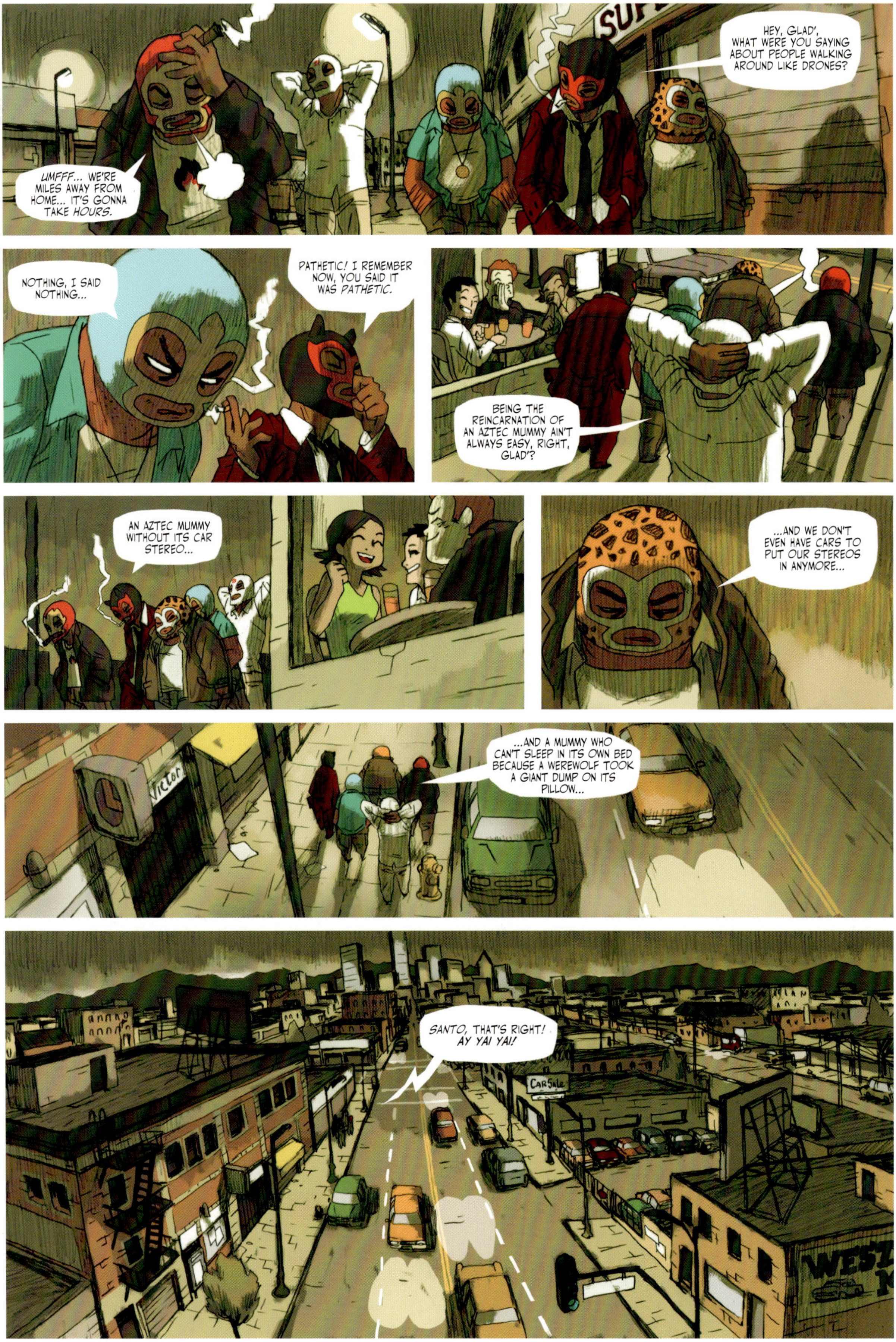
UMFFF... WE'RE MILES AWAY FROM HOME... IT'S GONNA TAKE HOURS.
HEY, GLAD', WHAT WERE YOU SAYING ABOUT PEOPLE WALKING AROUND LIKE DRONES?
NOTHING, I SAID NOTHING...
PATHETIC! I REMEMBER NOW, YOU SAID IT WAS PATHETIC.
BEING THE REINCARNATION OF AN AZTEC MUMMY AIN'T ALWAYS EASY, RIGHT, GLAD'?
AN AZTEC MUMMY WITHOUT ITS CAR STEREO...
...AND WE DON'T EVEN HAVE CARS TO PUT OUR STEREOS IN ANYMORE...
...AND A MUMMY WHO CAN'T SLEEP IN ITS OWN BED BECAUSE A WEREWOLF TOOK A GIANT DUMP ON ITS PILLOW...
SANTO, THAT'S RIGHT! AY YAI YAI!

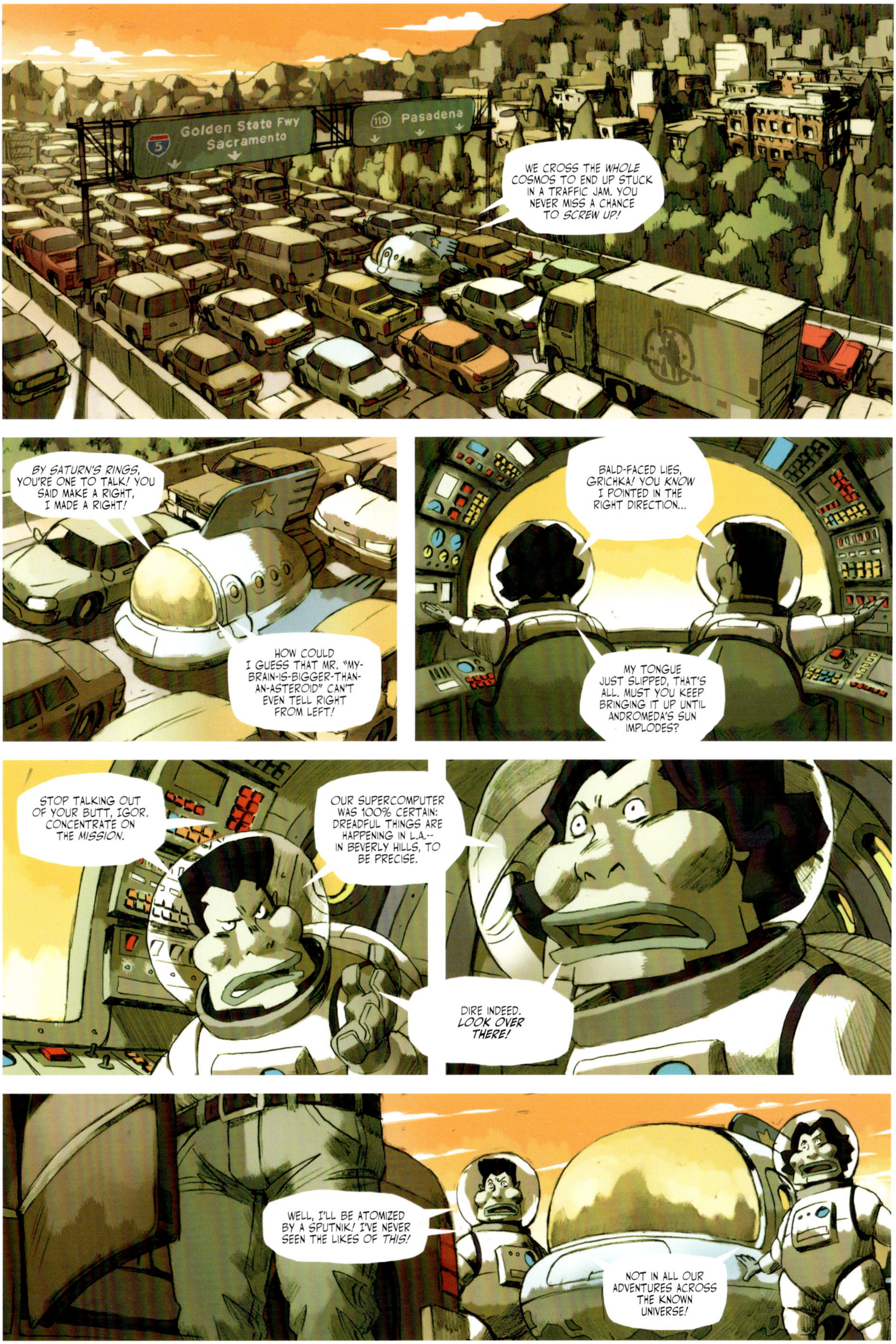
Golden State Fwy
5
Sacramento
110
Pasadena
WE CROSS THE WHOLE COSMOS TO END UP STUCK IN A TRAFFIC JAM. YOU NEVER MISS A CHANCE TO SCREW UP!
BY SATURN'S RINGS, YOU'RE ONE TO TALK! YOU SAID MAKE A RIGHT, I MADE A RIGHT!
HOW COULD I GUESS THAT MR. "MY-BRAIN-IS-BIGGER-THAN-AN-ASTEROID" CAN'T EVEN TELL RIGHT FROM LEFT!
BALD-FACED LIES, GRICHKA! YOU KNOW I POINTED IN THE RIGHT DIRECTION...
MY TONGUE JUST SLIPPED, THAT'S ALL. MUST YOU KEEP BRINGING IT UP UNTIL ANDROMEDA'S SUN IMPLODES?
STOP TALKING OUT OF YOUR BUTT, IGOR. CONCENTRATE ON THE MISSION.
OUR SUPERCOMPUTER WAS 100% CERTAIN: DREADFUL THINGS ARE HAPPENING IN L.A.-- IN BEVERLY HILLS, TO BE PRECISE.
DIRE INDEED. LOOK OVER THERE!
WELL, I'LL BE ATOMIZED BY A SPUTNIK! I'VE NEVER SEEN THE LIKES OF THIS!
NOT IN ALL OUR ADVENTURES ACROSS THE KNOWN UNIVERSE!

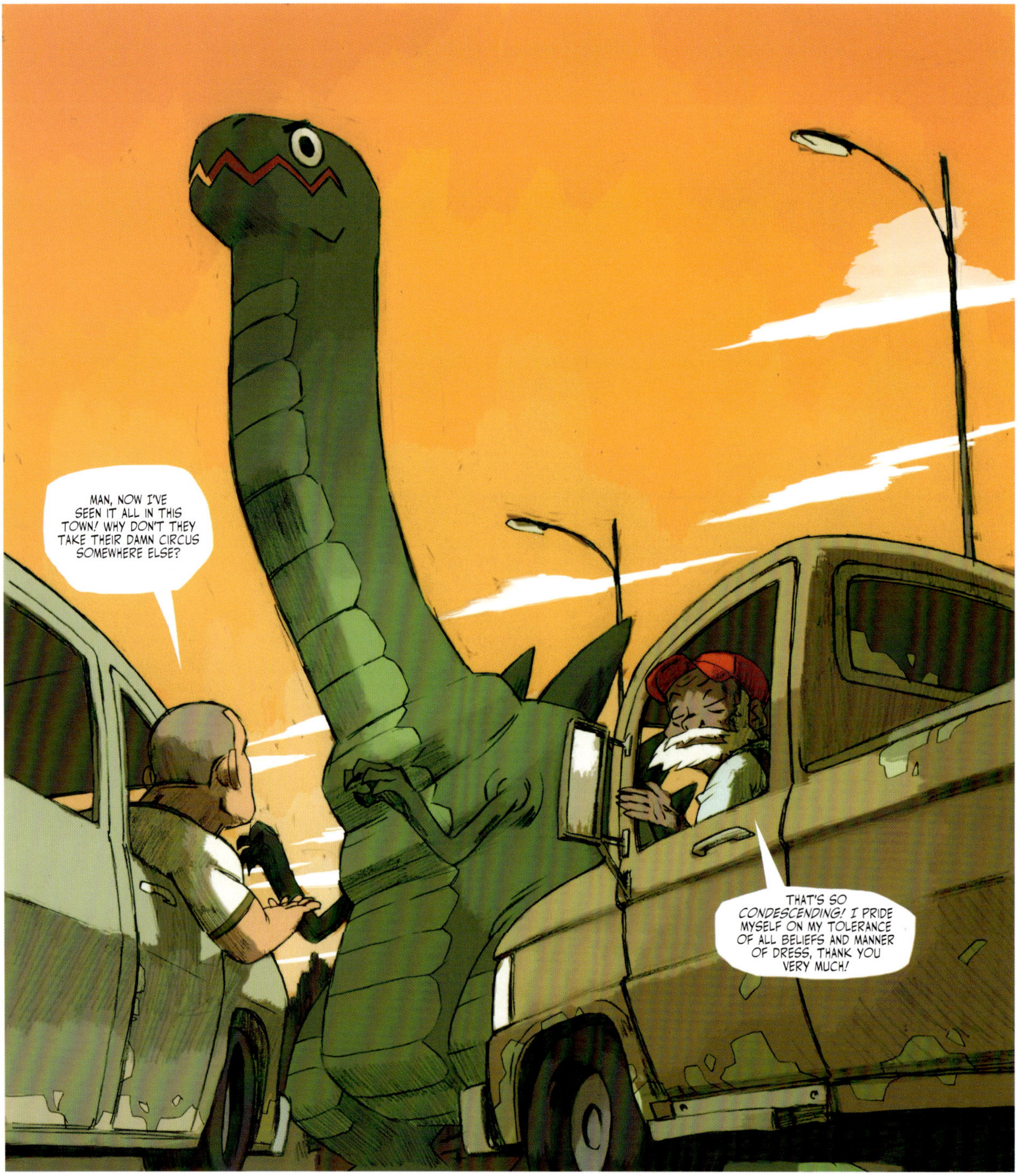
MAN, NOW I'VE SEEN IT ALL IN THIS TOWN! WHY DON'T THEY TAKE THEIR DAMN CIRCUS SOMEWHERE ELSE?
THAT'S SO CONDESCENDING! I PRIDE MYSELF ON MY TOLERANCE OF ALL BELIEFS AND MANNER OF DRESS, THANK YOU VERY MUCH!

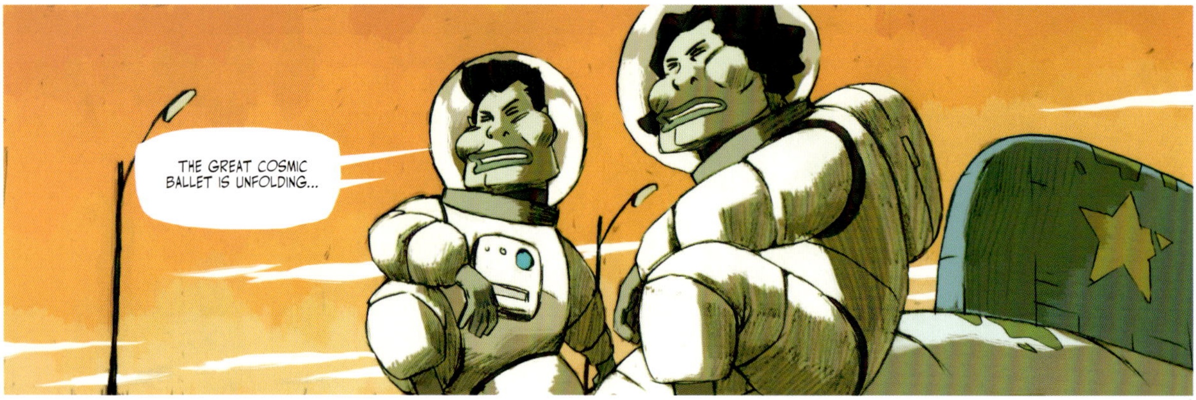
THE GREAT COSMIC BALLET IS UNFOLDING...

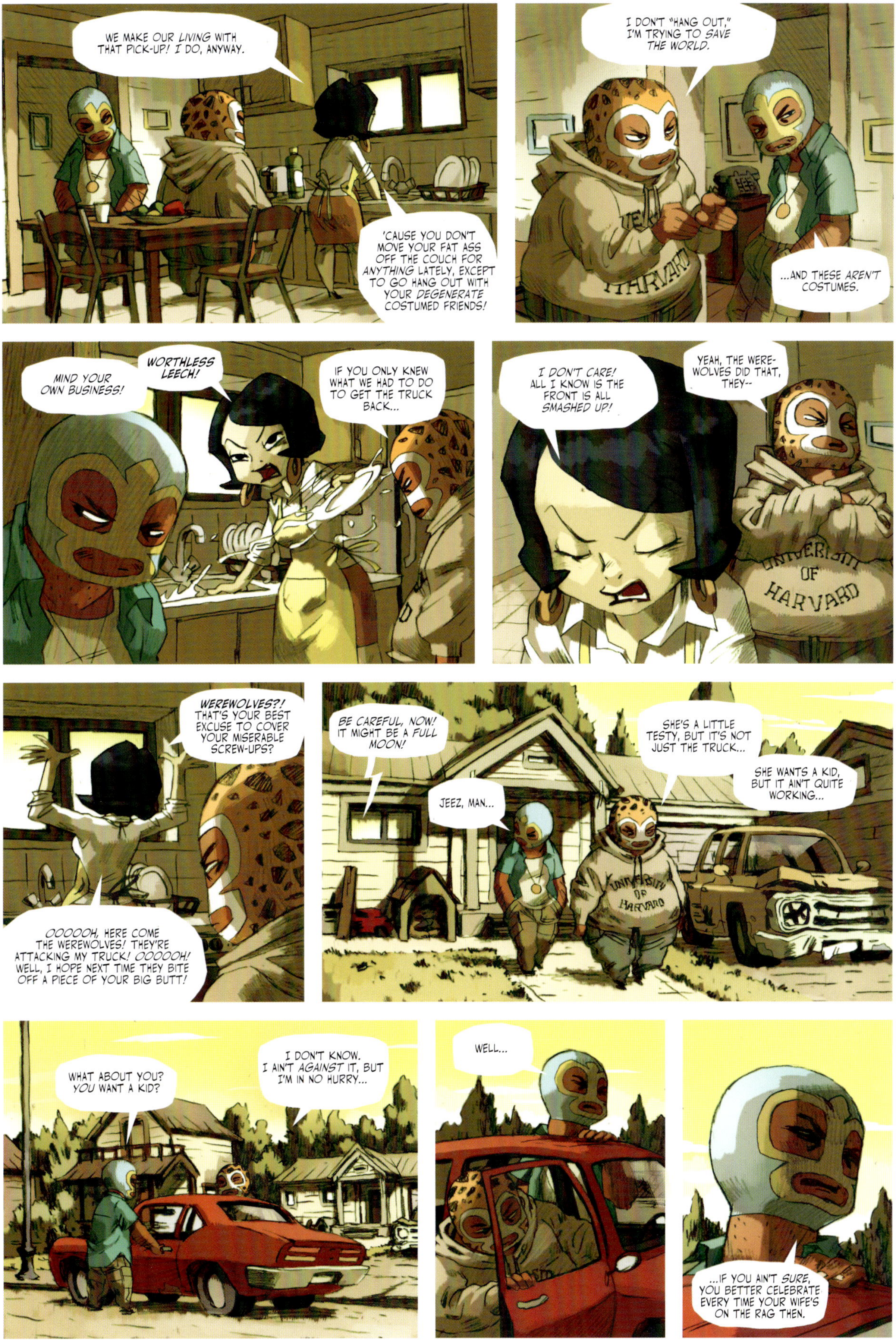
WE MAKE OUR *LIVING* WITH THAT PICK-UP! *I* DO, ANYWAY.
'CAUSE YOU DON'T MOVE YOUR FAT ASS OFF THE COUCH FOR *ANYTHING* LATELY, EXCEPT TO GO HANG OUT WITH YOUR *DEGENERATE* COSTUMED FRIENDS!
I DON'T "HANG OUT," I'M TRYING TO *SAVE* THE WORLD.
...AND THESE *AREN'T* COSTUMES.
MIND YOUR OWN BUSINESS!
WORTHLESS LEECH!
IF YOU ONLY KNEW WHAT WE HAD TO DO TO GET THE TRUCK BACK...
I DON'T CARE! ALL I KNOW IS THE FRONT IS ALL SMASHED UP!
YEAH, THE WERE-WOLVES DID THAT, THEY--
UNIVERSITY OF HARVARD
WEREWOLVES?! THAT'S YOUR BEST EXCUSE TO COVER YOUR MISERABLE SCREW-UPS?
OOOOOH, HERE COME THE WEREWOLVES! THEY'RE ATTACKING MY TRUCK! *OOOOOH!* WELL, I HOPE NEXT TIME THEY BITE OFF A PIECE OF YOUR BIG BUTT!
BE CAREFUL, NOW! IT MIGHT BE A *FULL MOON!*
JEEZ, MAN...
SHE'S A LITTLE TESTY, BUT IT'S NOT JUST THE TRUCK...
SHE WANTS A KID, BUT IT AIN'T QUITE WORKING...
WHAT ABOUT YOU? *YOU* WANT A KID?
I DON'T KNOW. I AIN'T *AGAINST* IT, BUT I'M IN NO HURRY...
WELL...
...IF YOU AIN'T *SURE*, YOU BETTER CELEBRATE EVERY TIME YOUR WIFE'S ON THE RAG THEN.

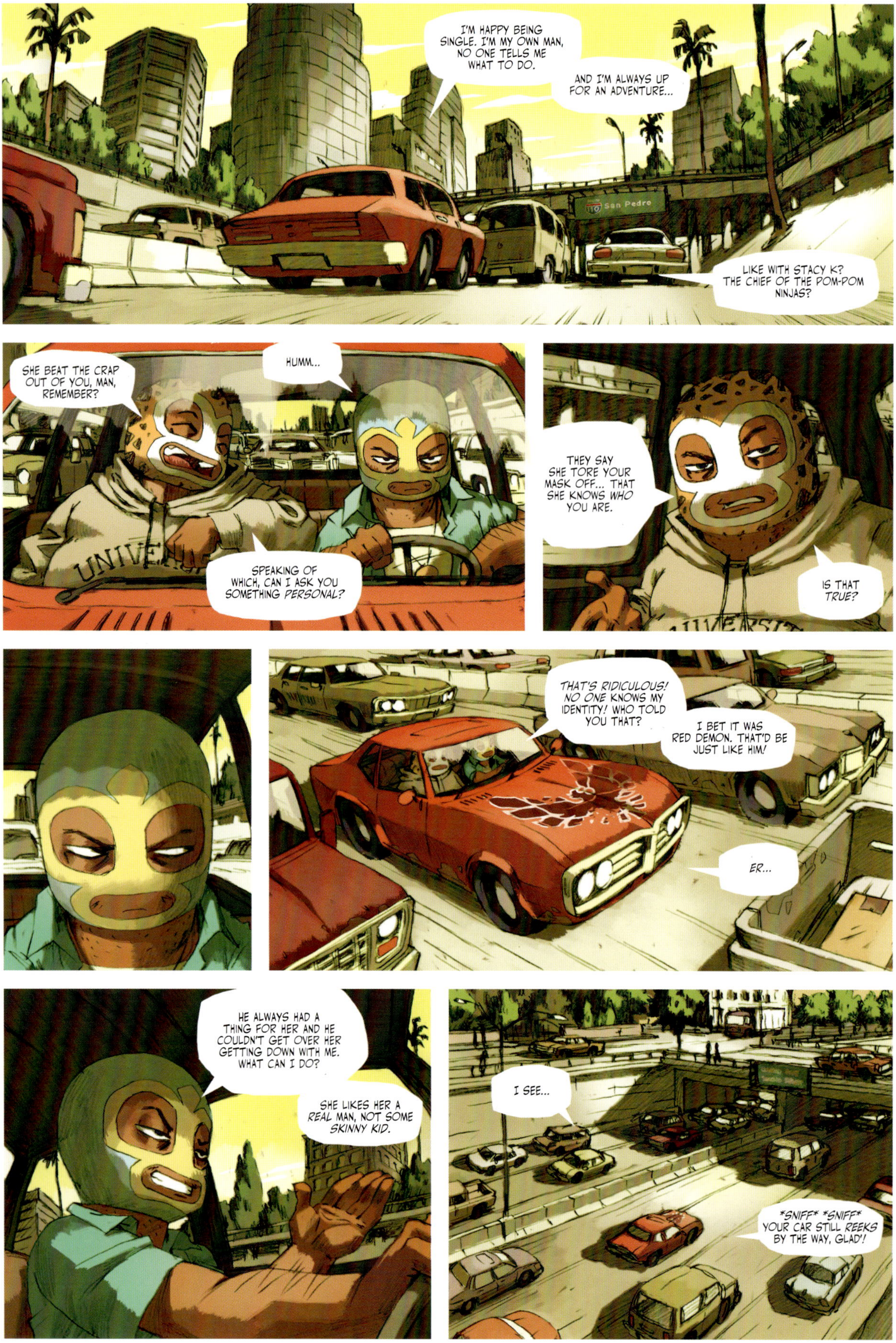
I'M HAPPY BEING SINGLE. I'M MY OWN MAN, NO ONE TELLS ME WHAT TO DO.
AND I'M ALWAYS UP FOR AN ADVENTURE...
San Pedro
LIKE WITH STACY K? THE CHIEF OF THE POM-POM NINJAS?
SHE BEAT THE CRAP OUT OF YOU, MAN, REMEMBER?
HUMM...
SPEAKING OF WHICH, CAN I ASK YOU SOMETHING *PERSONAL*?
THEY SAY SHE TORE YOUR MASK OFF... THAT SHE KNOWS *WHO* YOU ARE.
IS THAT *TRUE?*
THAT'S RIDICULOUS! NO ONE KNOWS MY IDENTITY! WHO TOLD YOU THAT?
I BET IT WAS RED DEMON. THAT'D BE JUST LIKE HIM!
ER...
HE ALWAYS HAD A THING FOR HER AND HE COULDN'T GET OVER HER GETTING DOWN WITH ME. WHAT CAN I DO?
SHE LIKES HER A *REAL* MAN, NOT SOME *SKINNY* KID.
I SEE...
SNIFF *SNIFF* YOUR CAR STILL *REEKS* BY THE WAY, GLAD'!

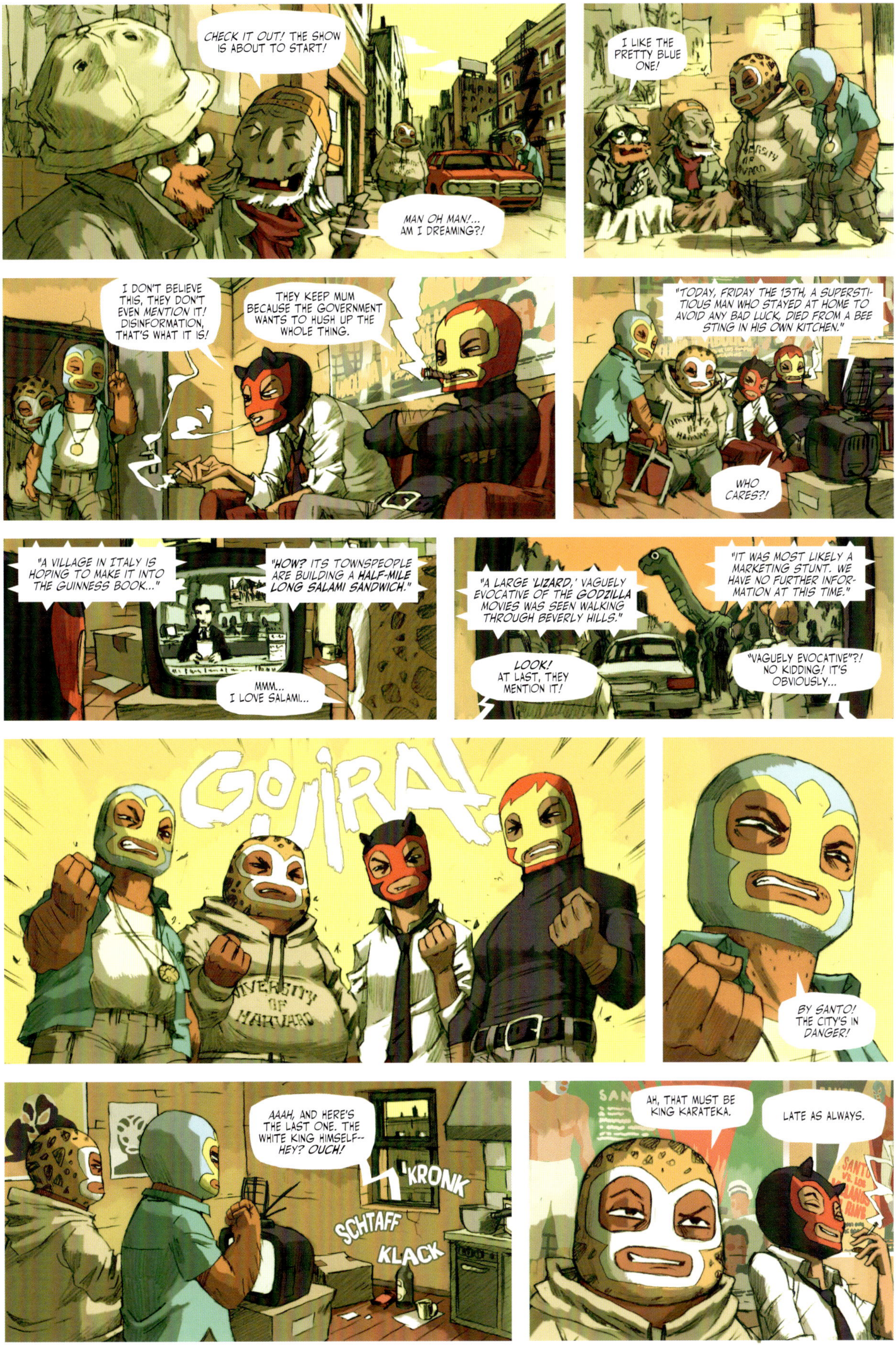
CHECK IT OUT! THE SHOW IS ABOUT TO START!
MAN OH MAN!... AM I DREAMING?!
I LIKE THE PRETTY BLUE ONE!
I DON'T BELIEVE THIS, THEY DON'T EVEN MENTION IT! DISINFORMATION, THAT'S WHAT IT IS!
THEY KEEP MUM BECAUSE THE GOVERNMENT WANTS TO HUSH UP THE WHOLE THING.
"TODAY, FRIDAY THE 13TH, A SUPERSTI-TIOUS MAN WHO STAYED AT HOME TO AVOID ANY BAD LUCK, DIED FROM A BEE STING IN HIS OWN KITCHEN."
WHO CARES?!
"A VILLAGE IN ITALY IS HOPING TO MAKE IT INTO THE GUINNESS BOOK..."
"HOW? ITS TOWNSPEOPLE ARE BUILDING A HALF-MILE LONG SALAMI SANDWICH."
MMM... I LOVE SALAMI...
"A LARGE 'LIZARD,' VAGUELY EVOCATIVE OF THE GODZILLA MOVIES WAS SEEN WALKING THROUGH BEVERLY HILLS."
"IT WAS MOST LIKELY A MARKETING STUNT. WE HAVE NO FURTHER INFOR-MATION AT THIS TIME."
LOOK! AT LAST, THEY MENTION IT!
"VAGUELY EVOCATIVE"?! NO KIDDING! IT'S OBVIOUSLY...
GOJIRA!
BY SANTO! THE CITY'S IN DANGER!
AAAH, AND HERE'S THE LAST ONE. THE WHITE KING HIMSELF-- HEY? OUCH!
KRONK
SCHTAFF
KLACK
AH, THAT MUST BE KING KARATEKA.
LATE AS ALWAYS.

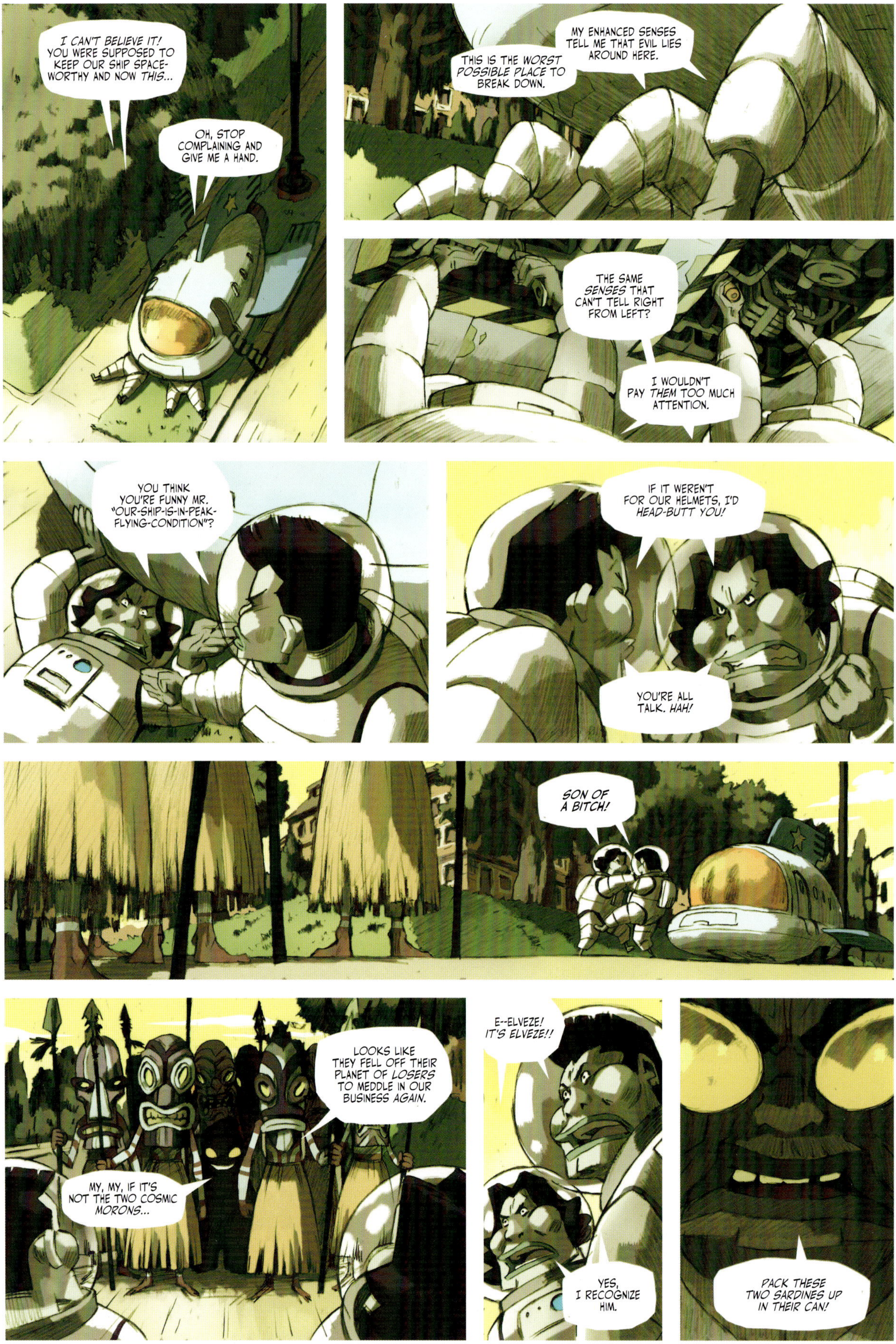
I CAN'T BELIEVE IT! YOU WERE SUPPOSED TO KEEP OUR SHIP SPACE-WORTHY AND NOW THIS...
OH, STOP COMPLAINING AND GIVE ME A HAND.
THIS IS THE WORST POSSIBLE PLACE TO BREAK DOWN.
MY ENHANCED SENSES TELL ME THAT EVIL LIES AROUND HERE.
THE SAME SENSES THAT CAN'T TELL RIGHT FROM LEFT?
I WOULDN'T PAY THEM TOO MUCH ATTENTION.
YOU THINK YOU'RE FUNNY MR. "OUR-SHIP-IS-IN-PEAK-FLYING-CONDITION"?
IF IT WEREN'T FOR OUR HELMETS, I'D HEAD-BUTT YOU!
YOU'RE ALL TALK. HAH!
SON OF A BITCH!
MY, MY, IF IT'S NOT THE TWO COSMIC MORONS...
LOOKS LIKE THEY FELL OFF THEIR PLANET OF LOSERS TO MEDDLE IN OUR BUSINESS AGAIN.
E--ELVEZE! IT'S ELVEZE!!
YES, I RECOGNIZE HIM.
PACK THESE TWO SARDINES UP IN THEIR CAN!

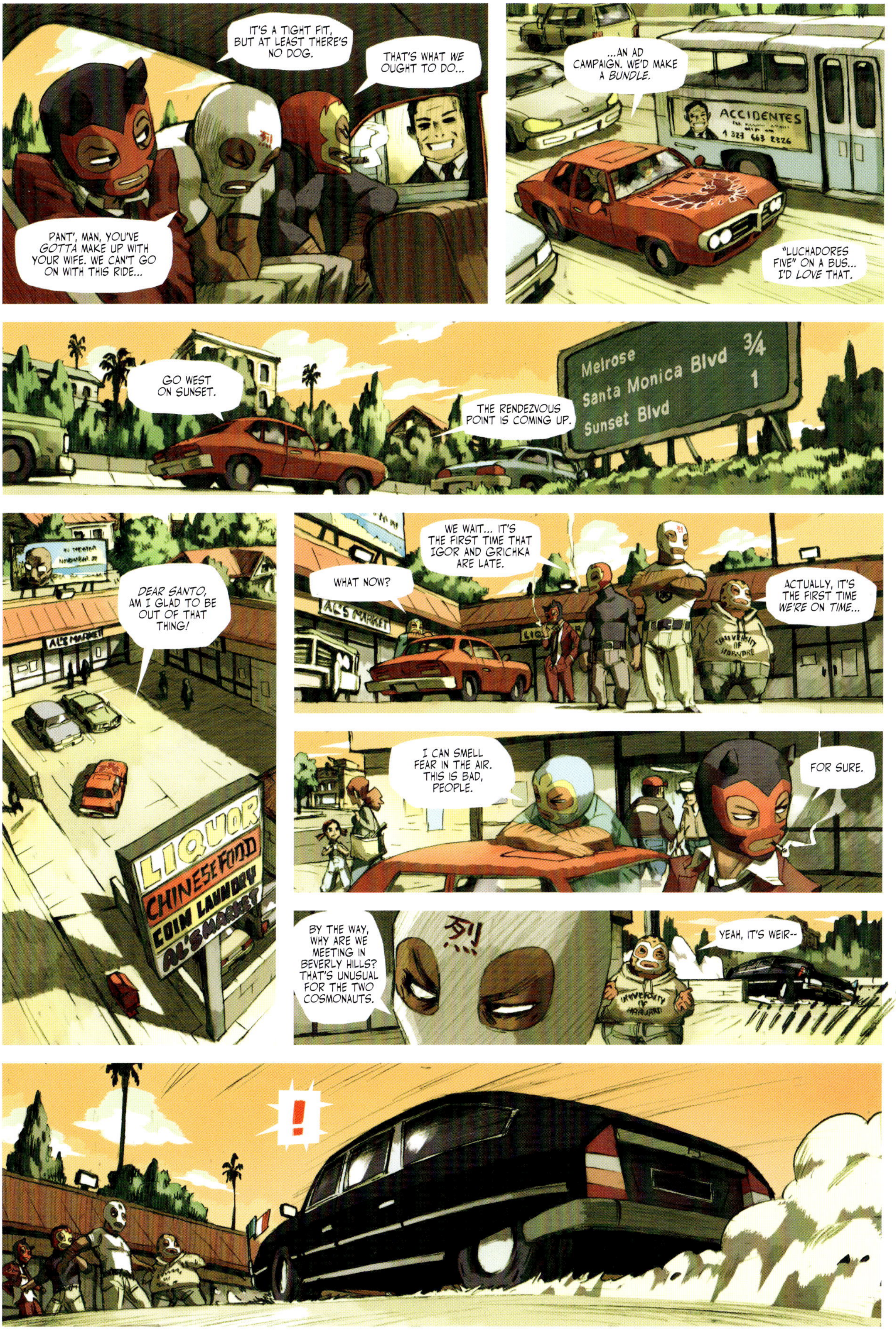
IT'S A TIGHT FIT, BUT AT LEAST THERE'S NO DOG.
THAT'S WHAT WE OUGHT TO DO...
PANT', MAN, YOU'VE GOTTA MAKE UP WITH YOUR WIFE. WE CAN'T GO ON WITH THIS RIDE...
...AN AD CAMPAIGN. WE'D MAKE A BUNDLE.
ACCIDENTES
"LUCHADORES FIVE" ON A BUS... I'D LOVE THAT.
GO WEST ON SUNSET.
THE RENDEZVOUS POINT IS COMING UP.
Melrose 3/4
Santa Monica Blvd 1
Sunset Blvd
DEAR SANTO, AM I GLAD TO BE OUT OF THAT THING!
LIQUOR
CHINESE FOOD
COIN LAUNDRY
AL'S MARKET
WHAT NOW?
WE WAIT... IT'S THE FIRST TIME THAT IGOR AND GRICHKA ARE LATE.
ACTUALLY, IT'S THE FIRST TIME WE'RE ON TIME...
I CAN SMELL FEAR IN THE AIR. THIS IS BAD, PEOPLE.
FOR SURE.
BY THE WAY, WHY ARE WE MEETING IN BEVERLY HILLS? THAT'S UNUSUAL FOR THE TWO COSMONAUTS.
YEAH, IT'S WEIR--
!

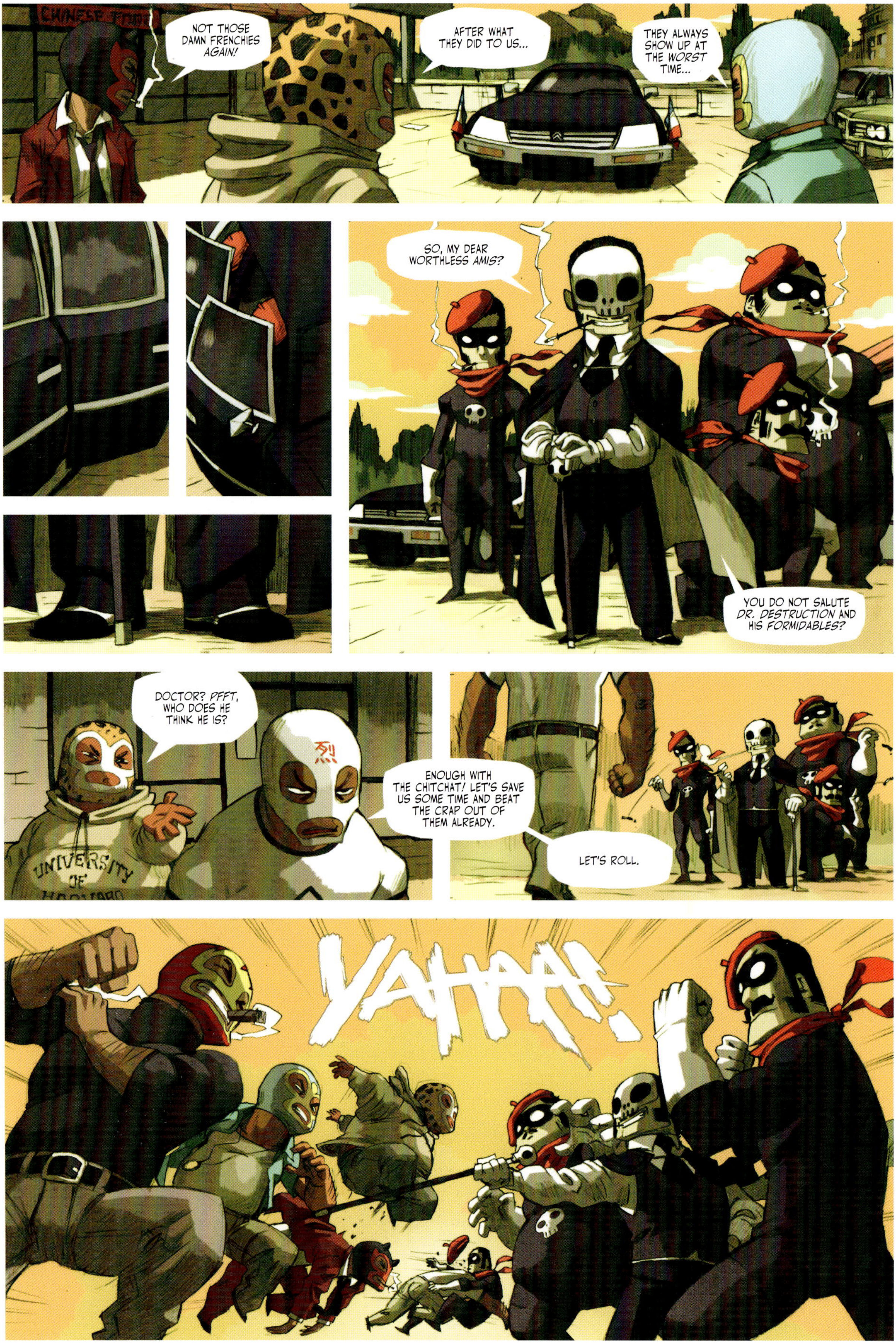
CHINESE FOOD
NOT THOSE DAMN FRENCHIES AGAIN!
AFTER WHAT THEY DID TO US...
THEY ALWAYS SHOW UP AT THE WORST TIME...
SO, MY DEAR WORTHLESS AMIS?
YOU DO NOT SALUTE DR. DESTRUCTION AND HIS FORMIDABLES?
DOCTOR? PFFT, WHO DOES HE THINK HE IS?
UNIVERSITY OF
ENOUGH WITH THE CHITCHAT! LET'S SAVE US SOME TIME AND BEAT THE CRAP OUT OF THEM ALREADY.
LET'S ROLL.
YAHAA!

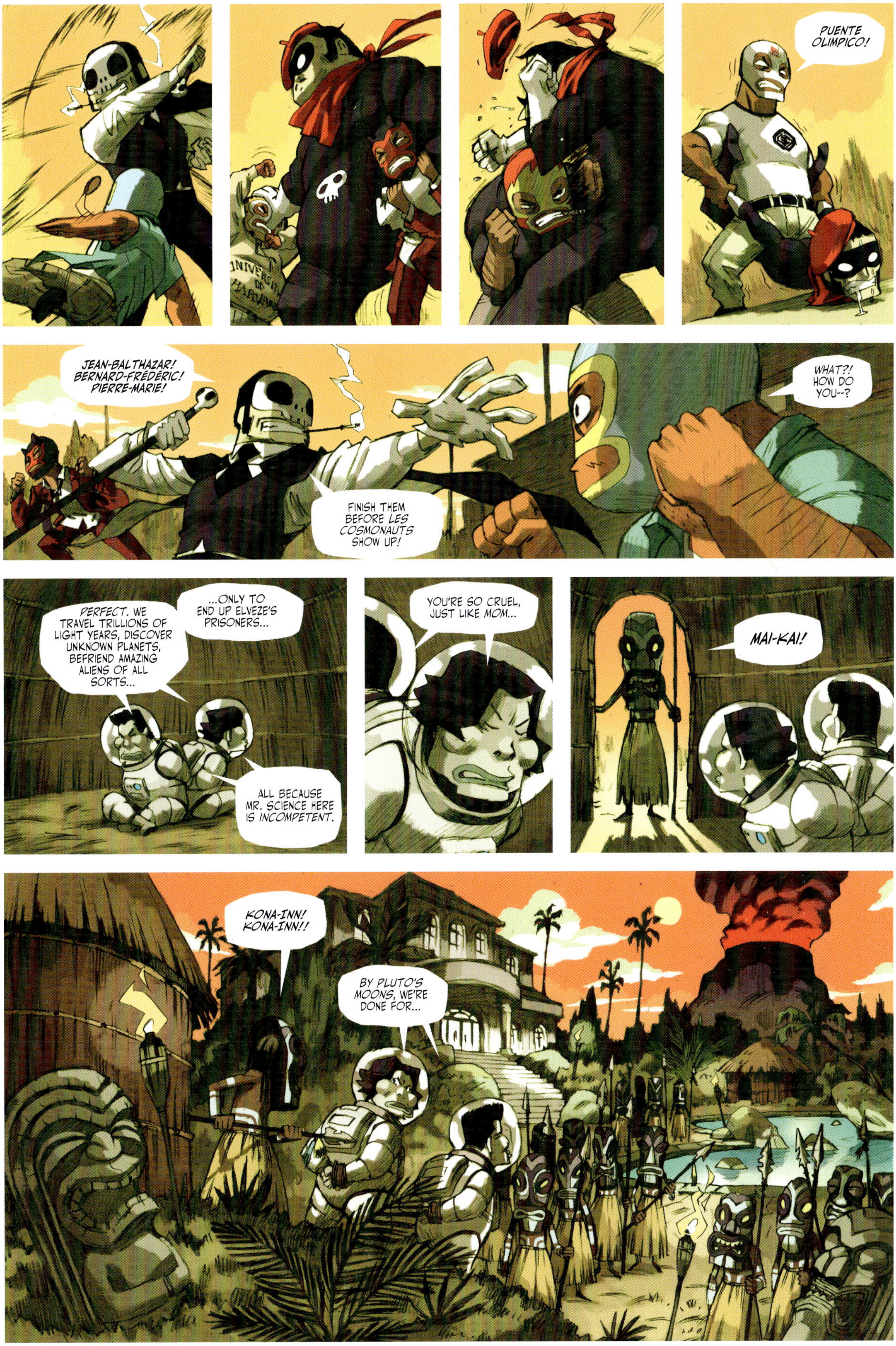
PUENTE OLIMPICO!
JEAN-BALTHAZAR! BERNARD-FRÉDÉRIC! PIERRE-MARIE!
FINISH THEM BEFORE LES COSMONAUTS SHOW UP!
WHAT?! HOW DO YOU--?
PERFECT. WE TRAVEL TRILLIONS OF LIGHT YEARS, DISCOVER UNKNOWN PLANETS, BEFRIEND AMAZING ALIENS OF ALL SORTS...
...ONLY TO END UP ELVEZE'S PRISONERS...
ALL BECAUSE MR. SCIENCE HERE IS INCOMPETENT.
YOU'RE SO CRUEL, JUST LIKE MOM...
MAI-KAI!
KONA-INN! KONA-INN!!
BY PLUTO'S MOONS, WE'RE DONE FOR...

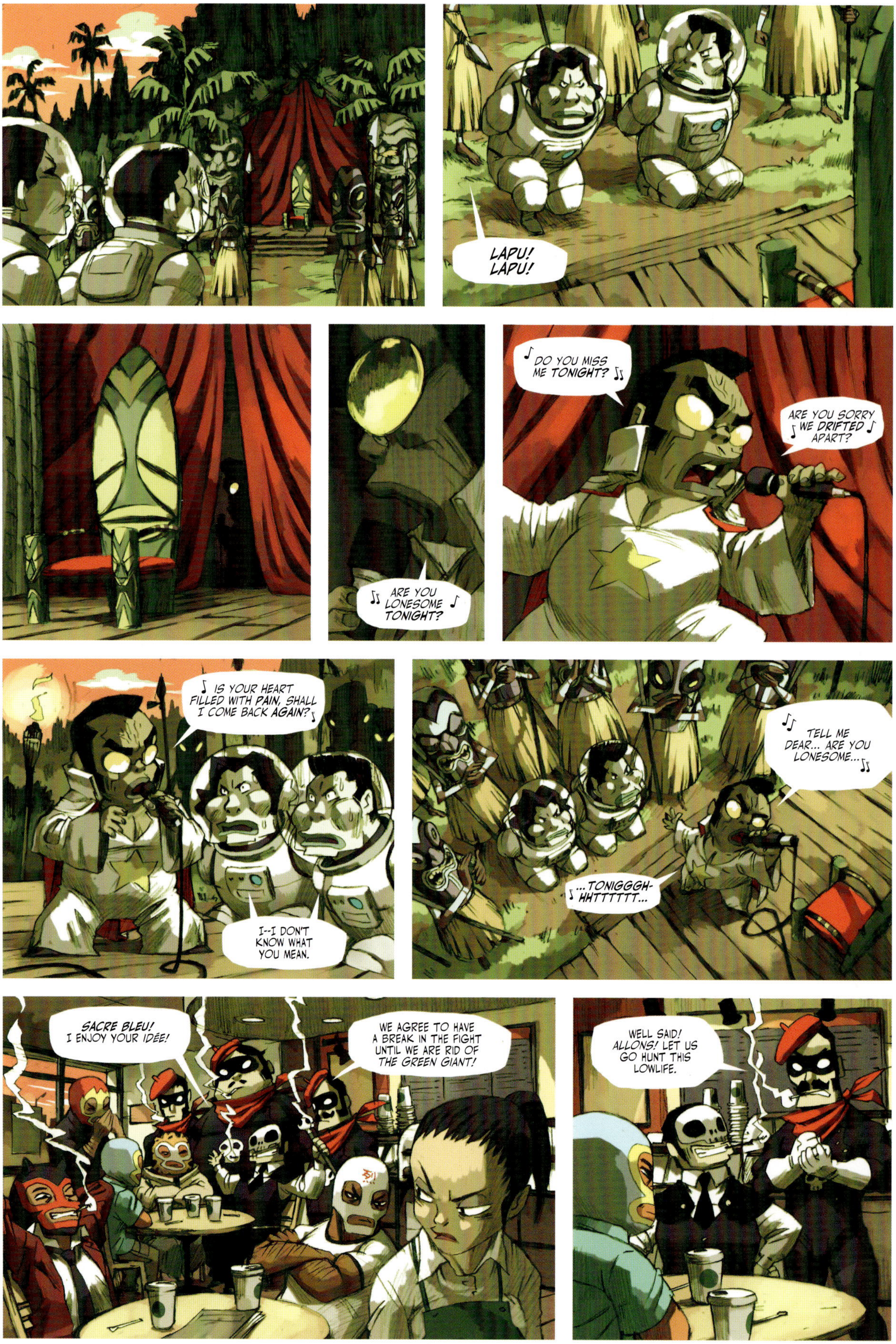
LAPU! LAPU!
DO YOU MISS ME TONIGHT?
ARE YOU LONESOME TONIGHT?
ARE YOU SORRY WE DRIFTED APART?
IS YOUR HEART FILLED WITH PAIN, SHALL I COME BACK AGAIN?
I--I DON'T KNOW WHAT YOU MEAN.
TELL ME DEAR... ARE YOU LONESOME...
...TONIGGGH-HHTTTTTTT...
SACRE BLEU! I ENJOY YOUR IDÉE!
WE AGREE TO HAVE A BREAK IN THE FIGHT UNTIL WE ARE RID OF THE GREEN GIANT!
WELL SAID! ALLONS! LET US GO HUNT THIS LOWLIFE.

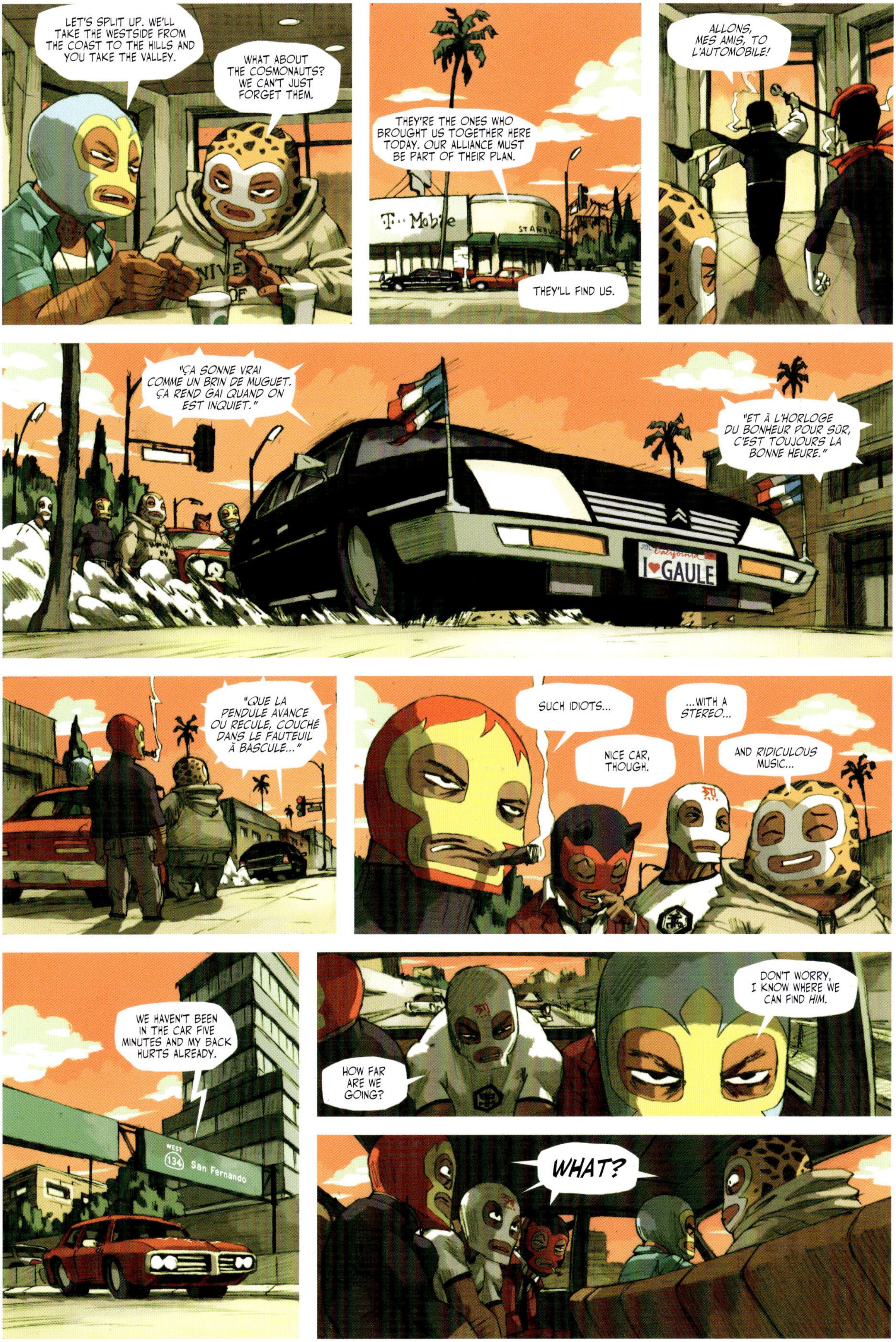
LET'S SPLIT UP. WE'LL TAKE THE WESTSIDE FROM THE COAST TO THE HILLS AND YOU TAKE THE VALLEY.
WHAT ABOUT THE COSMONAUTS? WE CAN'T JUST FORGET THEM.
THEY'RE THE ONES WHO BROUGHT US TOGETHER HERE TODAY. OUR ALLIANCE MUST BE PART OF THEIR PLAN.
T··Mobile
THEY'LL FIND US.
ALLONS, MES AMIS, TO L'AUTOMOBILE!
"ÇA SONNE VRAI COMME UN BRIN DE MUGUET. ÇA REND GAI QUAND ON EST INQUIET."
"ET À L'HORLOGE DU BONHEUR POUR SÛR, C'EST TOUJOURS LA BONNE HEURE."
I ♥ GAULE
"QUE LA PENDULE AVANCE OU RECULE, COUCHÉ DANS LE FAUTEUIL À BASCULE..."
SUCH IDIOTS...
NICE CAR, THOUGH.
...WITH A STEREO...
AND RIDICULOUS MUSIC...
WE HAVEN'T BEEN IN THE CAR FIVE MINUTES AND MY BACK HURTS ALREADY.
WEST 134 San Fernando
HOW FAR ARE WE GOING?
DON'T WORRY, I KNOW WHERE WE CAN FIND HIM.
WHAT?

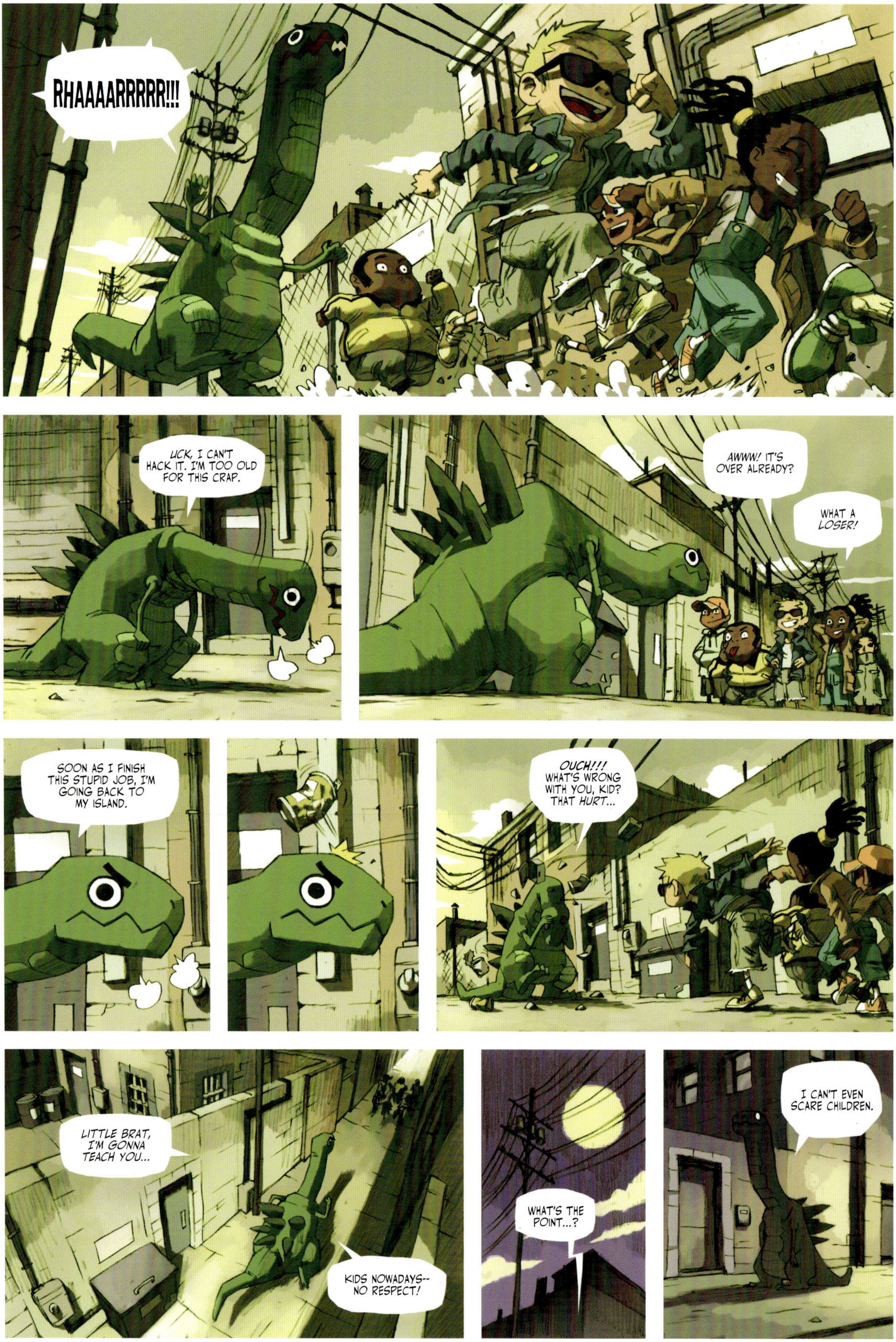
RHAAAARRRRR!!!
UCK, I CAN'T HACK IT. I'M TOO OLD FOR THIS CRAP.
AWW! IT'S OVER ALREADY?
WHAT A LOSER!
SOON AS I FINISH THIS STUPID JOB, I'M GOING BACK TO MY ISLAND.
OUCH!!! WHAT'S WRONG WITH YOU, KID? THAT HURT...
LITTLE BRAT, I'M GONNA TEACH YOU...
KIDS NOWADAYS-- NO RESPECT!
WHAT'S THE POINT...?
I CAN'T EVEN SCARE CHILDREN.

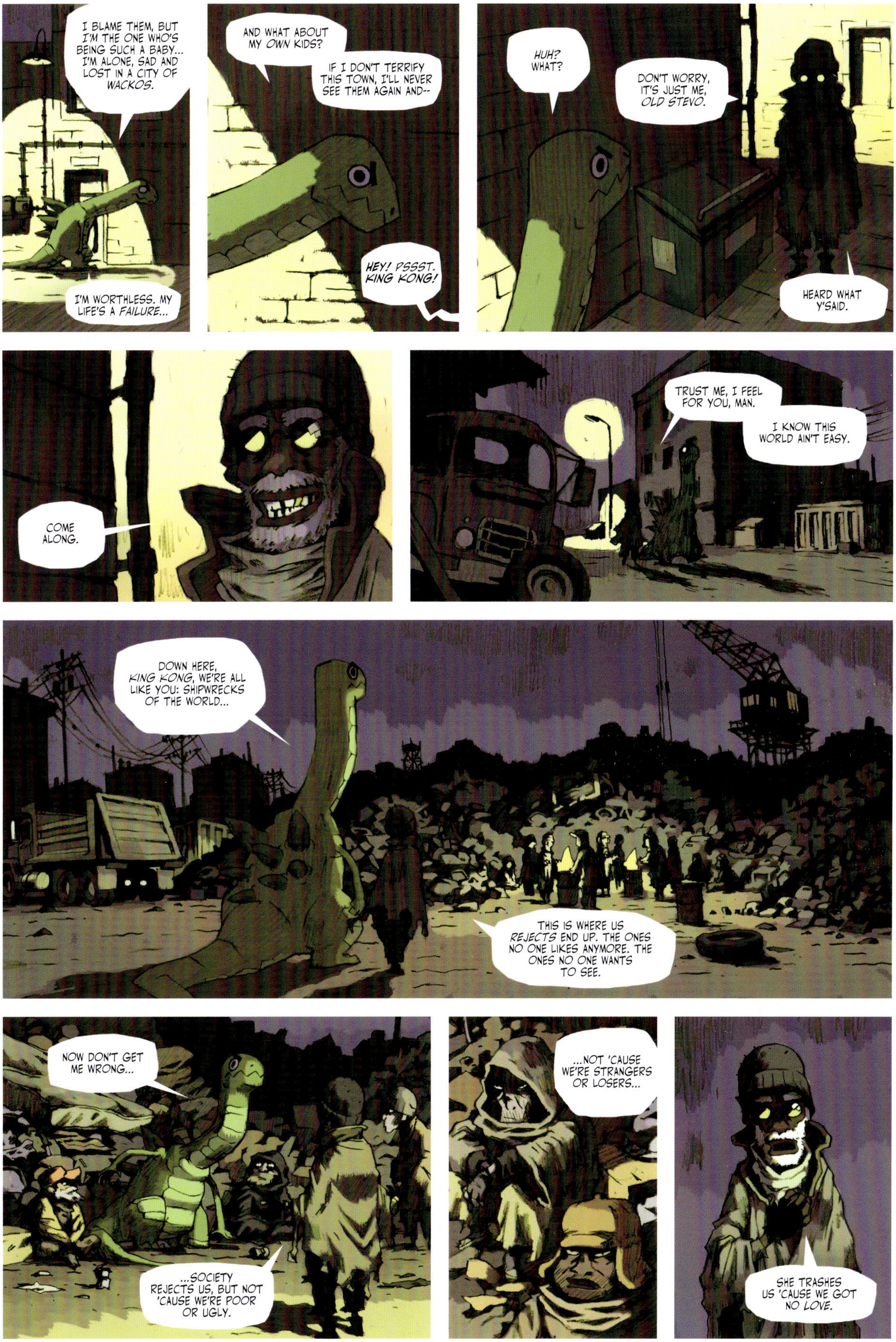
I BLAME THEM, BUT I'M THE ONE WHO'S BEING SUCH A BABY... I'M ALONE, SAD AND LOST IN A CITY OF WACKOS.
I'M WORTHLESS. MY LIFE'S A FAILURE...
AND WHAT ABOUT MY OWN KIDS?
IF I DON'T TERRIFY THIS TOWN, I'LL NEVER SEE THEM AGAIN AND--
HEY! PSSST. KING KONG!
HUH? WHAT?
DON'T WORRY, IT'S JUST ME, OLD STEVO.
HEARD WHAT Y'SAID.
COME ALONG.
TRUST ME, I FEEL FOR YOU, MAN.
I KNOW THIS WORLD AIN'T EASY.
DOWN HERE, KING KONG, WE'RE ALL LIKE YOU: SHIPWRECKS OF THE WORLD...
THIS IS WHERE US REJECTS END UP. THE ONES NO ONE LIKES ANYMORE. THE ONES NO ONE WANTS TO SEE.
NOW DON'T GET ME WRONG...
...SOCIETY REJECTS US, BUT NOT 'CAUSE WE'RE POOR OR UGLY.
...NOT 'CAUSE WE'RE STRANGERS OR LOSERS...
SHE TRASHES US 'CAUSE WE GOT NO LOVE.

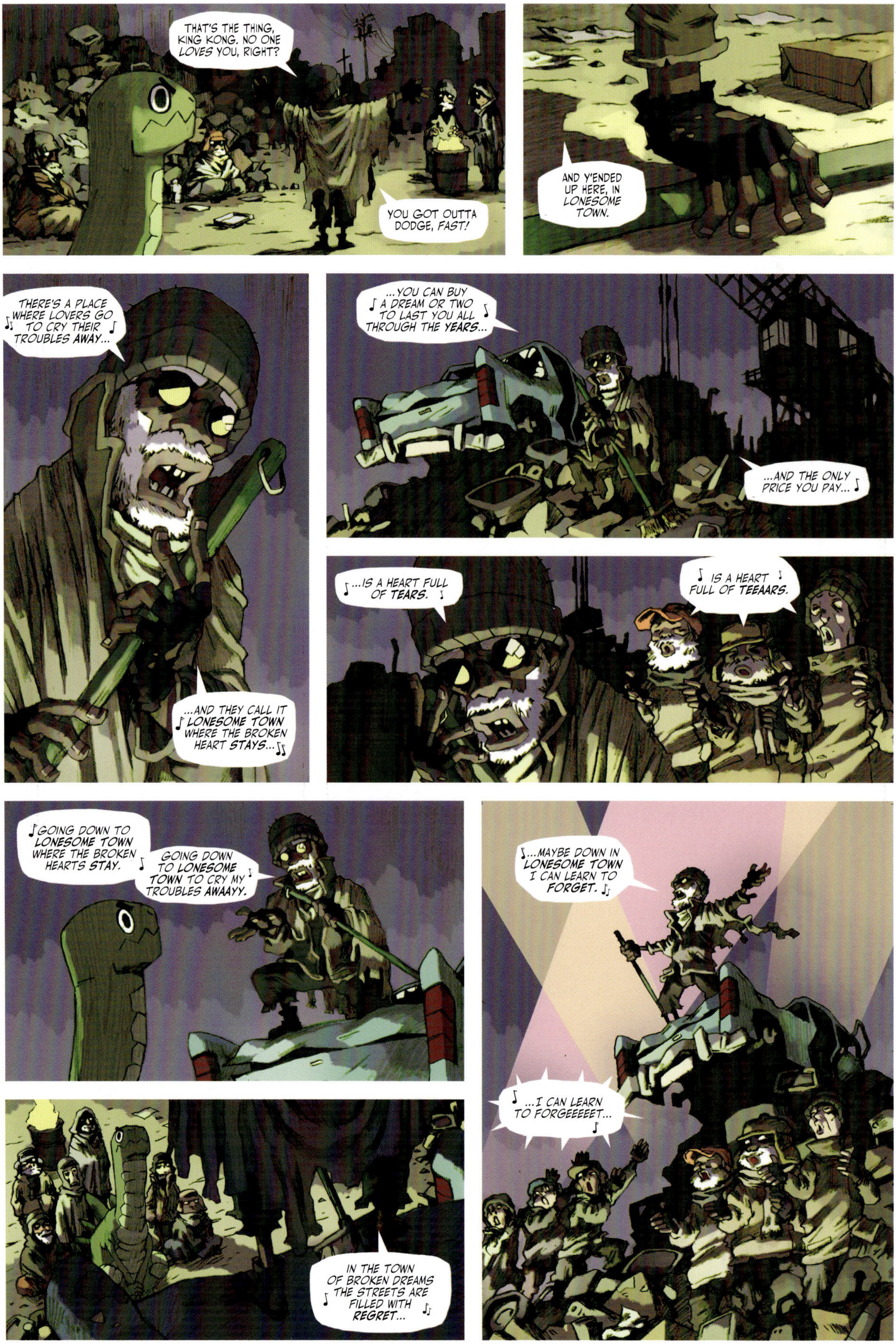
THAT'S THE THING, KING KONG. NO ONE LOVES YOU, RIGHT?
YOU GOT OUTTA DODGE, FAST!
AND Y'ENDED UP HERE, IN LONESOME TOWN.
THERE'S A PLACE WHERE LOVERS GO TO CRY THEIR TROUBLES AWAY...
...AND THEY CALL IT LONESOME TOWN WHERE THE BROKEN HEART STAYS...
...YOU CAN BUY A DREAM OR TWO TO LAST YOU ALL THROUGH THE YEARS...
...AND THE ONLY PRICE YOU PAY...
...IS A HEART FULL OF TEARS.
IS A HEART FULL OF TEEAARS.
GOING DOWN TO LONESOME TOWN WHERE THE BROKEN HEARTS STAY.
GOING DOWN TO LONESOME TOWN TO CRY MY TROUBLES AWAAYY.
IN THE TOWN OF BROKEN DREAMS THE STREETS ARE FILLED WITH REGRET...
...MAYBE DOWN IN LONESOME TOWN I CAN LEARN TO FORGET.
...I CAN LEARN TO FORGEEEEET...

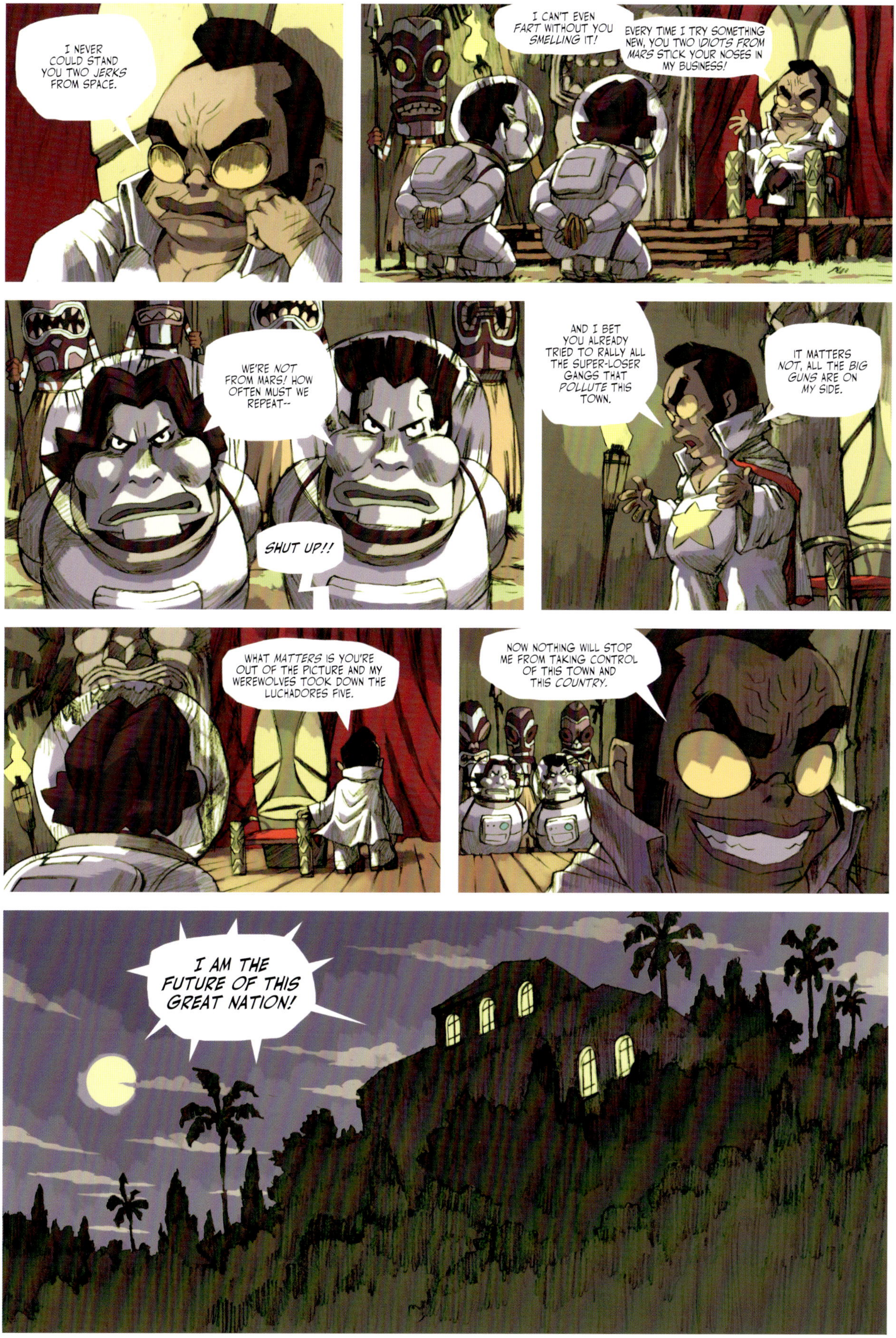
I NEVER COULD STAND YOU TWO JERKS FROM SPACE.
I CAN'T EVEN FART WITHOUT YOU SMELLING IT!
EVERY TIME I TRY SOMETHING NEW, YOU TWO IDIOTS FROM MARS STICK YOUR NOSES IN MY BUSINESS!
WE'RE NOT FROM MARS! HOW OFTEN MUST WE REPEAT--
SHUT UP!!
AND I BET YOU ALREADY TRIED TO RALLY ALL THE SUPER-LOSER GANGS THAT POLLUTE THIS TOWN.
IT MATTERS NOT, ALL THE BIG GUNS ARE ON MY SIDE.
WHAT MATTERS IS YOU'RE OUT OF THE PICTURE AND MY WEREWOLVES TOOK DOWN THE LUCHADORES FIVE.
NOW NOTHING WILL STOP ME FROM TAKING CONTROL OF THIS TOWN AND THIS COUNTRY.
I AM THE FUTURE OF THIS GREAT NATION!

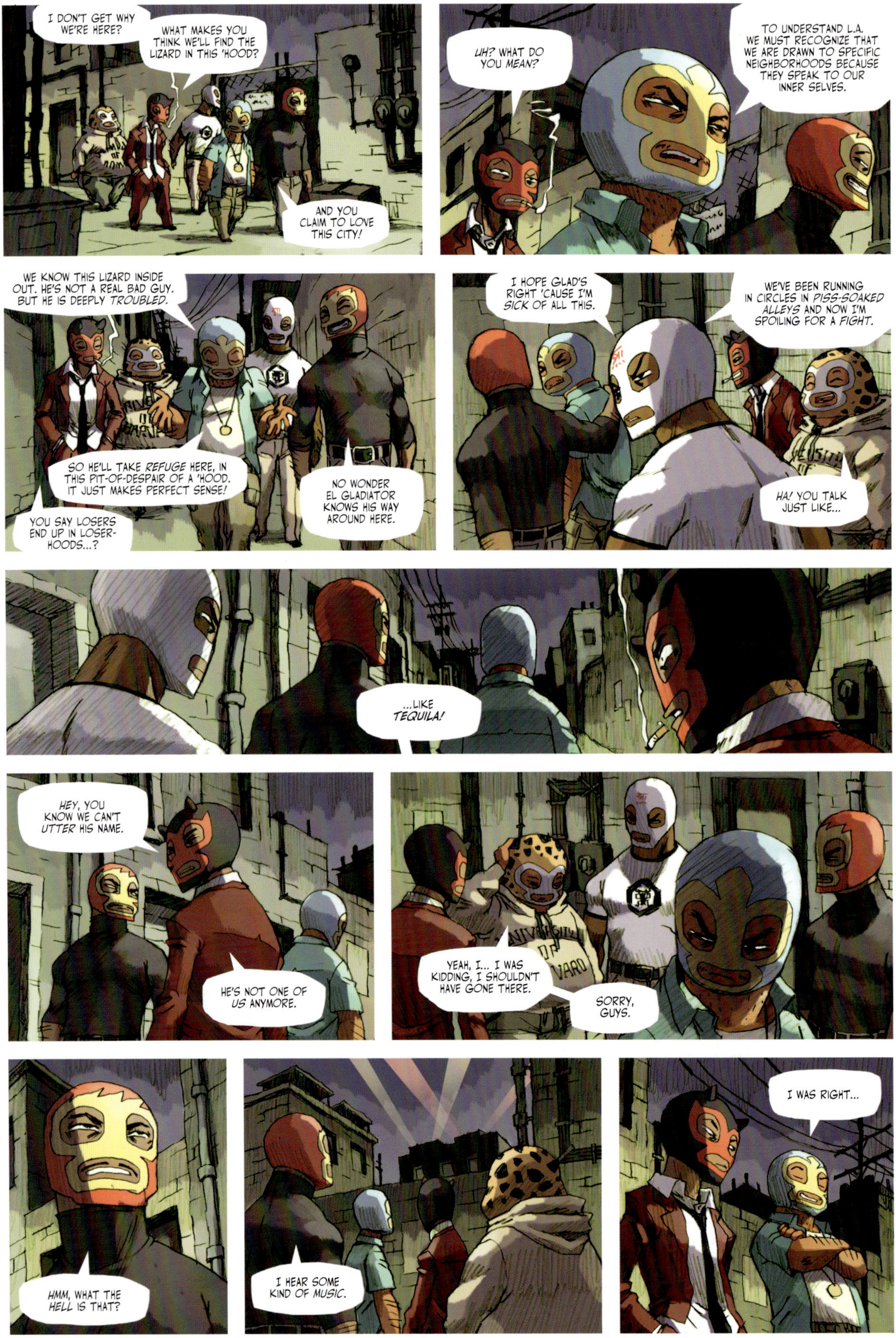
I DON'T GET WHY WE'RE HERE?
WHAT MAKES YOU THINK WE'LL FIND THE LIZARD IN THIS 'HOOD?
AND YOU CLAIM TO LOVE THIS CITY!
UH? WHAT DO YOU MEAN?
TO UNDERSTAND L.A. WE MUST RECOGNIZE THAT WE ARE DRAWN TO SPECIFIC NEIGHBORHOODS BECAUSE THEY SPEAK TO OUR INNER SELVES.
WE KNOW THIS LIZARD INSIDE OUT. HE'S NOT A REAL BAD GUY. BUT HE IS DEEPLY TROUBLED.
SO HE'LL TAKE REFUGE HERE, IN THIS PIT-OF-DESPAIR OF A 'HOOD. IT JUST MAKES PERFECT SENSE!
YOU SAY LOSERS END UP IN LOSER-HOODS...?
NO WONDER EL GLADIATOR KNOWS HIS WAY AROUND HERE.
I HOPE GLAD'S RIGHT 'CAUSE I'M SICK OF ALL THIS.
WE'VE BEEN RUNNING IN CIRCLES IN PISS-SOAKED ALLEYS AND NOW I'M SPOILING FOR A FIGHT.
HA! YOU TALK JUST LIKE...
...LIKE TEQUILA!
HEY, YOU KNOW WE CAN'T UTTER HIS NAME.
HE'S NOT ONE OF US ANYMORE.
YEAH, I... I WAS KIDDING, I SHOULDN'T HAVE GONE THERE.
SORRY, GUYS.
HMM, WHAT THE HELL IS THAT?
I HEAR SOME KIND OF MUSIC.
I WAS RIGHT...

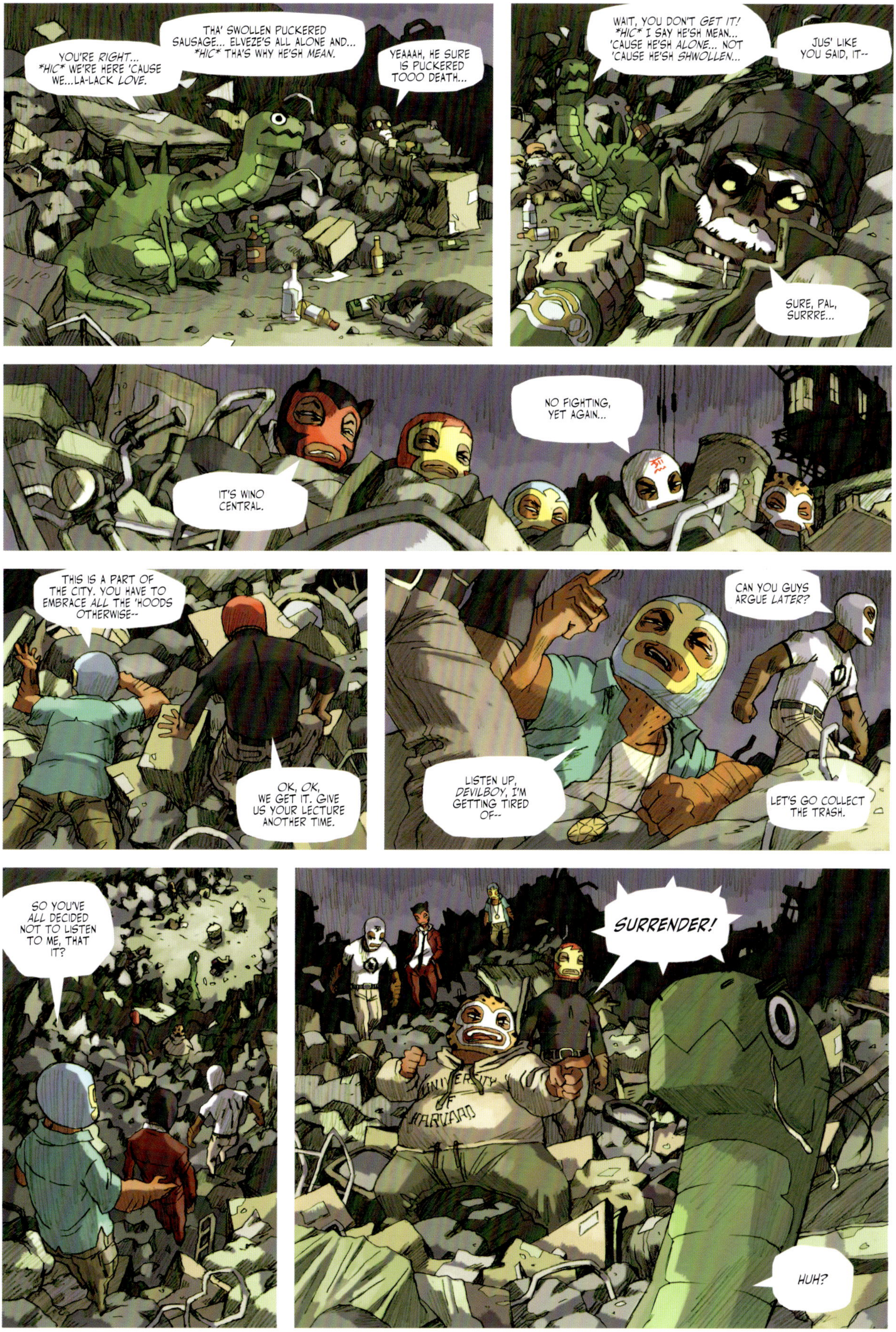
THA' SWOLLEN PUCKERED SAUSAGE... ELVEZE'S ALL ALONE AND... *HIC* THA'S WHY HE'SH MEAN.
YOU'RE RIGHT... *HIC* WE'RE HERE 'CAUSE WE...LA-LACK LOVE.
YEAAAH, HE SURE IS PUCKERED TOOO DEATH...
WAIT, YOU DON'T GET IT! *HIC* I SAY HE'SH MEAN... 'CAUSE HE'SH ALONE... NOT 'CAUSE HE'SH SHWOLLEN...
JUS' LIKE YOU SAID, IT--
SURE, PAL, SURRRE...
IT'S WINO CENTRAL.
NO FIGHTING, YET AGAIN...
THIS IS A PART OF THE CITY. YOU HAVE TO EMBRACE ALL THE 'HOODS OTHERWISE--
OK, OK, WE GET IT. GIVE US YOUR LECTURE ANOTHER TIME.
LISTEN UP, DEVILBOY, I'M GETTING TIRED OF--
CAN YOU GUYS ARGUE LATER?
LET'S GO COLLECT THE TRASH.
SO YOU'VE ALL DECIDED NOT TO LISTEN TO ME, THAT IT?
SURRENDER!
UNIVERSITY OF HARVARD
HUH?

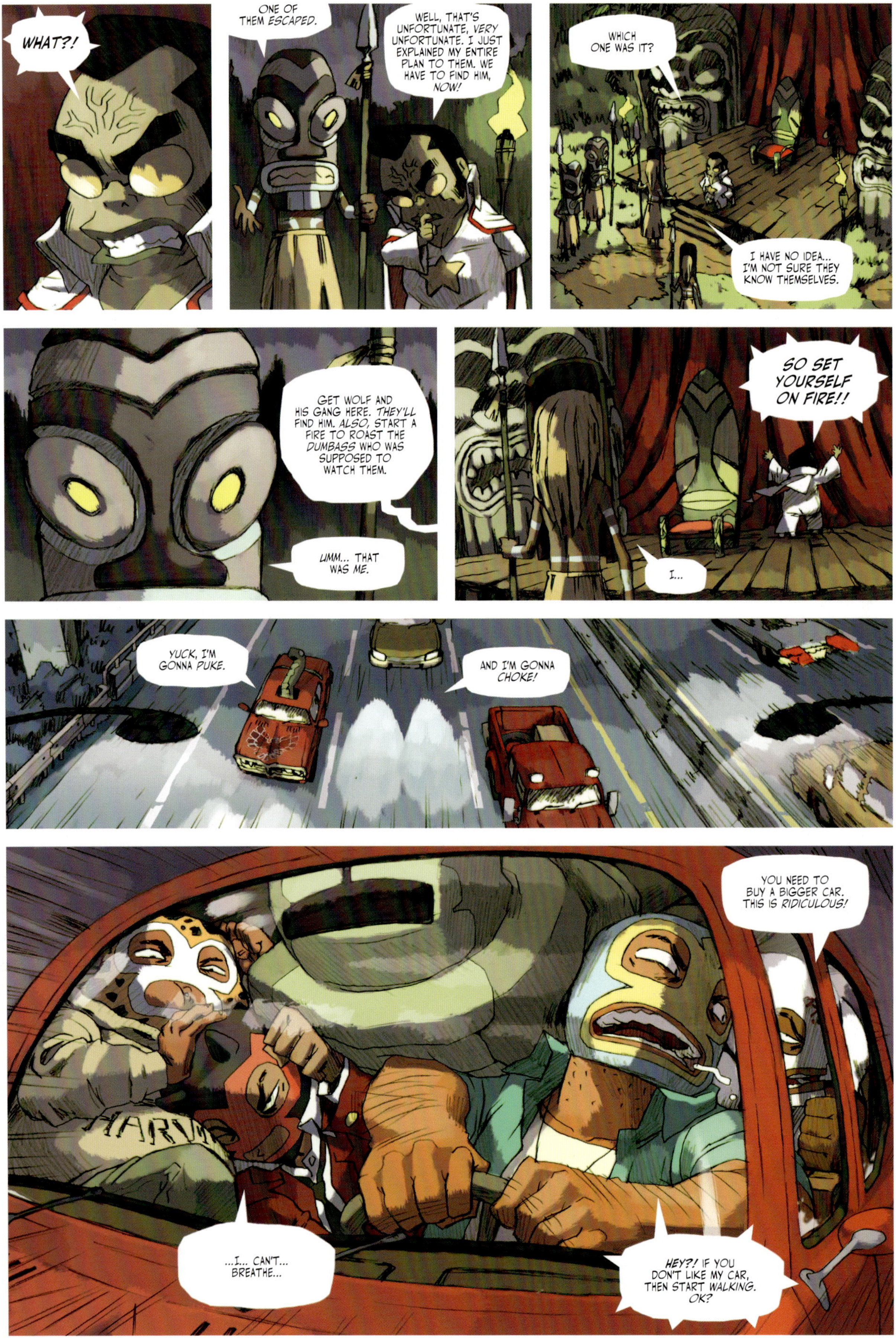
WHAT?!
ONE OF THEM ESCAPED.
WELL, THAT'S UNFORTUNATE, VERY UNFORTUNATE. I JUST EXPLAINED MY ENTIRE PLAN TO THEM. WE HAVE TO FIND HIM, NOW!
WHICH ONE WAS IT?
I HAVE NO IDEA... I'M NOT SURE THEY KNOW THEMSELVES.
GET WOLF AND HIS GANG HERE. THEY'LL FIND HIM. ALSO, START A FIRE TO ROAST THE DUMBASS WHO WAS SUPPOSED TO WATCH THEM.
UMM... THAT WAS ME.
SO SET YOURSELF ON FIRE!!
I...
YUCK, I'M GONNA PUKE.
AND I'M GONNA CHOKE!
YOU NEED TO BUY A BIGGER CAR. THIS IS RIDICULOUS!
...I... CAN'T... BREATHE...
HEY?! IF YOU DON'T LIKE MY CAR, THEN START WALKING. OK?

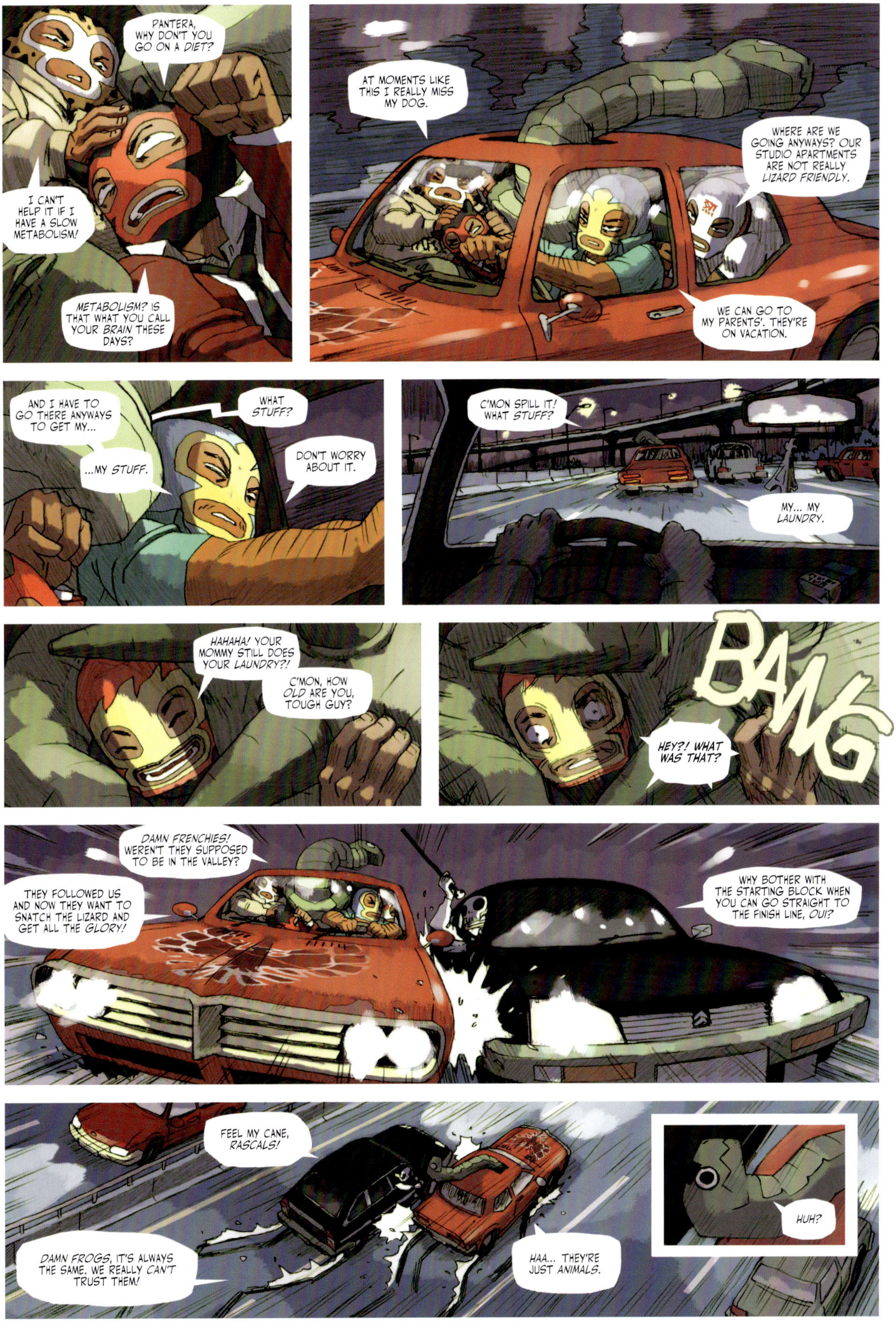
PANTERA, WHY DON'T YOU GO ON A DIET?
I CAN'T HELP IT IF I HAVE A SLOW METABOLISM!
METABOLISM? IS THAT WHAT YOU CALL YOUR BRAIN THESE DAYS?
AT MOMENTS LIKE THIS I REALLY MISS MY DOG.
WHERE ARE WE GOING ANYWAYS? OUR STUDIO APARTMENTS ARE NOT REALLY LIZARD FRIENDLY.
WE CAN GO TO MY PARENTS'. THEY'RE ON VACATION.
AND I HAVE TO GO THERE ANYWAYS TO GET MY...
...MY STUFF.
WHAT STUFF?
DON'T WORRY ABOUT IT.
C'MON SPILL IT! WHAT STUFF?
MY... MY LAUNDRY.
HAHAHA! YOUR MOMMY STILL DOES YOUR LAUNDRY?!
C'MON, HOW OLD ARE YOU, TOUGH GUY?
BANG
HEY?! WHAT WAS THAT?
DAMN FRENCHIES! WEREN'T THEY SUPPOSED TO BE IN THE VALLEY?
THEY FOLLOWED US AND NOW THEY WANT TO SNATCH THE LIZARD AND GET ALL THE GLORY!
WHY BOTHER WITH THE STARTING BLOCK WHEN YOU CAN GO STRAIGHT TO THE FINISH LINE, OUI?
FEEL MY CANE, RASCALS!
DAMN FROGS, IT'S ALWAYS THE SAME. WE REALLY CAN'T TRUST THEM!
HAA... THEY'RE JUST ANIMALS.
HUH?

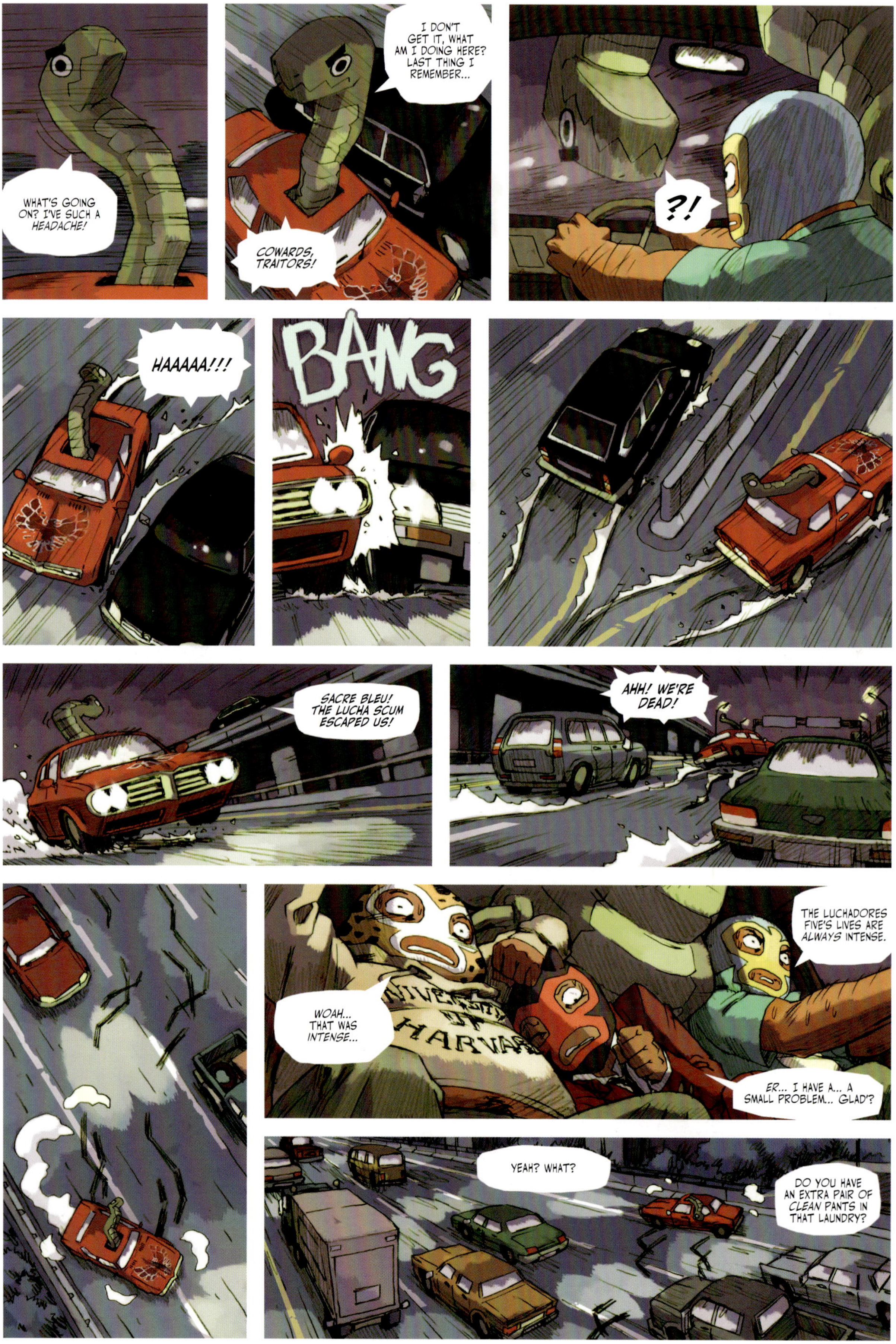
WHAT'S GOING ON? I'VE SUCH A HEADACHE!
I DON'T GET IT, WHAT AM I DOING HERE? LAST THING I REMEMBER...
COWARDS, TRAITORS!
?!
HAAAAA!!!
BANG
SACRE BLEU! THE LUCHA SCUM ESCAPED US!
AHH! WE'RE DEAD!
THE LUCHADORES FIVE'S LIVES ARE ALWAYS INTENSE.
WOAH... THAT WAS INTENSE...
ER... I HAVE A... A SMALL PROBLEM... GLAD'?
YEAH? WHAT?
DO YOU HAVE AN EXTRA PAIR OF CLEAN PANTS IN THAT LAUNDRY?

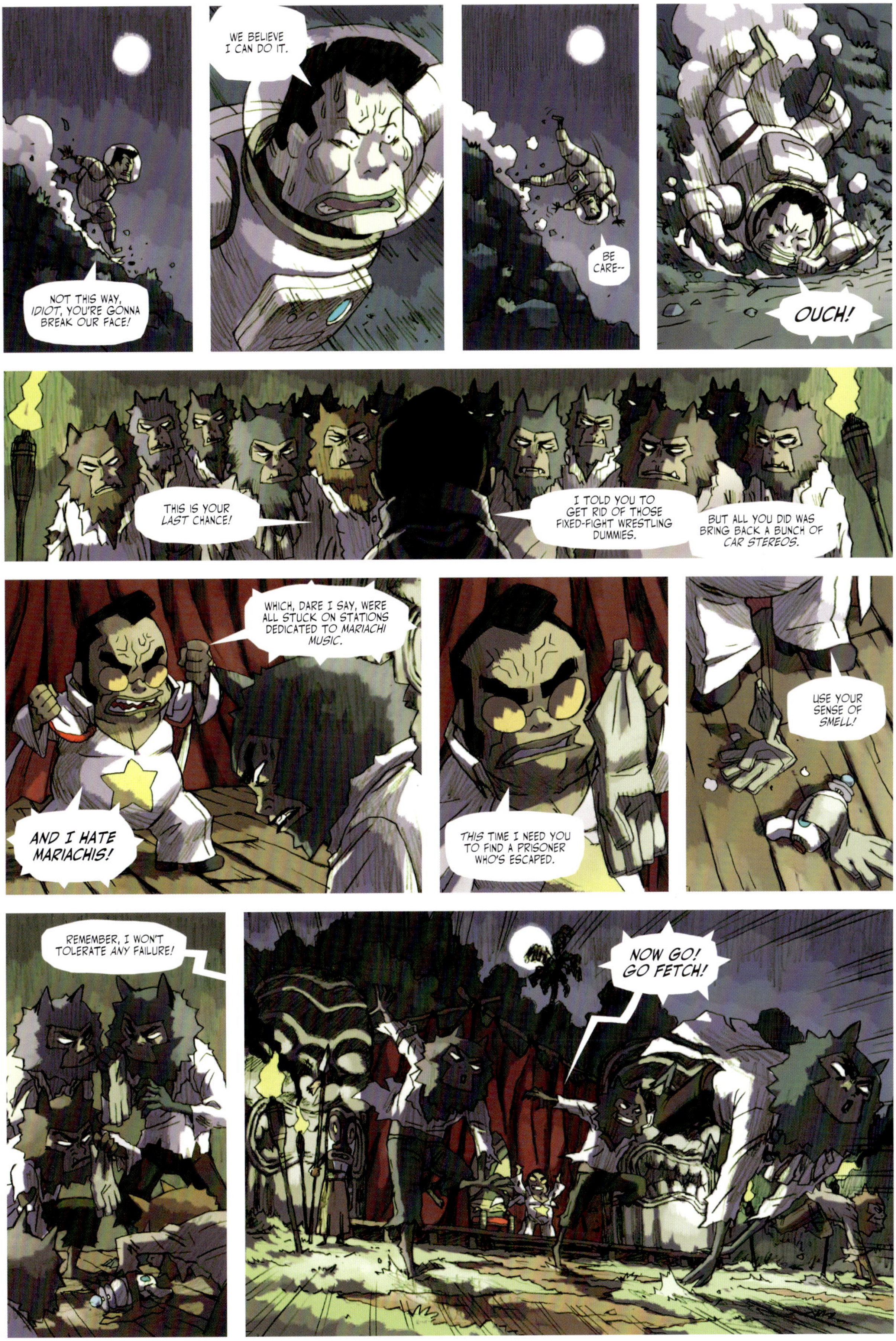
NOT THIS WAY, IDIOT, YOU'RE GONNA BREAK OUR FACE!
WE BELIEVE I CAN DO IT.
BE CARE--
OUCH!
THIS IS YOUR LAST CHANCE!
I TOLD YOU TO GET RID OF THOSE FIXED-FIGHT WRESTLING DUMMIES.
BUT ALL YOU DID WAS BRING BACK A BUNCH OF CAR STEREOS.
WHICH, DARE I SAY, WERE ALL STUCK ON STATIONS DEDICATED TO MARIACHI MUSIC.
AND I HATE MARIACHIS!
THIS TIME I NEED YOU TO FIND A PRISONER WHO'S ESCAPED.
USE YOUR SENSE OF SMELL!
REMEMBER, I WON'T TOLERATE ANY FAILURE!
NOW GO! GO FETCH!

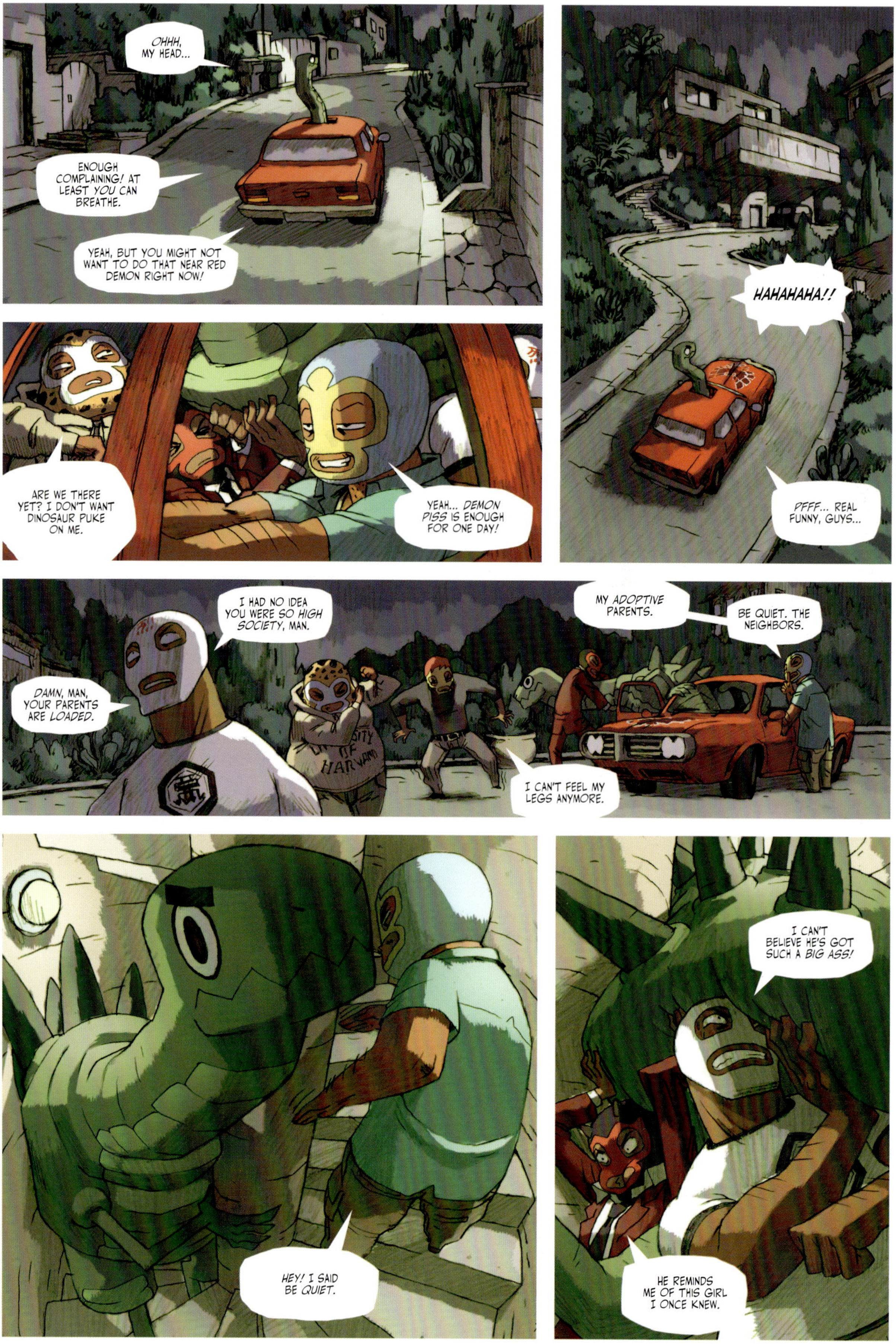
OHHH, MY HEAD...
ENOUGH COMPLAINING! AT LEAST YOU CAN BREATHE.
YEAH, BUT YOU MIGHT NOT WANT TO DO THAT NEAR RED DEMON RIGHT NOW!
HAHAHAHA!!
ARE WE THERE YET? I DON'T WANT DINOSAUR PUKE ON ME.
YEAH... DEMON PISS IS ENOUGH FOR ONE DAY!
PFFF... REAL FUNNY, GUYS...
DAMN, MAN, YOUR PARENTS ARE LOADED.
I HAD NO IDEA YOU WERE SO HIGH SOCIETY, MAN.
I CAN'T FEEL MY LEGS ANYMORE.
MY ADOPTIVE PARENTS.
BE QUIET. THE NEIGHBORS.
HEY! I SAID BE QUIET.
I CAN'T BELIEVE HE'S GOT SUCH A BIG ASS!
HE REMINDS ME OF THIS GIRL I ONCE KNEW.

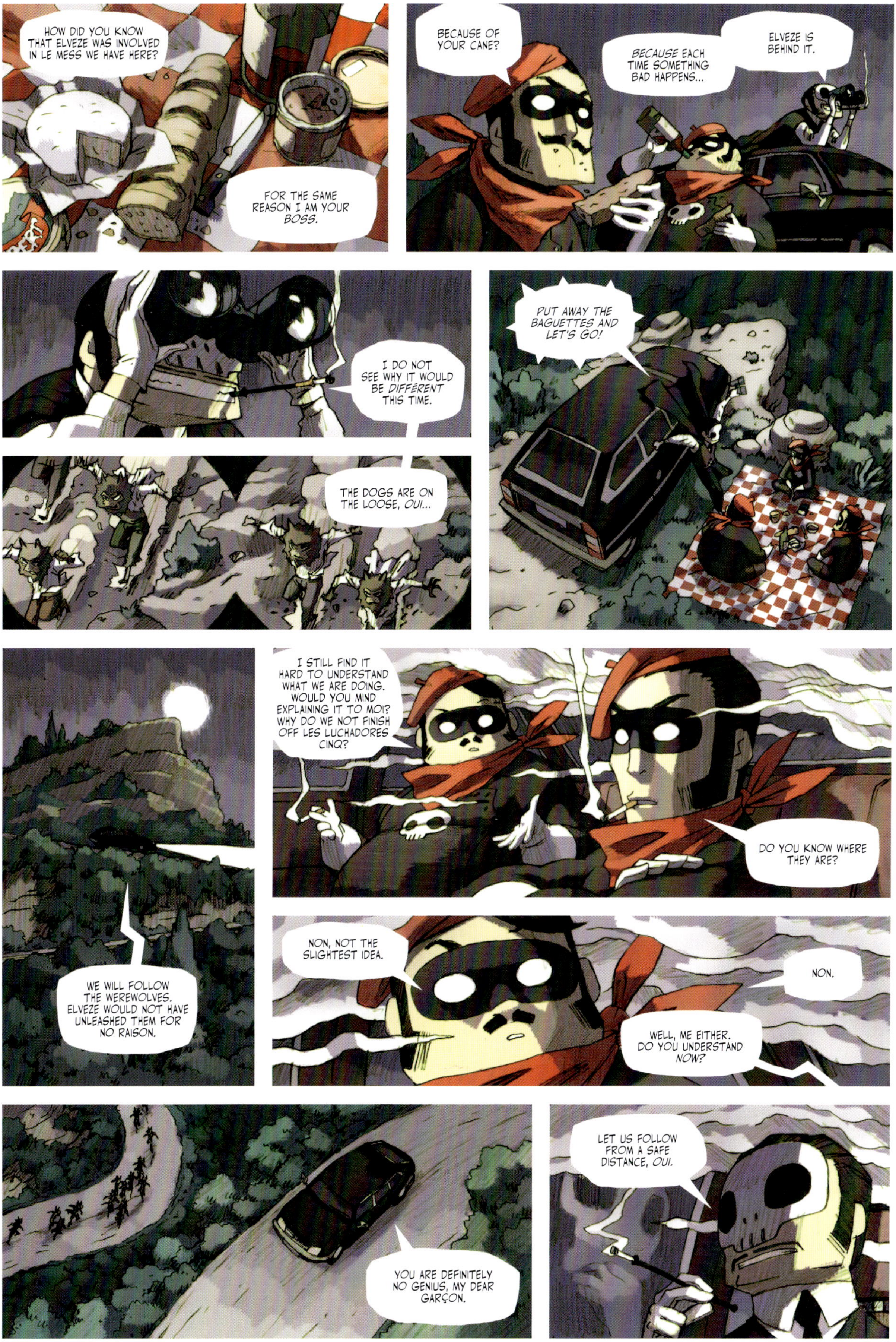
HOW DID YOU KNOW THAT ELVEZE WAS INVOLVED IN LE MESS WE HAVE HERE?
FOR THE SAME REASON I AM YOUR BOSS.
BECAUSE OF YOUR CANE?
BECAUSE EACH TIME SOMETHING BAD HAPPENS...
ELVEZE IS BEHIND IT.
I DO NOT SEE WHY IT WOULD BE DIFFERENT THIS TIME.
THE DOGS ARE ON THE LOOSE, OUI...
PUT AWAY THE BAGUETTES AND LET'S GO!
WE WILL FOLLOW THE WEREWOLVES. ELVEZE WOULD NOT HAVE UNLEASHED THEM FOR NO RAISON.
I STILL FIND IT HARD TO UNDERSTAND WHAT WE ARE DOING. WOULD YOU MIND EXPLAINING IT TO MOI? WHY DO WE NOT FINISH OFF LES LUCHADORES CINQ?
DO YOU KNOW WHERE THEY ARE?
NON, NOT THE SLIGHTEST IDEA.
NON.
WELL, ME EITHER. DO YOU UNDERSTAND NOW?
YOU ARE DEFINITELY NO GENIUS, MY DEAR GARÇON.
LET US FOLLOW FROM A SAFE DISTANCE, OUI.

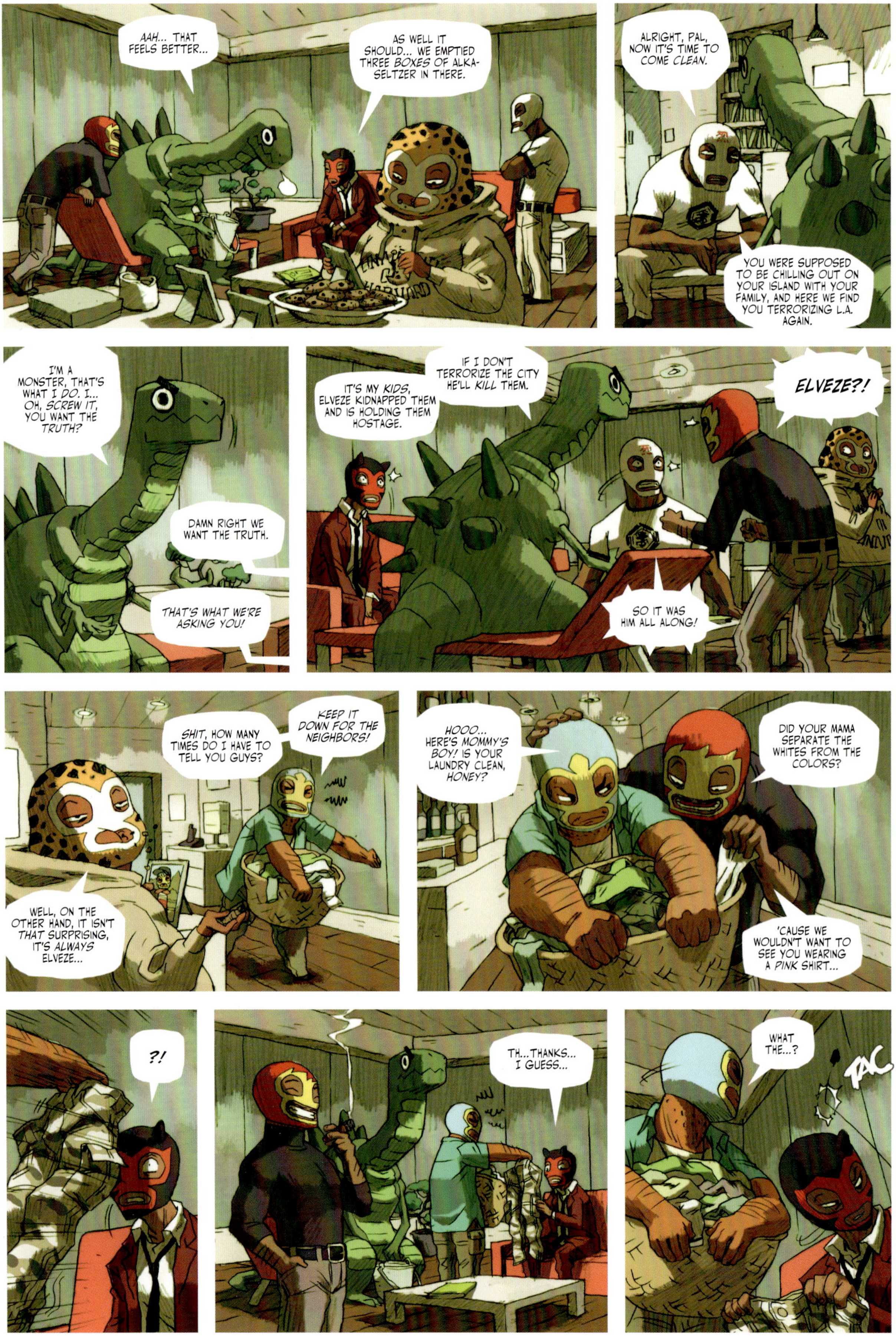
AAH... THAT FEELS BETTER...
AS WELL IT SHOULD... WE EMPTIED THREE BOXES OF ALKA-SELTZER IN THERE.
ALRIGHT, PAL, NOW IT'S TIME TO COME CLEAN.
YOU WERE SUPPOSED TO BE CHILLING OUT ON YOUR ISLAND WITH YOUR FAMILY, AND HERE WE FIND YOU TERRORIZING L.A. AGAIN.
I'M A MONSTER, THAT'S WHAT I DO. I... OH, SCREW IT, YOU WANT THE TRUTH?
DAMN RIGHT WE WANT THE TRUTH.
THAT'S WHAT WE'RE ASKING YOU!
IT'S MY KIDS, ELVEZE KIDNAPPED THEM AND IS HOLDING THEM HOSTAGE.
IF I DON'T TERRORIZE THE CITY HE'LL KILL THEM.
ELVEZE?!
SO IT WAS HIM ALL ALONG!
WELL, ON THE OTHER HAND, IT ISN'T THAT SURPRISING, IT'S ALWAYS ELVEZE...
SHIT, HOW MANY TIMES DO I HAVE TO TELL YOU GUYS?
KEEP IT DOWN FOR THE NEIGHBORS!
HOOO... HERE'S MOMMY'S BOY! IS YOUR LAUNDRY CLEAN, HONEY?
DID YOUR MAMA SEPARATE THE WHITES FROM THE COLORS?
'CAUSE WE WOULDN'T WANT TO SEE YOU WEARING A PINK SHIRT...
?!
TH...THANKS... I GUESS...
WHAT THE...?
TAC

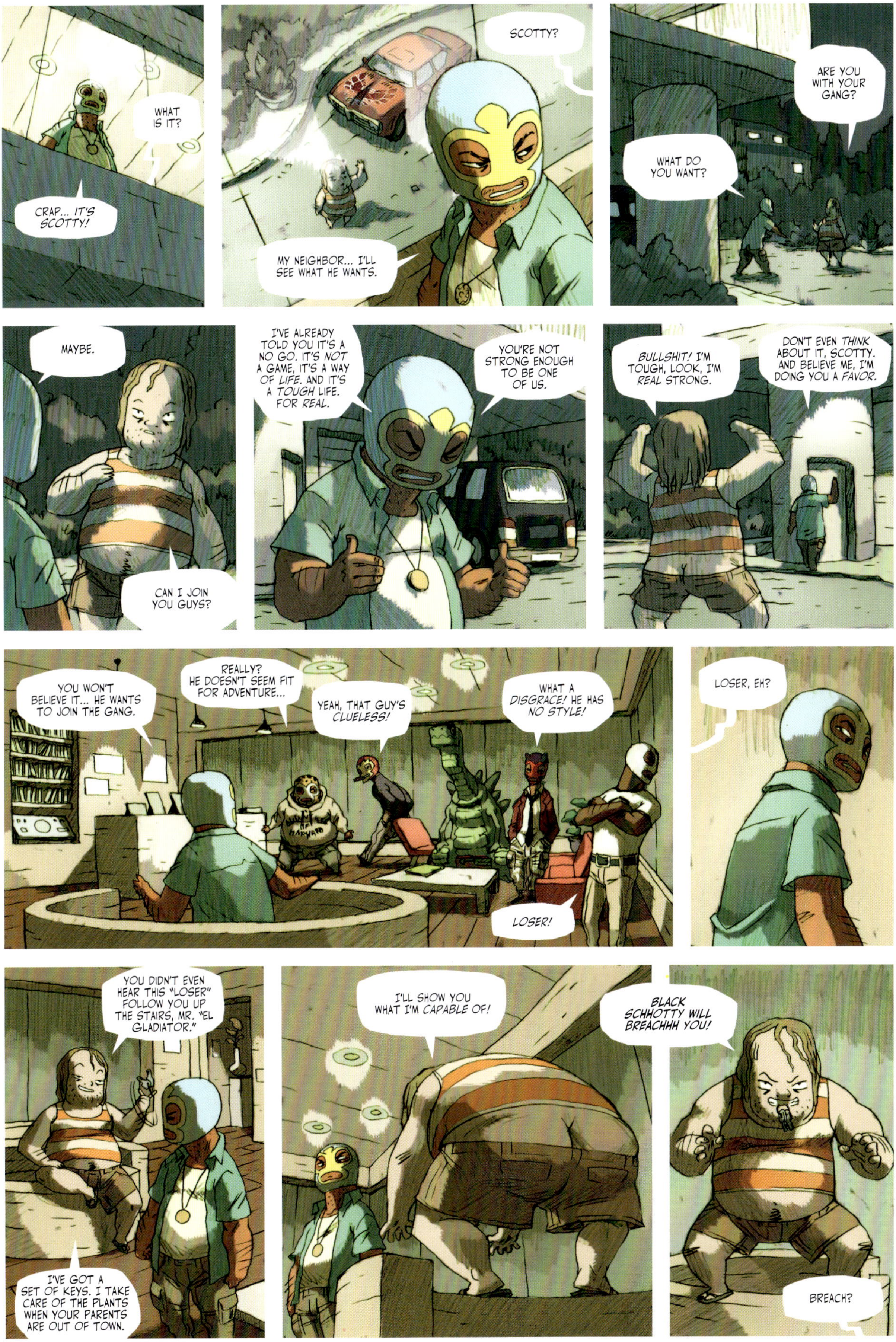
WHAT IS IT?
CRAP... IT'S SCOTTY!
SCOTTY?
MY NEIGHBOR... I'LL SEE WHAT HE WANTS.
WHAT DO YOU WANT?
ARE YOU WITH YOUR GANG?
MAYBE.
CAN I JOIN YOU GUYS?
I'VE ALREADY TOLD YOU IT'S A NO GO. IT'S NOT A GAME, IT'S A WAY OF LIFE. AND IT'S A TOUGH LIFE. FOR REAL.
YOU'RE NOT STRONG ENOUGH TO BE ONE OF US.
BULLSHIT! I'M TOUGH, LOOK, I'M REAL STRONG.
DON'T EVEN THINK ABOUT IT, SCOTTY. AND BELIEVE ME, I'M DOING YOU A FAVOR.
YOU WON'T BELIEVE IT... HE WANTS TO JOIN THE GANG.
REALLY? HE DOESN'T SEEM FIT FOR ADVENTURE...
YEAH, THAT GUY'S CLUELESS!
WHAT A DISGRACE! HE HAS NO STYLE!
LOSER!
LOSER, EH?
YOU DIDN'T EVEN HEAR THIS "LOSER" FOLLOW YOU UP THE STAIRS, MR. "EL GLADIATOR."
I'VE GOT A SET OF KEYS. I TAKE CARE OF THE PLANTS WHEN YOUR PARENTS ARE OUT OF TOWN.
I'LL SHOW YOU WHAT I'M CAPABLE OF!
BLACK SCHHOTTY WILL BREACHHH YOU!
BREACH?

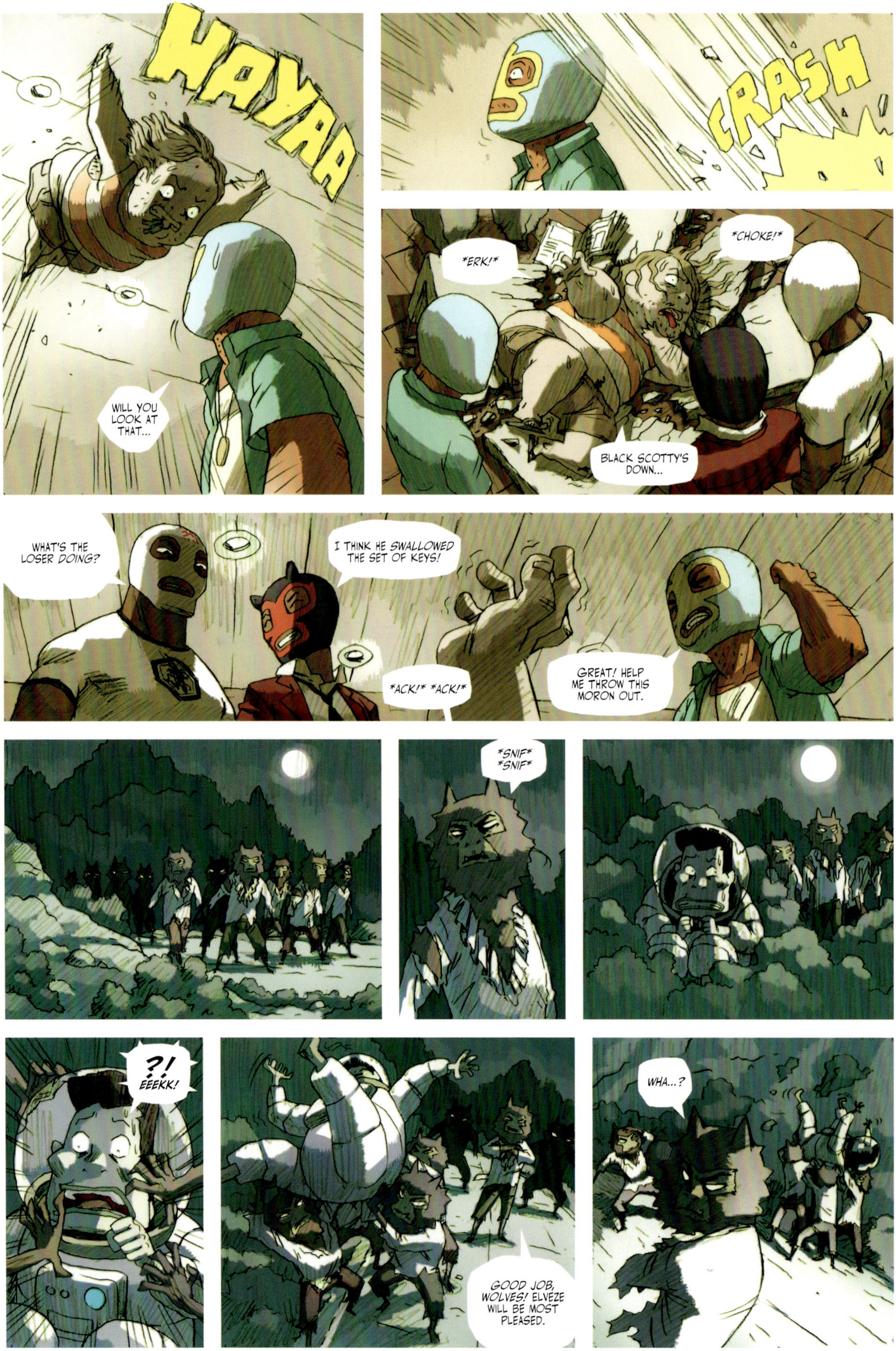
HAYAA
WILL YOU LOOK AT THAT...
CRASH
ERK!
CHOKE!
BLACK SCOTTY'S DOWN...
WHAT'S THE LOSER DOING?
I THINK HE SWALLOWED THE SET OF KEYS!
ACK! *ACK!*
GREAT! HELP ME THROW THIS MORON OUT.
SNIF *SNIF*
?! EEEKK!
GOOD JOB, WOLVES! ELVEZE WILL BE MOST PLEASED.
WHA...?

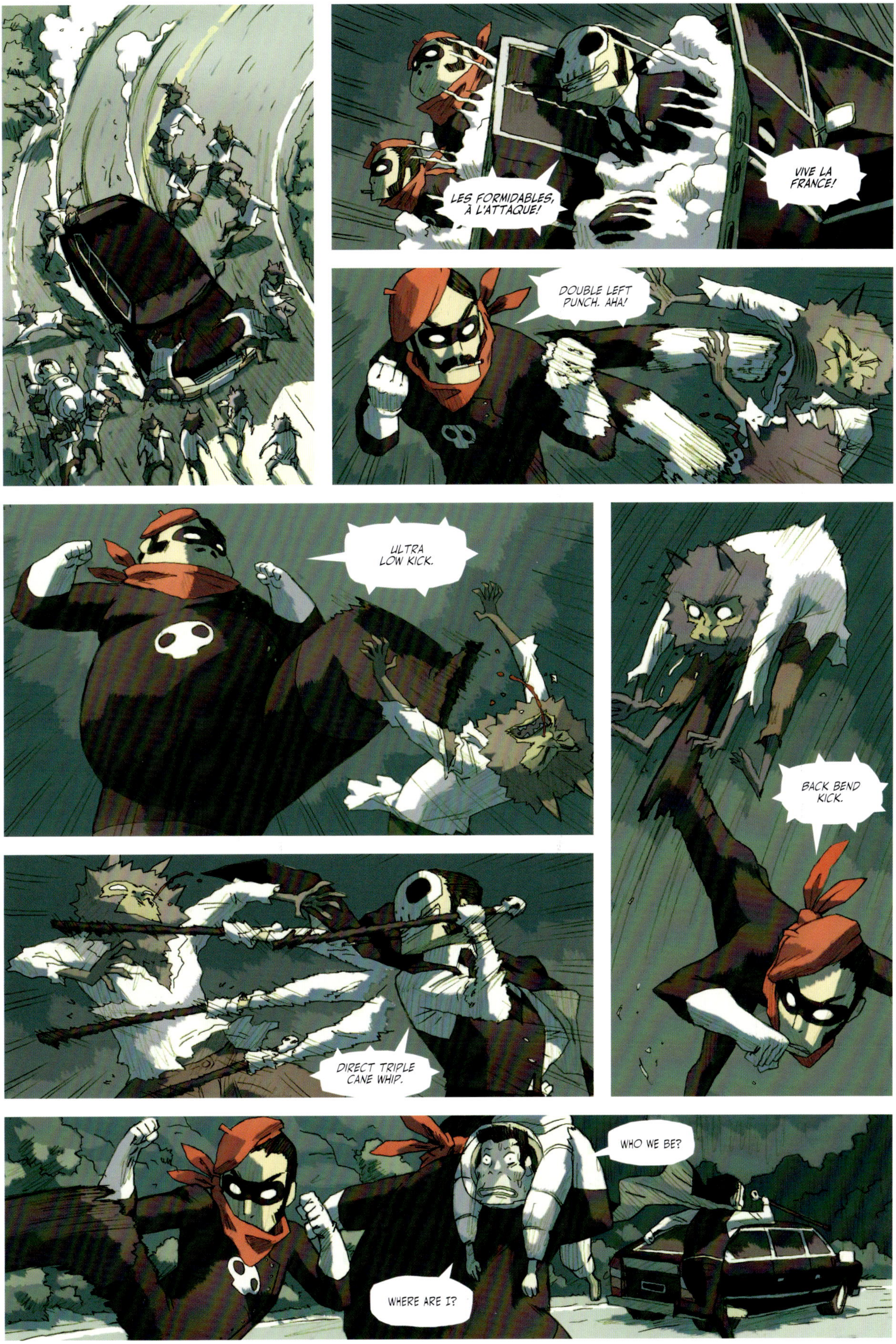
LES FORMIDABLES, À L'ATTAQUE!
VIVE LA FRANCE!
DOUBLE LEFT PUNCH. AHA!
ULTRA LOW KICK.
BACK BEND KICK.
DIRECT TRIPLE CANE WHIP.
WHO WE BE?
WHERE ARE I?

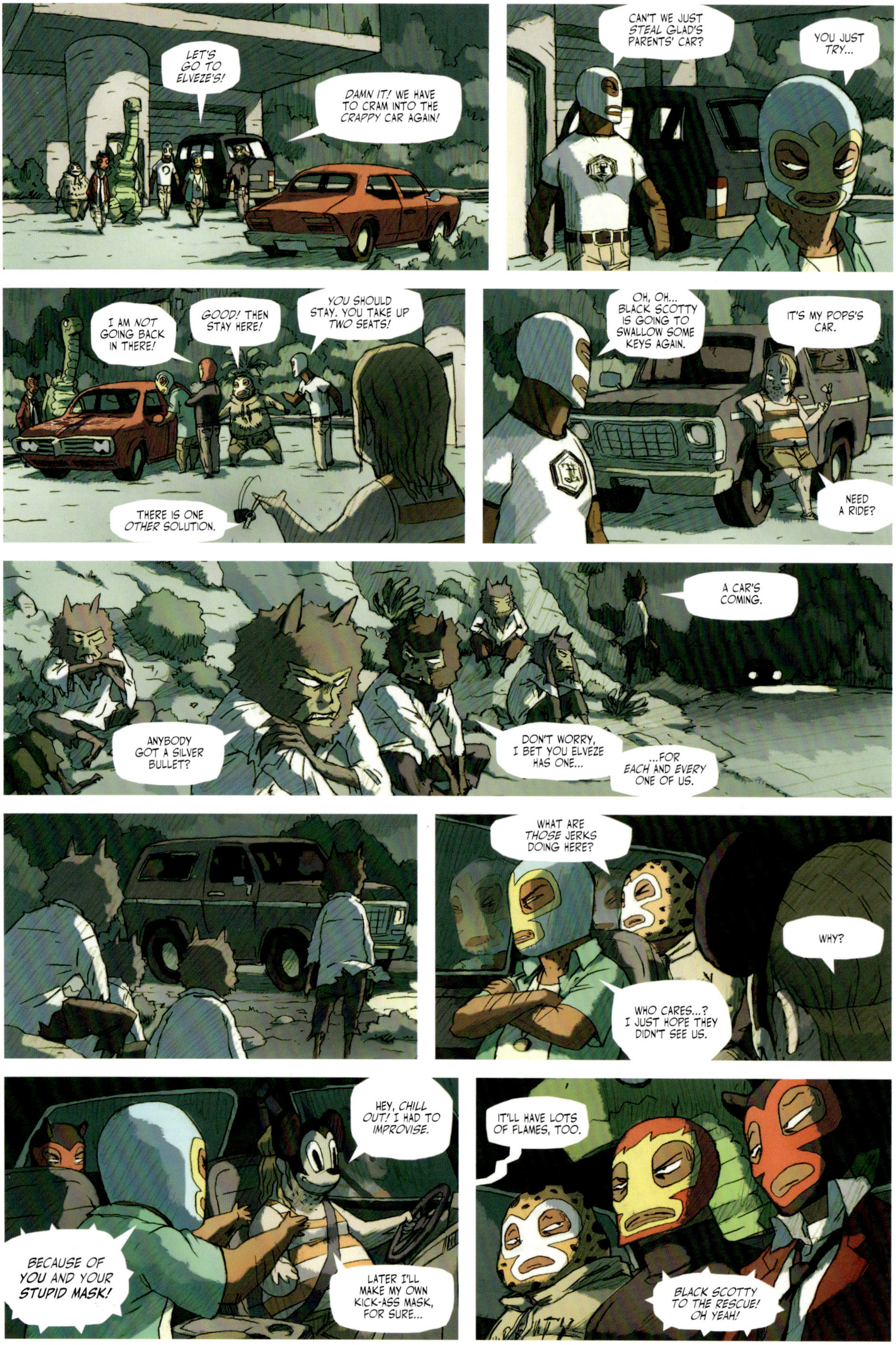
LET'S GO TO ELVEZE'S!
DAMN IT! WE HAVE TO CRAM INTO THE CRAPPY CAR AGAIN!
CAN'T WE JUST STEAL GLAD'S PARENTS' CAR?
YOU JUST TRY...
I AM NOT GOING BACK IN THERE!
GOOD! THEN STAY HERE!
YOU SHOULD STAY. YOU TAKE UP TWO SEATS!
THERE IS ONE OTHER SOLUTION.
OH, OH... BLACK SCOTTY IS GOING TO SWALLOW SOME KEYS AGAIN.
IT'S MY POPS'S CAR.
NEED A RIDE?
A CAR'S COMING.
ANYBODY GOT A SILVER BULLET?
DON'T WORRY, I BET YOU ELVEZE HAS ONE...
...FOR EACH AND EVERY ONE OF US.
WHAT ARE THOSE JERKS DOING HERE?
WHY?
WHO CARES...? I JUST HOPE THEY DIDN'T SEE US.
HEY, CHILL OUT! I HAD TO IMPROVISE.
BECAUSE OF YOU AND YOUR STUPID MASK!
LATER I'LL MAKE MY OWN KICK-ASS MASK, FOR SURE...
IT'LL HAVE LOTS OF FLAMES, TOO.
BLACK SCOTTY TO THE RESCUE! OH YEAH!

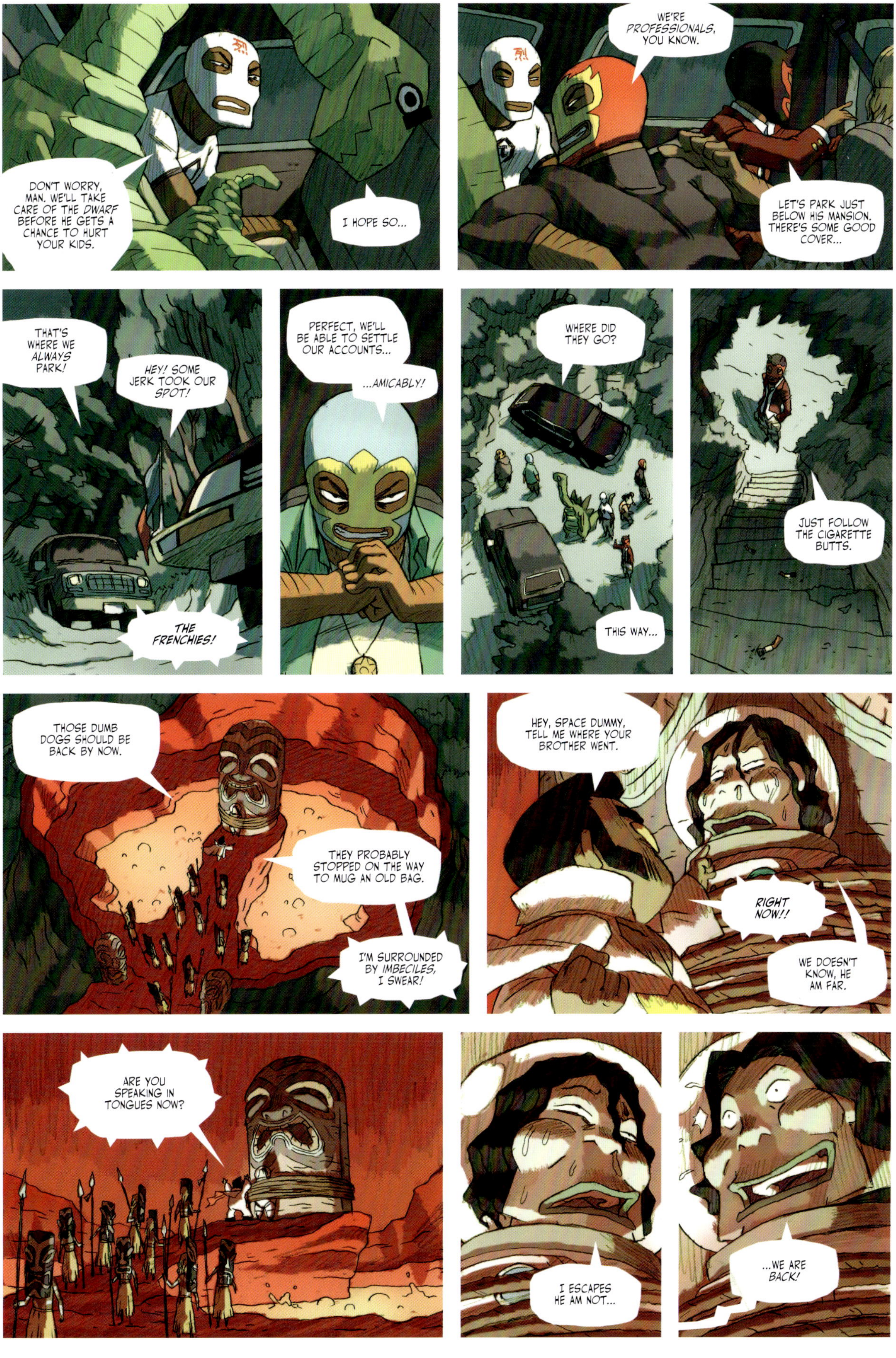

DON'T WORRY, MAN. WE'LL TAKE CARE OF THE DWARF BEFORE HE GETS A CHANCE TO HURT YOUR KIDS.
I HOPE SO...
WE'RE PROFESSIONALS, YOU KNOW.
LET'S PARK JUST BELOW HIS MANSION. THERE'S SOME GOOD COVER...
THAT'S WHERE WE ALWAYS PARK!
HEY! SOME JERK TOOK OUR SPOT!
THE FRENCHIES!
PERFECT, WE'LL BE ABLE TO SETTLE OUR ACCOUNTS...
...AMICABLY!
WHERE DID THEY GO?
THIS WAY...
JUST FOLLOW THE CIGARETTE BUTTS.
THOSE DUMB DOGS SHOULD BE BACK BY NOW.
THEY PROBABLY STOPPED ON THE WAY TO MUG AN OLD BAG.
I'M SURROUNDED BY IMBECILES, I SWEAR!
HEY, SPACE DUMMY, TELL ME WHERE YOUR BROTHER WENT.
RIGHT NOW!!
WE DOESN'T KNOW, HE AM FAR.
ARE YOU SPEAKING IN TONGUES NOW?
I ESCAPES HE AM NOT...
...WE ARE BACK!

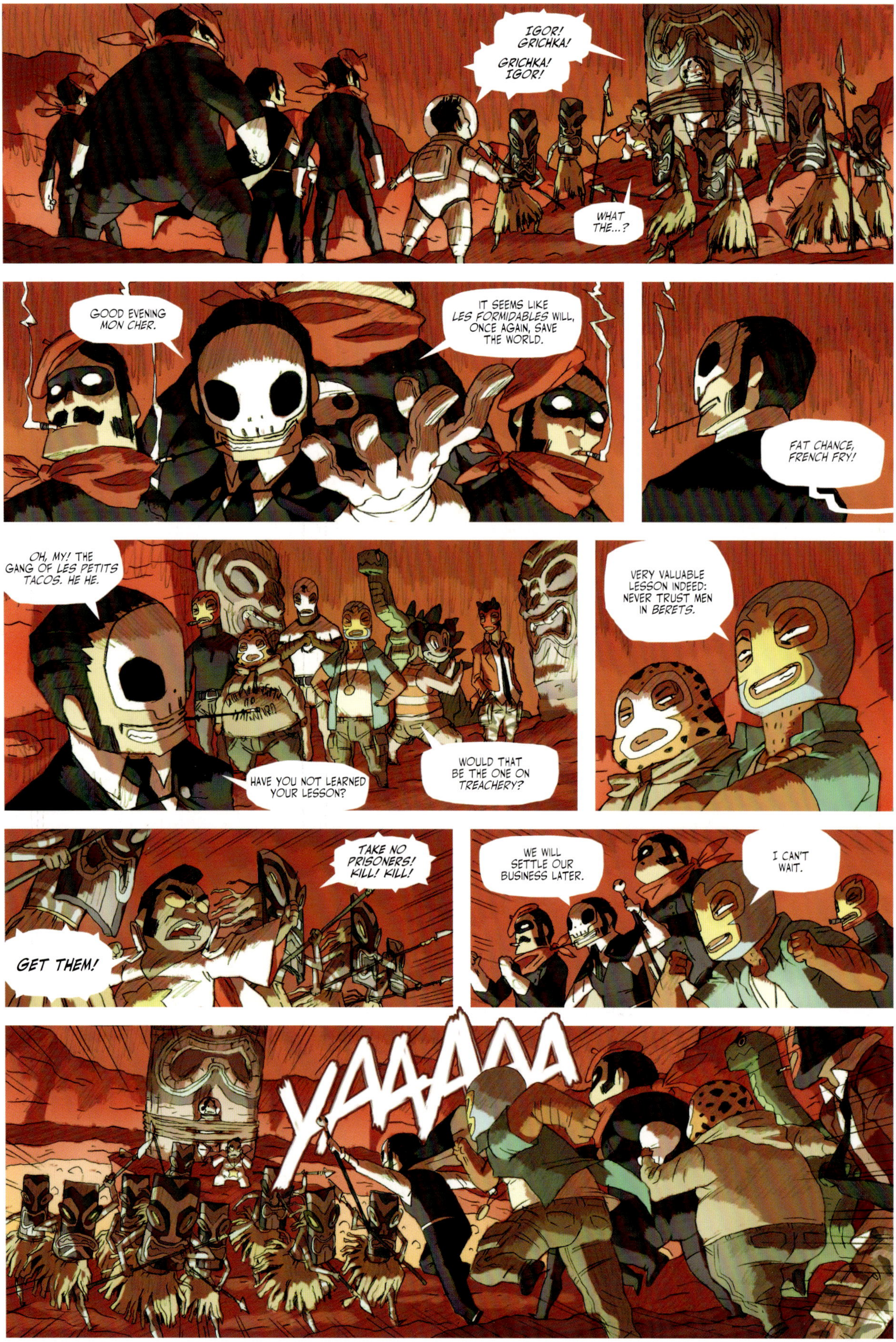
IGOR! GRICHKA!
GRICHKA! IGOR!
WHAT THE...?
GOOD EVENING MON CHER.
IT SEEMS LIKE LES FORMIDABLES WILL, ONCE AGAIN, SAVE THE WORLD.
FAT CHANCE, FRENCH FRY!
OH, MY! THE GANG OF LES PETITS TACOS. HE HE.
HAVE YOU NOT LEARNED YOUR LESSON?
WOULD THAT BE THE ONE ON TREACHERY?
VERY VALUABLE LESSON INDEED: NEVER TRUST MEN IN BERETS.
TAKE NO PRISONERS! KILL! KILL!
GET THEM!
WE WILL SETTLE OUR BUSINESS LATER.
I CAN'T WAIT.
YAAAAA

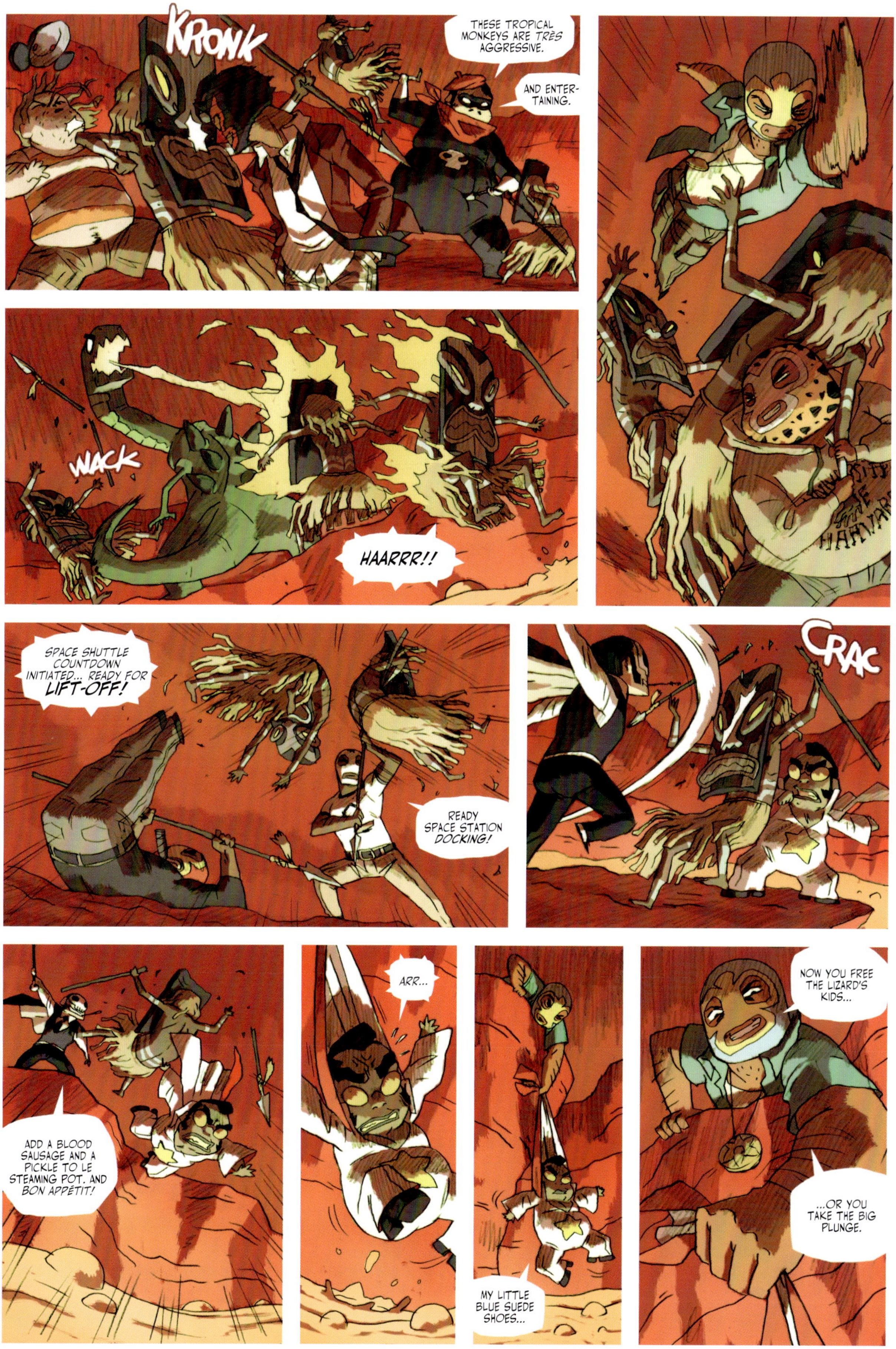
KRONK
THESE TROPICAL MONKEYS ARE TRÈS AGGRESSIVE.
AND ENTERTAINING.
WACK
HAARRR!!
SPACE SHUTTLE COUNTDOWN INITIATED... READY FOR LIFT-OFF!
READY SPACE STATION DOCKING!
CRAC
ADD A BLOOD SAUSAGE AND A PICKLE TO LE STEAMING POT. AND BON APPÉTIT!
ARR...
MY LITTLE BLUE SUEDE SHOES...
NOW YOU FREE THE LIZARD'S KIDS...
...OR YOU TAKE THE BIG PLUNGE.

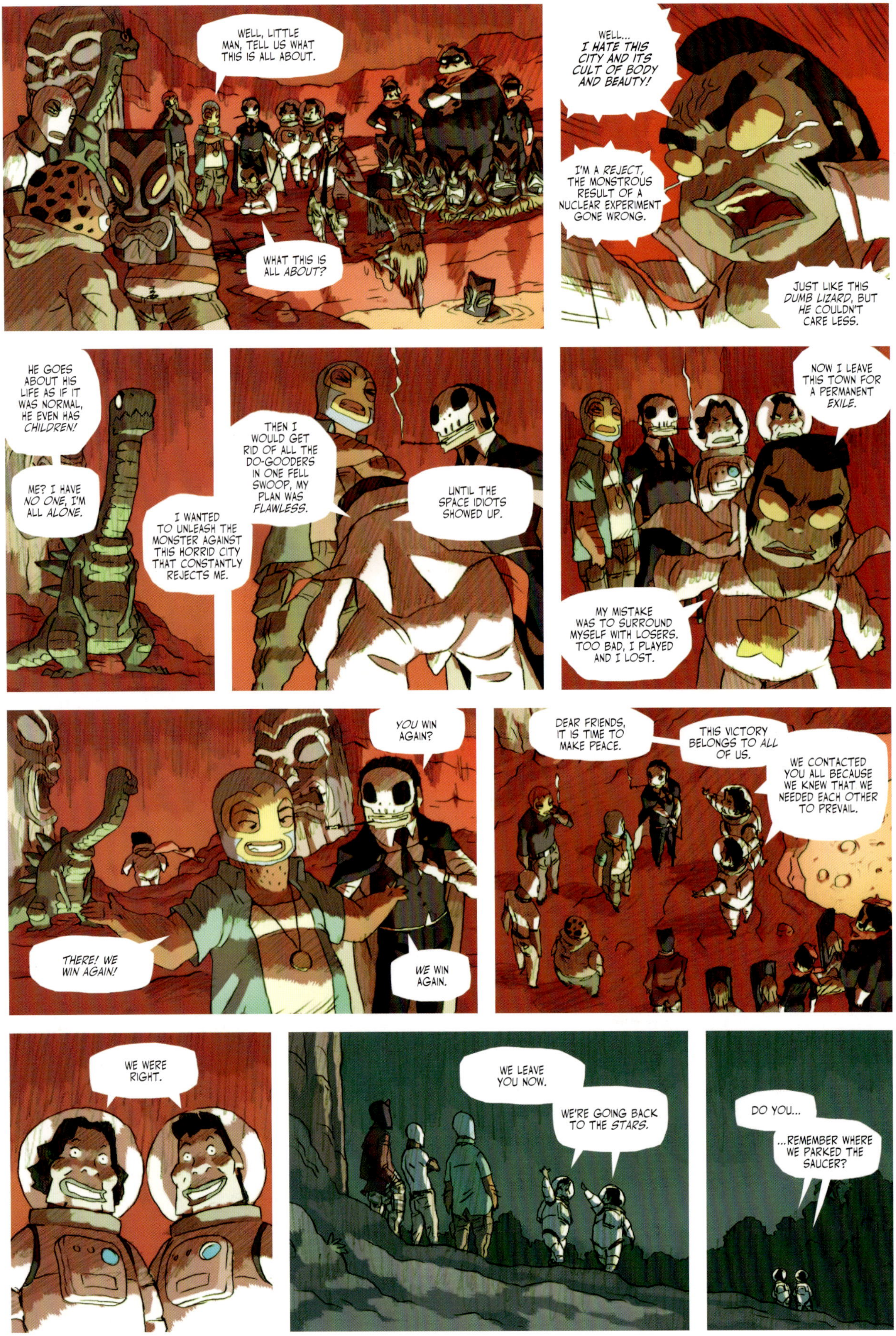
WELL, LITTLE MAN, TELL US WHAT THIS IS ALL ABOUT.
WHAT THIS IS ALL ABOUT?
WELL... I HATE THIS CITY AND ITS CULT OF BODY AND BEAUTY!
I'M A REJECT, THE MONSTROUS RESULT OF A NUCLEAR EXPERIMENT GONE WRONG.
JUST LIKE THIS DUMB LIZARD, BUT HE COULDN'T CARE LESS.
HE GOES ABOUT HIS LIFE AS IF IT WAS NORMAL, HE EVEN HAS CHILDREN!
ME? I HAVE NO ONE, I'M ALL ALONE.
I WANTED TO UNLEASH THE MONSTER AGAINST THIS HORRID CITY THAT CONSTANTLY REJECTS ME.
THEN I WOULD GET RID OF ALL THE DO-GOODERS IN ONE FELL SWOOP, MY PLAN WAS FLAWLESS.
UNTIL THE SPACE IDIOTS SHOWED UP.
NOW I LEAVE THIS TOWN FOR A PERMANENT EXILE.
MY MISTAKE WAS TO SURROUND MYSELF WITH LOSERS. TOO BAD, I PLAYED AND I LOST.
YOU WIN AGAIN?
THERE! WE WIN AGAIN!
WE WIN AGAIN.
DEAR FRIENDS, IT IS TIME TO MAKE PEACE.
THIS VICTORY BELONGS TO ALL OF US.
WE CONTACTED YOU ALL BECAUSE WE KNEW THAT WE NEEDED EACH OTHER TO PREVAIL.
WE WERE RIGHT.
WE LEAVE YOU NOW.
WE'RE GOING BACK TO THE STARS.
DO YOU...
...REMEMBER WHERE WE PARKED THE SAUCER?

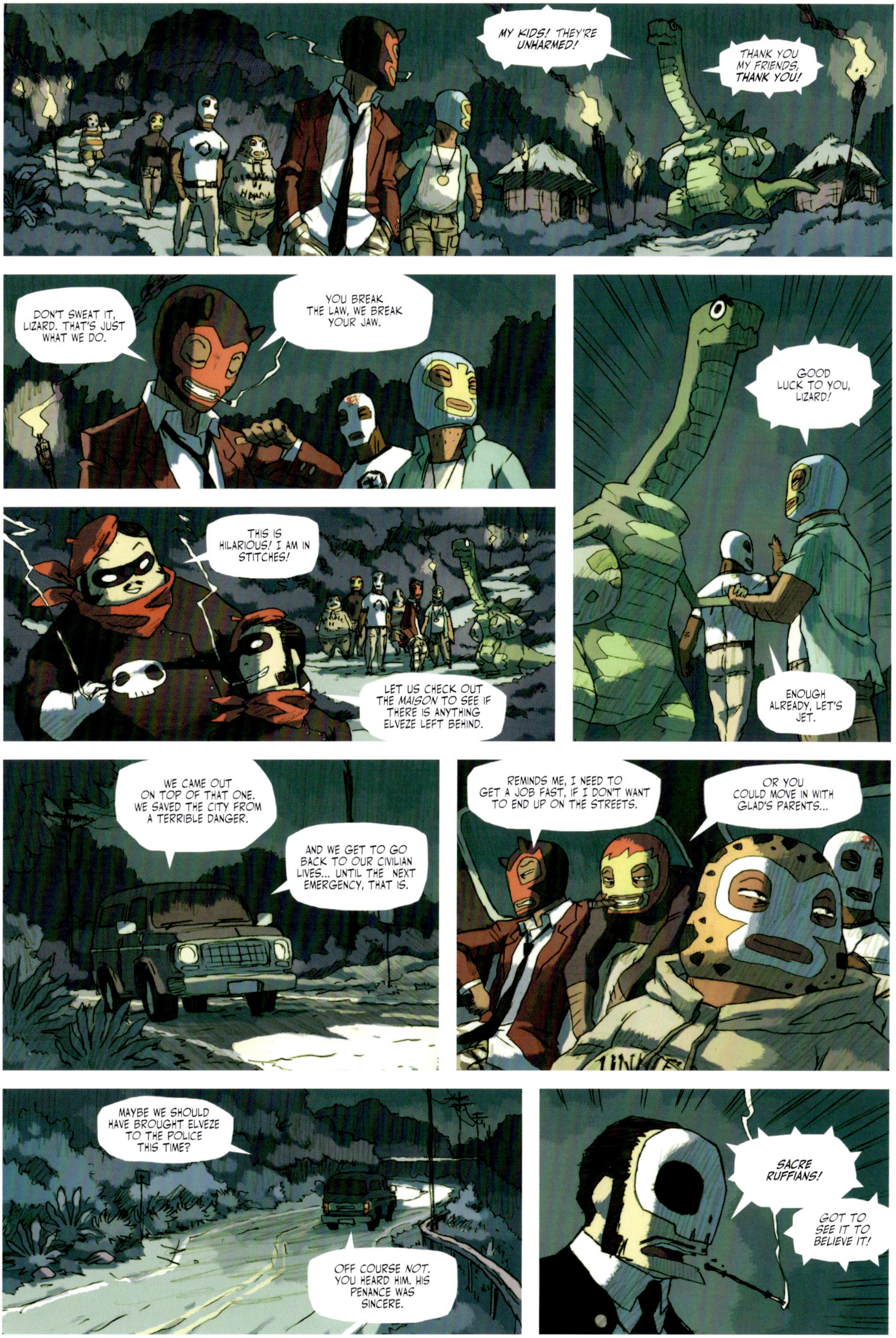
MY KIDS! THEY'RE UNHARMED!
THANK YOU MY FRIENDS, THANK YOU!
DON'T SWEAT IT, LIZARD. THAT'S JUST WHAT WE DO.
YOU BREAK THE LAW, WE BREAK YOUR JAW.
GOOD LUCK TO YOU, LIZARD!
THIS IS HILARIOUS! I AM IN STITCHES!
LET US CHECK OUT THE MAISON TO SEE IF THERE IS ANYTHING ELVEZE LEFT BEHIND.
ENOUGH ALREADY, LET'S JET.
WE CAME OUT ON TOP OF THAT ONE. WE SAVED THE CITY FROM A TERRIBLE DANGER.
AND WE GET TO GO BACK TO OUR CIVILIAN LIVES... UNTIL THE NEXT EMERGENCY, THAT IS.
REMINDS ME, I NEED TO GET A JOB FAST, IF I DON'T WANT TO END UP ON THE STREETS.
OR YOU COULD MOVE IN WITH GLAD'S PARENTS...
MAYBE WE SHOULD HAVE BROUGHT ELVEZE TO THE POLICE THIS TIME?
OFF COURSE NOT. YOU HEARD HIM. HIS PENANCE WAS SINCERE.
SACRE RUFFIANS!
GOT TO SEE IT TO BELIEVE IT!

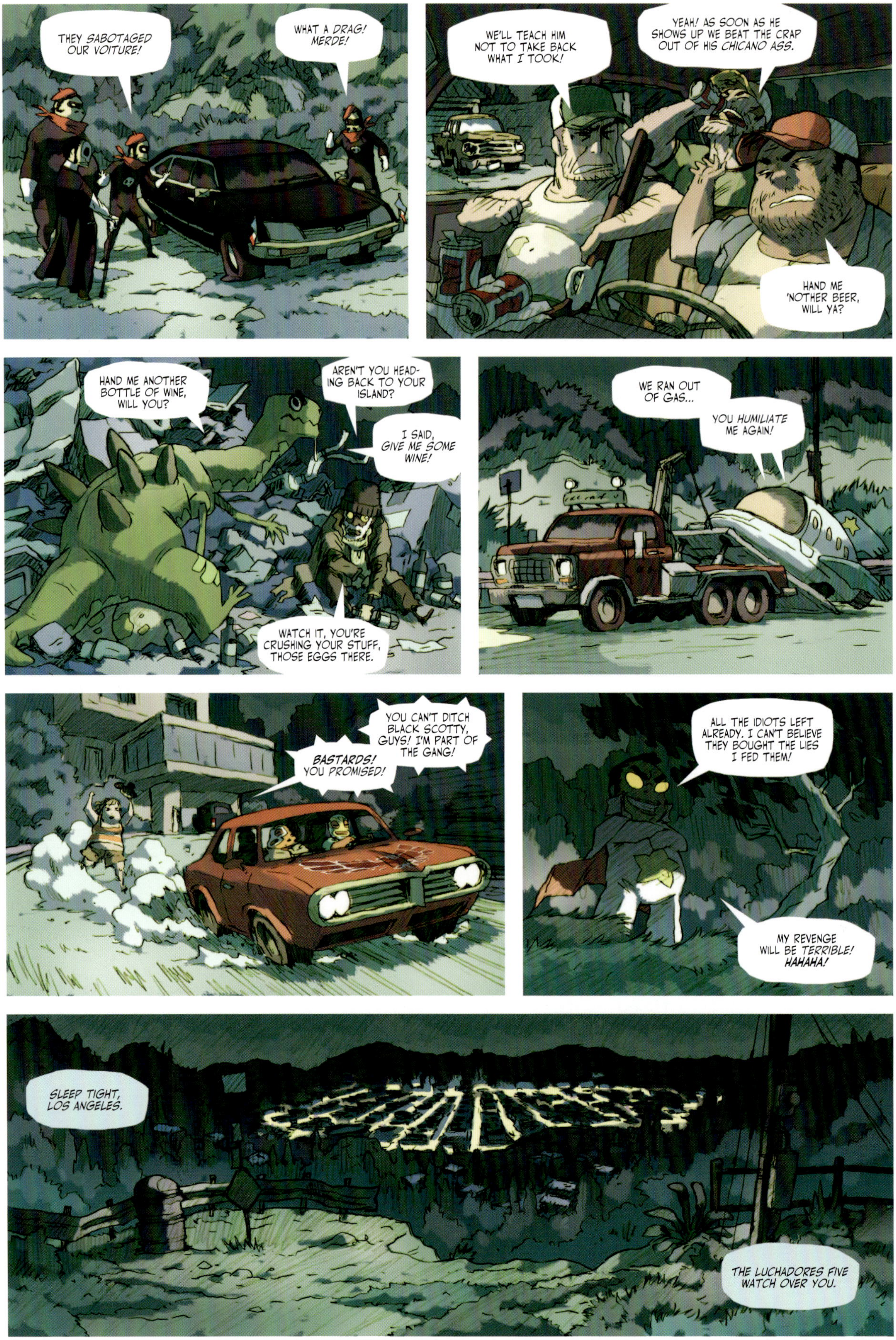
THEY SABOTAGED OUR VOITURE!
WHAT A DRAG! MERDE!
WE'LL TEACH HIM NOT TO TAKE BACK WHAT I TOOK!
YEAH! AS SOON AS HE SHOWS UP WE BEAT THE CRAP OUT OF HIS CHICANO ASS.
HAND ME 'NOTHER BEER, WILL YA?
HAND ME ANOTHER BOTTLE OF WINE, WILL YOU?
AREN'T YOU HEADING BACK TO YOUR ISLAND?
I SAID, GIVE ME SOME WINE!
WATCH IT, YOU'RE CRUSHING YOUR STUFF, THOSE EGGS THERE.
WE RAN OUT OF GAS...
YOU HUMILIATE ME AGAIN!
YOU CAN'T DITCH BLACK SCOTTY, GUYS! I'M PART OF THE GANG!
BASTARDS! YOU PROMISED!
ALL THE IDIOTS LEFT ALREADY. I CAN'T BELIEVE THEY BOUGHT THE LIES I FED THEM!
MY REVENGE WILL BE TERRIBLE! HAHAHA!
SLEEP TIGHT, LOS ANGELES.
THE LUCHADORES FIVE WATCH OVER YOU.

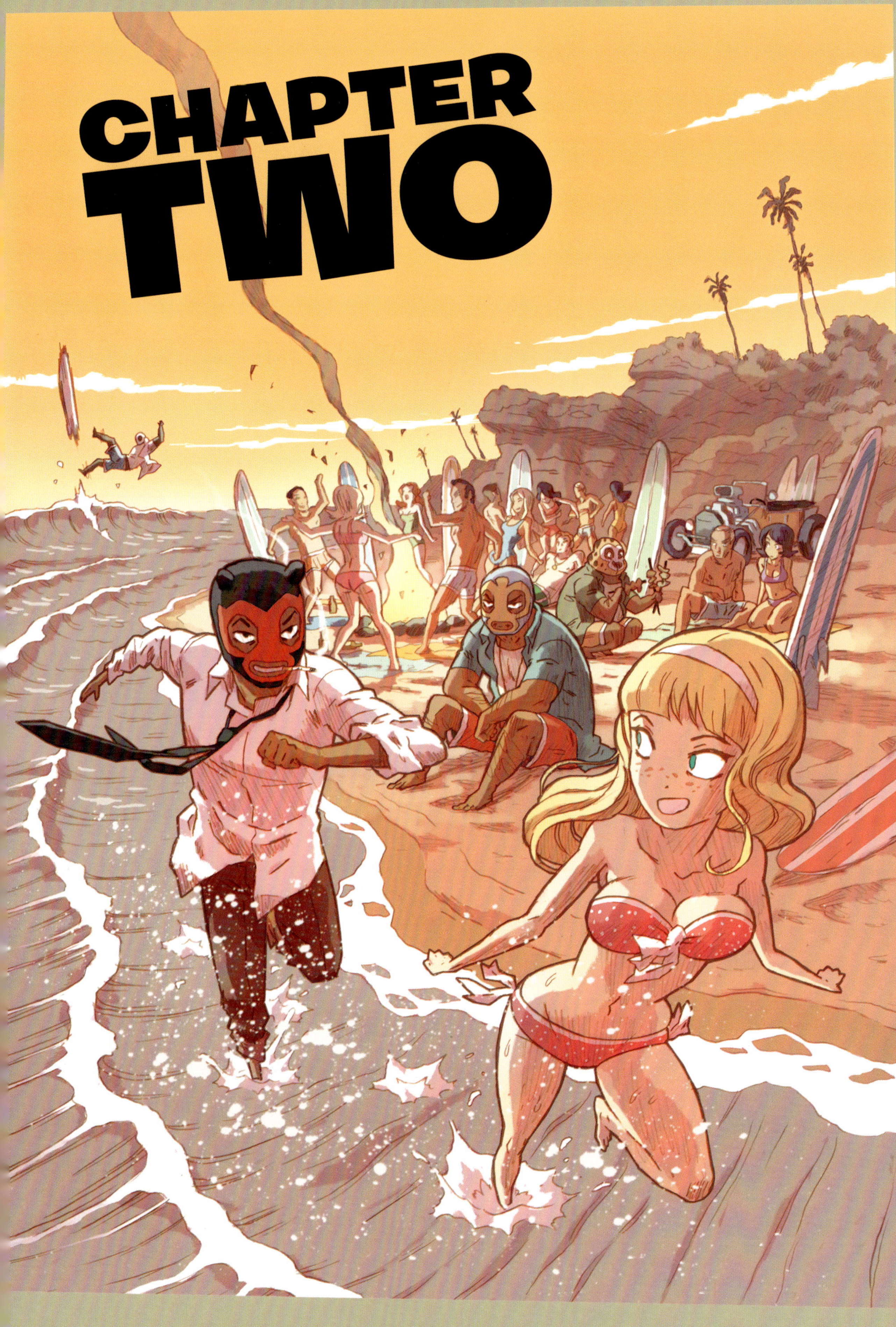
CHAPTER
TWO

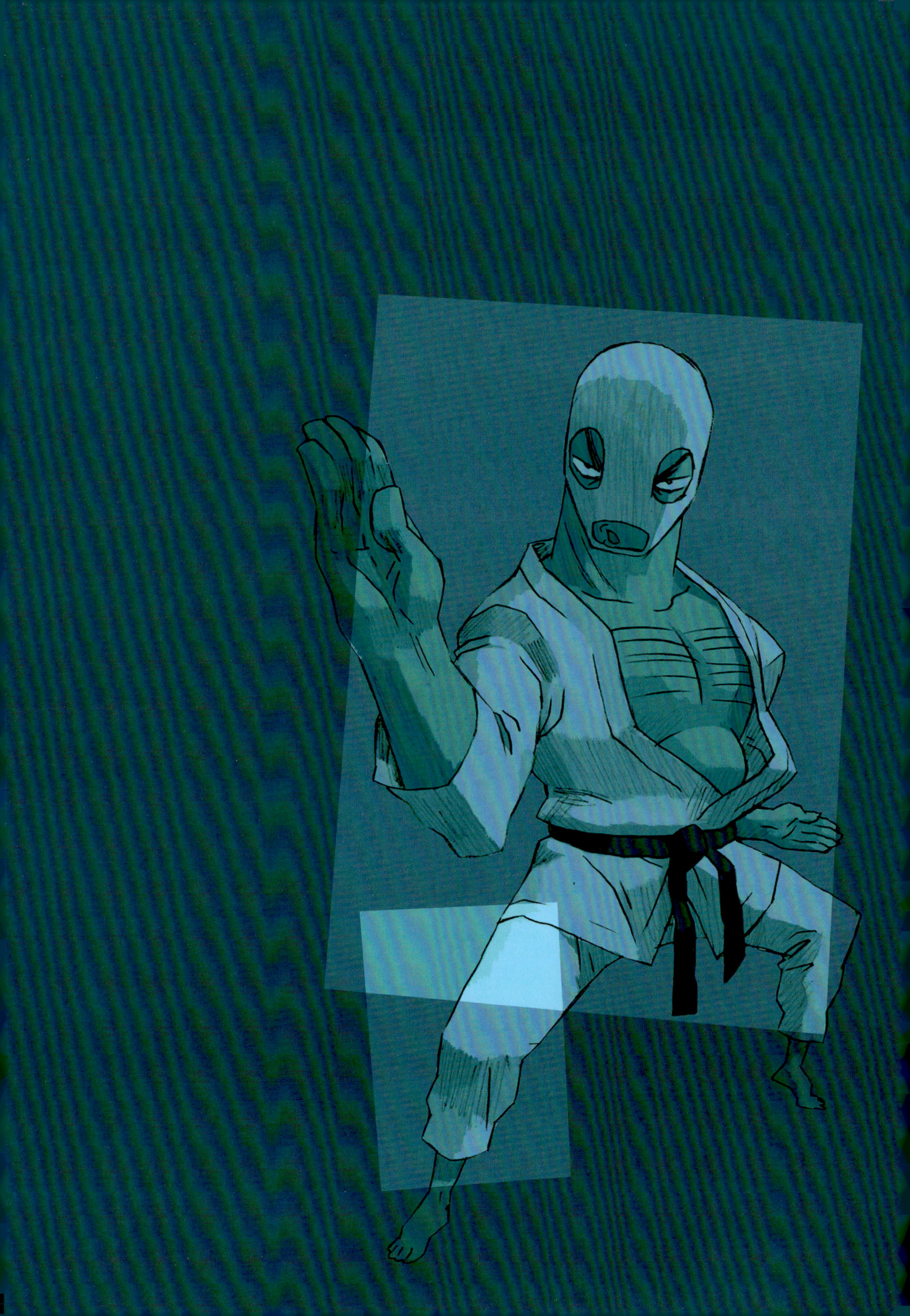

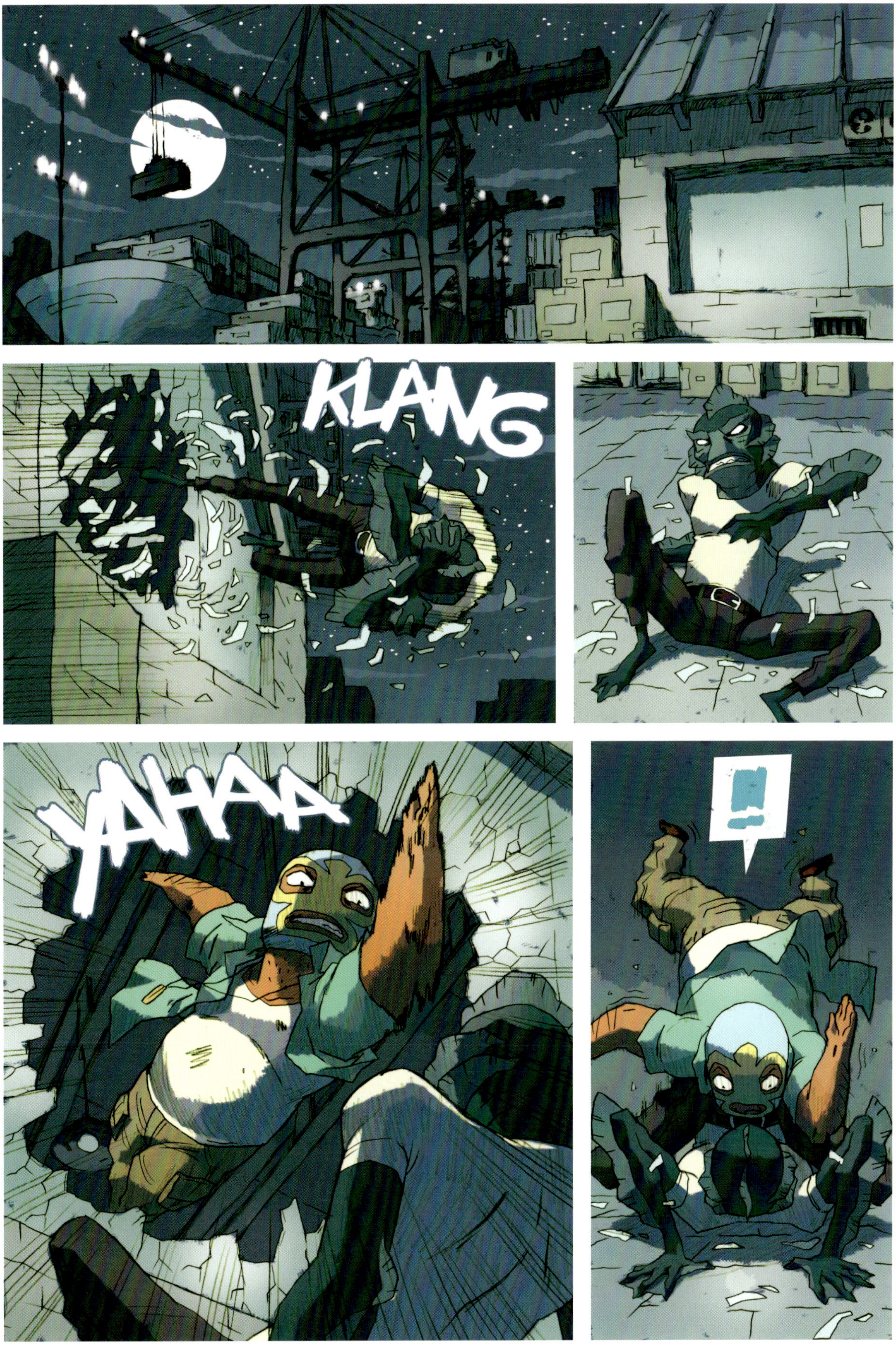
KLANG
YAHAA
!

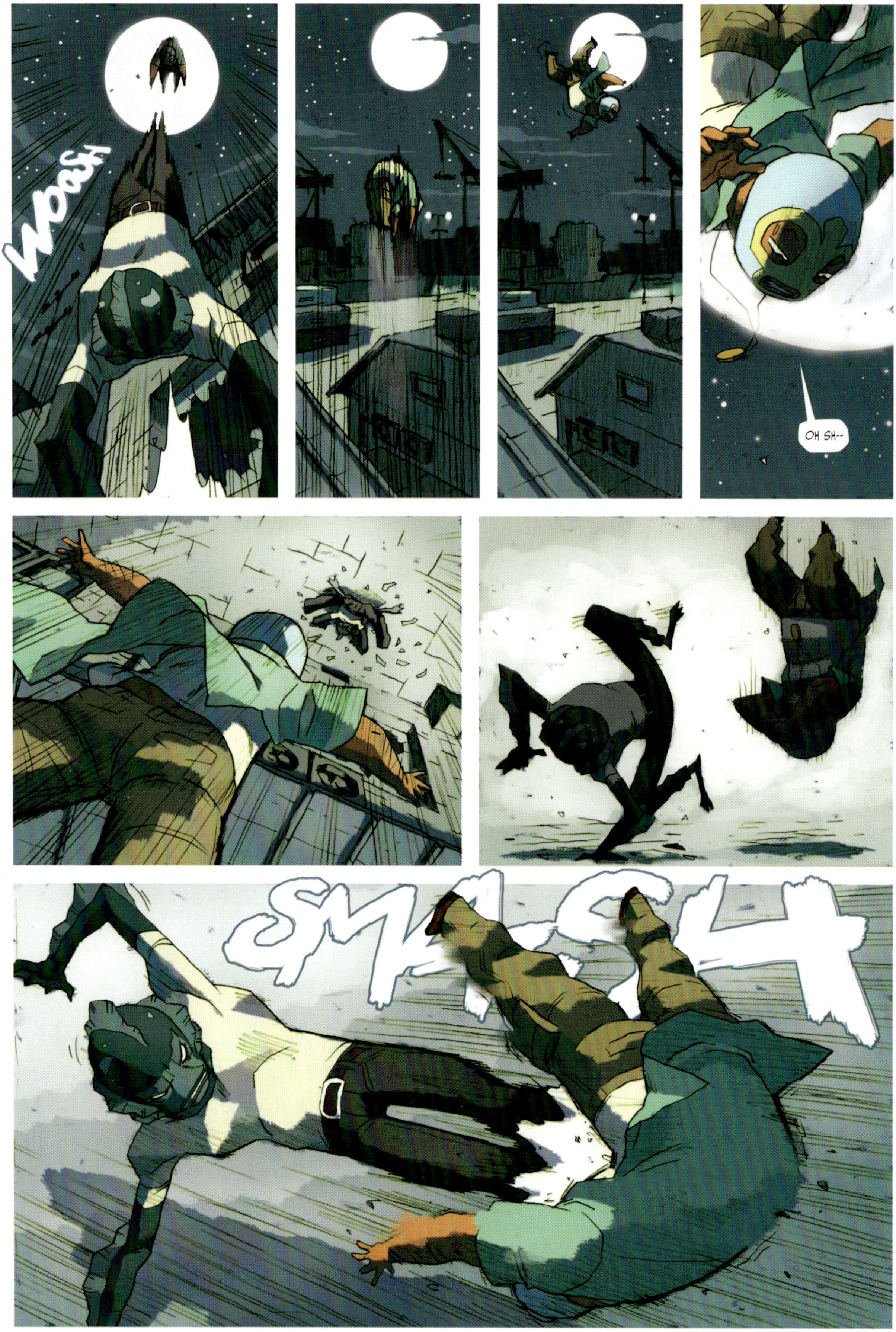
WOOSH
OH SH--
SMASH

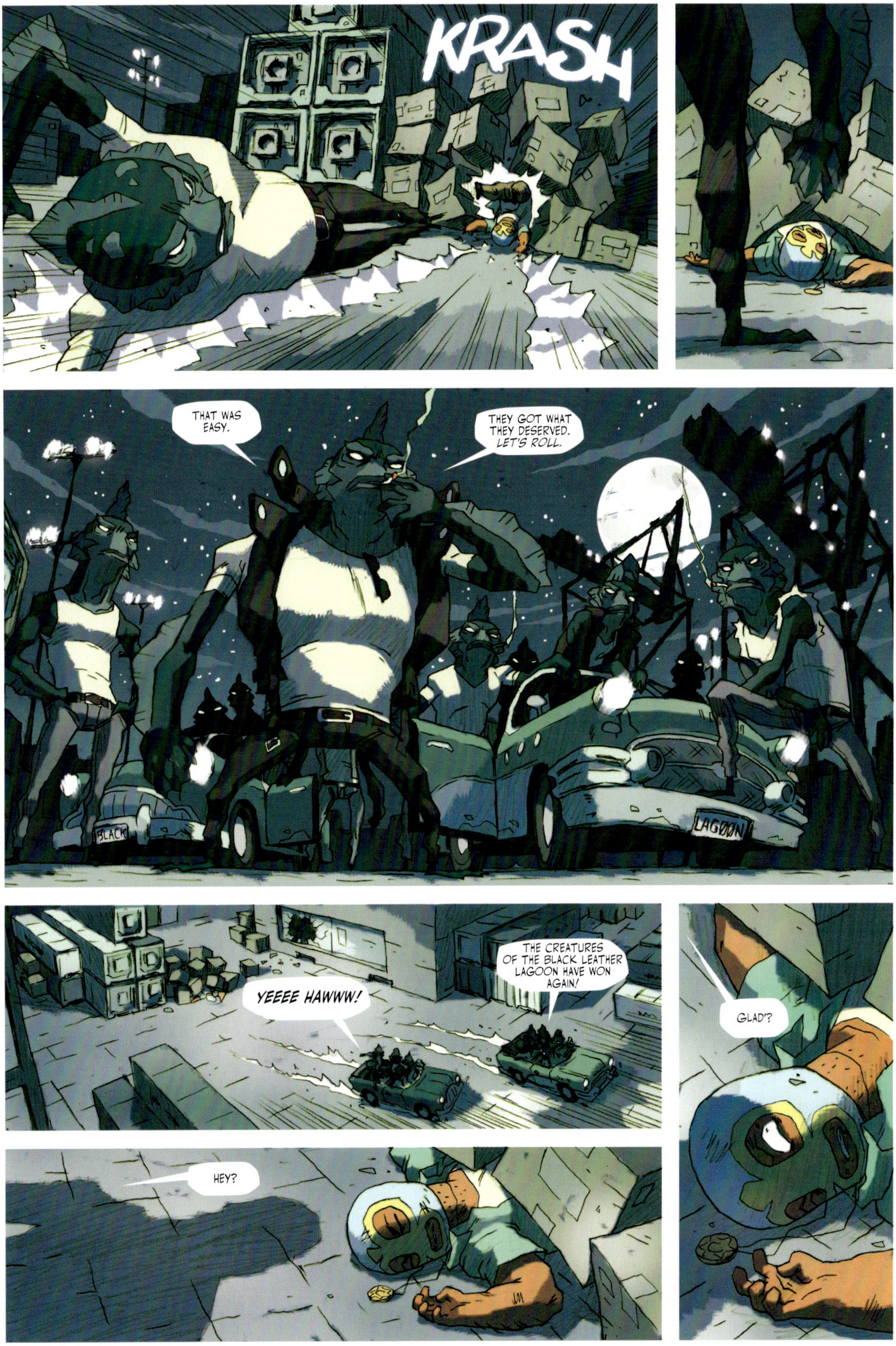
KRASH
THAT WAS EASY.
THEY GOT WHAT THEY DESERVED. LET'S ROLL.
BLACK
LAGOON
YEEEE HAWWW!
THE CREATURES OF THE BLACK LEATHER LAGOON HAVE WON AGAIN!
GLAD?
HEY?

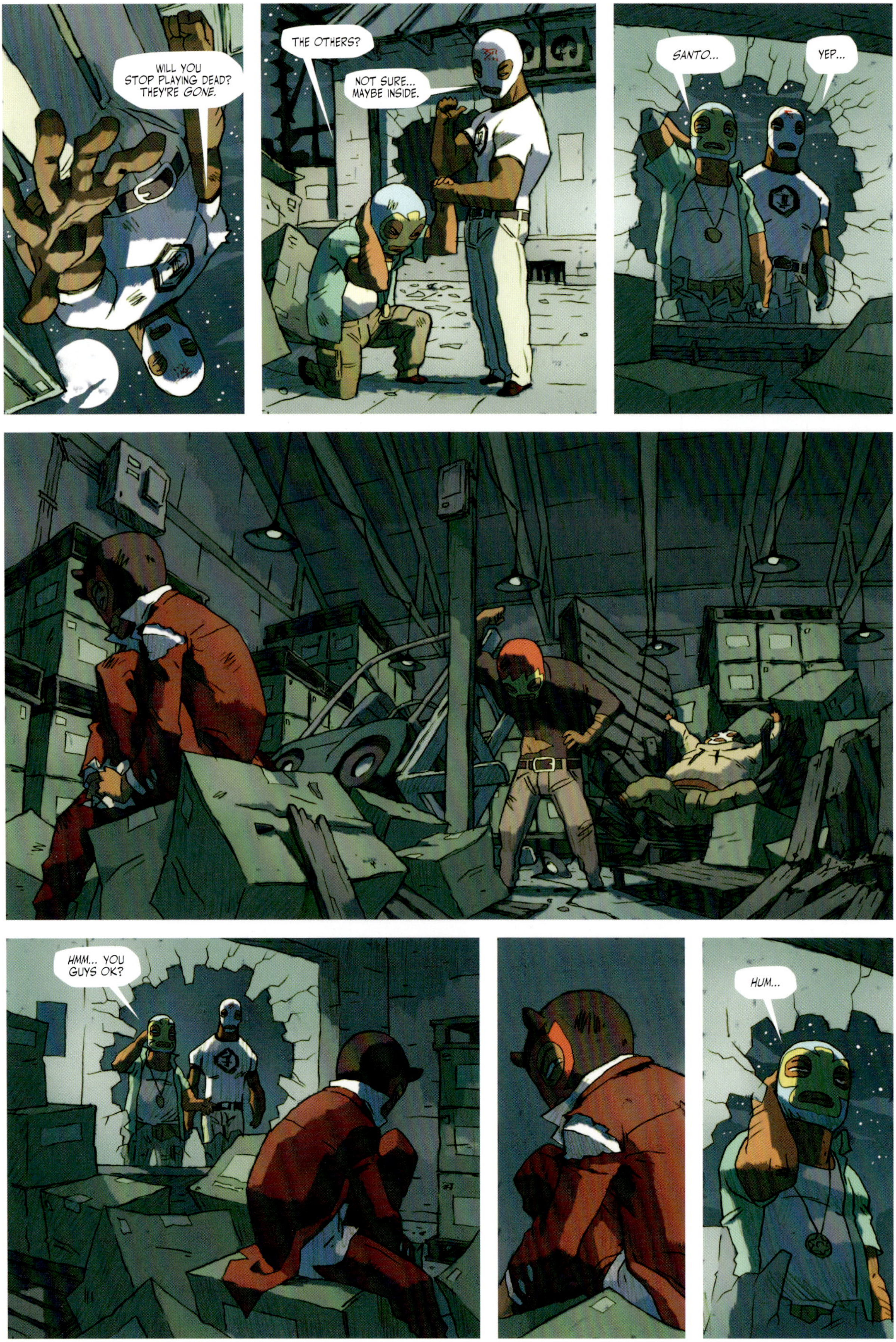
WILL YOU STOP PLAYING DEAD? THEY'RE GONE.
THE OTHERS?
NOT SURE... MAYBE INSIDE.
SANTO...
YEP...
HMM... YOU GUYS OK?
HUM...

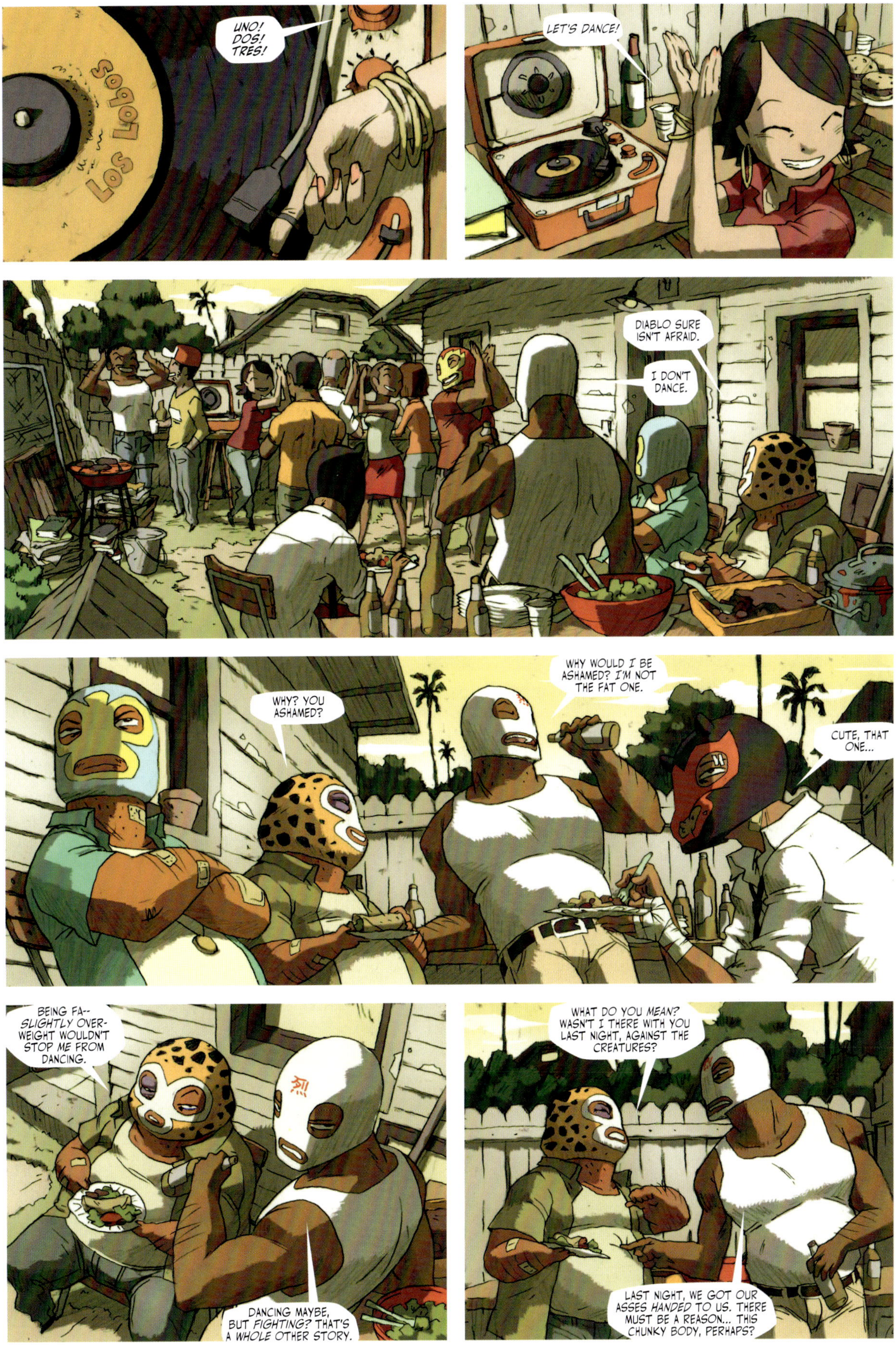
UNO! DOS! TRES!
Los Lobos
LET'S DANCE!
DIABLO SURE ISN'T AFRAID.
I DON'T DANCE.
WHY? YOU ASHAMED?
WHY WOULD I BE ASHAMED? I'M NOT THE FAT ONE.
CUTE, THAT ONE...
BEING FA-- SLIGHTLY OVER-WEIGHT WOULDN'T STOP ME FROM DANCING.
DANCING MAYBE, BUT FIGHTING? THAT'S A WHOLE OTHER STORY.
WHAT DO YOU MEAN? WASN'T I THERE WITH YOU LAST NIGHT, AGAINST THE CREATURES?
LAST NIGHT, WE GOT OUR ASSES HANDED TO US. THERE MUST BE A REASON... THIS CHUNKY BODY, PERHAPS?

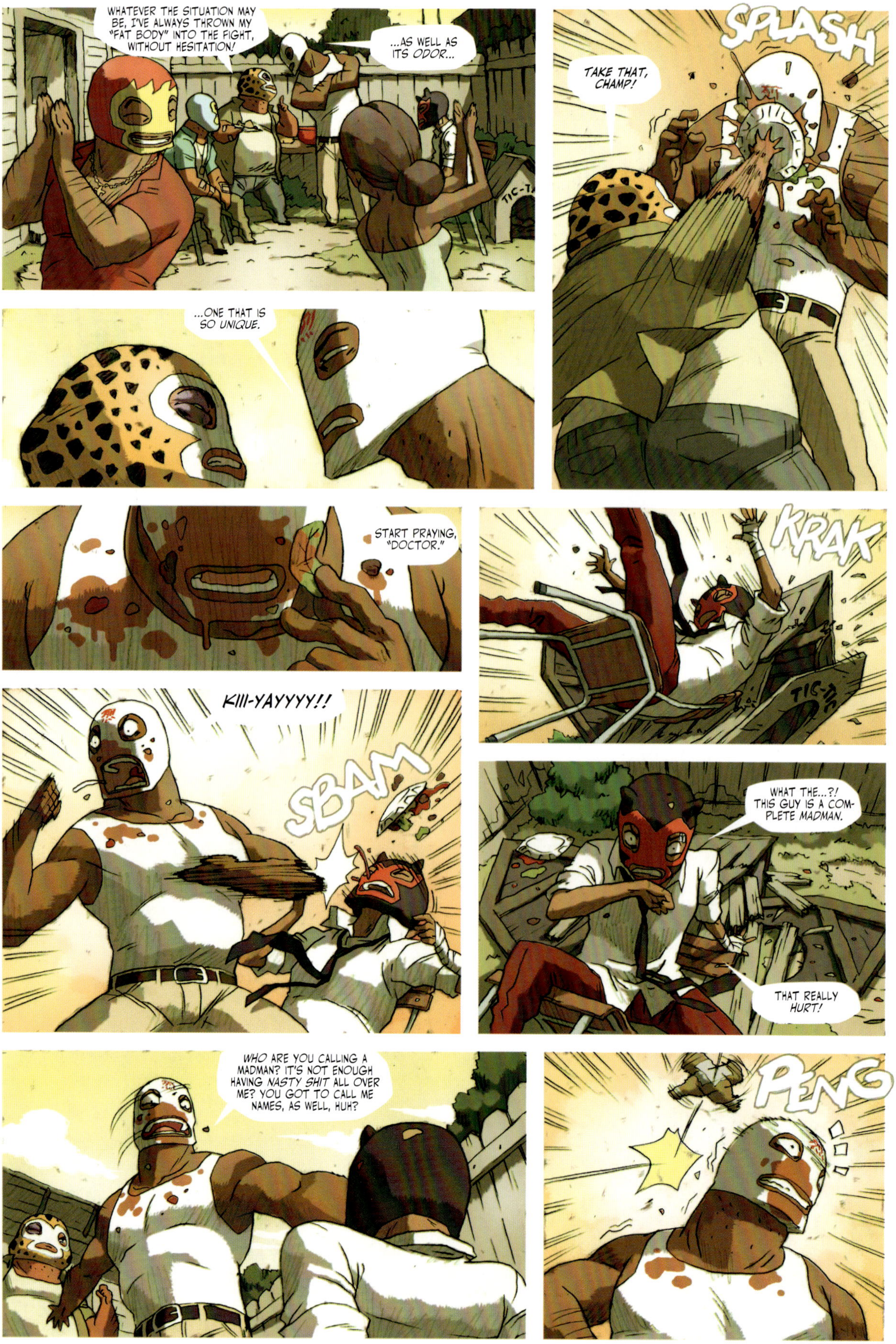
WHATEVER THE SITUATION MAY BE, I'VE ALWAYS THROWN MY "FAT BODY" INTO THE FIGHT, WITHOUT HESITATION!
...AS WELL AS ITS ODOR...
SPLASH
TAKE THAT, CHAMP!
...ONE THAT IS SO UNIQUE.
START PRAYING, "DOCTOR."
KRAK
KIII-YAYYYY!!
SBAM
WHAT THE...?! THIS GUY IS A COMPLETE MADMAN.
THAT REALLY HURT!
WHO ARE YOU CALLING A MADMAN? IT'S NOT ENOUGH HAVING NASTY SHIT ALL OVER ME? YOU GOT TO CALL ME NAMES, AS WELL, HUH?
PENG

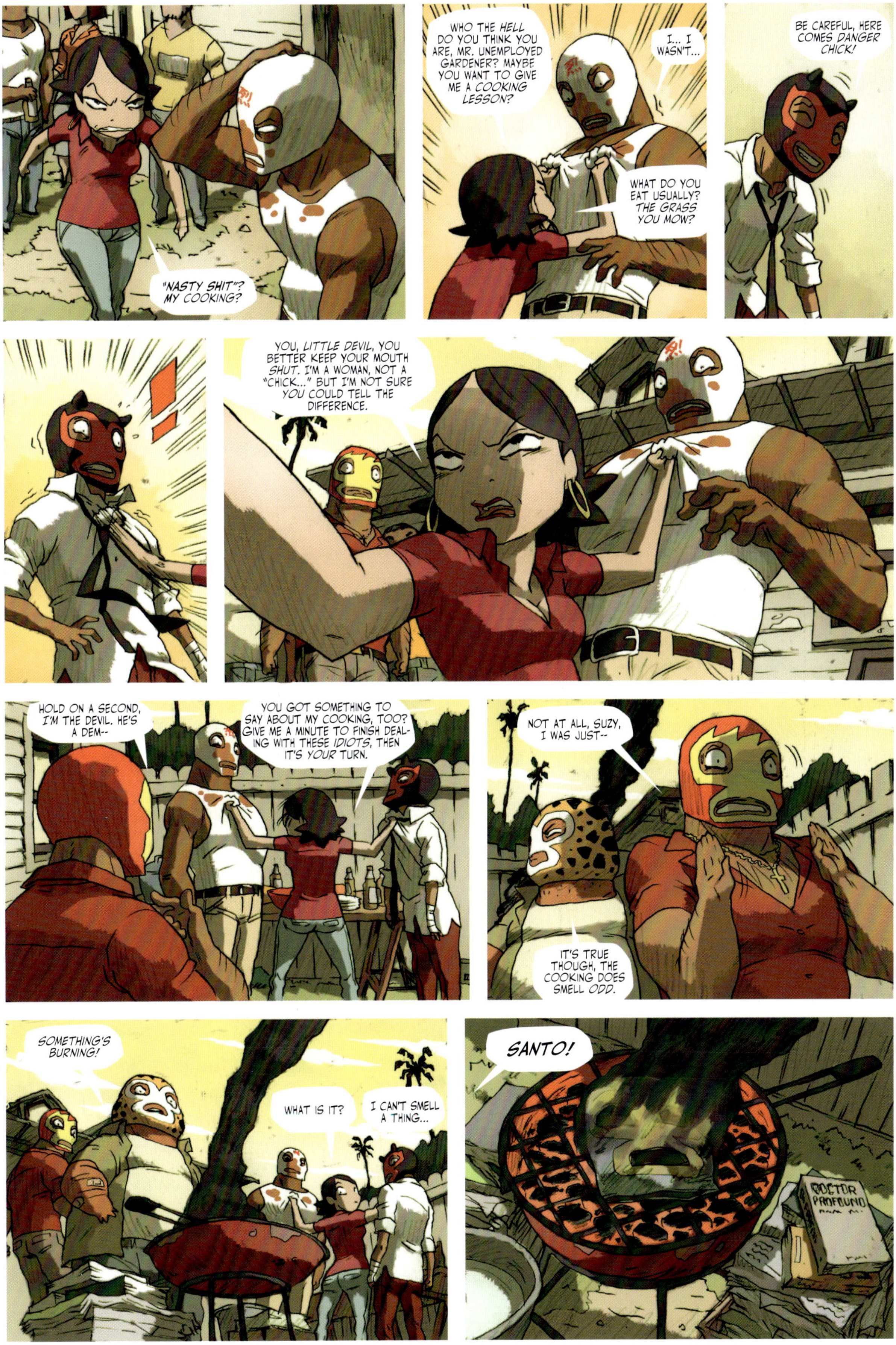
"NASTY SHIT"? MY COOKING?
WHO THE HELL DO YOU THINK YOU ARE, MR. UNEMPLOYED GARDENER? MAYBE YOU WANT TO GIVE ME A COOKING LESSON?
I... I WASN'T...
WHAT DO YOU EAT USUALLY? THE GRASS YOU MOW?
BE CAREFUL, HERE COMES DANGER CHICK!
YOU, LITTLE DEVIL, YOU BETTER KEEP YOUR MOUTH SHUT. I'M A WOMAN, NOT A "CHICK..." BUT I'M NOT SURE YOU COULD TELL THE DIFFERENCE.
HOLD ON A SECOND, I'M THE DEVIL. HE'S A DEM--
YOU GOT SOMETHING TO SAY ABOUT MY COOKING, TOO? GIVE ME A MINUTE TO FINISH DEALING WITH THESE IDIOTS, THEN IT'S YOUR TURN.
NOT AT ALL, SUZY, I WAS JUST--
IT'S TRUE THOUGH, THE COOKING DOES SMELL ODD.
SOMETHING'S BURNING!
WHAT IS IT?
I CAN'T SMELL A THING...
SANTO!
DOCTOR PROFOUND

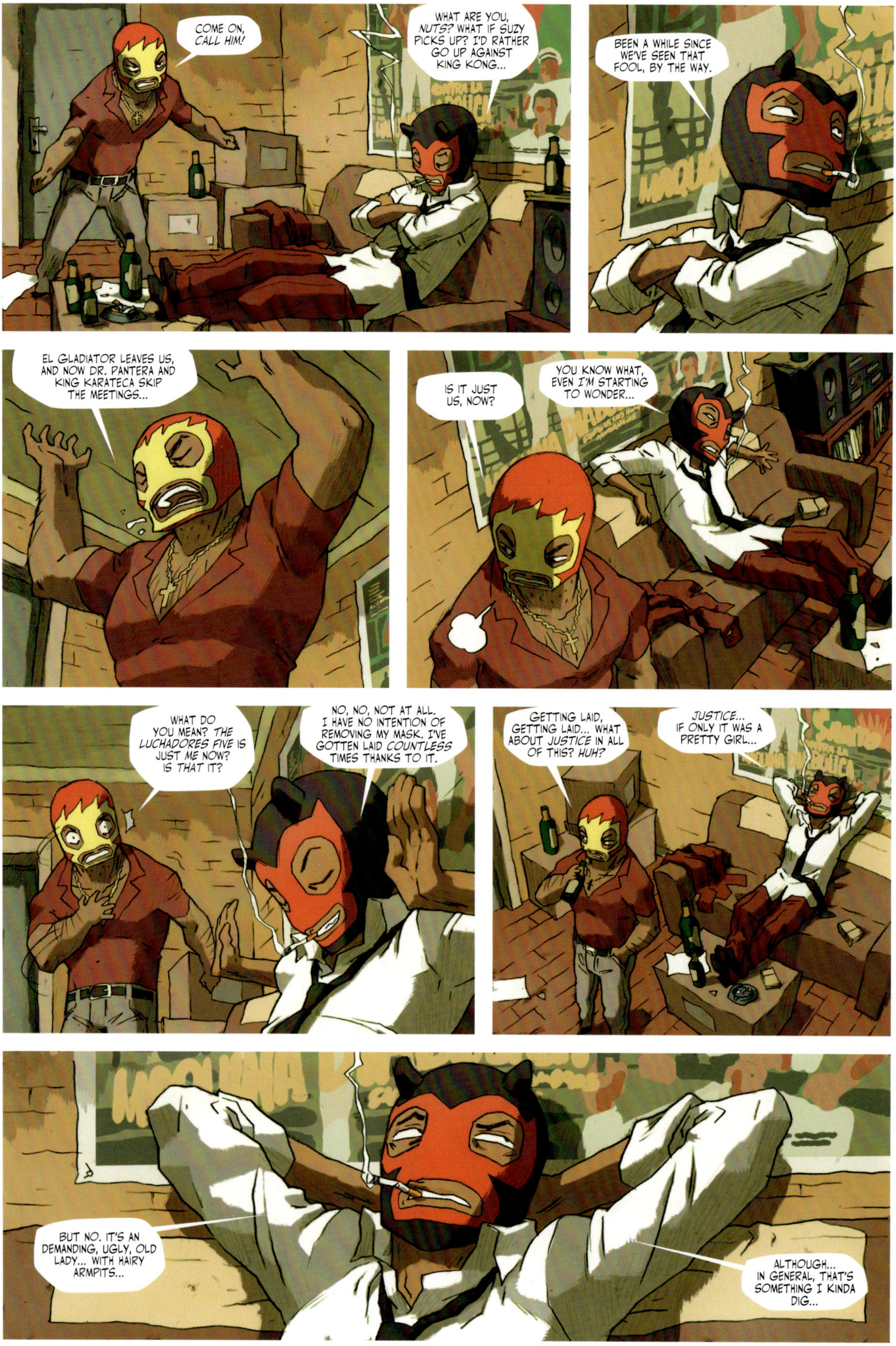
COME ON, CALL HIM!
WHAT ARE YOU, NUTS? WHAT IF SUZY PICKS UP? I'D RATHER GO UP AGAINST KING KONG...
BEEN A WHILE SINCE WE'VE SEEN THAT FOOL, BY THE WAY.
EL GLADIATOR LEAVES US, AND NOW DR. PANTERA AND KING KARATECA SKIP THE MEETINGS...
IS IT JUST US, NOW?
YOU KNOW WHAT, EVEN I'M STARTING TO WONDER...
WHAT DO YOU MEAN? THE LUCHADORES FIVE IS JUST ME NOW? IS THAT IT?
NO, NO, NOT AT ALL. I HAVE NO INTENTION OF REMOVING MY MASK. I'VE GOTTEN LAID COUNTLESS TIMES THANKS TO IT.
GETTING LAID, GETTING LAID... WHAT ABOUT JUSTICE IN ALL OF THIS? HUH?
JUSTICE... IF ONLY IT WAS A PRETTY GIRL...
BUT NO. IT'S AN DEMANDING, UGLY, OLD LADY... WITH HAIRY ARMPITS...
ALTHOUGH... IN GENERAL, THAT'S SOMETHING I KINDA DIG...

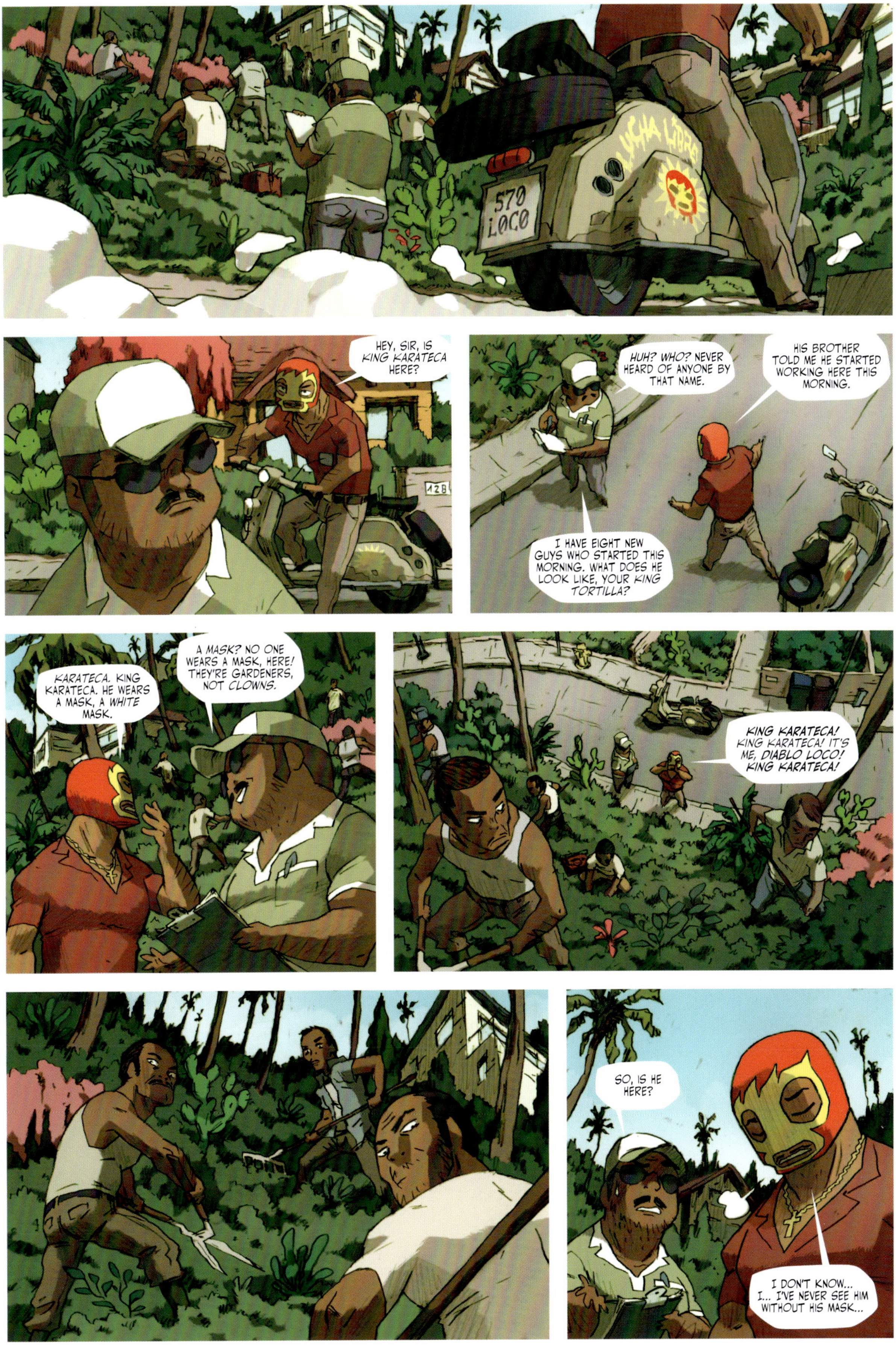
570 LOCO
LUCHA LIBRE
HEY, SIR, IS KING KARATECA HERE?
128
HUH? WHO? NEVER HEARD OF ANYONE BY THAT NAME.
HIS BROTHER TOLD ME HE STARTED WORKING HERE THIS MORNING.
I HAVE EIGHT NEW GUYS WHO STARTED THIS MORNING. WHAT DOES HE LOOK LIKE, YOUR KING TORTILLA?
KARATECA. KING KARATECA. HE WEARS A MASK, A WHITE MASK.
A MASK? NO ONE WEARS A MASK, HERE! THEY'RE GARDENERS, NOT CLOWNS.
KING KARATECA! KING KARATECA! IT'S ME, DIABLO LOCO! KING KARATECA!
SO, IS HE HERE?
I DON'T KNOW... I... I'VE NEVER SEE HIM WITHOUT HIS MASK...

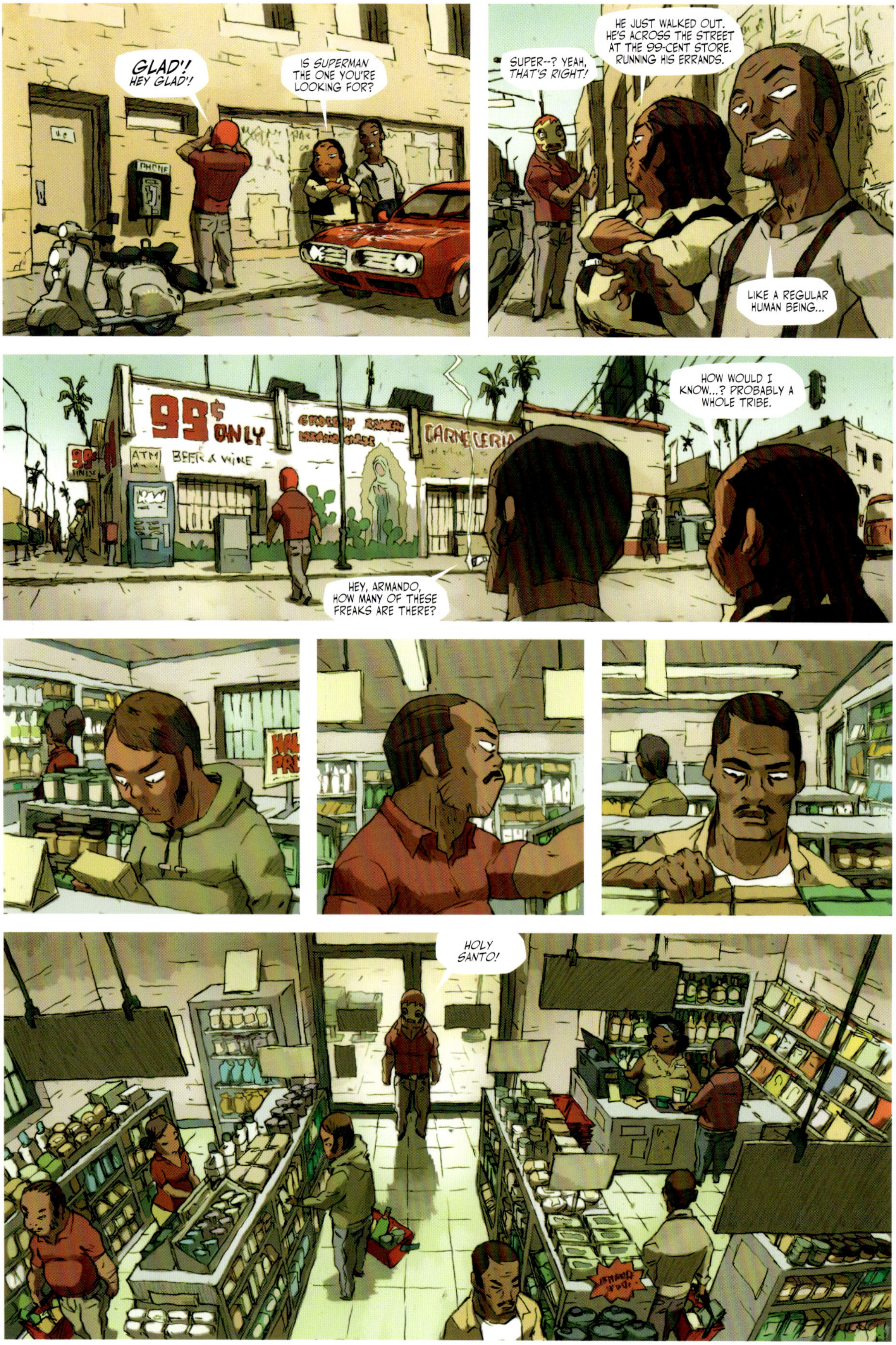
GLAD'! HEY GLAD'!
IS SUPERMAN THE ONE YOU'RE LOOKING FOR?
SUPER--? YEAH, THAT'S RIGHT!
HE JUST WALKED OUT. HE'S ACROSS THE STREET AT THE 99-CENT STORE. RUNNING HIS ERRANDS.
LIKE A REGULAR HUMAN BEING...
99¢ ONLY
ATM
BEER & WINE
CARNECERIA
HEY, ARMANDO, HOW MANY OF THESE FREAKS ARE THERE?
HOW WOULD I KNOW...? PROBABLY A WHOLE TRIBE.
HOLY SANTO!

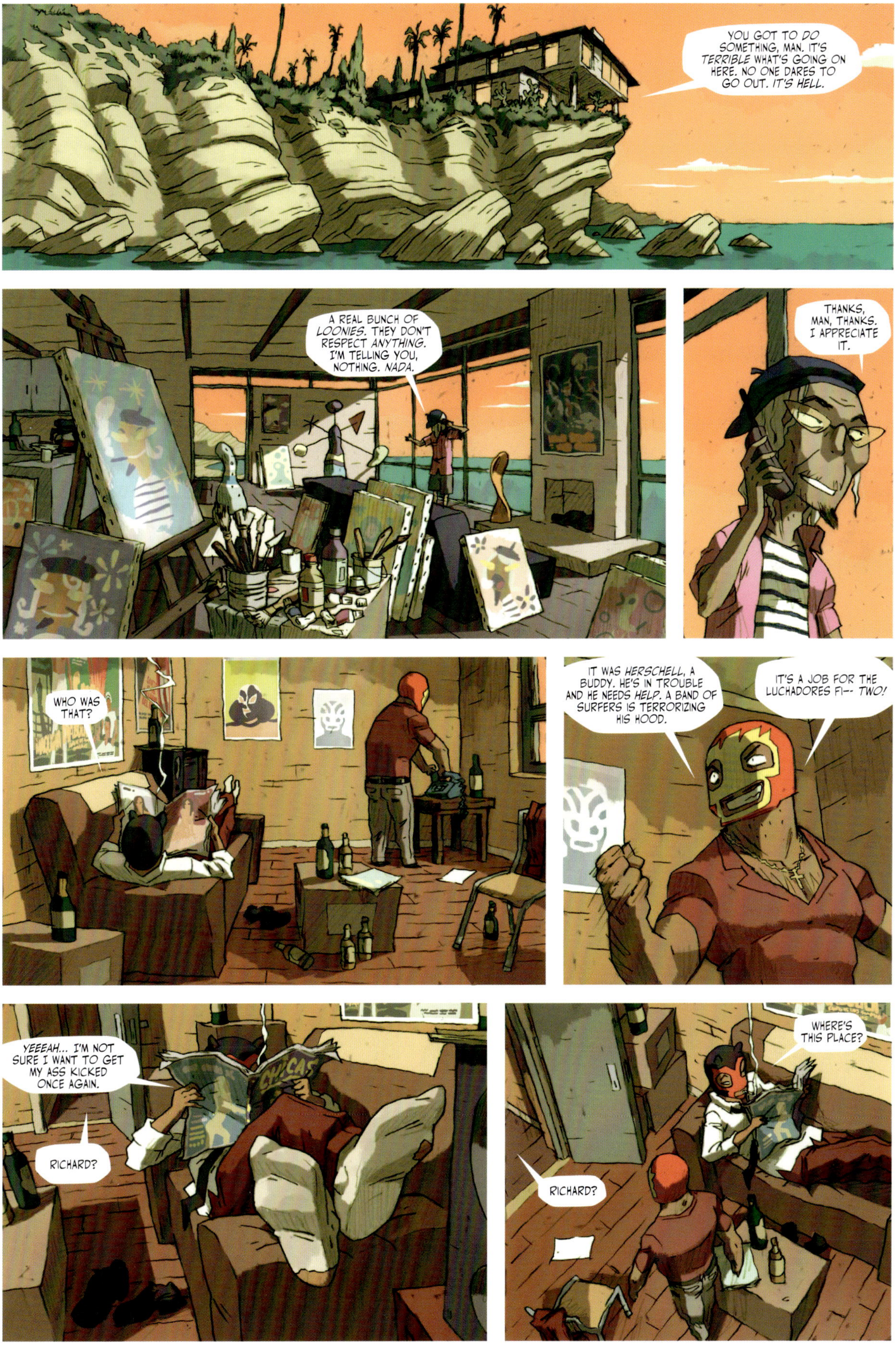
YOU GOT TO DO SOMETHING, MAN. IT'S TERRIBLE WHAT'S GOING ON HERE. NO ONE DARES TO GO OUT. IT'S HELL.
A REAL BUNCH OF LOONIES. THEY DON'T RESPECT ANYTHING. I'M TELLING YOU, NOTHING. NADA.
THANKS, MAN, THANKS. I APPRECIATE IT.
WHO WAS THAT?
IT WAS HERSCHELL, A BUDDY. HE'S IN TROUBLE AND HE NEEDS HELP. A BAND OF SURFERS IS TERRORIZING HIS HOOD.
IT'S A JOB FOR THE LUCHADORES FI-- TWO!
YEEEAH... I'M NOT SURE I WANT TO GET MY ASS KICKED ONCE AGAIN.
RICHARD?
WHERE'S THIS PLACE?
RICHARD?

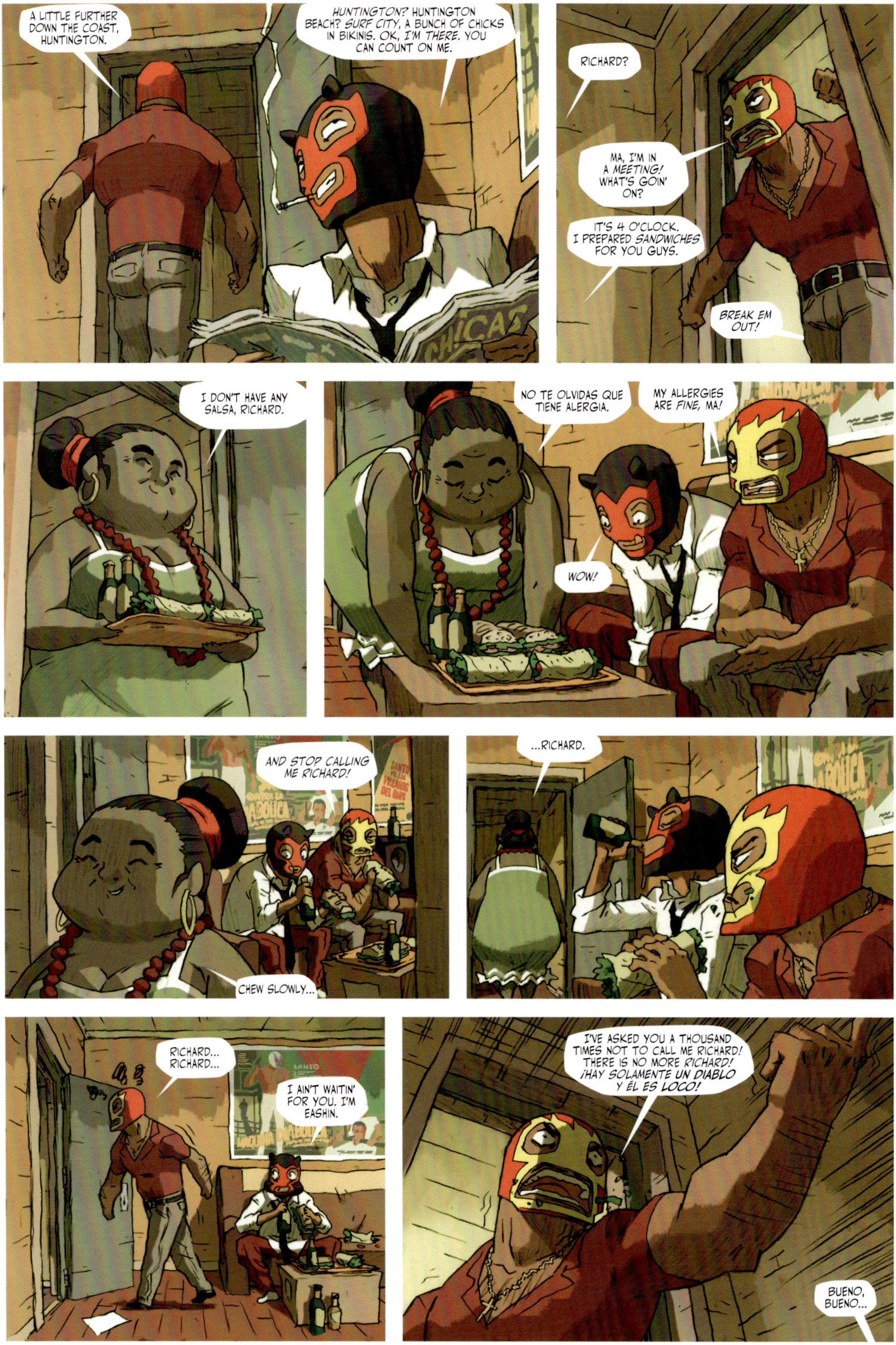

A LITTLE FURTHER DOWN THE COAST, HUNTINGTON.
HUNTINGTON? HUNTINGTON BEACH? SURF CITY, A BUNCH OF CHICKS IN BIKINIS. OK, I'M THERE. YOU CAN COUNT ON ME.
CHICAS
RICHARD?
MA, I'M IN A MEETING! WHAT'S GOIN' ON?
IT'S 4 O'CLOCK. I PREPARED SANDWICHES FOR YOU GUYS.
BREAK EM OUT!
I DON'T HAVE ANY SALSA, RICHARD.
NO TE OLVIDAS QUE TIENE ALERGIA.
MY ALLERGIES ARE FINE, MA!
WOW!
AND STOP CALLING ME RICHARD!
CHEW SLOWLY...
...RICHARD.
RICHARD... RICHARD...
I AIN'T WAITIN' FOR YOU. I'M EASHIN.
I'VE ASKED YOU A THOUSAND TIMES NOT TO CALL ME RICHARD! THERE IS NO MORE RICHARD! ¡HAY SOLAMENTE UN DIABLO Y ÉL ES LOCO!
BUENO, BUENO...

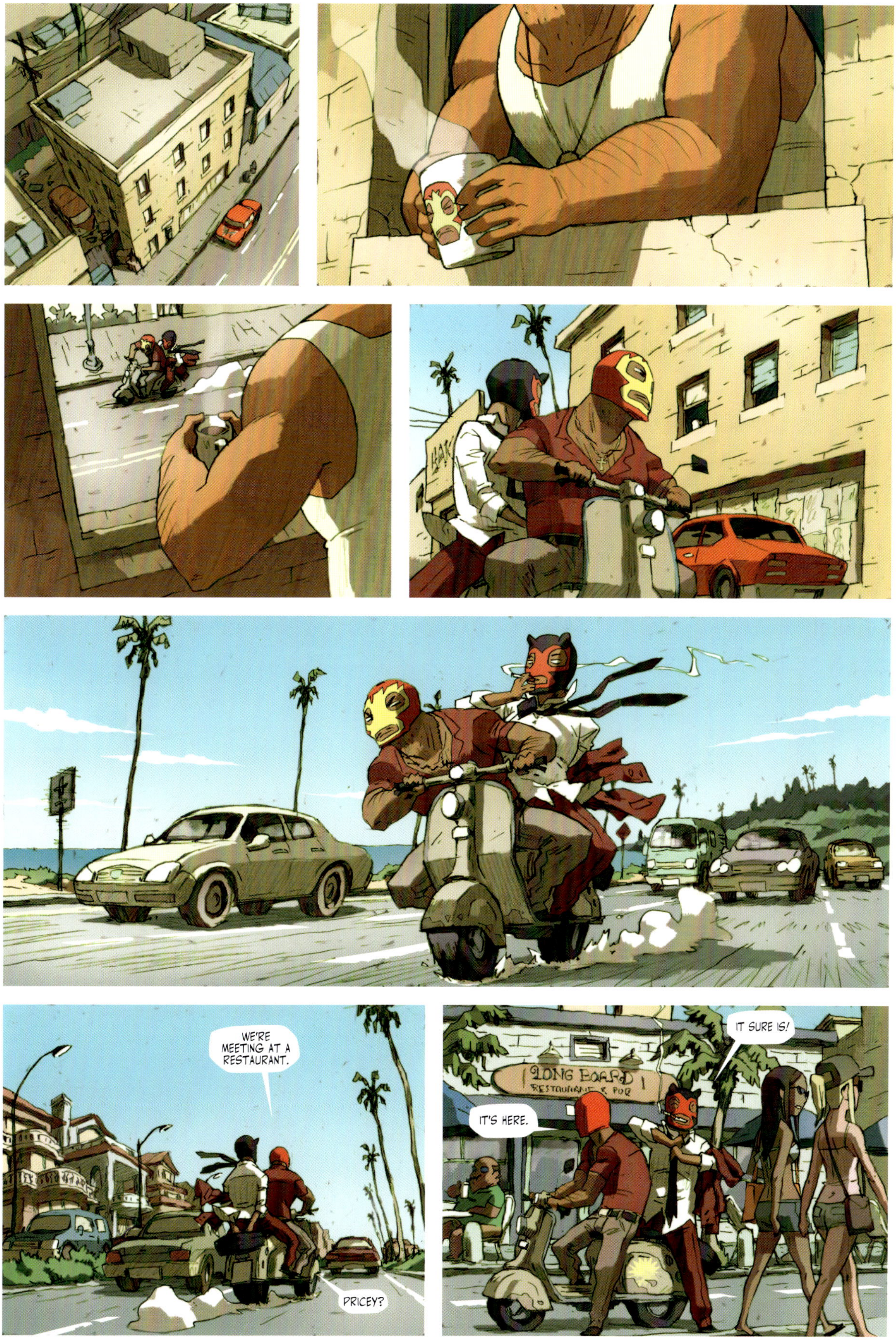
WE'RE MEETING AT A RESTAURANT.
PRICEY?
IT'S HERE.
IT SURE IS!
LONG BOARD RESTAURANT & PUB

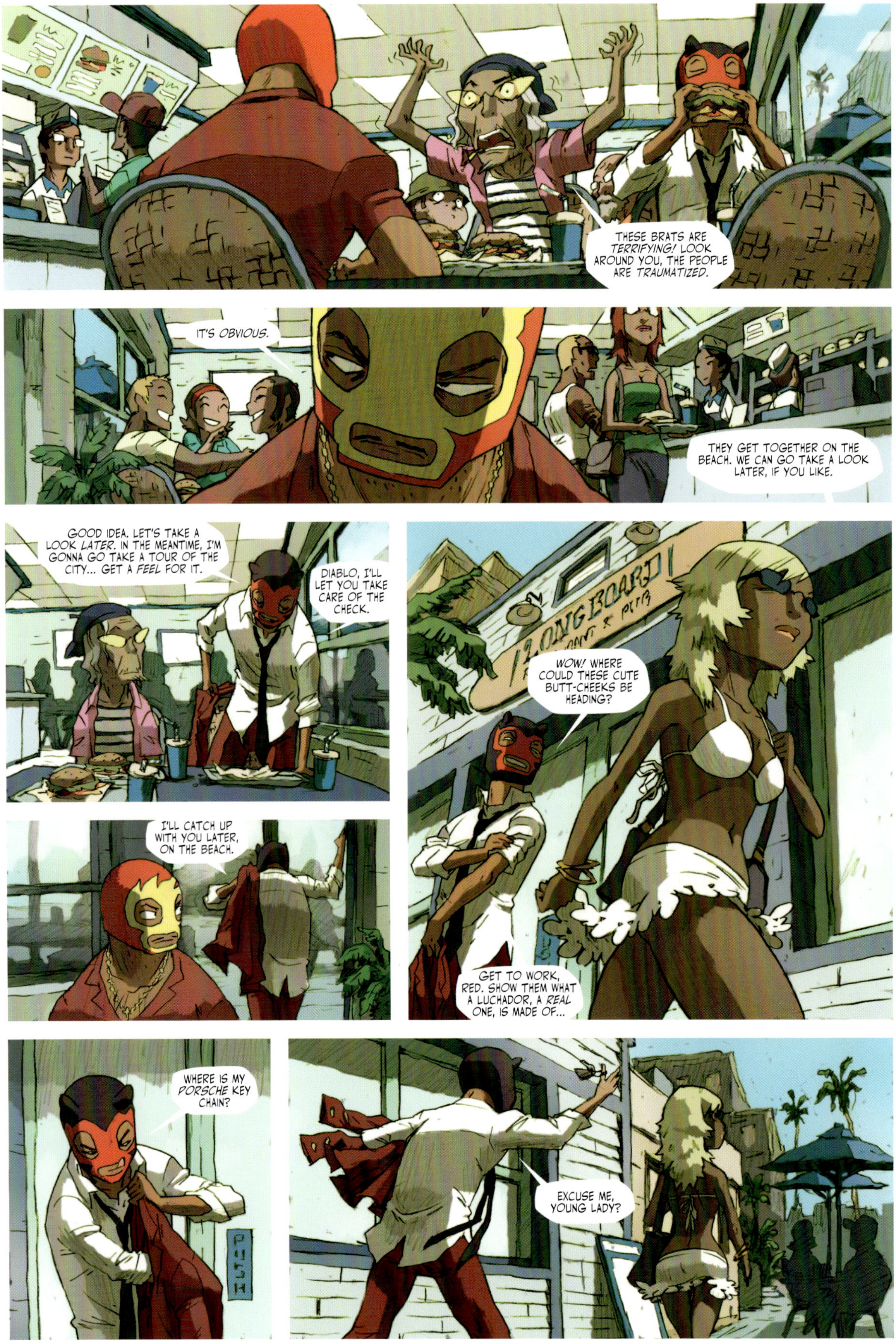
THESE BRATS ARE TERRIFYING! LOOK AROUND YOU, THE PEOPLE ARE TRAUMATIZED.
IT'S OBVIOUS.
THEY GET TOGETHER ON THE BEACH. WE CAN GO TAKE A LOOK LATER, IF YOU LIKE.
GOOD IDEA. LET'S TAKE A LOOK LATER. IN THE MEANTIME, I'M GONNA GO TAKE A TOUR OF THE CITY... GET A FEEL FOR IT.
DIABLO, I'LL LET YOU TAKE CARE OF THE CHECK.
I'LL CATCH UP WITH YOU LATER, ON THE BEACH.
LONGBOARD
WOW! WHERE COULD THESE CUTE BUTT-CHEEKS BE HEADING?
GET TO WORK, RED. SHOW THEM WHAT A LUCHADOR, A REAL ONE, IS MADE OF...
WHERE IS MY PORSCHE KEY CHAIN?
PUSH
EXCUSE ME, YOUNG LADY?

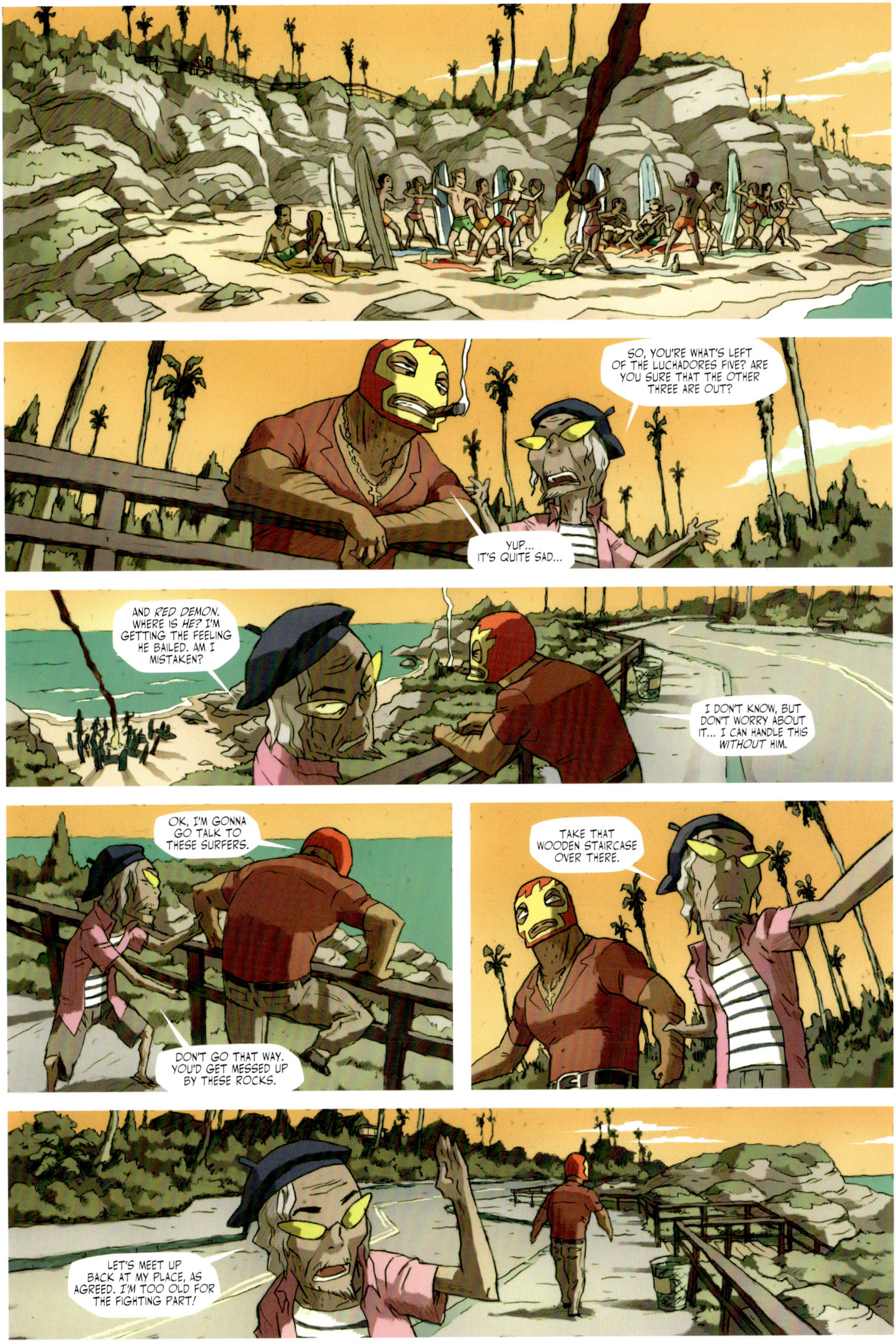

SO, YOU'RE WHAT'S LEFT OF THE LUCHADORES FIVE? ARE YOU SURE THAT THE OTHER THREE ARE OUT?
YUP... IT'S QUITE SAD...
AND *RED DEMON*. WHERE IS *HE*? I'M GETTING THE FEELING HE BAILED. AM I MISTAKEN?
I DON'T KNOW, BUT DON'T WORRY ABOUT IT... I CAN HANDLE THIS *WITHOUT* HIM.
OK, I'M GONNA GO TALK TO THESE SURFERS.
DON'T GO THAT WAY. YOU'D GET MESSED UP BY THESE ROCKS.
TAKE THAT WOODEN STAIRCASE OVER THERE.
LET'S MEET UP BACK AT MY PLACE, AS AGREED. I'M TOO OLD FOR THE FIGHTING PART!

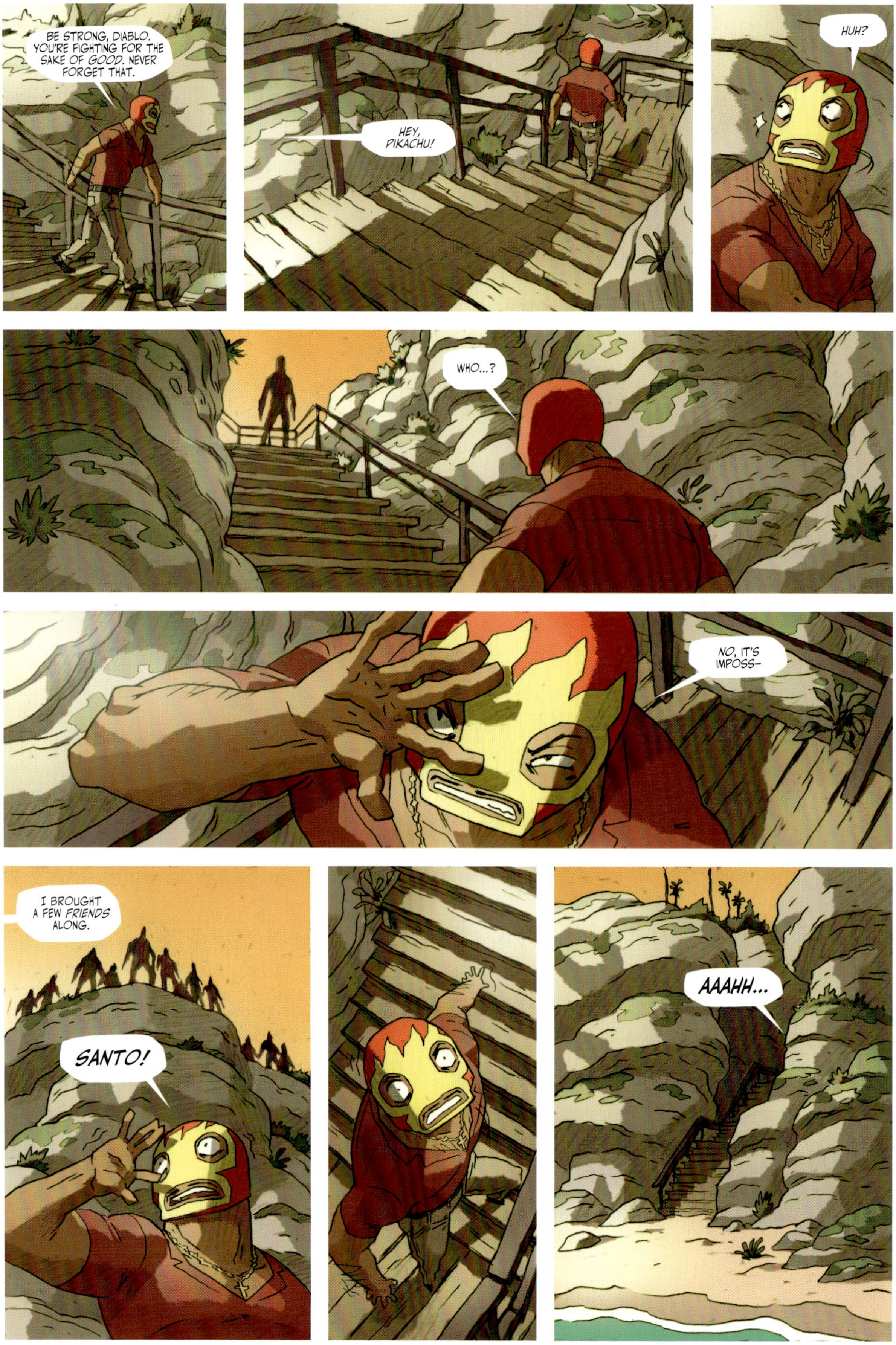
BE STRONG, DIABLO. YOU'RE FIGHTING FOR THE SAKE OF GOOD. NEVER FORGET THAT.
HEY, PIKACHU!
HUH?
WHO...?
NO, IT'S IMPOSS-
I BROUGHT A FEW FRIENDS ALONG.
SANTO!
AAAHH...

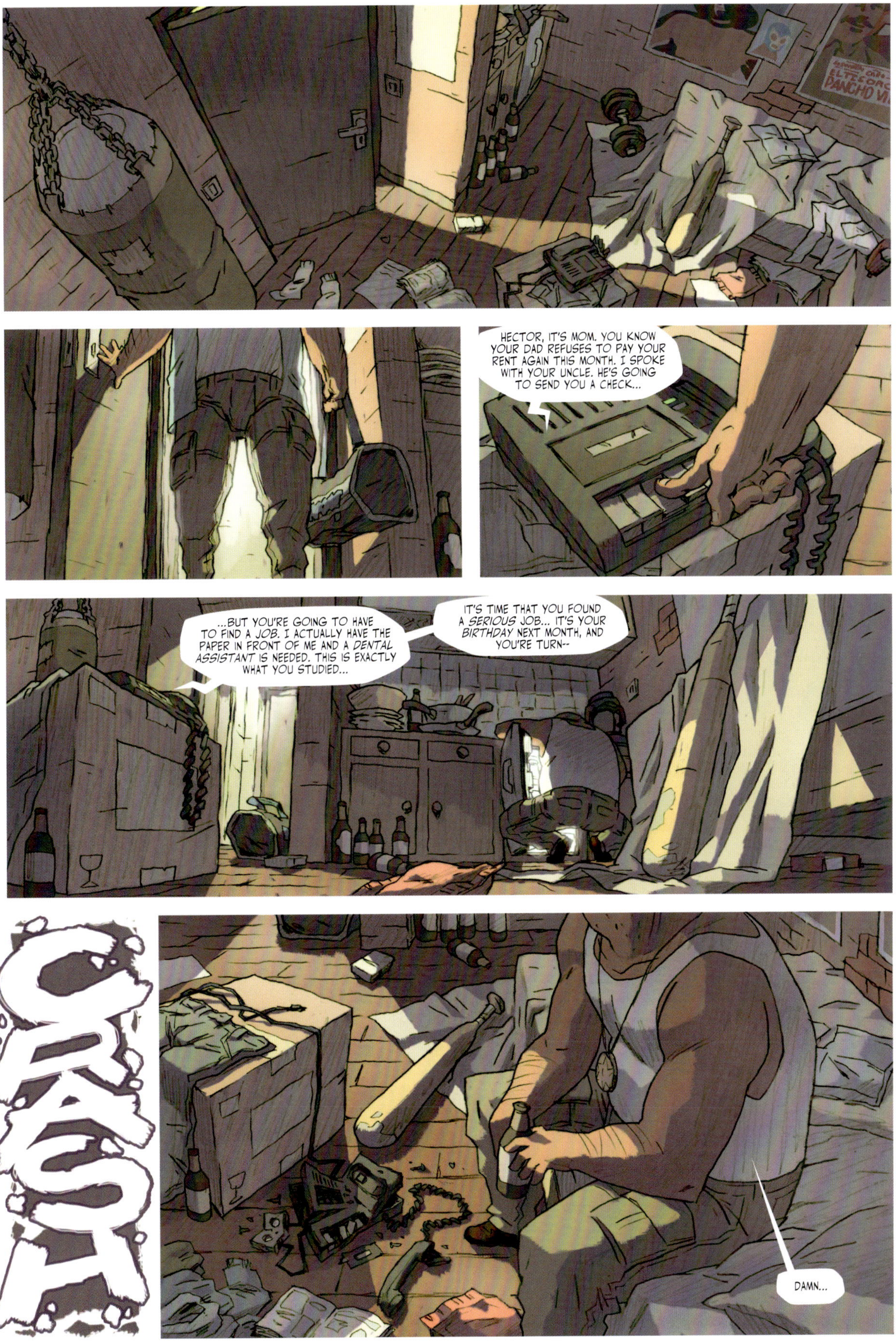
HECTOR, IT'S MOM. YOU KNOW YOUR DAD REFUSES TO PAY YOUR RENT AGAIN THIS MONTH. I SPOKE WITH YOUR UNCLE. HE'S GOING TO SEND YOU A CHECK...
...BUT YOU'RE GOING TO HAVE TO FIND A *JOB*. I ACTUALLY HAVE THE PAPER IN FRONT OF ME AND A *DENTAL ASSISTANT* IS NEEDED. THIS IS EXACTLY WHAT YOU STUDIED...
IT'S TIME THAT YOU FOUND A *SERIOUS* JOB... IT'S YOUR *BIRTHDAY* NEXT MONTH, AND YOU'RE TURN--
DAMN...

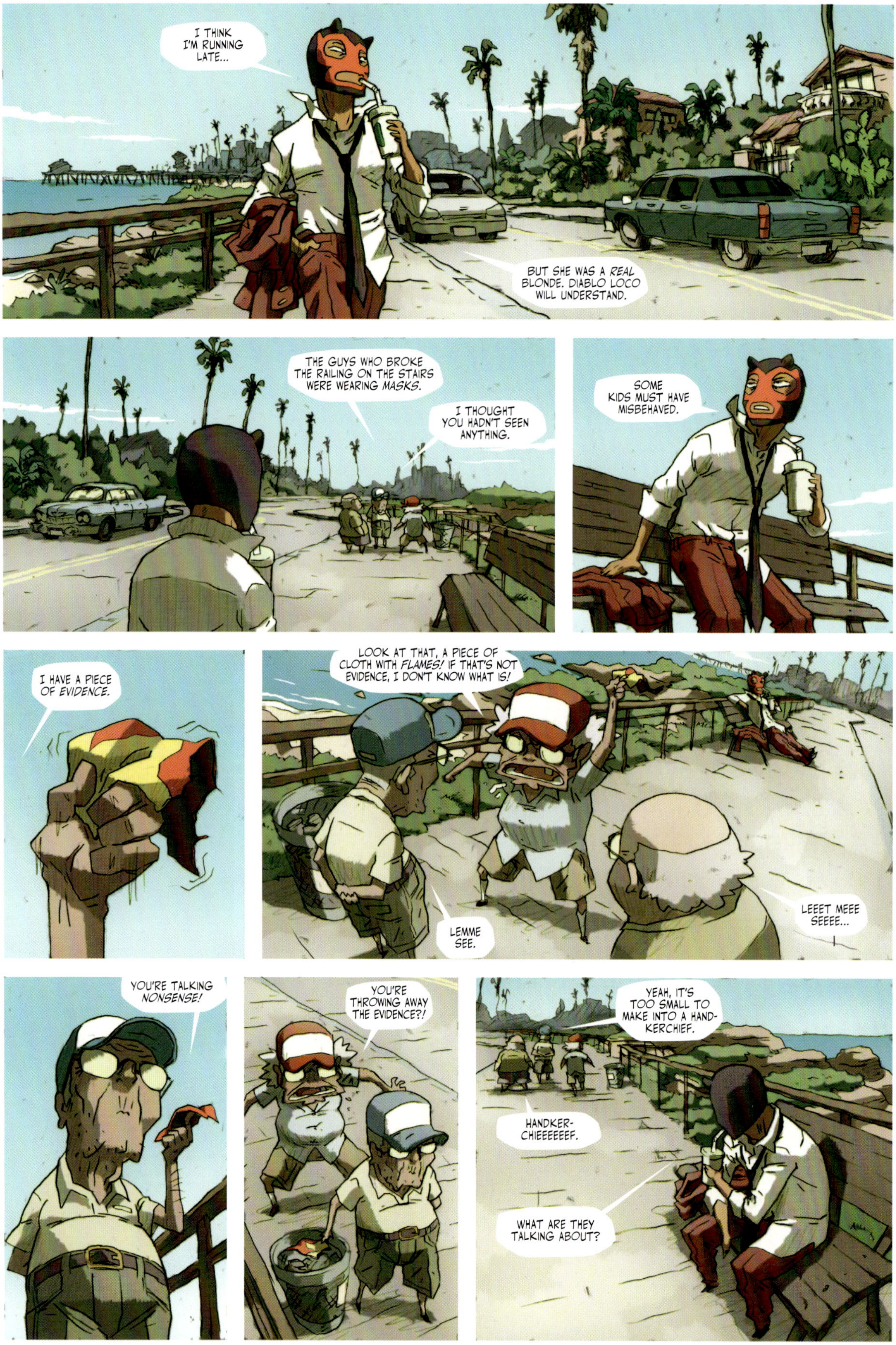
I THINK I'M RUNNING LATE...
BUT SHE WAS A *REAL* BLONDE. DIABLO LOCO WILL UNDERSTAND.
THE GUYS WHO BROKE THE RAILING ON THE STAIRS WERE WEARING *MASKS*.
I THOUGHT YOU HADN'T SEEN ANYTHING.
SOME KIDS MUST HAVE MISBEHAVED.
I HAVE A PIECE OF *EVIDENCE*.
LOOK AT THAT, A PIECE OF CLOTH WITH *FLAMES!* IF THAT'S NOT EVIDENCE, I DON'T KNOW WHAT IS!
LEMME SEE.
LEEET MEEE SEEEE...
YOU'RE TALKING *NONSENSE!*
YOU'RE THROWING AWAY THE EVIDENCE?!
YEAH, IT'S TOO SMALL TO MAKE INTO A HAND-KERCHIEF.
HANDKER-CHIEEEEEEF.
WHAT ARE THEY TALKING ABOUT?

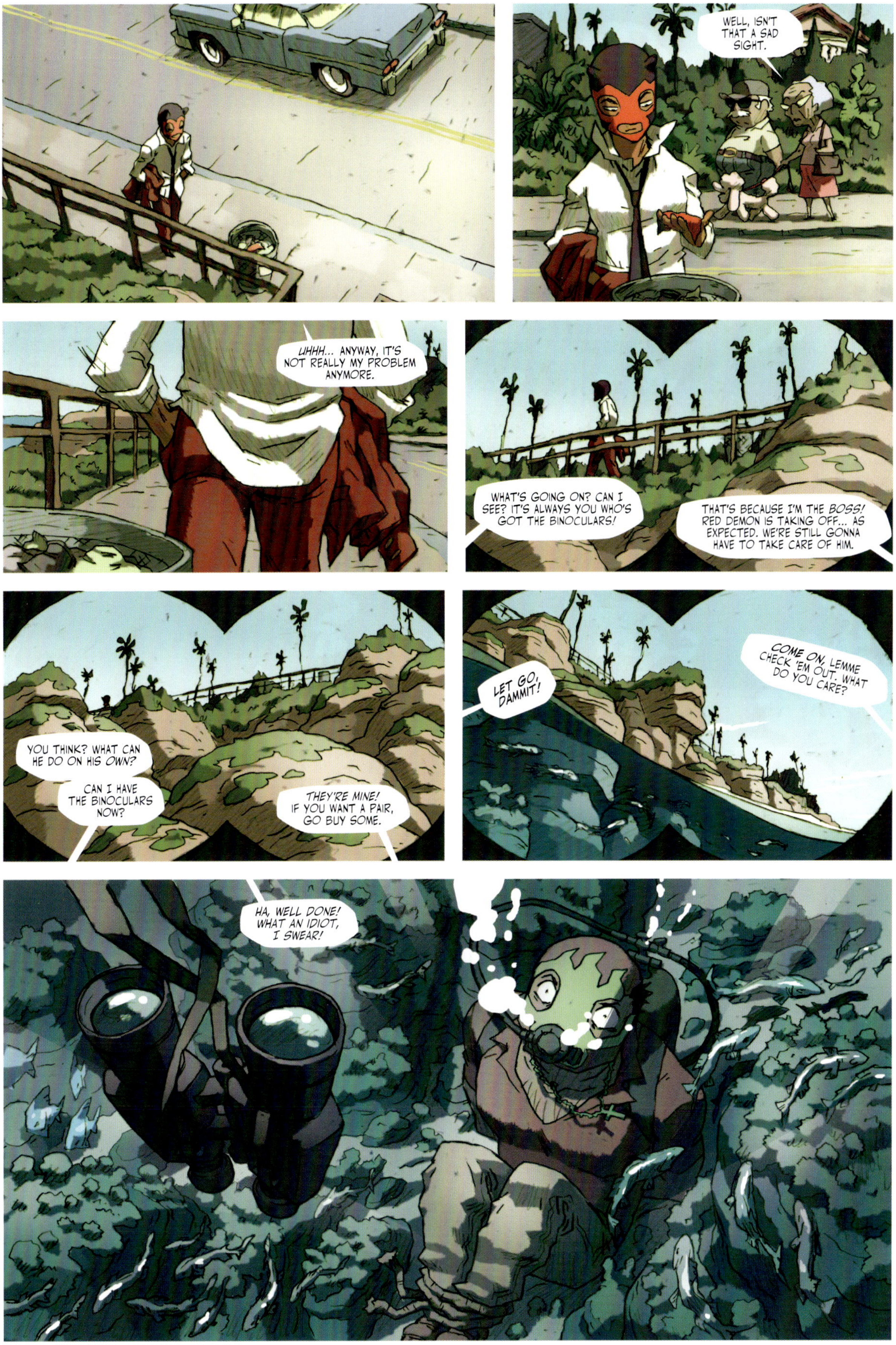
WELL, ISN'T THAT A SAD SIGHT.
UHHH... ANYWAY, IT'S NOT REALLY MY PROBLEM ANYMORE.
WHAT'S GOING ON? CAN I SEE? IT'S ALWAYS YOU WHO'S GOT THE BINOCULARS!
THAT'S BECAUSE I'M THE BOSS! RED DEMON IS TAKING OFF... AS EXPECTED. WE'RE STILL GONNA HAVE TO TAKE CARE OF HIM.
YOU THINK? WHAT CAN HE DO ON HIS OWN?
CAN I HAVE THE BINOCULARS NOW?
THEY'RE MINE! IF YOU WANT A PAIR, GO BUY SOME.
COME ON, LEMME CHECK 'EM OUT. WHAT DO YOU CARE?
LET GO, DAMMIT!
HA, WELL DONE! WHAT AN IDIOT, I SWEAR!

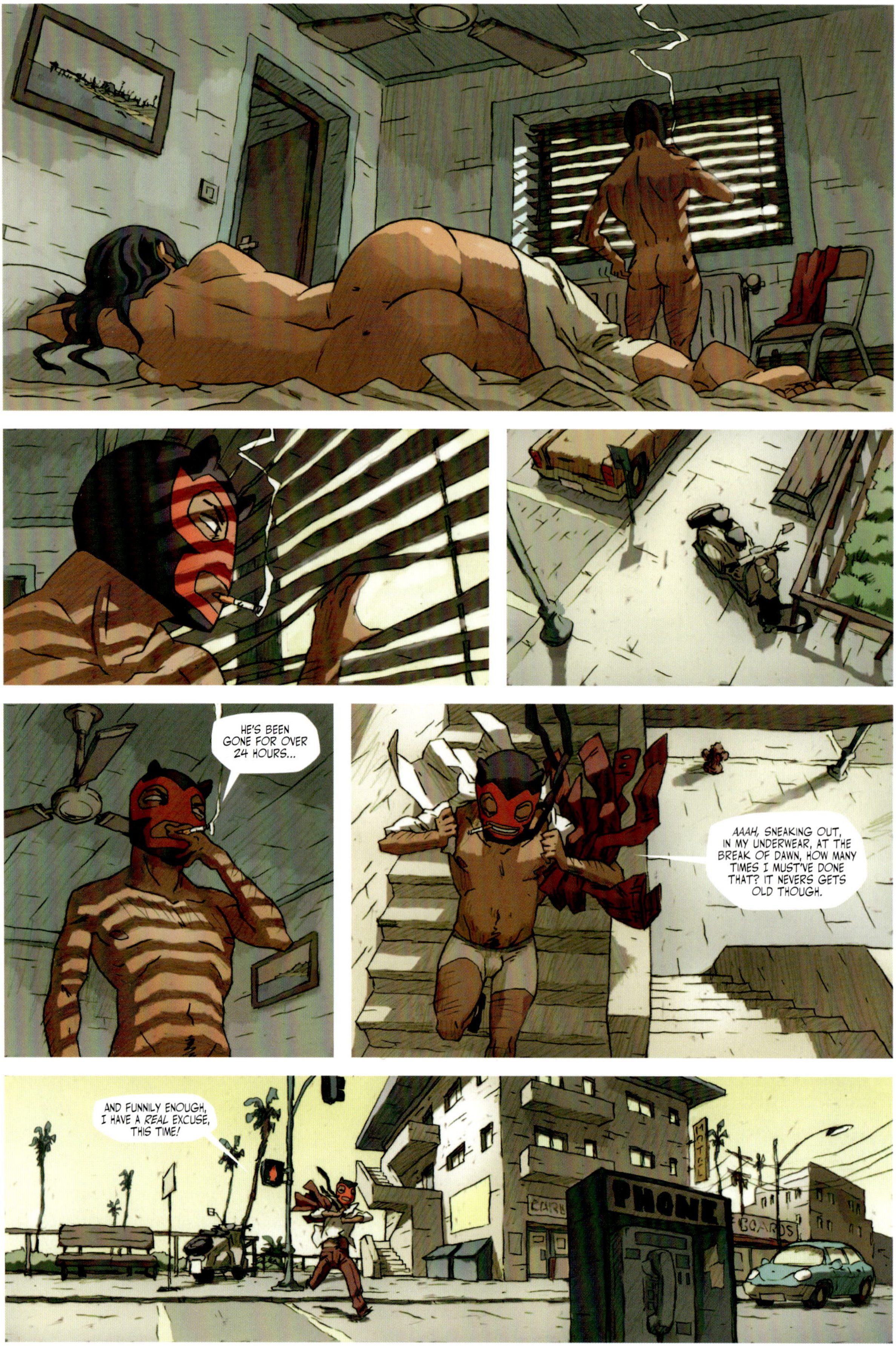
HE'S BEEN GONE FOR OVER 24 HOURS...
AAAH, SNEAKING OUT, IN MY UNDERWEAR, AT THE BREAK OF DAWN, HOW MANY TIMES I MUST'VE DONE THAT? IT NEVERS GETS OLD THOUGH.
AND FUNNILY ENOUGH, I HAVE A REAL EXCUSE, THIS TIME!
PHONE

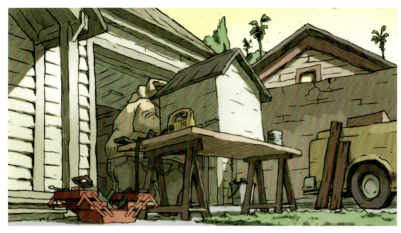

FAN-TAS-TIC! TIC-TAC WILL BE VERY HAPPY IN HIS NEW DOGHOUSE...

HE'LL SURELY STOP VOMITING ON THE BED NOW.

RRRIIINNNGGG... RRRIIINNNGGG...

I'LL GET IT. YOU CAN RELAX.

AWW, MY LITTLE HUBBY!

I'VE LEARNED A LOT IN MY CLOSE CONTACT WITH PLANTS. I'VE EVEN DEVELOPED WHAT CAN BE CALLED A PHILOSOPHY... "THE DOCTRINE OF BAD HERBS."

SEE, WE CAN LEARN A LOT FROM WATCHING A PLANT GROW...

BEEBEELEEPP... BEEBEELEEPP...

...AND EVEN MORE BY RIPPING IT OUT!

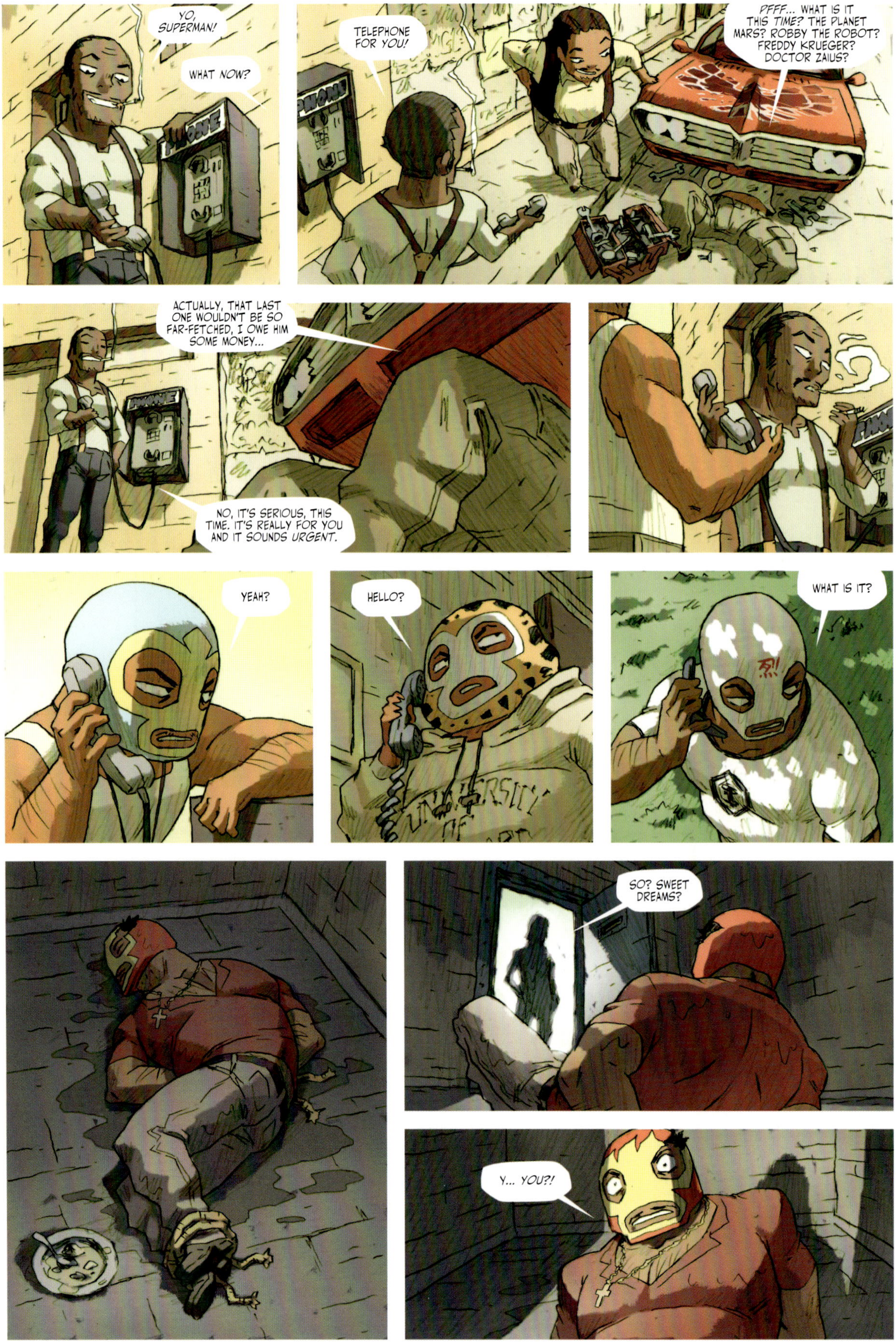
YO, SUPERMAN!
WHAT NOW?
TELEPHONE FOR YOU!
PFFF... WHAT IS IT THIS TIME? THE PLANET MARS? ROBBY THE ROBOT? FREDDY KRUEGER? DOCTOR ZAIUS?
ACTUALLY, THAT LAST ONE WOULDN'T BE SO FAR-FETCHED, I OWE HIM SOME MONEY...
NO, IT'S SERIOUS, THIS TIME. IT'S REALLY FOR YOU AND IT SOUNDS URGENT.
YEAH?
HELLO?
WHAT IS IT?
SO? SWEET DREAMS?
Y... YOU?!

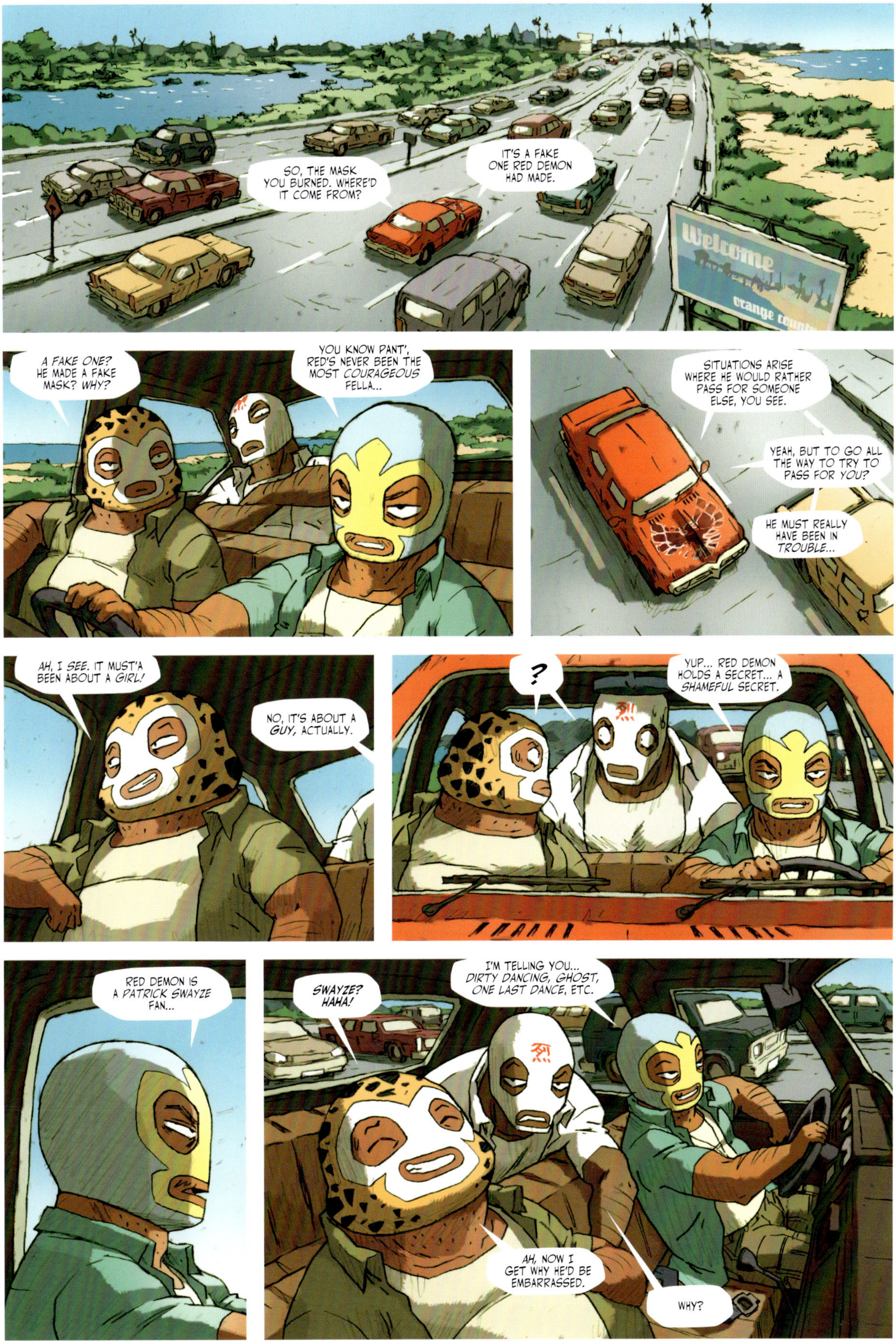
SO, THE MASK YOU BURNED. WHERE'D IT COME FROM?
IT'S A FAKE ONE RED DEMON HAD MADE.
Welcome
orange county
A FAKE ONE? HE MADE A FAKE MASK? WHY?
YOU KNOW PANT', RED'S NEVER BEEN THE MOST COURAGEOUS FELLA...
SITUATIONS ARISE WHERE HE WOULD RATHER PASS FOR SOMEONE ELSE, YOU SEE.
YEAH, BUT TO GO ALL THE WAY TO TRY TO PASS FOR YOU?
HE MUST REALLY HAVE BEEN IN TROUBLE...
AH, I SEE. IT MUST'A BEEN ABOUT A GIRL!
NO, IT'S ABOUT A GUY, ACTUALLY.
?
YUP... RED DEMON HOLDS A SECRET... A SHAMEFUL SECRET.
RED DEMON IS A PATRICK SWAYZE FAN...
SWAYZE? HAHA!
I'M TELLING YOU... DIRTY DANCING, GHOST, ONE LAST DANCE, ETC.
AH, NOW I GET WHY HE'D BE EMBARRASSED.
WHY?

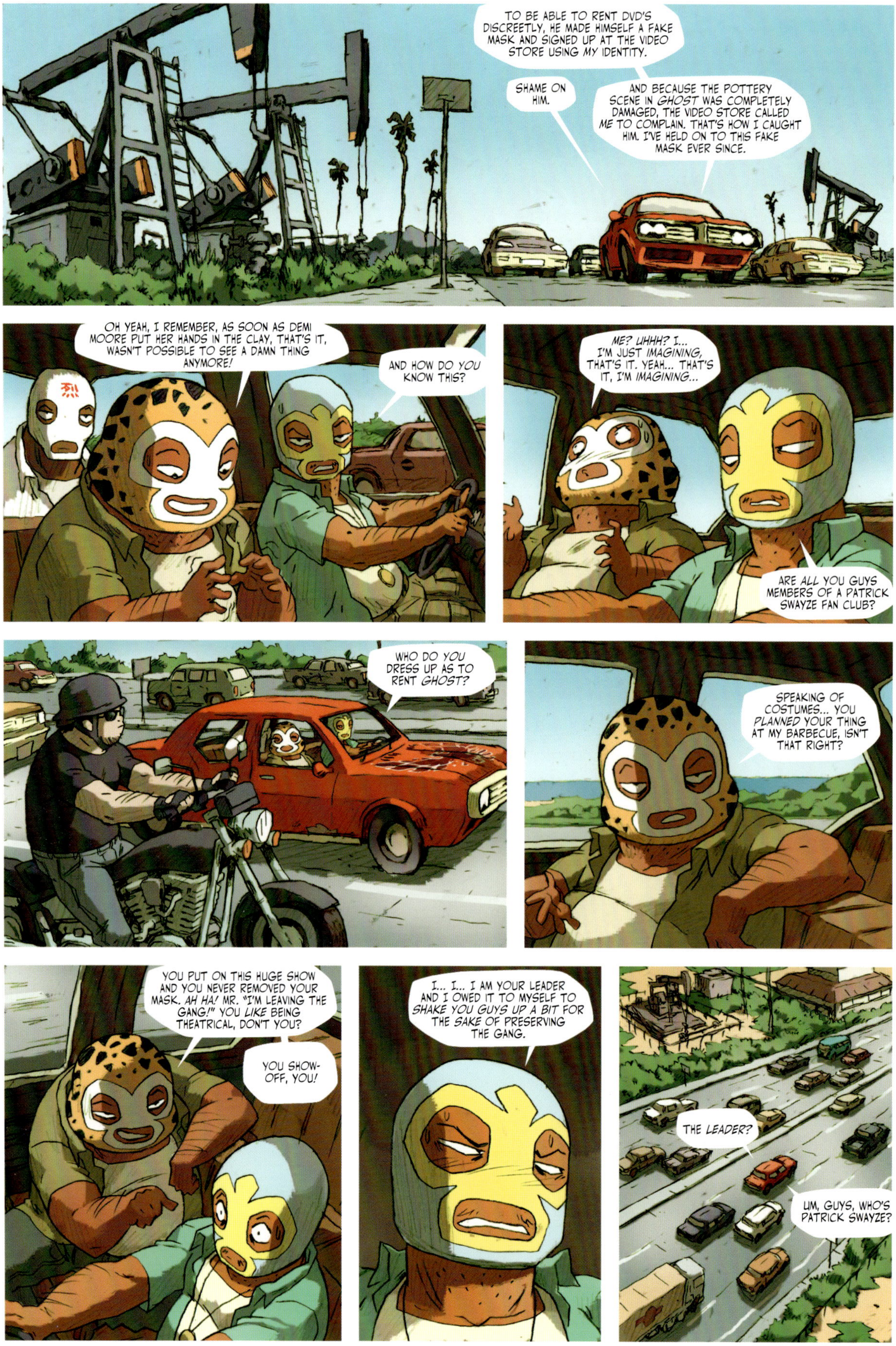
TO BE ABLE TO RENT DVD'S DISCREETLY, HE MADE HIMSELF A FAKE MASK AND SIGNED UP AT THE VIDEO STORE USING MY IDENTITY.
SHAME ON HIM.
AND BECAUSE THE POTTERY SCENE IN GHOST WAS COMPLETELY DAMAGED, THE VIDEO STORE CALLED ME TO COMPLAIN. THAT'S HOW I CAUGHT HIM. I'VE HELD ON TO THIS FAKE MASK EVER SINCE.
OH YEAH, I REMEMBER, AS SOON AS DEMI MOORE PUT HER HANDS IN THE CLAY, THAT'S IT, WASN'T POSSIBLE TO SEE A DAMN THING ANYMORE!
AND HOW DO YOU KNOW THIS?
ME? UHHH? I... I'M JUST IMAGINING, THAT'S IT. YEAH... THAT'S IT, I'M IMAGINING...
ARE ALL YOU GUYS MEMBERS OF A PATRICK SWAYZE FAN CLUB?
WHO DO YOU DRESS UP AS TO RENT GHOST?
SPEAKING OF COSTUMES... YOU PLANNED YOUR THING AT MY BARBECUE, ISN'T THAT RIGHT?
YOU PUT ON THIS HUGE SHOW AND YOU NEVER REMOVED YOUR MASK. AH HA! MR. "I'M LEAVING THE GANG!" YOU LIKE BEING THEATRICAL, DON'T YOU?
YOU SHOW-OFF, YOU!
I... I... I AM YOUR LEADER AND I OWED IT TO MYSELF TO SHAKE YOU GUYS UP A BIT FOR THE SAKE OF PRESERVING THE GANG.
THE LEADER?
UM, GUYS, WHO'S PATRICK SWAYZE?

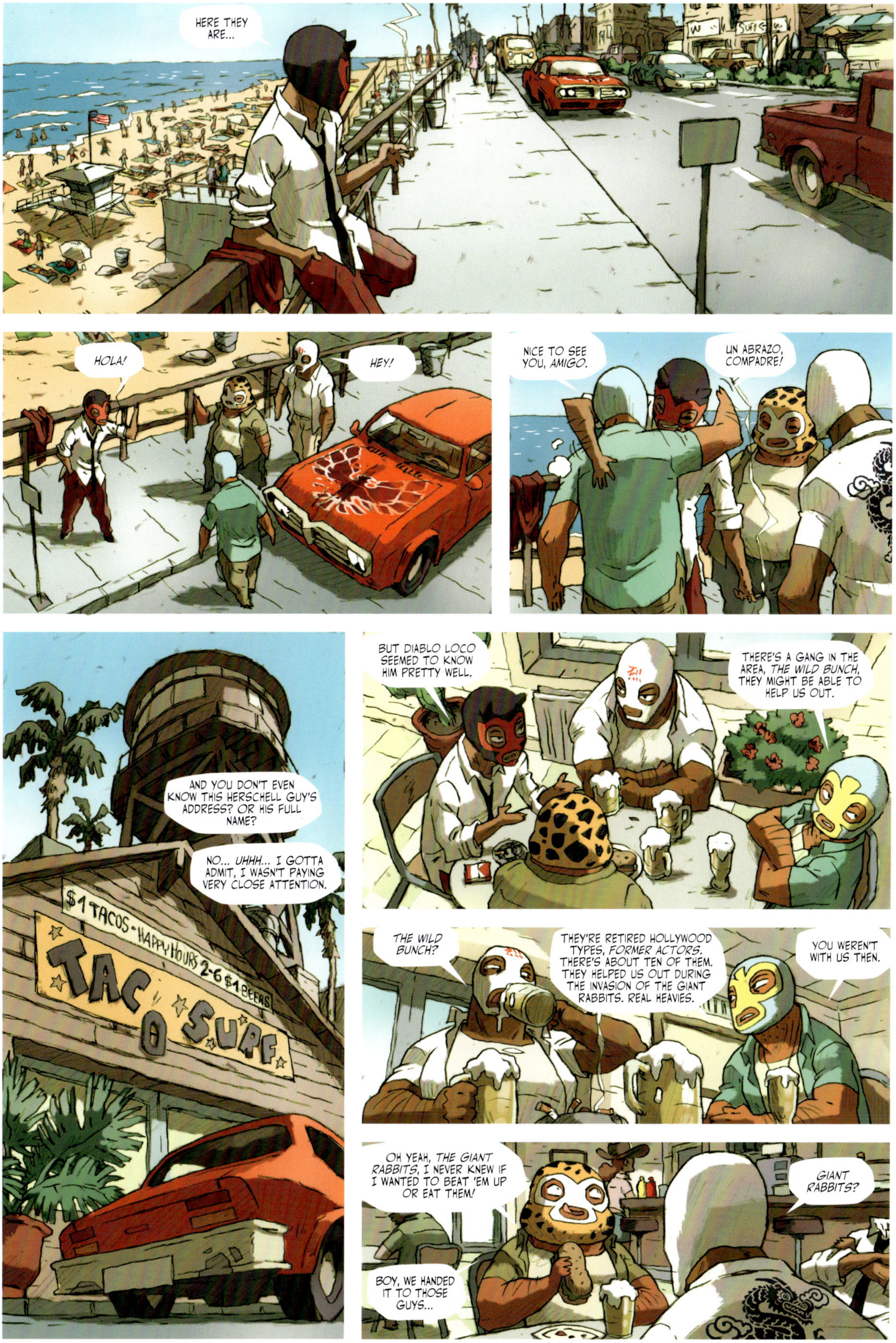
HERE THEY ARE...
HOLA!
HEY!
NICE TO SEE YOU, AMIGO.
UN ABRAZO, COMPADRE!
AND YOU DON'T EVEN KNOW THIS HERSCHELL GUY'S ADDRESS? OR HIS FULL NAME?
NO... UHHH... I GOTTA ADMIT, I WASN'T PAYING VERY CLOSE ATTENTION.
$1 TACOS - HAPPY HOURS 2-6 $1 BEERS
TACO SURF
BUT DIABLO LOCO SEEMED TO KNOW HIM PRETTY WELL.
THERE'S A GANG IN THE AREA, THE WILD BUNCH, THEY MIGHT BE ABLE TO HELP US OUT.
THE WILD BUNCH?
THEY'RE RETIRED HOLLYWOOD TYPES, FORMER ACTORS. THERE'S ABOUT TEN OF THEM. THEY HELPED US OUT DURING THE INVASION OF THE GIANT RABBITS. REAL HEAVIES.
YOU WEREN'T WITH US THEN.
OH YEAH, THE GIANT RABBITS, I NEVER KNEW IF I WANTED TO BEAT 'EM UP OR EAT THEM!
GIANT RABBITS?
BOY, WE HANDED IT TO THOSE GUYS...

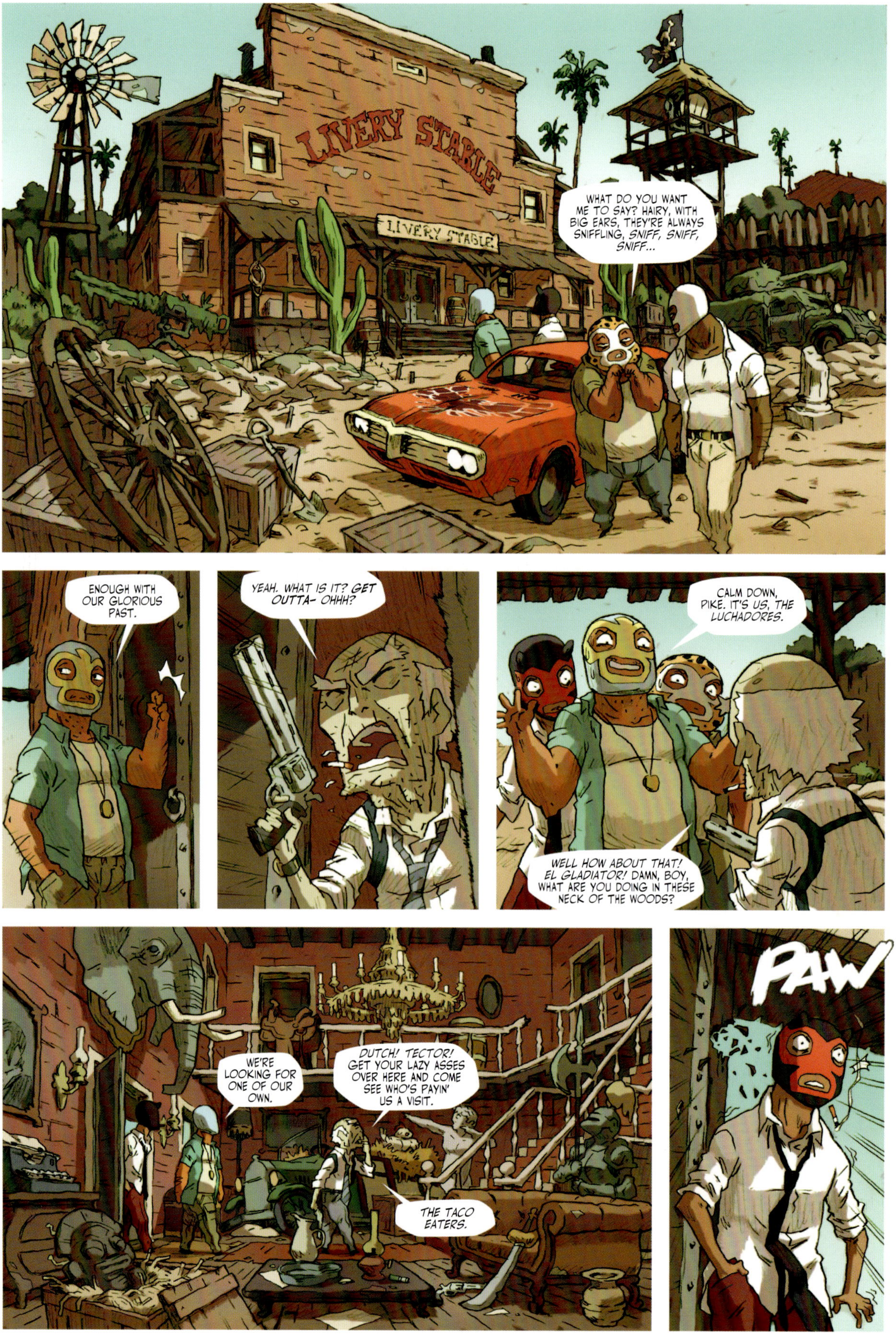
LIVERY STABLE
LIVERY STABLE
WHAT DO YOU WANT ME TO SAY? HAIRY, WITH BIG EARS, THEY'RE ALWAYS SNIFFLING, SNIFF, SNIFF, SNIFF...
ENOUGH WITH OUR GLORIOUS PAST.
YEAH. WHAT IS IT? GET OUTTA- OHHH?
CALM DOWN, PIKE. IT'S US, THE LUCHADORES.
WELL HOW ABOUT THAT! EL GLADIATOR! DAMN, BOY, WHAT ARE YOU DOING IN THESE NECK OF THE WOODS?
WE'RE LOOKING FOR ONE OF OUR OWN.
DUTCH! TECTOR! GET YOUR LAZY ASSES OVER HERE AND COME SEE WHO'S PAYIN' US A VISIT.
THE TACO EATERS.
PAW

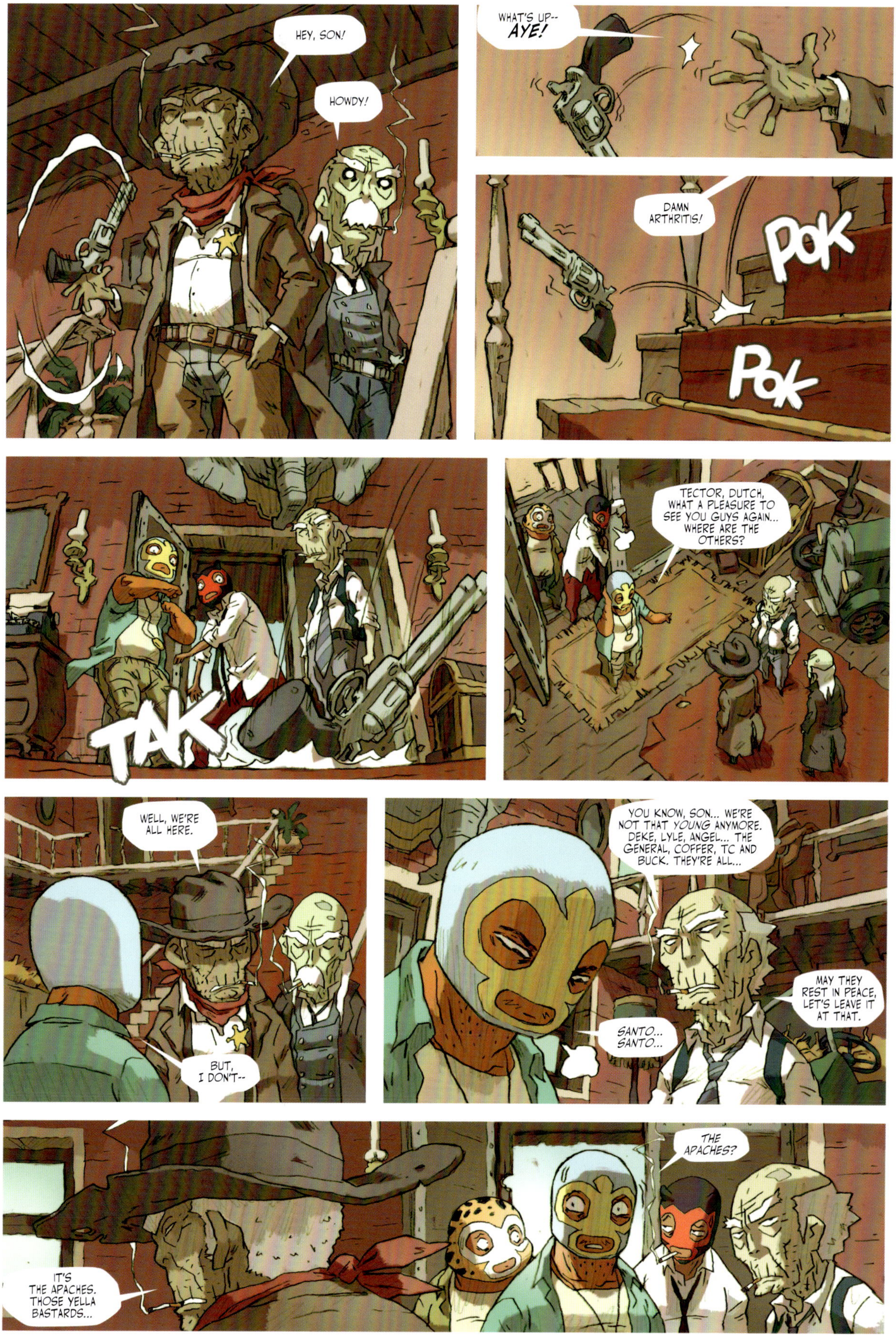
HEY, SON!
HOWDY!
WHAT'S UP-- AYE!
DAMN ARTHRITIS!
POK
POK
TAK
TECTOR, DUTCH, WHAT A PLEASURE TO SEE YOU GUYS AGAIN... WHERE ARE THE OTHERS?
WELL, WE'RE ALL HERE.
BUT, I DON'T--
YOU KNOW, SON... WE'RE NOT THAT YOUNG ANYMORE. DEKE, LYLE, ANGEL... THE GENERAL, COFFER, TC AND BUCK. THEY'RE ALL...
SANTO... SANTO...
MAY THEY REST IN PEACE, LET'S LEAVE IT AT THAT.
THE APACHES?
IT'S THE APACHES. THOSE YELLA BASTARDS...

YEAH, SON. THE APACHES. THEY ATTACKED THE FORT AND THEY *SCALPED* THEM.

THEY STRUNG THE REVEREND TO A CHARIOT AND DRAGGED HIM AWAY UNTIL THERE WAS NOTHING LEFT OF HIM... NOTHING AT ALL.

WHAT'S HE TALKING ABOUT? THAT'S FROM A MOVIE, *NO?*

HE'S PROBABLY NOT ALL *THERE* ANYMORE.

I'M SORRY TO HEAR ABOUT YOUR FRIENDS... AND THE APACHES...

BUT WE HAVE AN *EMERGENCY.* WE'RE SEARCHING FOR ONE OF OUR PALS, DIABLO LOCO.

GOTTA FORGIVE THE OLD DUTCH. HE CAN'T REALLY TELL THE DIFFERENCE BETWEEN THE MOVIES HE WAS IN AND REALITY.

OH OK, I GET IT. BUT WHAT ABOUT DIABLO LOCO?

THE APACHES! *BULLSHIT.* WE ALL KNOW THE *GERMANS* WERE BEHIND THE HITS.

THE... THE *GERMANS?*

YEAH, THE HEINIES, THE HUNS, THE SCHMEISSERS, THE JERRIES, THE NAZIS, THE DAMN *GERMANS!*

THOSE BASTARDS GOT US WITH THEIR FLAME-THROWERS. THE ENTIRE HILL WAS BURNING.

ONE DAY, WE'LL FIND THAT HOFFMAN SON-OF-A-BITCH.

MAYBE WE SHOULDN'T OVERSTAY OUR WELCOME?

THANKS, PIKE. SEE YOU NEXT TIME.

I HAVE A HARD TIME BELIEVING THEY WERE MEANER THAN THE GIANT RABBITS.

THE APACHES...!

HEY KID, DIABLO LOCO IS A MASKED GUY, LIKE YOU, HUH? THE ONE WHO DISAPPEARED AT THE BEACH?

HUH? UHH... YEAH, THAT'S CORRECT.

COME BACK LATER. GOT SOMETHING FOR YOU. BUT DON'T SAY A WORD TO YOUR GUYS. NOTHING, GOT IT?

UHHH...

TO NOBODY!

OK, OK.

YOUR FRIENDS ARE REALLY SOMETHING, GLAD'. YOU GOT OTHERS LIKE THOSE IN RESERVE? 'CAUSE THE INVESTIGATION'S NOT REALLY PROGRESSING...

THE ONLY LEAD WE HAVE ARE THE SURFERS. THEY'RE PROBABLY THE ONES RESPONSIBLE FOR LOCO'S DISAPPEARANCE.

THEY ALL MEET UP EVERY NIGHT AT THE BEACH. THAT'S WHAT HERSCHELL TOLD US AT LEAST.

BRADBURY

ONE WAY

LD CR AT RES OF TH BLO D BEACH

Lyric Ave.

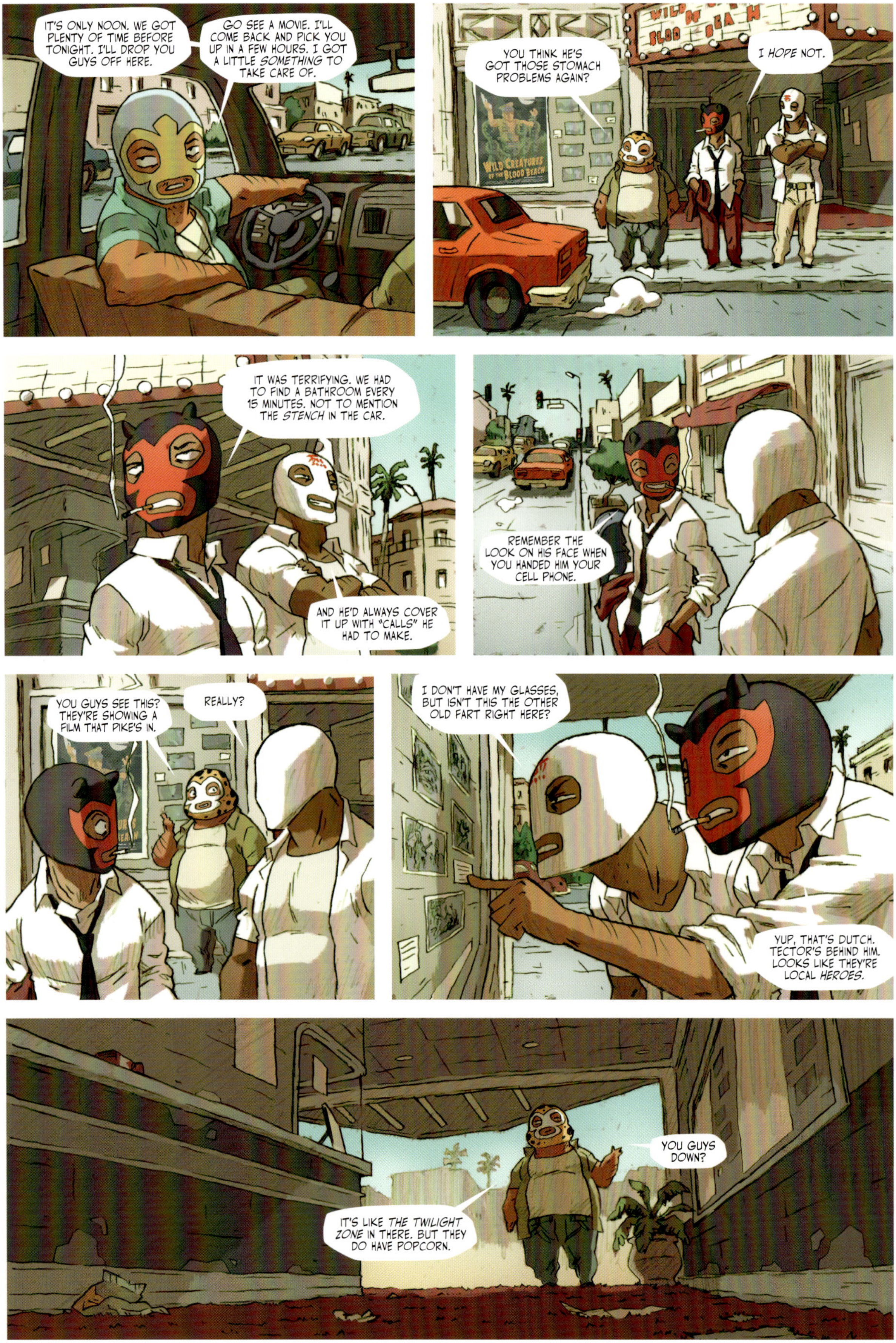

IT'S ONLY NOON. WE GOT PLENTY OF TIME BEFORE TONIGHT. I'LL DROP YOU GUYS OFF HERE.
GO SEE A MOVIE. I'LL COME BACK AND PICK YOU UP IN A FEW HOURS. I GOT A LITTLE *SOMETHING* TO TAKE CARE OF.
WILD CREATURES OF THE BLOOD BEACH
YOU THINK HE'S GOT THOSE STOMACH PROBLEMS AGAIN?
I *HOPE* NOT.
IT WAS TERRIFYING. WE HAD TO FIND A BATHROOM EVERY 15 MINUTES. NOT TO MENTION THE *STENCH* IN THE CAR.
AND HE'D ALWAYS COVER IT UP WITH "CALLS" HE HAD TO MAKE.
REMEMBER THE LOOK ON HIS FACE WHEN YOU HANDED HIM YOUR CELL PHONE.
YOU GUYS SEE THIS? THEY'RE SHOWING A FILM THAT PIKE'S IN.
REALLY?
I DON'T HAVE MY GLASSES, BUT ISN'T THIS THE OTHER OLD FART RIGHT HERE?
YUP, THAT'S DUTCH. TECTOR'S BEHIND HIM. LOOKS LIKE THEY'RE LOCAL *HEROES*.
YOU GUYS DOWN?
IT'S LIKE *THE TWILIGHT ZONE* IN THERE. BUT THEY DO HAVE POPCORN.

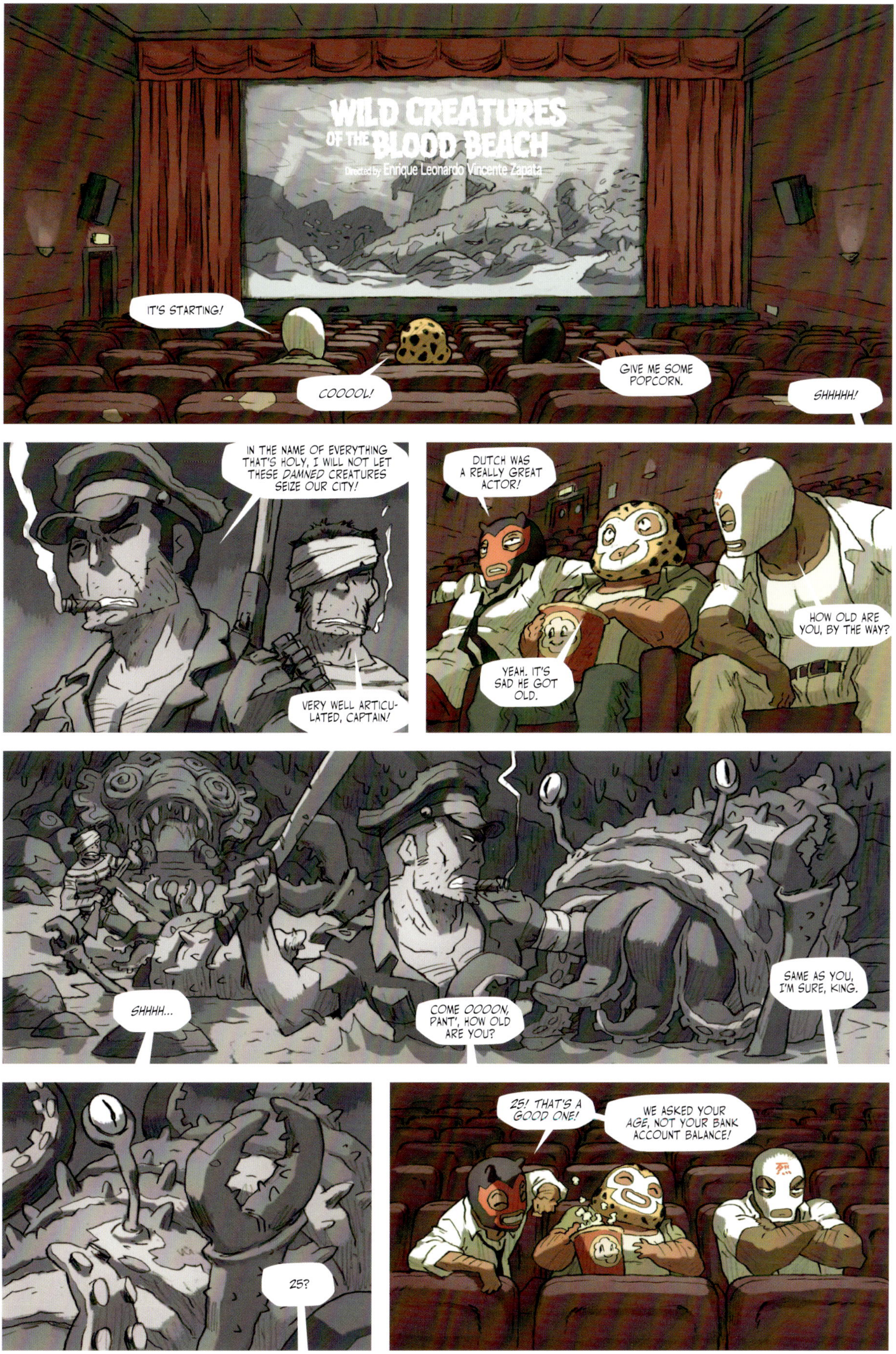
WILD CREATURES OF THE BLOOD BEACH
Directed by Enrique Leonardo Vincente Zapata
IT'S STARTING!
COOOOL!
GIVE ME SOME POPCORN.
SHHHHH!
IN THE NAME OF EVERYTHING THAT'S HOLY, I WILL NOT LET THESE DAMNED CREATURES SEIZE OUR CITY!
VERY WELL ARTICU-LATED, CAPTAIN!
DUTCH WAS A REALLY GREAT ACTOR!
YEAH. IT'S SAD HE GOT OLD.
HOW OLD ARE YOU, BY THE WAY?
SHHHH...
COME OOOON, PANT', HOW OLD ARE YOU?
SAME AS YOU, I'M SURE, KING.
25?
25! THAT'S A GOOD ONE!
WE ASKED YOUR AGE, NOT YOUR BANK ACCOUNT BALANCE!

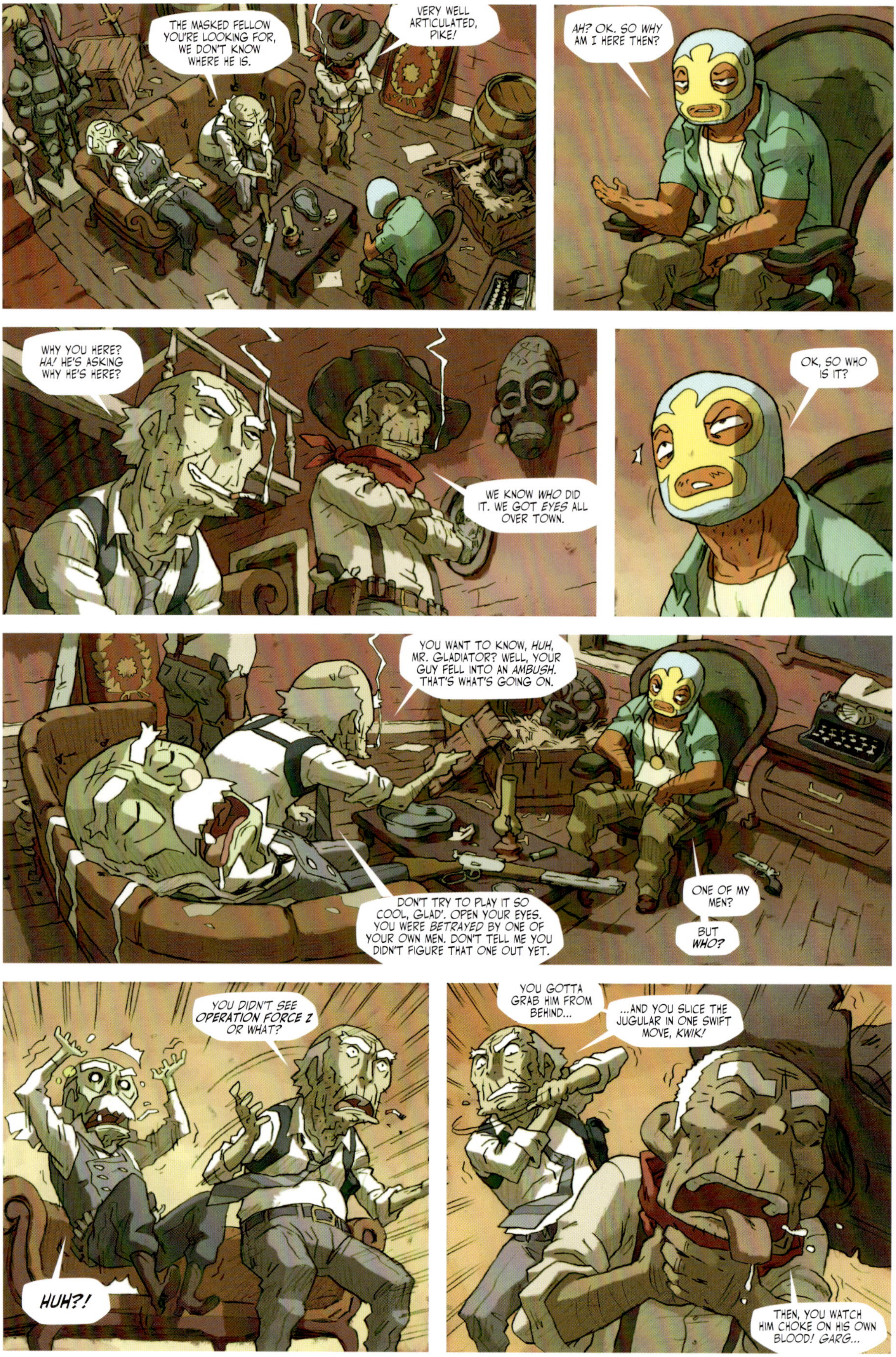
THE MASKED FELLOW YOU'RE LOOKING FOR, WE DON'T KNOW WHERE HE IS.
VERY WELL ARTICULATED, PIKE!
AH? OK. SO WHY AM I HERE THEN?
WHY YOU HERE? HA! HE'S ASKING WHY HE'S HERE?
WE KNOW WHO DID IT. WE GOT EYES ALL OVER TOWN.
OK, SO WHO IS IT?
YOU WANT TO KNOW, HUH, MR. GLADIATOR? WELL, YOUR GUY FELL INTO AN AMBUSH. THAT'S WHAT'S GOING ON.
DON'T TRY TO PLAY IT SO COOL, GLAD'. OPEN YOUR EYES. YOU WERE BETRAYED BY ONE OF YOUR OWN MEN. DON'T TELL ME YOU DIDN'T FIGURE THAT ONE OUT YET.
ONE OF MY MEN?
BUT WHO?
YOU DIDN'T SEE OPERATION FORCE Z OR WHAT?
HUH?!
YOU GOTTA GRAB HIM FROM BEHIND...
...AND YOU SLICE THE JUGULAR IN ONE SWIFT MOVE, KWIK!
THEN, YOU WATCH HIM CHOKE ON HIS OWN BLOOD! GARG...

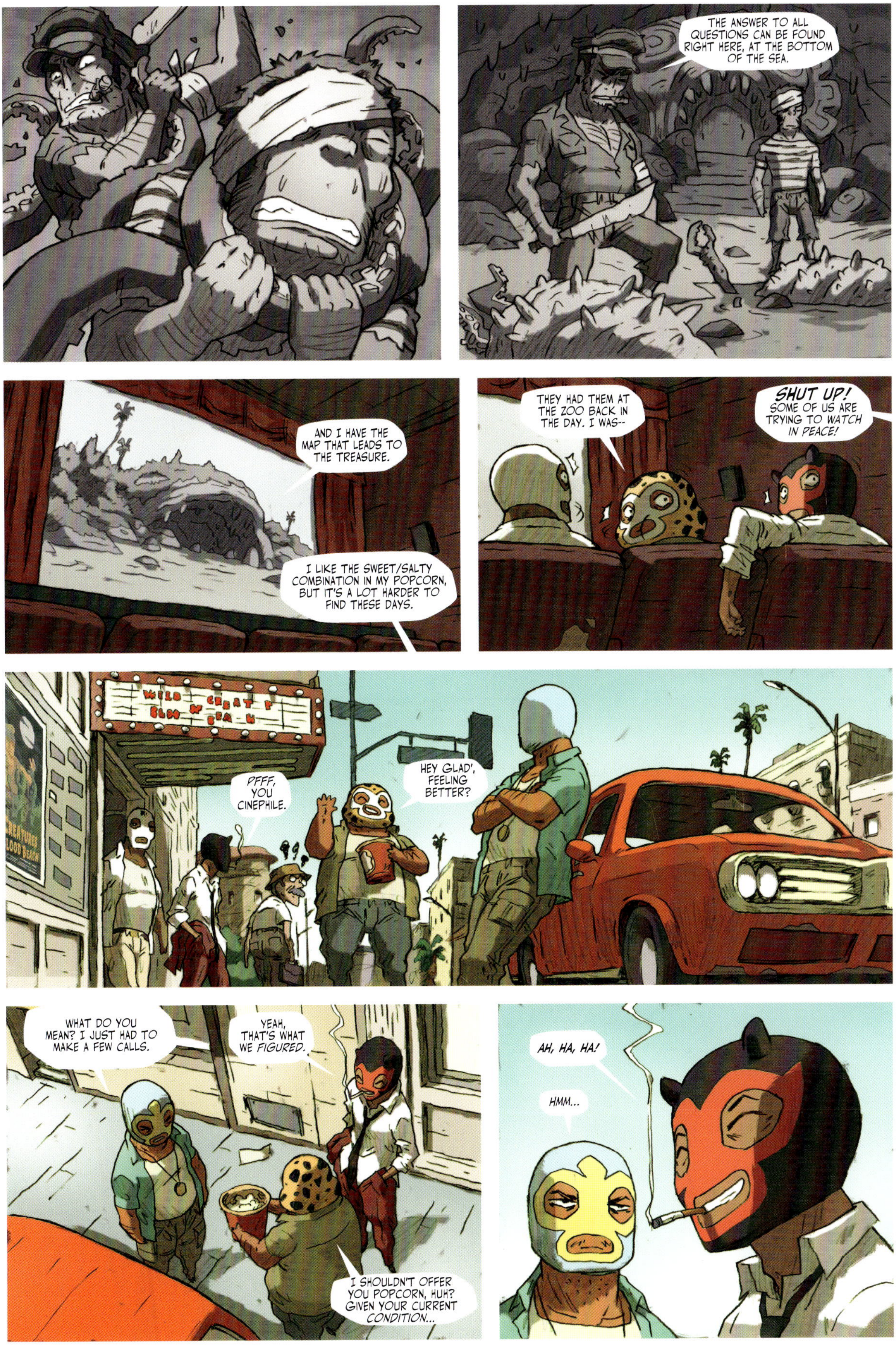
THE ANSWER TO ALL QUESTIONS CAN BE FOUND RIGHT HERE, AT THE BOTTOM OF THE SEA.
AND I HAVE THE MAP THAT LEADS TO THE TREASURE.
I LIKE THE SWEET/SALTY COMBINATION IN MY POPCORN, BUT IT'S A LOT HARDER TO FIND THESE DAYS.
THEY HAD THEM AT THE ZOO BACK IN THE DAY. I WAS--
SHUT UP! SOME OF US ARE TRYING TO WATCH IN PEACE!
PFFF, YOU CINEPHILE.
HEY GLAD', FEELING BETTER?
WHAT DO YOU MEAN? I JUST HAD TO MAKE A FEW CALLS.
YEAH, THAT'S WHAT WE FIGURED.
I SHOULDN'T OFFER YOU POPCORN, HUH? GIVEN YOUR CURRENT CONDITION...
AH, HA, HA!
HMM...

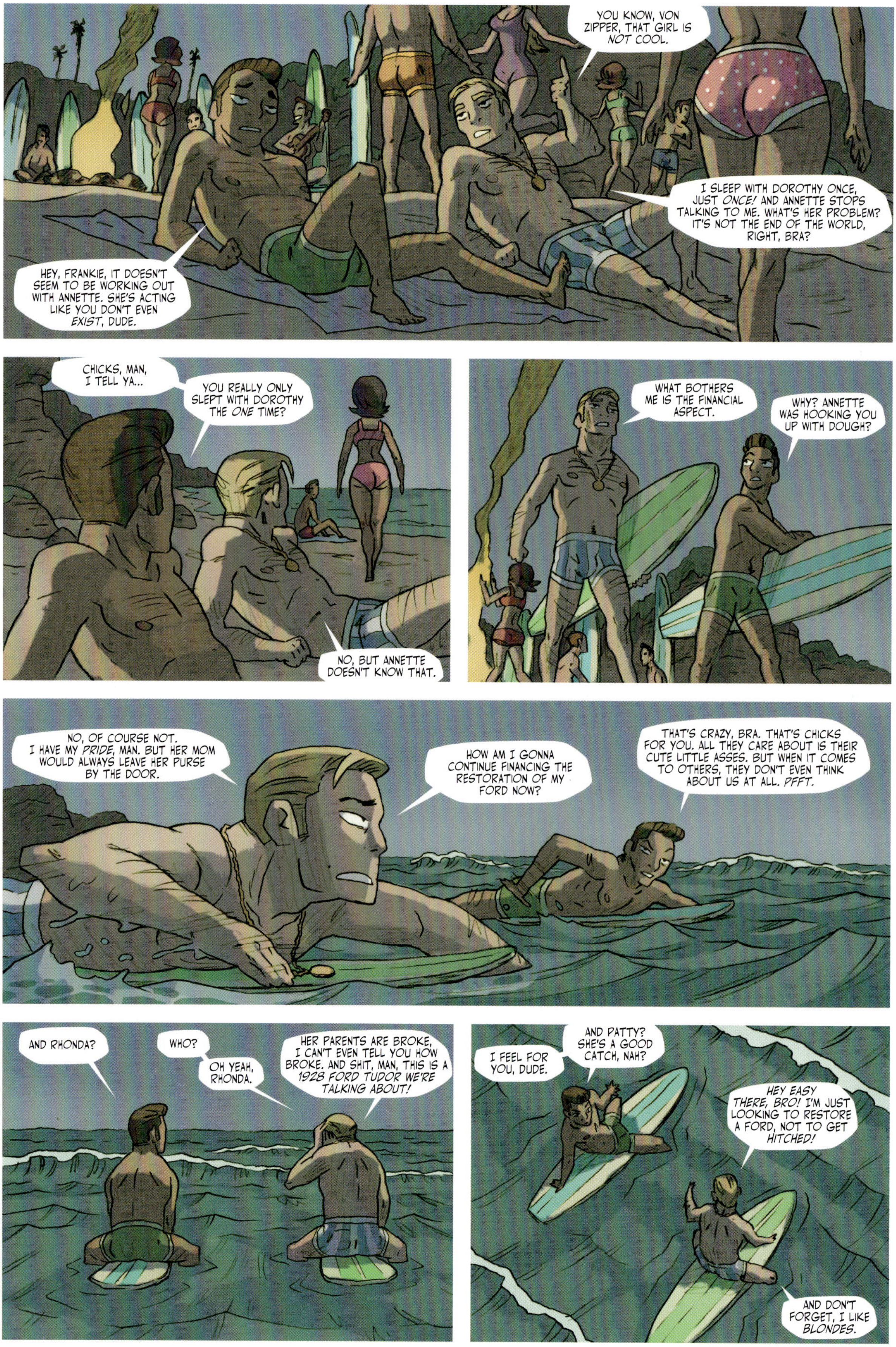

HEY, FRANKIE, IT DOESN'T SEEM TO BE WORKING OUT WITH ANNETTE. SHE'S ACTING LIKE YOU DON'T EVEN EXIST, DUDE.
YOU KNOW, VON ZIPPER, THAT GIRL IS NOT COOL.
I SLEEP WITH DOROTHY ONCE, JUST ONCE! AND ANNETTE STOPS TALKING TO ME. WHAT'S HER PROBLEM? IT'S NOT THE END OF THE WORLD, RIGHT, BRA?
CHICKS, MAN, I TELL YA...
YOU REALLY ONLY SLEPT WITH DOROTHY THE ONE TIME?
NO, BUT ANNETTE DOESN'T KNOW THAT.
WHAT BOTHERS ME IS THE FINANCIAL ASPECT.
WHY? ANNETTE WAS HOOKING YOU UP WITH DOUGH?
NO, OF COURSE NOT. I HAVE MY PRIDE, MAN. BUT HER MOM WOULD ALWAYS LEAVE HER PURSE BY THE DOOR.
HOW AM I GONNA CONTINUE FINANCING THE RESTORATION OF MY FORD NOW?
THAT'S CRAZY, BRA. THAT'S CHICKS FOR YOU. ALL THEY CARE ABOUT IS THEIR CUTE LITTLE ASSES. BUT WHEN IT COMES TO OTHERS, THEY DON'T EVEN THINK ABOUT US AT ALL. PFFT.
AND RHONDA?
WHO?
OH YEAH, RHONDA.
HER PARENTS ARE BROKE, I CAN'T EVEN TELL YOU HOW BROKE. AND SHIT, MAN, THIS IS A 1928 FORD TUDOR WE'RE TALKING ABOUT!
I FEEL FOR YOU, DUDE.
AND PATTY? SHE'S A GOOD CATCH, NAH?
HEY EASY THERE, BRO! I'M JUST LOOKING TO RESTORE A FORD, NOT TO GET HITCHED!
AND DON'T FORGET, I LIKE BLONDES.

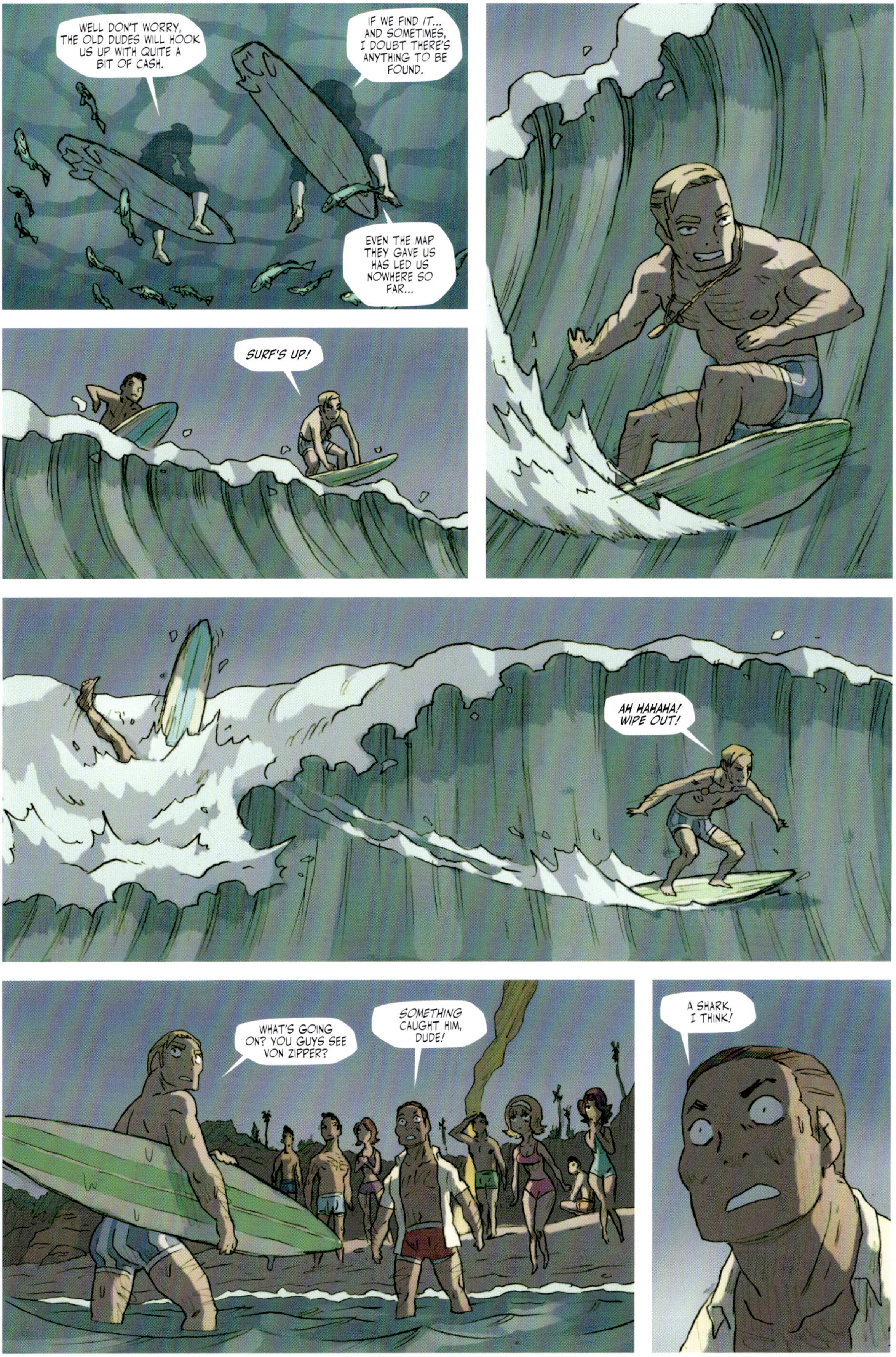
WELL DON'T WORRY, THE OLD DUDES WILL HOOK US UP WITH QUITE A BIT OF CASH.
IF WE FIND IT... AND SOMETIMES, I DOUBT THERE'S ANYTHING TO BE FOUND.
EVEN THE MAP THEY GAVE US HAS LED US NOWHERE SO FAR...
SURF'S UP!
AH HAHAHA! WIPE OUT!
WHAT'S GOING ON? YOU GUYS SEE VON ZIPPER?
SOMETHING CAUGHT HIM, DUDE!
A SHARK, I THINK!

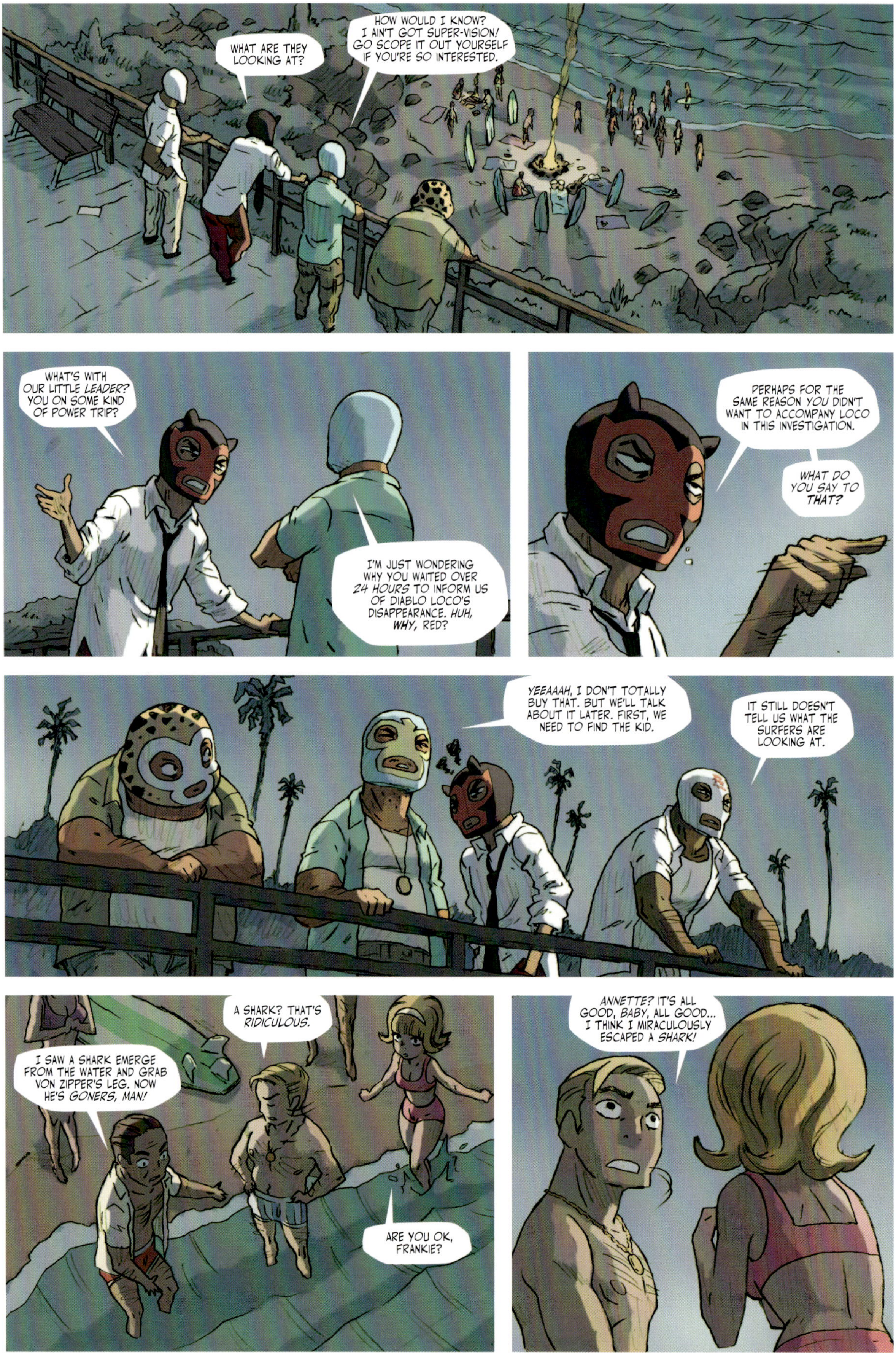
WHAT ARE THEY LOOKING AT?
HOW WOULD I KNOW? I AIN'T GOT SUPER-VISION! GO SCOPE IT OUT YOURSELF IF YOU'RE SO INTERESTED.
WHAT'S WITH OUR LITTLE *LEADER*? YOU ON SOME KIND OF POWER TRIP?
I'M JUST WONDERING WHY YOU WAITED OVER *24 HOURS* TO INFORM US OF DIABLO LOCO'S DISAPPEARANCE. *HUH, WHY,* RED?
PERHAPS FOR THE SAME REASON *YOU* DIDN'T WANT TO ACCOMPANY LOCO IN THIS INVESTIGATION.
WHAT DO YOU SAY TO ***THAT?***
YEEAAAH, I DON'T TOTALLY BUY THAT. BUT WE'LL TALK ABOUT IT LATER. FIRST, WE NEED TO FIND THE KID.
IT STILL DOESN'T TELL US WHAT THE SURFERS ARE LOOKING AT.
I SAW A SHARK EMERGE FROM THE WATER AND GRAB VON ZIPPER'S LEG. NOW HE'S *GONERS, MAN!*
A SHARK? THAT'S *RIDICULOUS.*
ARE YOU OK, FRANKIE?
ANNETTE? IT'S ALL GOOD, BABY, ALL GOOD... I THINK I MIRACULOUSLY ESCAPED A *SHARK!*

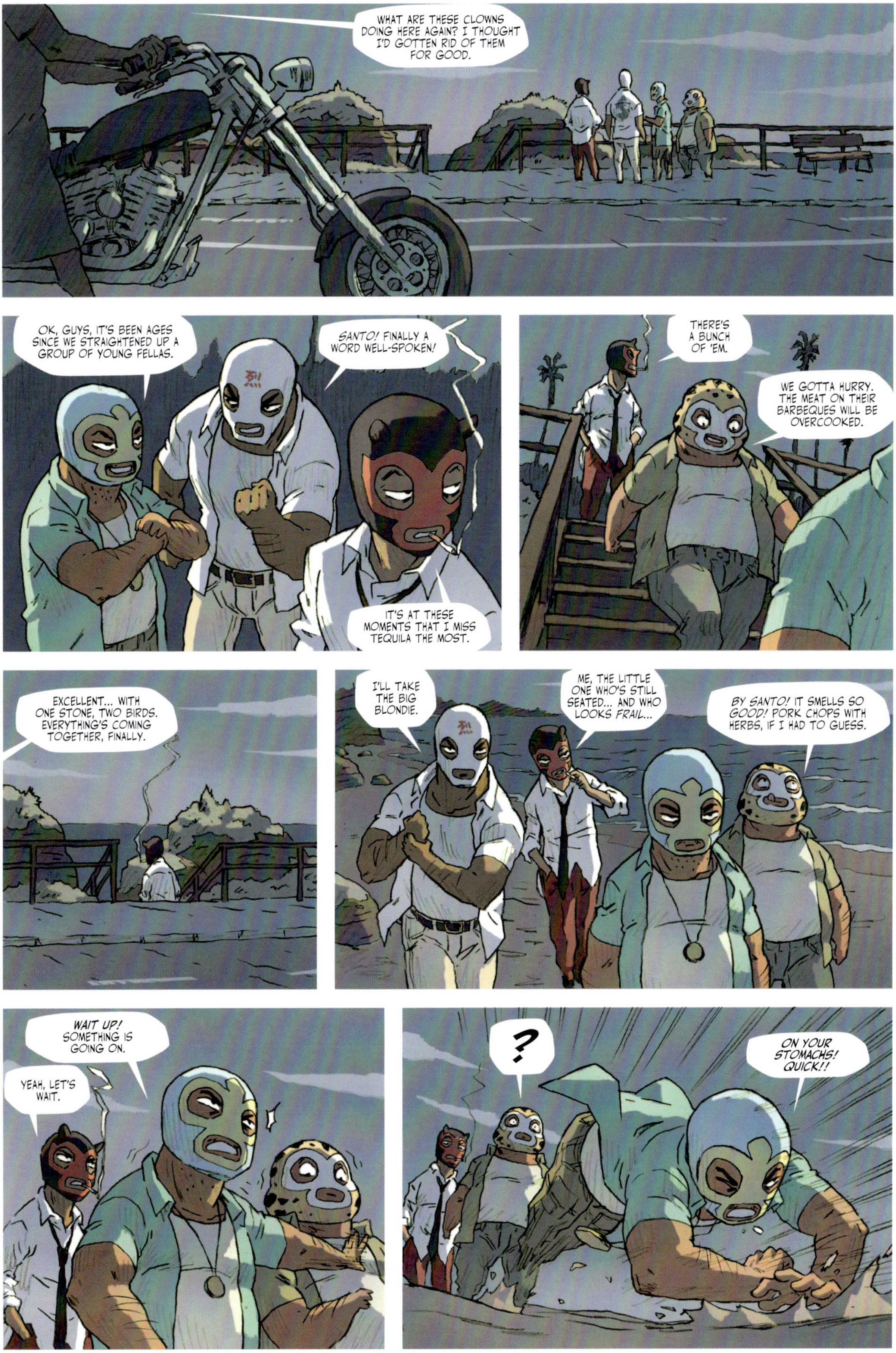
WHAT ARE THESE CLOWNS DOING HERE AGAIN? I THOUGHT I'D GOTTEN RID OF THEM FOR GOOD.
OK, GUYS, IT'S BEEN AGES SINCE WE STRAIGHTENED UP A GROUP OF YOUNG FELLAS.
SANTO! FINALLY A WORD WELL-SPOKEN!
IT'S AT THESE MOMENTS THAT I MISS TEQUILA THE MOST.
THERE'S A BUNCH OF 'EM.
WE GOTTA HURRY. THE MEAT ON THEIR BARBEQUES WILL BE OVERCOOKED.
EXCELLENT... WITH ONE STONE, TWO BIRDS. EVERYTHING'S COMING TOGETHER, FINALLY.
I'LL TAKE THE BIG BLONDIE.
ME, THE LITTLE ONE WHO'S STILL SEATED... AND WHO LOOKS FRAIL...
BY SANTO! IT SMELLS SO GOOD! PORK CHOPS WITH HERBS, IF I HAD TO GUESS.
WAIT UP! SOMETHING IS GOING ON.
YEAH, LET'S WAIT.
?
ON YOUR STOMACHS! QUICK!!

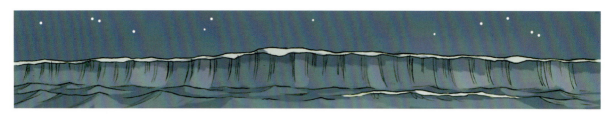

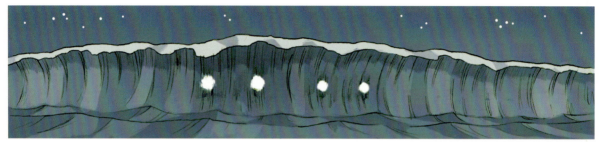

THEY WEREN'T SHARKS...

NO, BUT JUST AS NASTY.

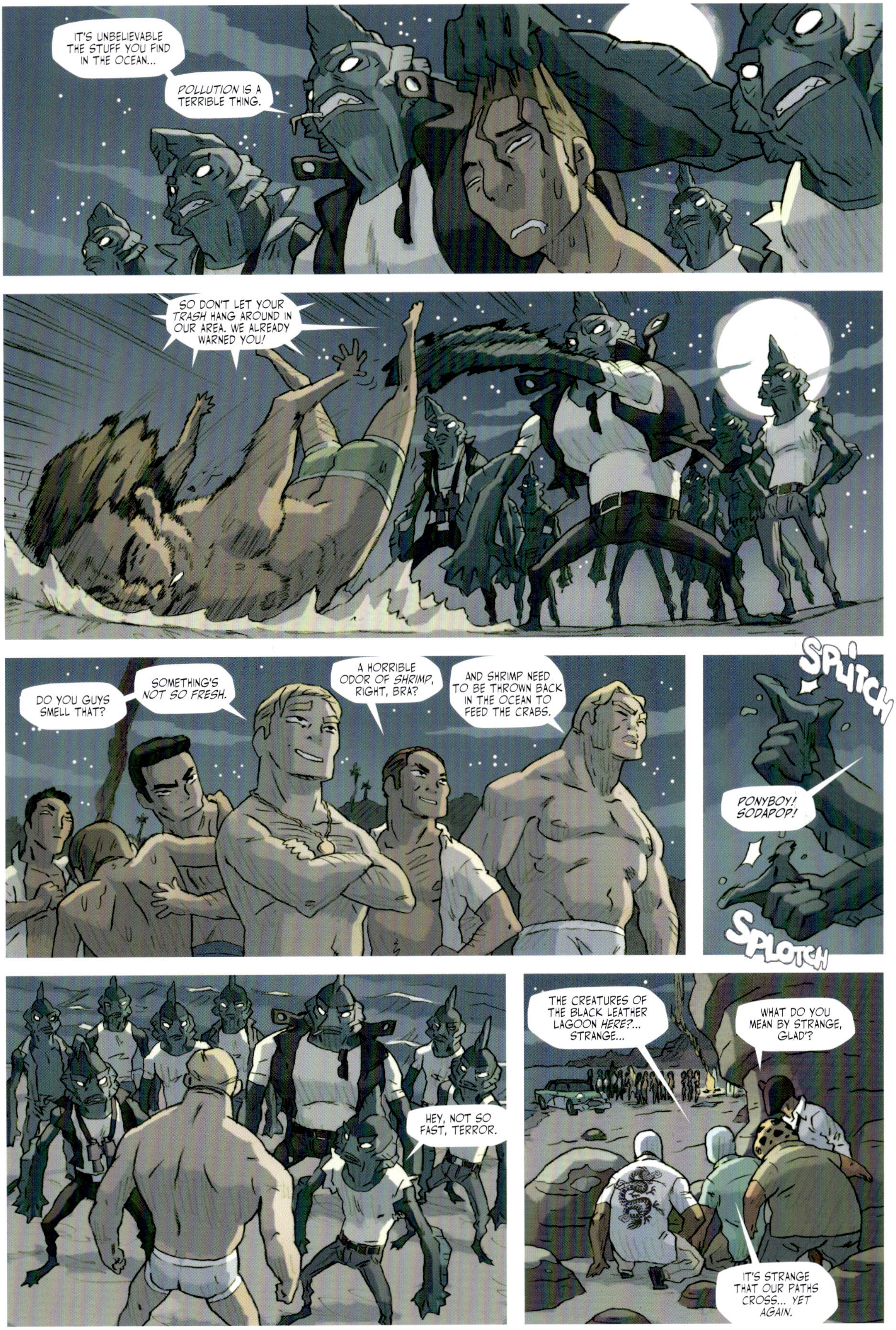
IT'S UNBELIEVABLE THE STUFF YOU FIND IN THE OCEAN...
POLLUTION IS A TERRIBLE THING.
SO DON'T LET YOUR TRASH HANG AROUND IN OUR AREA. WE ALREADY WARNED YOU!
DO YOU GUYS SMELL THAT?
SOMETHING'S NOT SO FRESH.
A HORRIBLE ODOR OF SHRIMP, RIGHT, BRA?
AND SHRIMP NEED TO BE THROWN BACK IN THE OCEAN TO FEED THE CRABS.
SPLITCH
PONYBOY! SODAPOP!
SPLOTCH
HEY, NOT SO FAST, TERROR.
THE CREATURES OF THE BLACK LEATHER LAGOON HERE?... STRANGE...
WHAT DO YOU MEAN BY STRANGE, GLAD?
IT'S STRANGE THAT OUR PATHS CROSS... YET AGAIN.

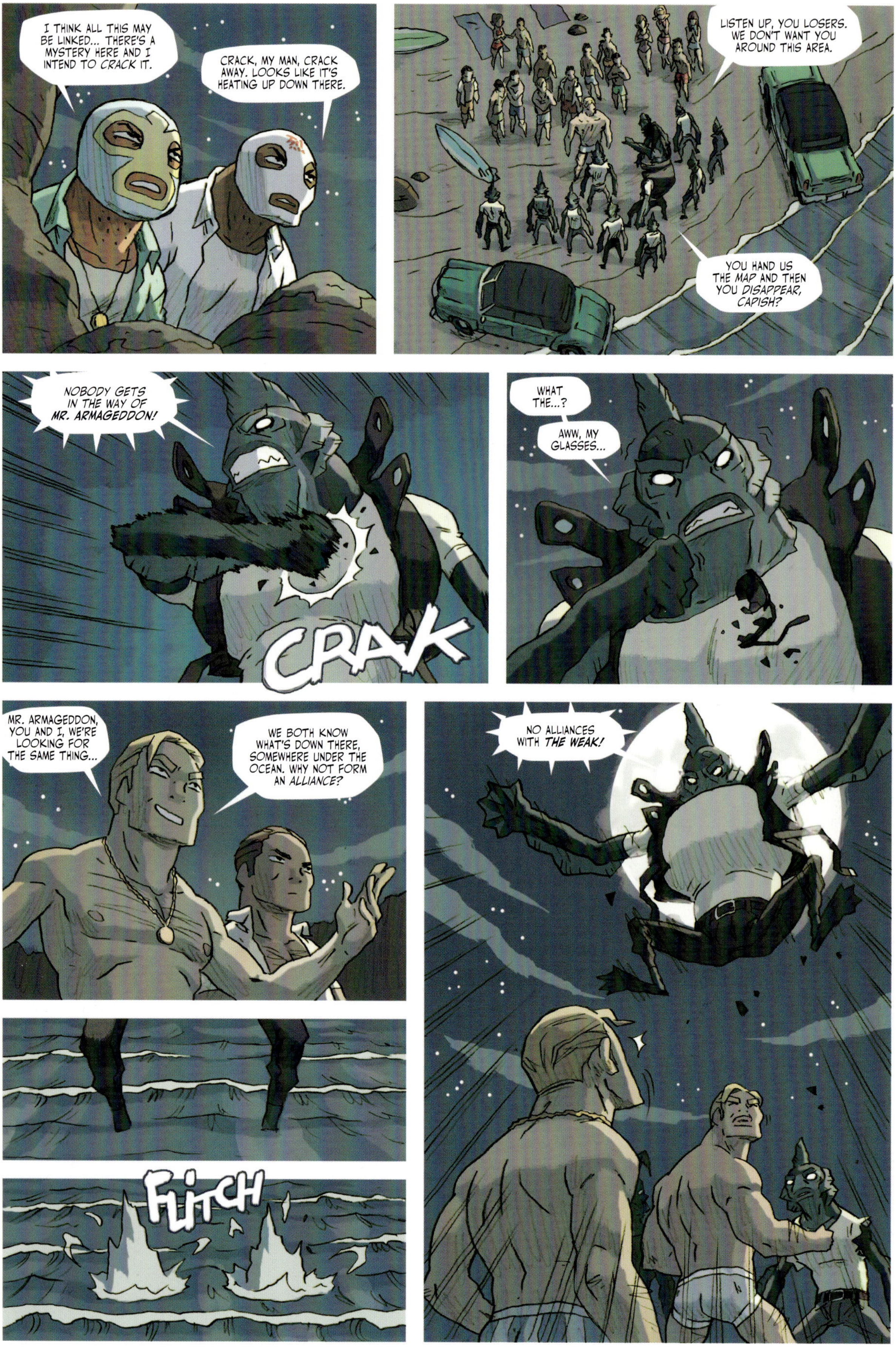
I THINK ALL THIS MAY BE LINKED... THERE'S A MYSTERY HERE AND I INTEND TO CRACK IT.
CRACK, MY MAN, CRACK AWAY. LOOKS LIKE IT'S HEATING UP DOWN THERE.
LISTEN UP, YOU LOSERS. WE DON'T WANT YOU AROUND THIS AREA.
YOU HAND US THE MAP AND THEN YOU DISAPPEAR, CAPISH?
NOBODY GETS IN THE WAY OF MR. ARMAGEDDON!
CRAK
WHAT THE...?
AWW, MY GLASSES...
MR. ARMAGEDDON, YOU AND I, WE'RE LOOKING FOR THE SAME THING...
WE BOTH KNOW WHAT'S DOWN THERE, SOMEWHERE UNDER THE OCEAN. WHY NOT FORM AN ALLIANCE?
FLITCH
NO ALLIANCES WITH THE WEAK!

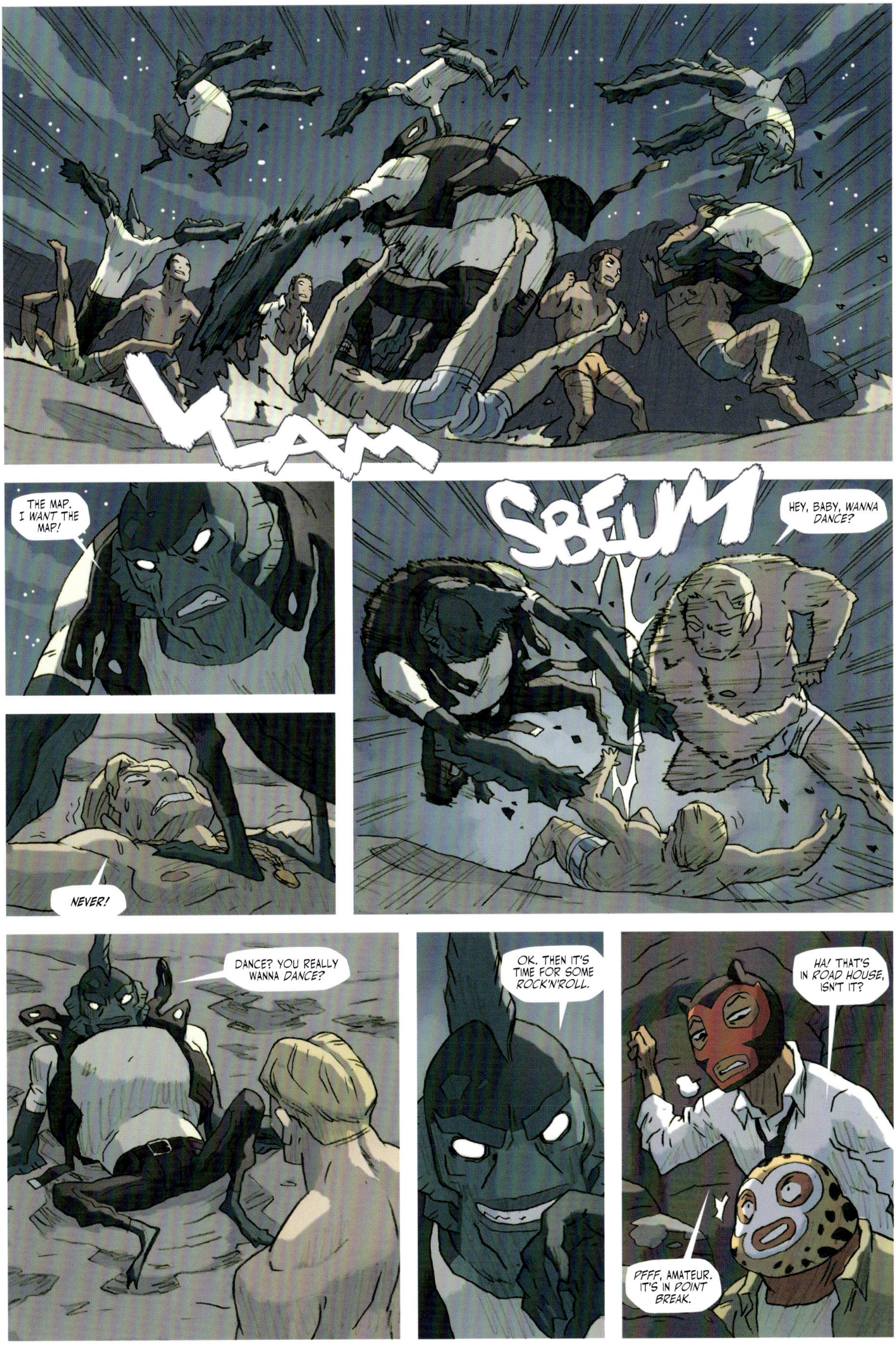
KLAM
THE MAP. I WANT THE MAP!
NEVER!
SBEUM
HEY, BABY, WANNA DANCE?
DANCE? YOU REALLY WANNA DANCE?
OK. THEN IT'S TIME FOR SOME ROCK'N'ROLL.
HA! THAT'S IN ROAD HOUSE, ISN'T IT?
PFFF, AMATEUR. IT'S IN POINT BREAK.

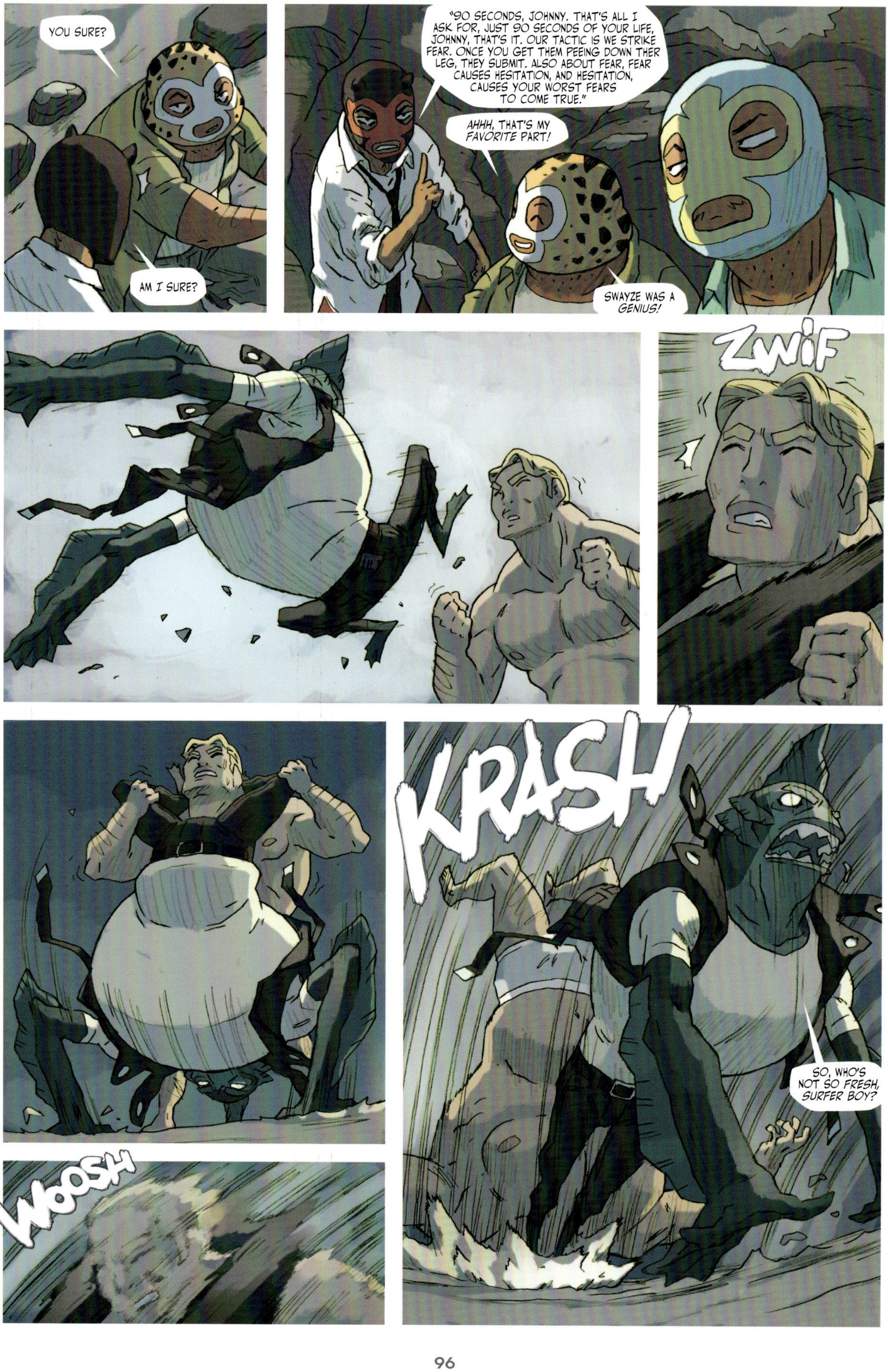
YOU SURE?
AM I SURE?
"90 SECONDS, JOHNNY. THAT'S ALL I ASK FOR, JUST 90 SECONDS OF YOUR LIFE, JOHNNY, THAT'S IT. OUR TACTIC IS WE STRIKE FEAR. ONCE YOU GET THEM PEEING DOWN THEIR LEG, THEY SUBMIT. ALSO ABOUT FEAR, FEAR CAUSES HESITATION, AND HESITATION, CAUSES YOUR WORST FEARS TO COME TRUE."
AHHH, THAT'S MY FAVORITE PART!
SWAYZE WAS A GENIUS!
ZWIF
KRASH
SO, WHO'S NOT SO FRESH, SURFER BOY?
WOOSH

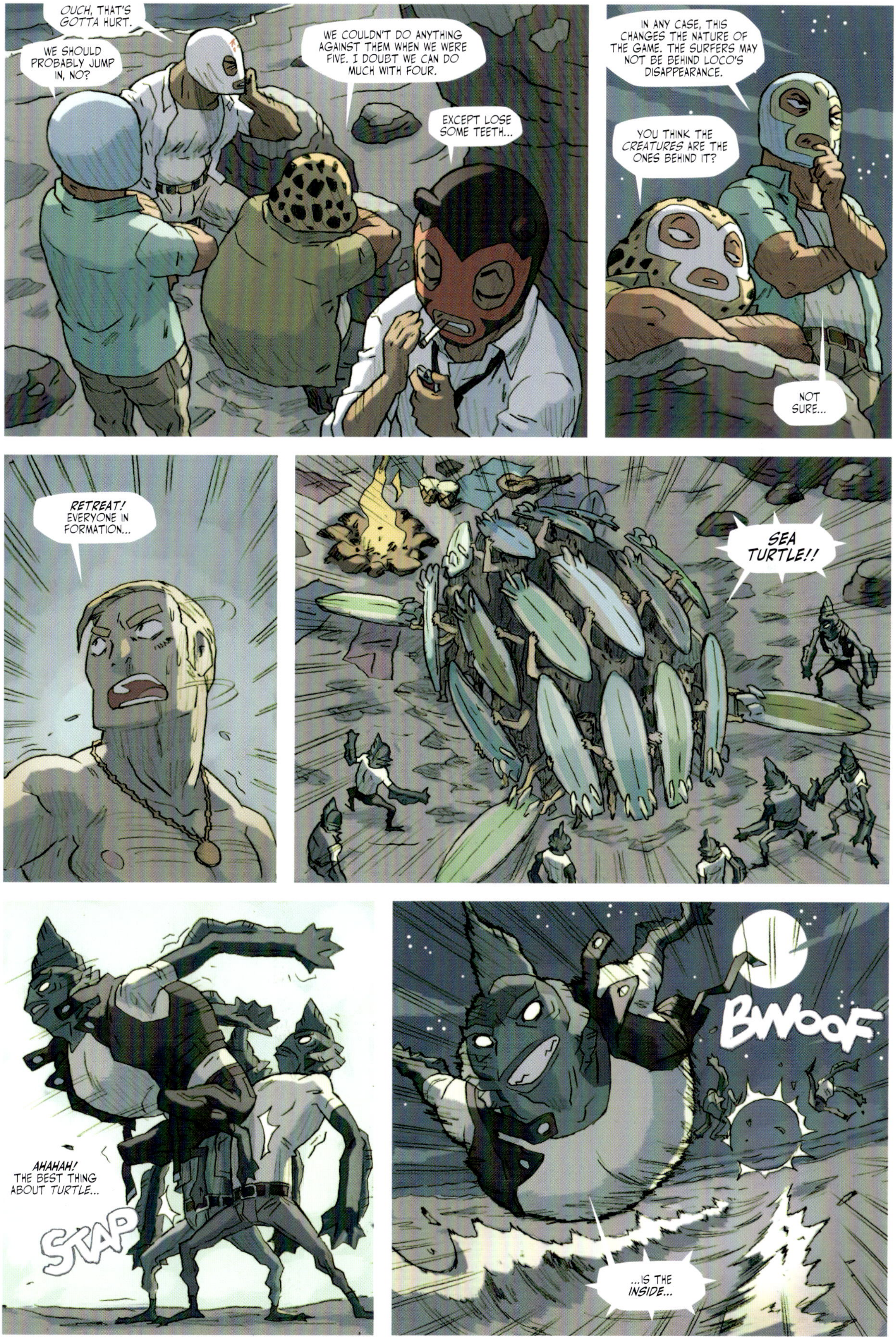
OUCH, THAT'S GOTTA HURT.
WE SHOULD PROBABLY JUMP IN, NO?
WE COULDN'T DO ANYTHING AGAINST THEM WHEN WE WERE FIVE. I DOUBT WE CAN DO MUCH WITH FOUR.
EXCEPT LOSE SOME TEETH...
IN ANY CASE, THIS CHANGES THE NATURE OF THE GAME. THE SURFERS MAY NOT BE BEHIND LOCO'S DISAPPEARANCE.
YOU THINK THE CREATURES ARE THE ONES BEHIND IT?
NOT SURE...
RETREAT! EVERYONE IN FORMATION...
SEA TURTLE!!
AHAHAH! THE BEST THING ABOUT TURTLE...
STAP
BWOOF
...IS THE INSIDE...

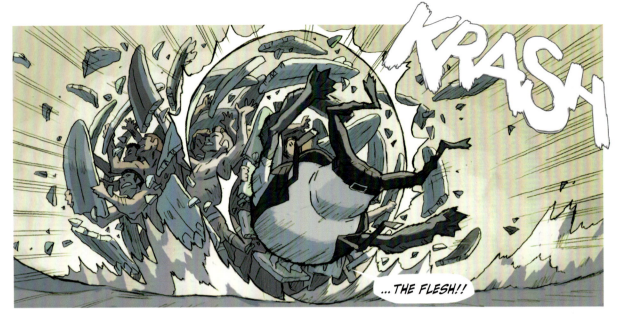

...THE FLESH!!

HA HA HA!! WE ARE THE UNDISPUTED MASTERS OF THE SEA!

THAT'S WHAT I WAS LOOKING FOR.

YOU CAN TELL YOUR SILENT PARTNERS THAT IT'S OVER FOR THEM. THAT IF THEY SEND YOU AGAIN IN SEARCH OF...YOU KNOW WHAT...WE'LL HAVE TO DEAL WITH THEM DIRECTLY.

LET'S MEET BACK AT THE CAVE, BOYS.

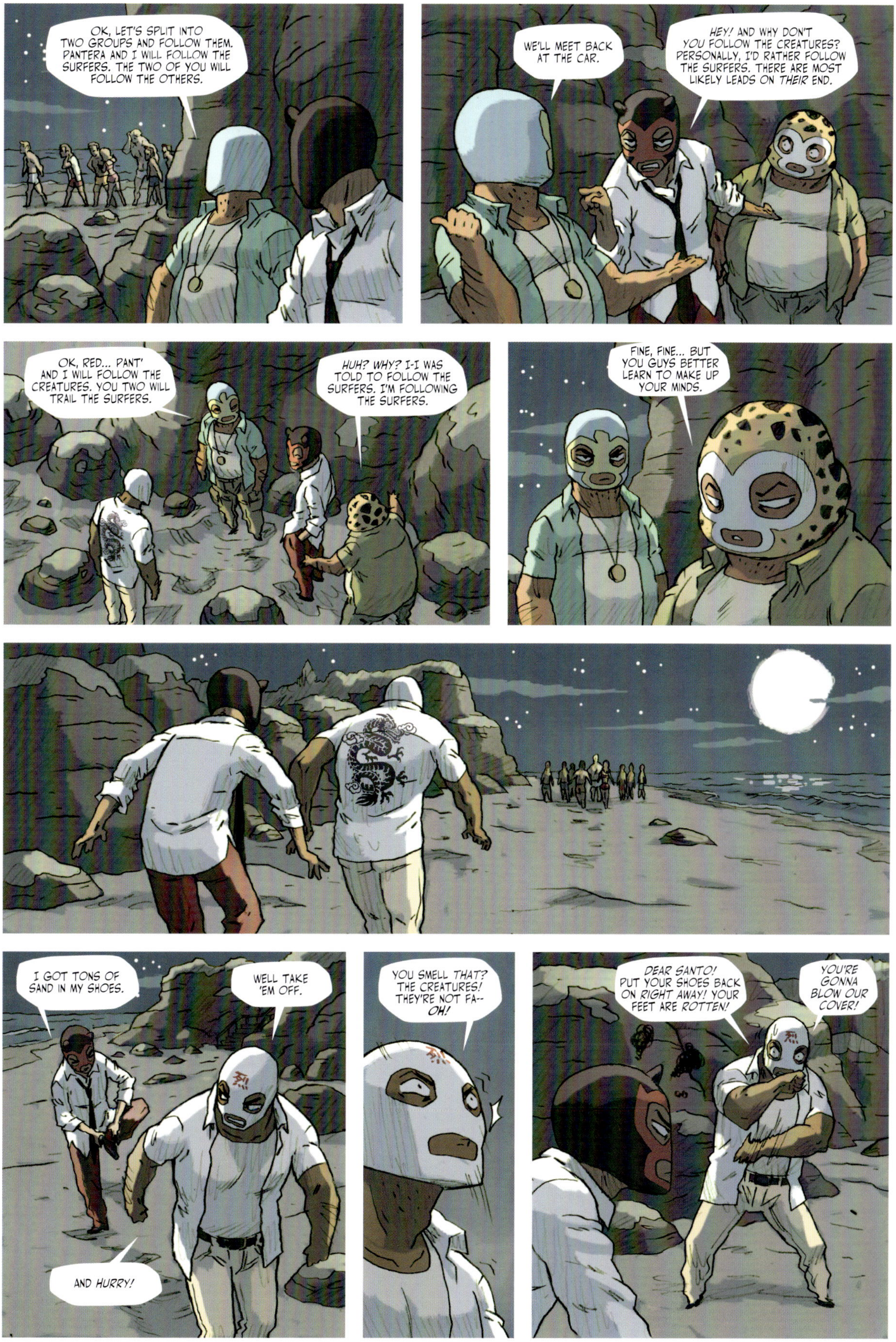
OK, LET'S SPLIT INTO TWO GROUPS AND FOLLOW THEM. PANTERA AND I WILL FOLLOW THE SURFERS. THE TWO OF YOU WILL FOLLOW THE OTHERS.
WE'LL MEET BACK AT THE CAR.
HEY! AND WHY DON'T YOU FOLLOW THE CREATURES? PERSONALLY, I'D RATHER FOLLOW THE SURFERS. THERE ARE MOST LIKELY LEADS ON THEIR END.
OK, RED... PANT' AND I WILL FOLLOW THE CREATURES. YOU TWO WILL TRAIL THE SURFERS.
HUH? WHY? I-I WAS TOLD TO FOLLOW THE SURFERS. I'M FOLLOWING THE SURFERS.
FINE, FINE... BUT YOU GUYS BETTER LEARN TO MAKE UP YOUR MINDS.
I GOT TONS OF SAND IN MY SHOES.
WELL TAKE 'EM OFF.
AND HURRY!
YOU SMELL THAT? THE CREATURES! THEY'RE NOT FA-- OH!
DEAR SANTO! PUT YOUR SHOES BACK ON RIGHT AWAY! YOUR FEET ARE ROTTEN!
YOU'RE GONNA BLOW OUR COVER!

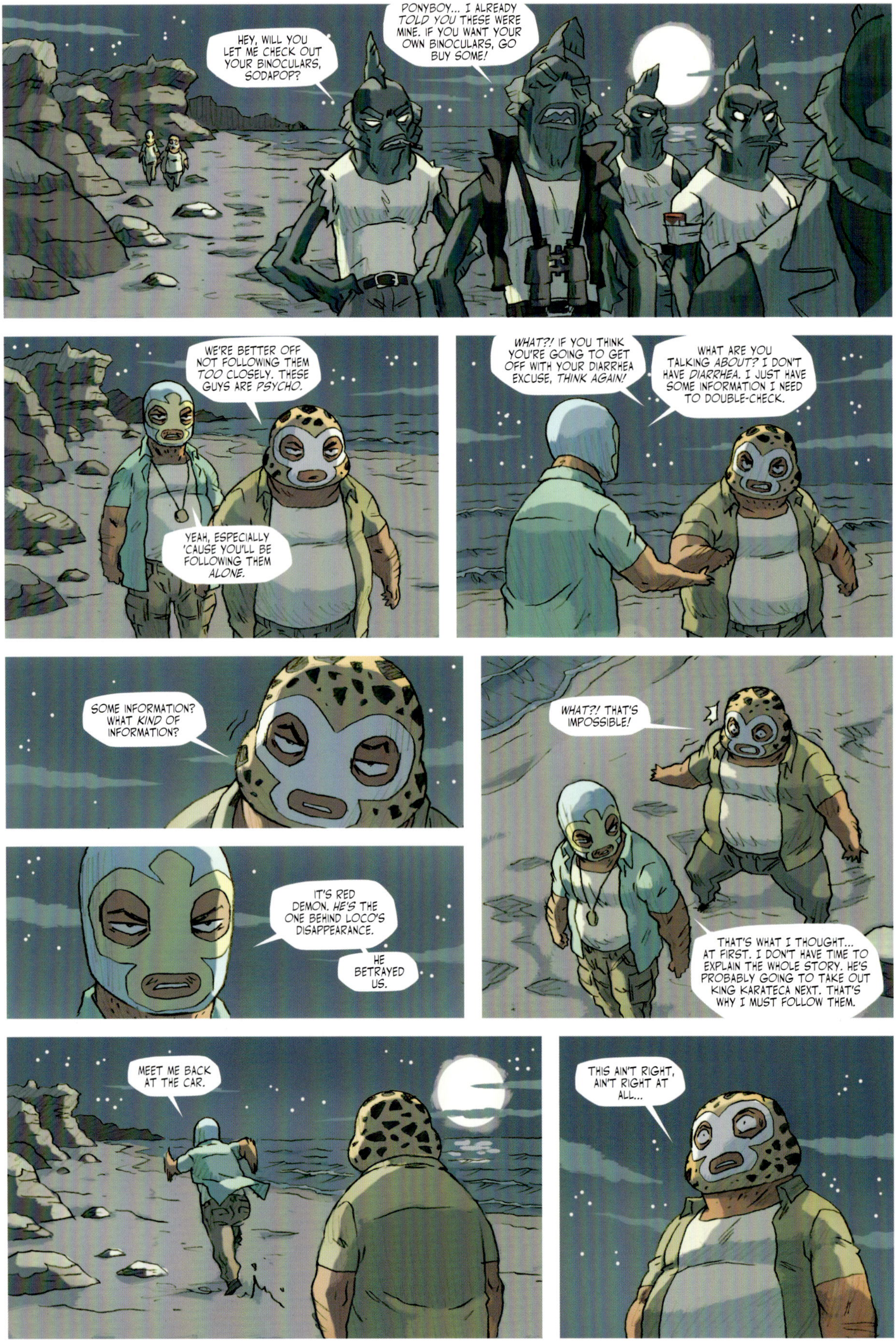
HEY, WILL YOU LET ME CHECK OUT YOUR BINOCULARS, SODAPOP?
PONYBOY... I ALREADY TOLD YOU THESE WERE MINE. IF YOU WANT YOUR OWN BINOCULARS, GO BUY SOME!
WE'RE BETTER OFF NOT FOLLOWING THEM TOO CLOSELY. THESE GUYS ARE PSYCHO.
YEAH, ESPECIALLY 'CAUSE YOU'LL BE FOLLOWING THEM ALONE.
WHAT?! IF YOU THINK YOU'RE GOING TO GET OFF WITH YOUR DIARRHEA EXCUSE, THINK AGAIN!
WHAT ARE YOU TALKING ABOUT? I DON'T HAVE DIARRHEA. I JUST HAVE SOME INFORMATION I NEED TO DOUBLE-CHECK.
SOME INFORMATION? WHAT KIND OF INFORMATION?
IT'S RED DEMON. HE'S THE ONE BEHIND LOCO'S DISAPPEARANCE.
HE BETRAYED US.
WHAT?! THAT'S IMPOSSIBLE!
THAT'S WHAT I THOUGHT... AT FIRST. I DON'T HAVE TIME TO EXPLAIN THE WHOLE STORY. HE'S PROBABLY GOING TO TAKE OUT KING KARATECA NEXT. THAT'S WHY I MUST FOLLOW THEM.
MEET ME BACK AT THE CAR.
THIS AIN'T RIGHT, AIN'T RIGHT AT ALL...

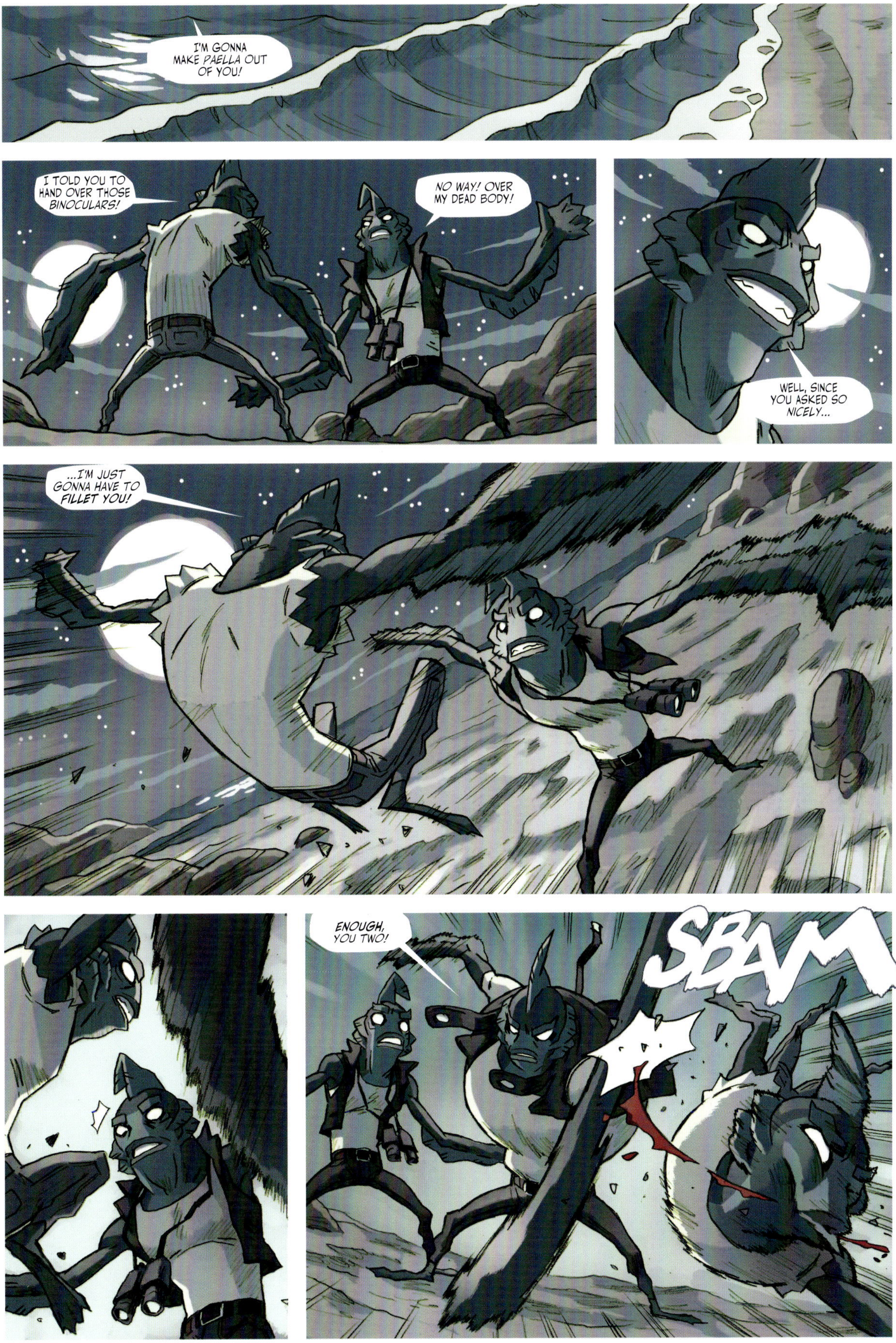
I'M GONNA MAKE PAELLA OUT OF YOU!
I TOLD YOU TO HAND OVER THOSE BINOCULARS!
NO WAY! OVER MY DEAD BODY!
WELL, SINCE YOU ASKED SO NICELY...
...I'M JUST GONNA HAVE TO FILLET YOU!
ENOUGH, YOU TWO!
SBAM

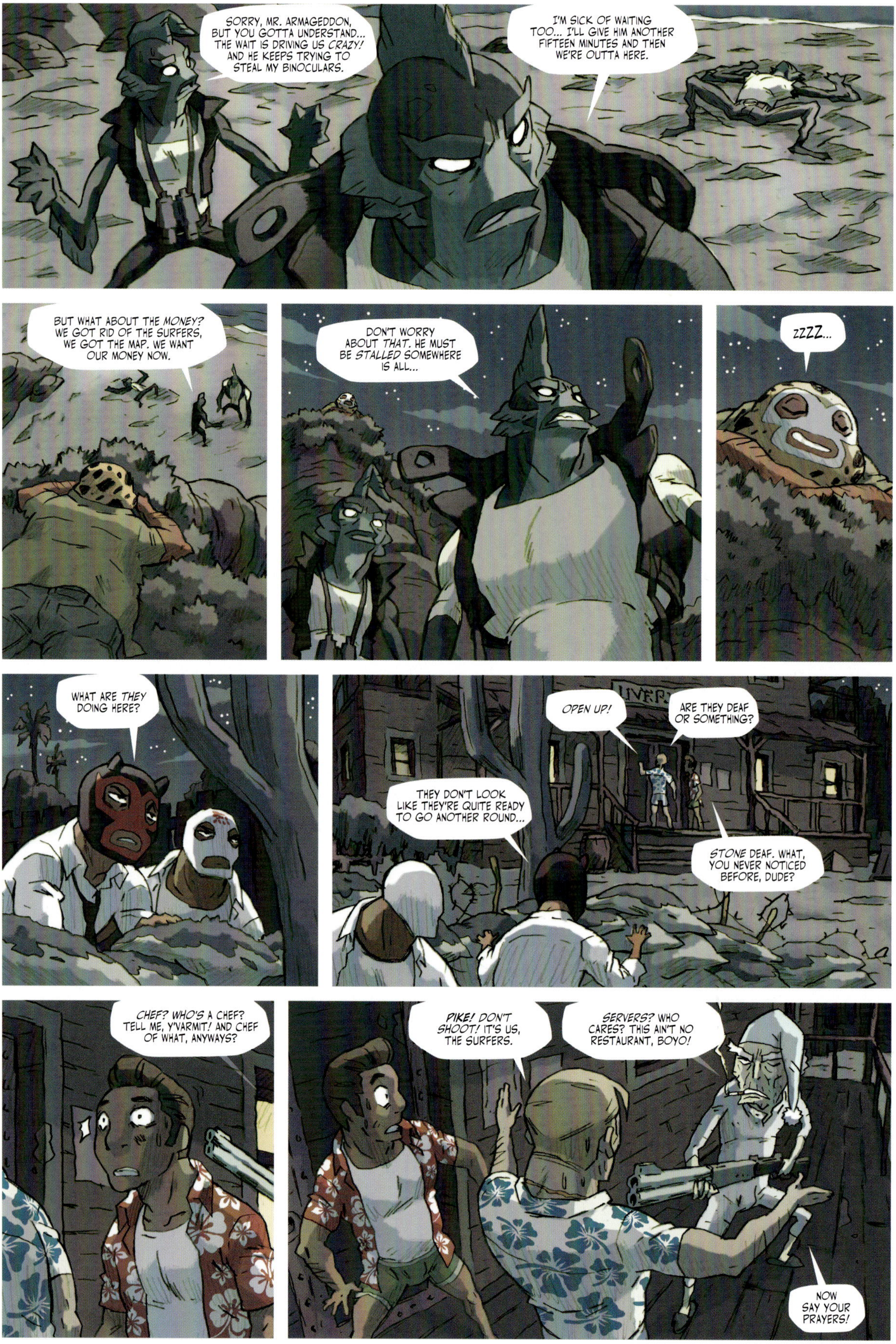
SORRY, MR. ARMAGEDDON, BUT YOU GOTTA UNDERSTAND... THE WAIT IS DRIVING US CRAZY! AND HE KEEPS TRYING TO STEAL MY BINOCULARS.
I'M SICK OF WAITING TOO... I'LL GIVE HIM ANOTHER FIFTEEN MINUTES AND THEN WE'RE OUTTA HERE.
BUT WHAT ABOUT THE MONEY? WE GOT RID OF THE SURFERS, WE GOT THE MAP. WE WANT OUR MONEY NOW.
DON'T WORRY ABOUT THAT. HE MUST BE STALLED SOMEWHERE IS ALL...
ZZZZ...
WHAT ARE THEY DOING HERE?
OPEN UP!
ARE THEY DEAF OR SOMETHING?
THEY DON'T LOOK LIKE THEY'RE QUITE READY TO GO ANOTHER ROUND...
STONE DEAF. WHAT, YOU NEVER NOTICED BEFORE, DUDE?
CHEF? WHO'S A CHEF? TELL ME, Y'VARMIT! AND CHEF OF WHAT, ANYWAYS?
PIKE! DON'T SHOOT! IT'S US, THE SURFERS.
SERVERS? WHO CARES? THIS AIN'T NO RESTAURANT, BOYO!
NOW SAY YOUR PRAYERS!

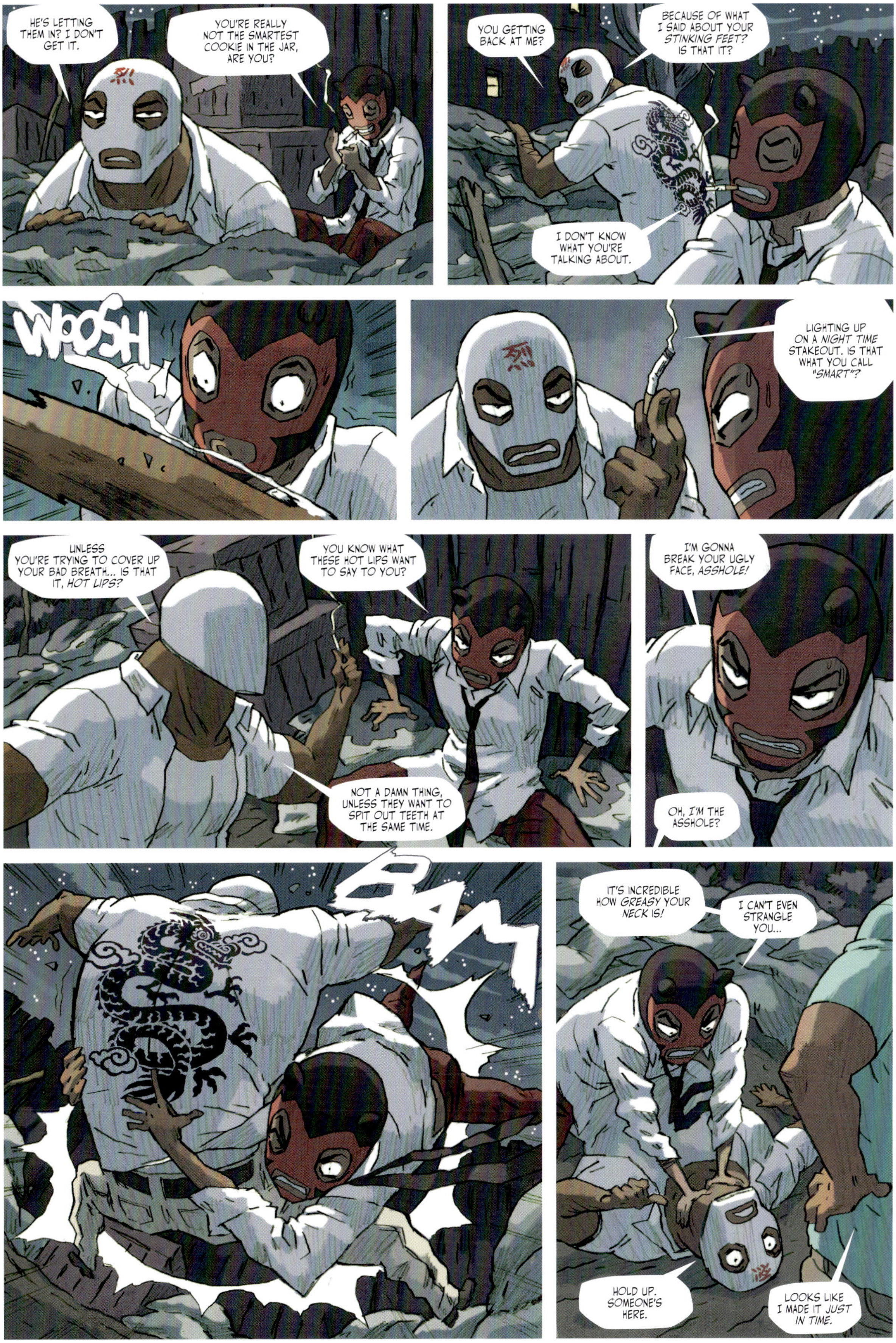
HE'S LETTING THEM IN? I DON'T GET IT.
YOU'RE REALLY NOT THE SMARTEST COOKIE IN THE JAR, ARE YOU?
YOU GETTING BACK AT ME?
BECAUSE OF WHAT I SAID ABOUT YOUR STINKING FEET? IS THAT IT?
I DON'T KNOW WHAT YOU'RE TALKING ABOUT.
WOOSH
LIGHTING UP ON A NIGHT TIME STAKEOUT. IS THAT WHAT YOU CALL "SMART"?
UNLESS YOU'RE TRYING TO COVER UP YOUR BAD BREATH... IS THAT IT, HOT LIPS?
YOU KNOW WHAT THESE HOT LIPS WANT TO SAY TO YOU?
NOT A DAMN THING, UNLESS THEY WANT TO SPIT OUT TEETH AT THE SAME TIME.
I'M GONNA BREAK YOUR UGLY FACE, ASSHOLE!
OH, I'M THE ASSHOLE?
BAM
IT'S INCREDIBLE HOW GREASY YOUR NECK IS!
I CAN'T EVEN STRANGLE YOU...
HOLD UP. SOMEONE'S HERE.
LOOKS LIKE I MADE IT JUST IN TIME.

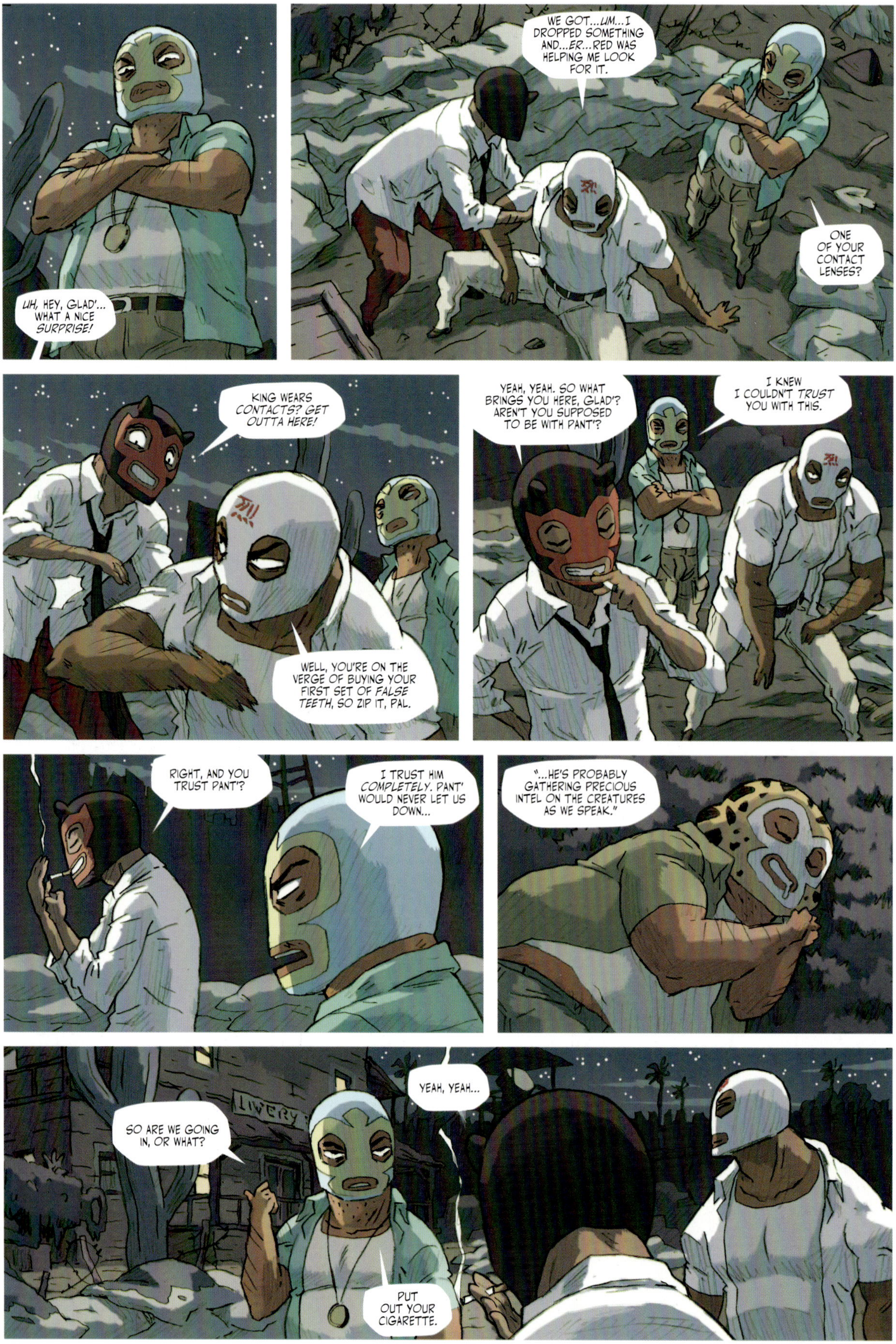
UH, HEY, GLAD'... WHAT A NICE SURPRISE!
WE GOT...UM...I DROPPED SOMETHING AND...ER...RED WAS HELPING ME LOOK FOR IT.
ONE OF YOUR CONTACT LENSES?
KING WEARS CONTACTS? GET OUTTA HERE!
WELL, YOU'RE ON THE VERGE OF BUYING YOUR FIRST SET OF FALSE TEETH, SO ZIP IT, PAL.
YEAH, YEAH. SO WHAT BRINGS YOU HERE, GLAD'? AREN'T YOU SUPPOSED TO BE WITH PANT'?
I KNEW I COULDN'T TRUST YOU WITH THIS.
RIGHT, AND YOU TRUST PANT'?
I TRUST HIM COMPLETELY. PANT' WOULD NEVER LET US DOWN...
"...HE'S PROBABLY GATHERING PRECIOUS INTEL ON THE CREATURES AS WE SPEAK."
SO ARE WE GOING IN, OR WHAT?
LIVERY
YEAH, YEAH...
PUT OUT YOUR CIGARETTE.

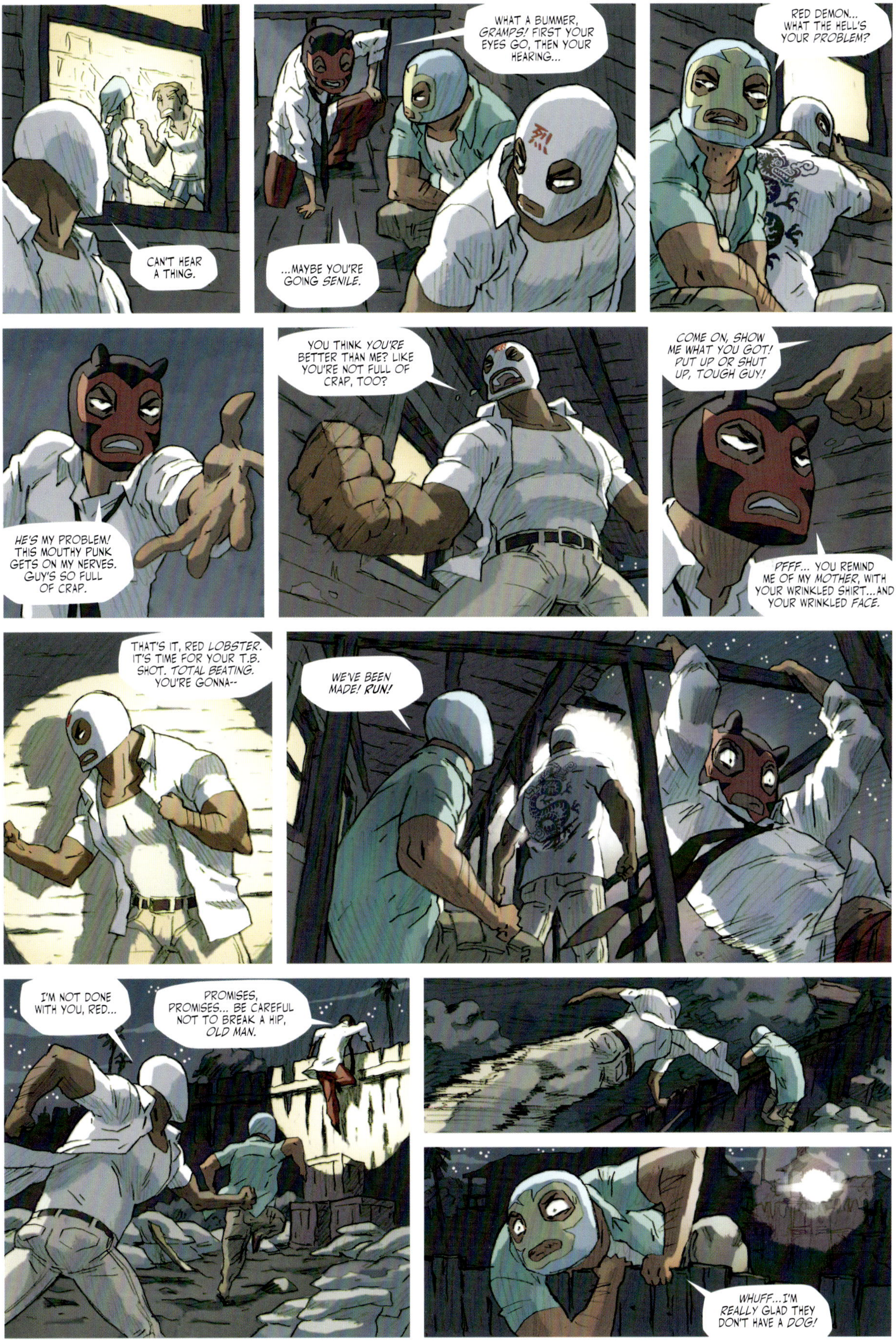
CAN'T HEAR A THING.
WHAT A BUMMER, GRAMPS! FIRST YOUR EYES GO, THEN YOUR HEARING...
...MAYBE YOU'RE GOING SENILE.
RED DEMON... WHAT THE HELL'S YOUR PROBLEM?
HE'S MY PROBLEM! THIS MOUTHY PUNK GETS ON MY NERVES. GUY'S SO FULL OF CRAP.
YOU THINK YOU'RE BETTER THAN ME? LIKE YOU'RE NOT FULL OF CRAP, TOO?
COME ON, SHOW ME WHAT YOU GOT! PUT UP OR SHUT UP, TOUGH GUY!
PFFF... YOU REMIND ME OF MY MOTHER, WITH YOUR WRINKLED SHIRT...AND YOUR WRINKLED FACE.
THAT'S IT, RED LOBSTER. IT'S TIME FOR YOUR T.B. SHOT. TOTAL BEATING. YOU'RE GONNA--
WE'VE BEEN MADE! RUN!
I'M NOT DONE WITH YOU, RED...
PROMISES, PROMISES... BE CAREFUL NOT TO BREAK A HIP, OLD MAN.
WHUFF...I'M REALLY GLAD THEY DON'T HAVE A DOG!

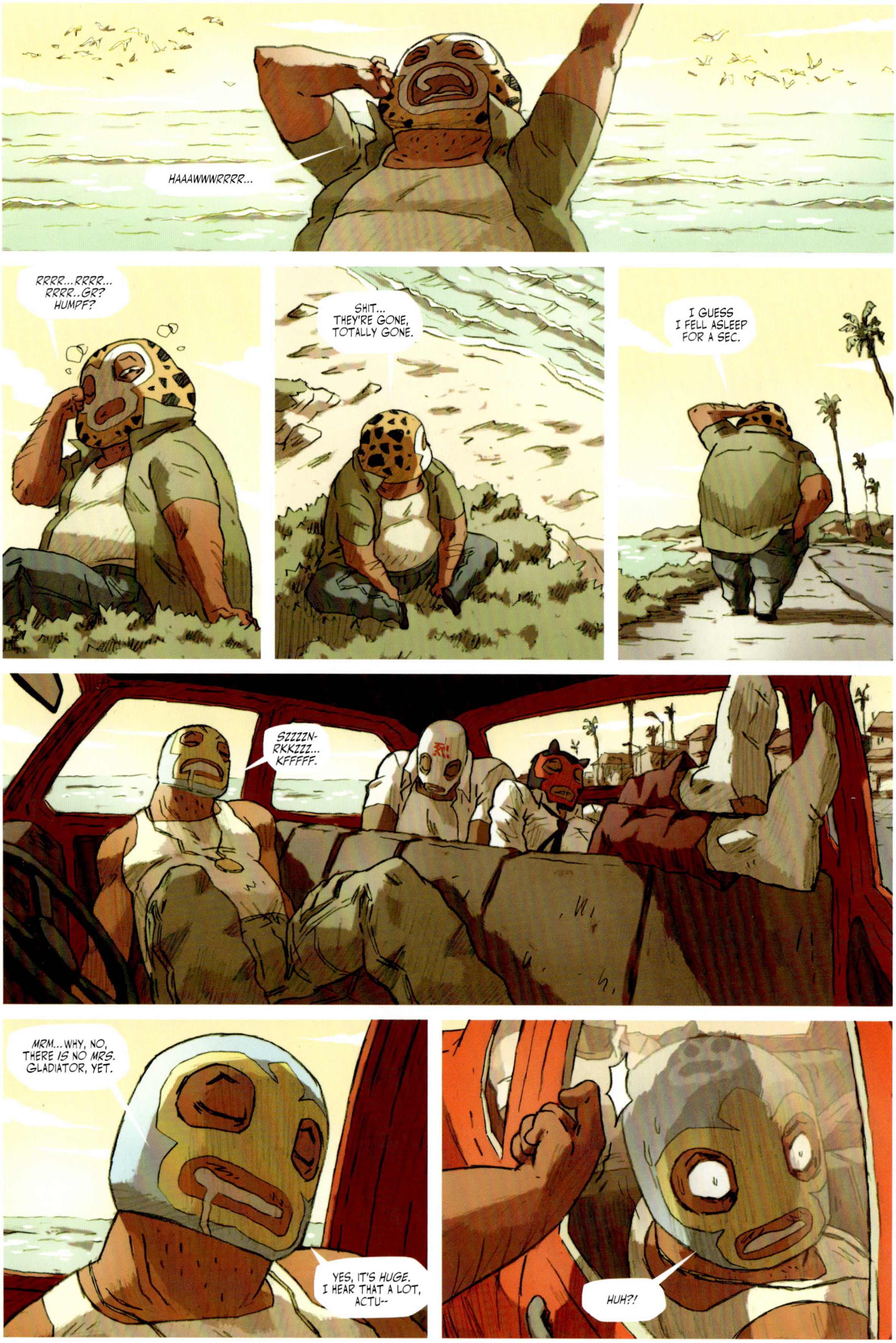

HAAAWWWRRRR...
RRRR...RRRR... RRRR..GR? HUMPF?
SHIT... THEY'RE GONE, TOTALLY GONE.
I GUESS I FELL ASLEEP FOR A SEC.
SZZZZN-RKKZZZ... KFFFFF.
MRM...WHY, NO, THERE *IS* NO MRS. GLADIATOR, YET.
YES, IT'S *HUGE*. I HEAR THAT A LOT, ACTU--
HUH?!

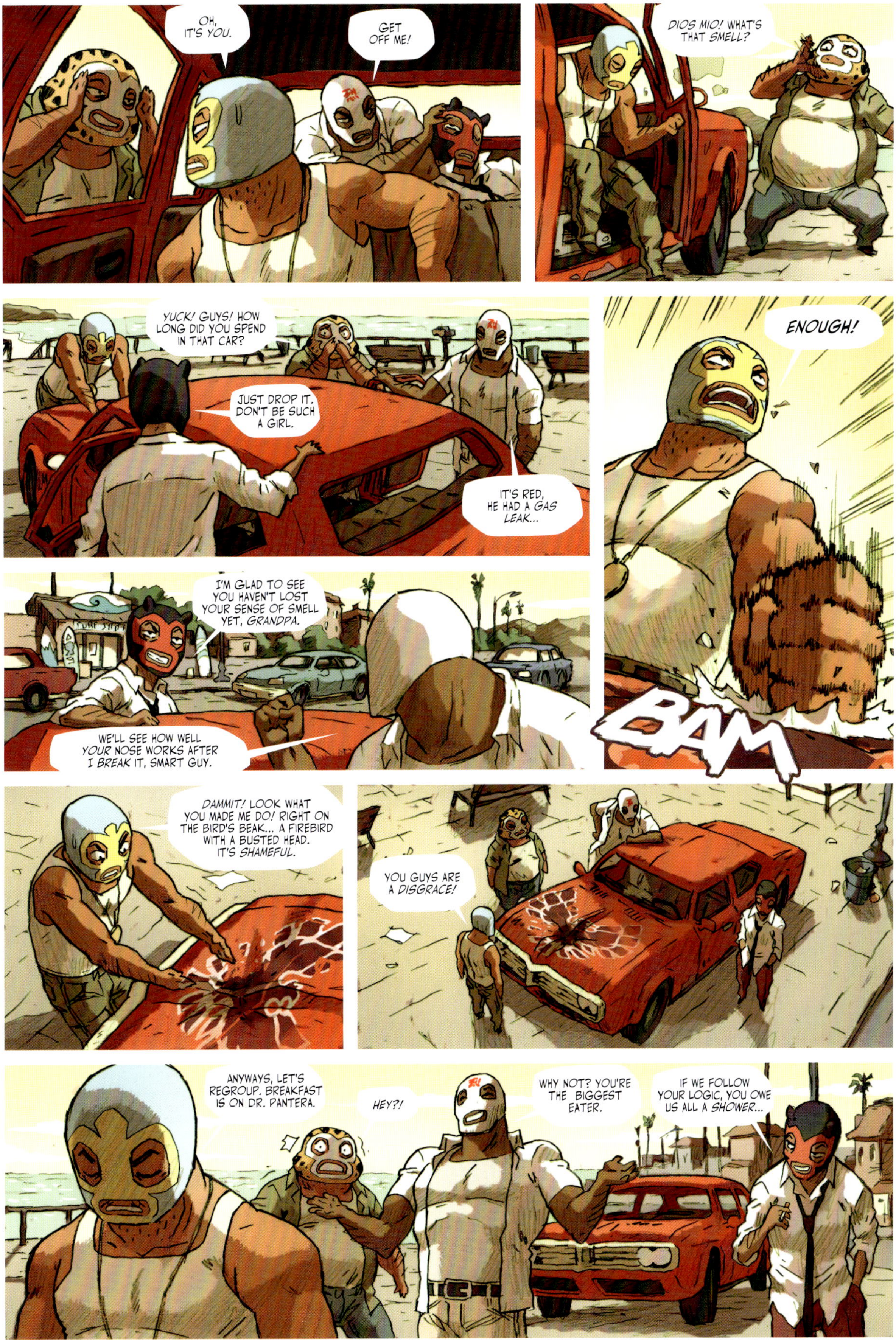
OH, IT'S YOU.
GET OFF ME!
DIOS MIO! WHAT'S THAT SMELL?
YUCK! GUYS! HOW LONG DID YOU SPEND IN THAT CAR?
JUST DROP IT. DON'T BE SUCH A GIRL.
IT'S RED, HE HAD A GAS LEAK...
I'M GLAD TO SEE YOU HAVEN'T LOST YOUR SENSE OF SMELL YET, GRANDPA.
WE'LL SEE HOW WELL YOUR NOSE WORKS AFTER I BREAK IT, SMART GUY.
ENOUGH!
BAM
DAMMIT! LOOK WHAT YOU MADE ME DO! RIGHT ON THE BIRD'S BEAK... A FIREBIRD WITH A BUSTED HEAD. IT'S SHAMEFUL.
YOU GUYS ARE A DISGRACE!
ANYWAYS, LET'S REGROUP. BREAKFAST IS ON DR. PANTERA.
HEY?!
WHY NOT? YOU'RE THE BIGGEST EATER.
IF WE FOLLOW YOUR LOGIC, YOU OWE US ALL A SHOWER...

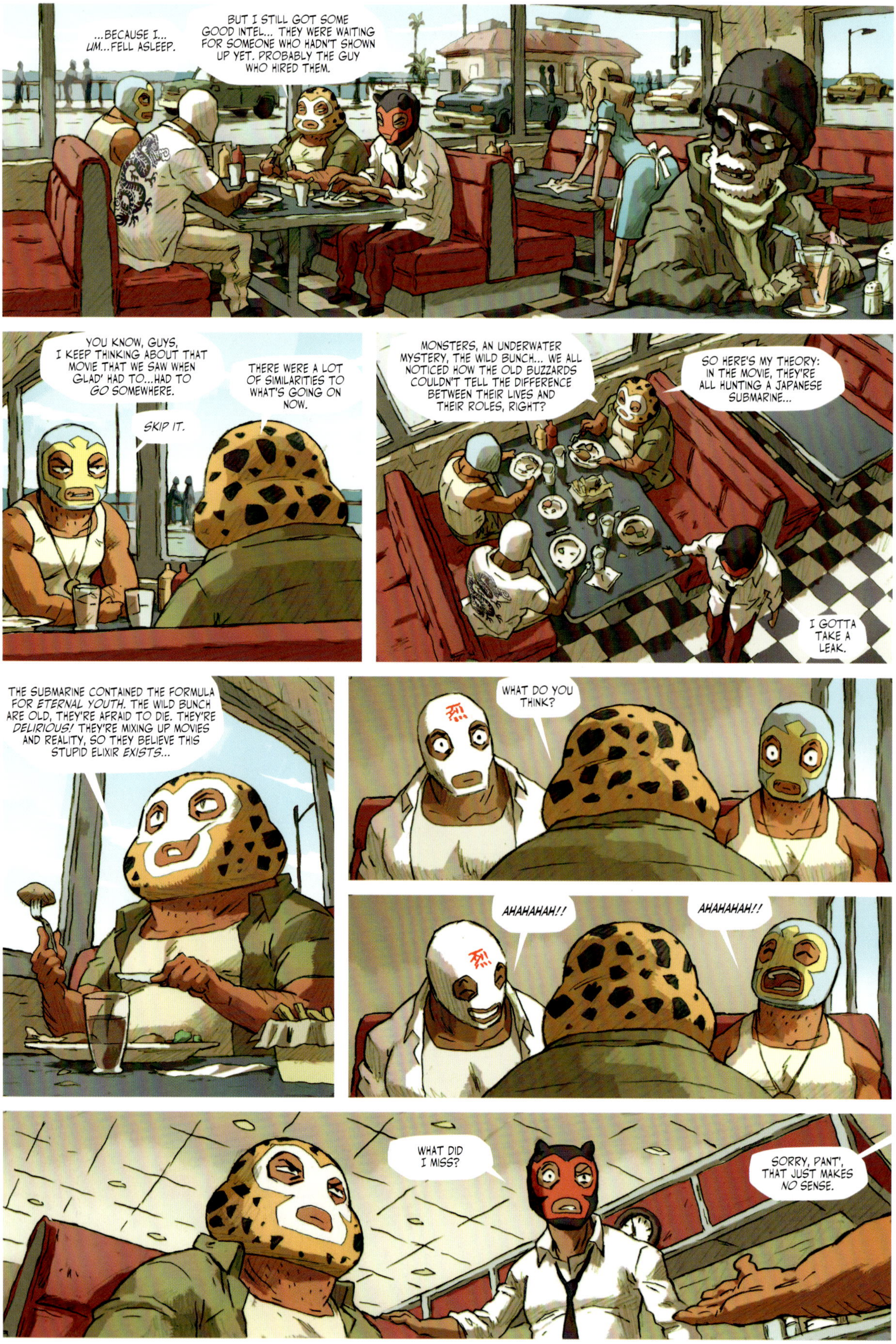
...BECAUSE I... UM...FELL ASLEEP.
BUT I STILL GOT SOME GOOD INTEL... THEY WERE WAITING FOR SOMEONE WHO HADN'T SHOWN UP YET. PROBABLY THE GUY WHO HIRED THEM.
YOU KNOW, GUYS, I KEEP THINKING ABOUT THAT MOVIE THAT WE SAW WHEN GLAD' HAD TO...HAD TO GO SOMEWHERE.
SKIP IT.
THERE WERE A LOT OF SIMILARITIES TO WHAT'S GOING ON NOW.
MONSTERS, AN UNDERWATER MYSTERY, THE WILD BUNCH... WE ALL NOTICED HOW THE OLD BUZZARDS COULDN'T TELL THE DIFFERENCE BETWEEN THEIR LIVES AND THEIR ROLES, RIGHT?
SO HERE'S MY THEORY: IN THE MOVIE, THEY'RE ALL HUNTING A JAPANESE SUBMARINE...
I GOTTA TAKE A LEAK.
THE SUBMARINE CONTAINED THE FORMULA FOR ETERNAL YOUTH. THE WILD BUNCH ARE OLD, THEY'RE AFRAID TO DIE. THEY'RE DELIRIOUS! THEY'RE MIXING UP MOVIES AND REALITY, SO THEY BELIEVE THIS STUPID ELIXIR EXISTS...
WHAT DO YOU THINK?
AHAHAHAH!!
AHAHAHAH!!
WHAT DID I MISS?
SORRY, PANT', THAT JUST MAKES NO SENSE.

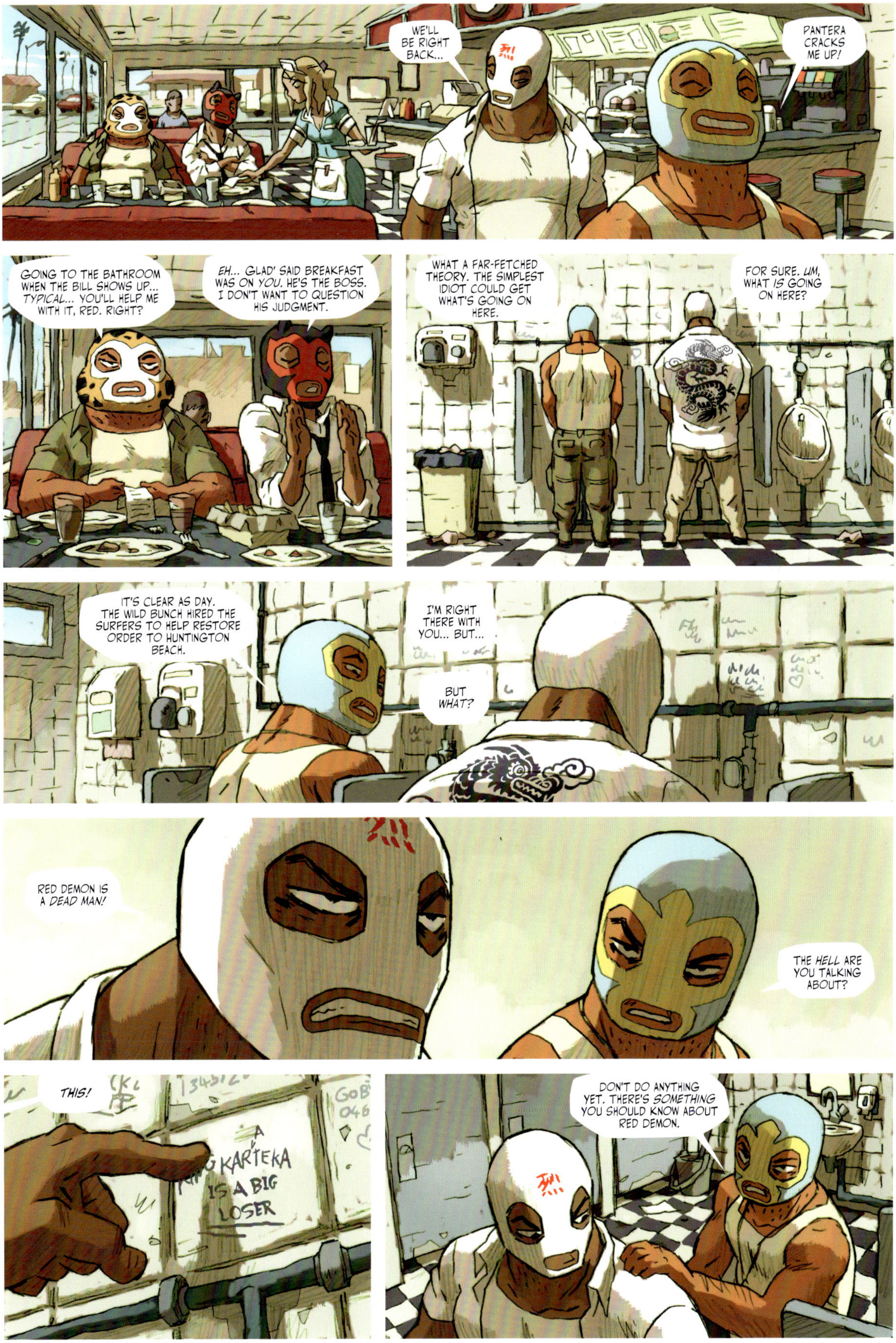
WE'LL BE RIGHT BACK...
PANTERA CRACKS ME UP!
GOING TO THE BATHROOM WHEN THE BILL SHOWS UP... TYPICAL... YOU'LL HELP ME WITH IT, RED. RIGHT?
EH... GLAD' SAID BREAKFAST WAS ON YOU. HE'S THE BOSS. I DON'T WANT TO QUESTION HIS JUDGMENT.
WHAT A FAR-FETCHED THEORY. THE SIMPLEST IDIOT COULD GET WHAT'S GOING ON HERE.
FOR SURE. UM, WHAT IS GOING ON HERE?
IT'S CLEAR AS DAY. THE WILD BUNCH HIRED THE SURFERS TO HELP RESTORE ORDER TO HUNTINGTON BEACH.
I'M RIGHT THERE WITH YOU... BUT...
BUT WHAT?
RED DEMON IS A DEAD MAN!
THE HELL ARE YOU TALKING ABOUT?
THIS!
A
KARTEKA
IS A BIG
LOSER
DON'T DO ANYTHING YET. THERE'S SOMETHING YOU SHOULD KNOW ABOUT RED DEMON.

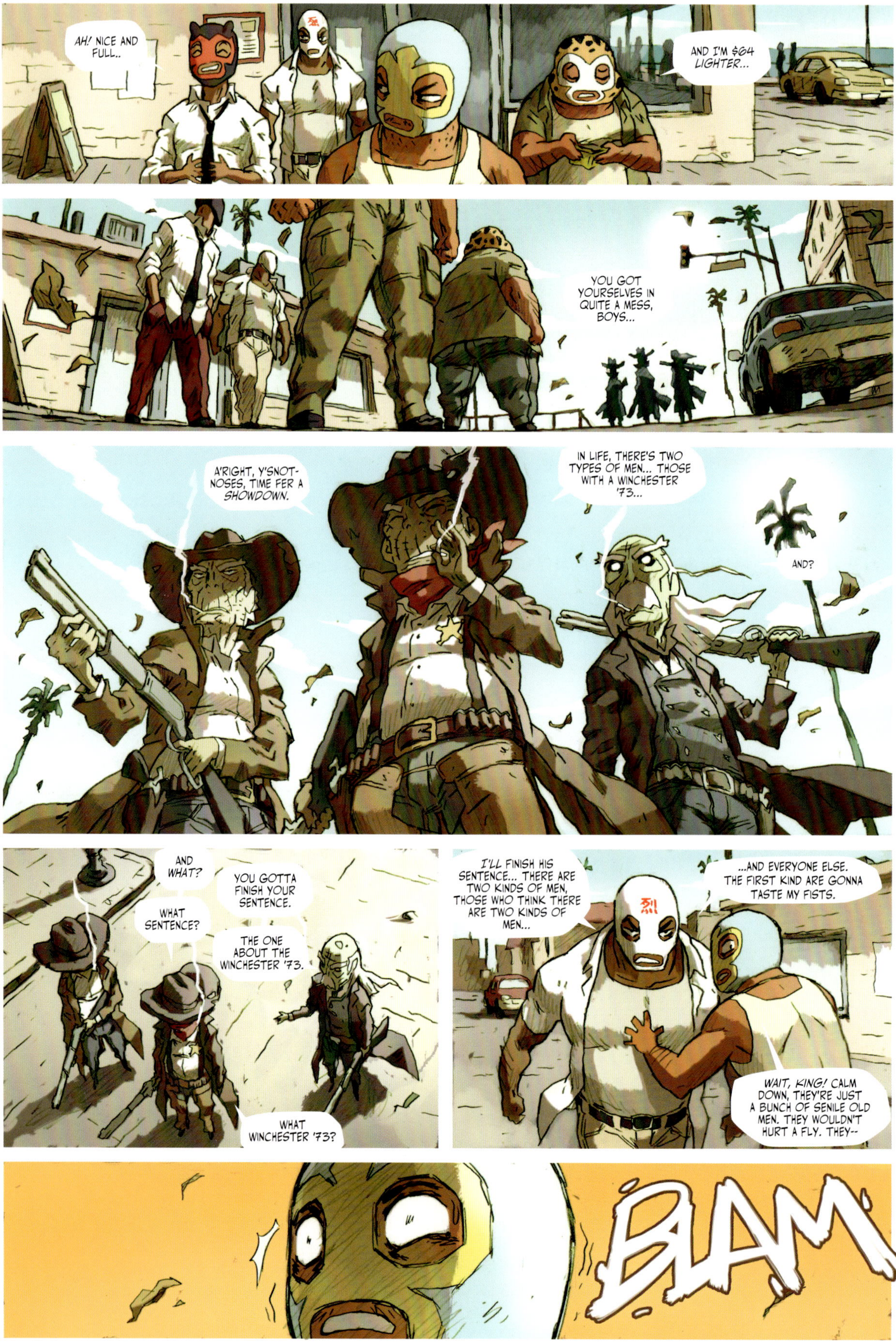
AH! NICE AND FULL..
AND I'M $64 LIGHTER...
YOU GOT YOURSELVES IN QUITE A MESS, BOYS...
A'RIGHT, Y'SNOT-NOSES, TIME FER A SHOWDOWN.
IN LIFE, THERE'S TWO TYPES OF MEN... THOSE WITH A WINCHESTER '73...
AND?
AND WHAT?
YOU GOTTA FINISH YOUR SENTENCE.
WHAT SENTENCE?
THE ONE ABOUT THE WINCHESTER '73.
WHAT WINCHESTER '73?
I'LL FINISH HIS SENTENCE... THERE ARE TWO KINDS OF MEN, THOSE WHO THINK THERE ARE TWO KINDS OF MEN...
...AND EVERYONE ELSE. THE FIRST KIND ARE GONNA TASTE MY FISTS.
WAIT, KING! CALM DOWN, THEY'RE JUST A BUNCH OF SENILE OLD MEN. THEY WOULDN'T HURT A FLY. THEY--
BLAM

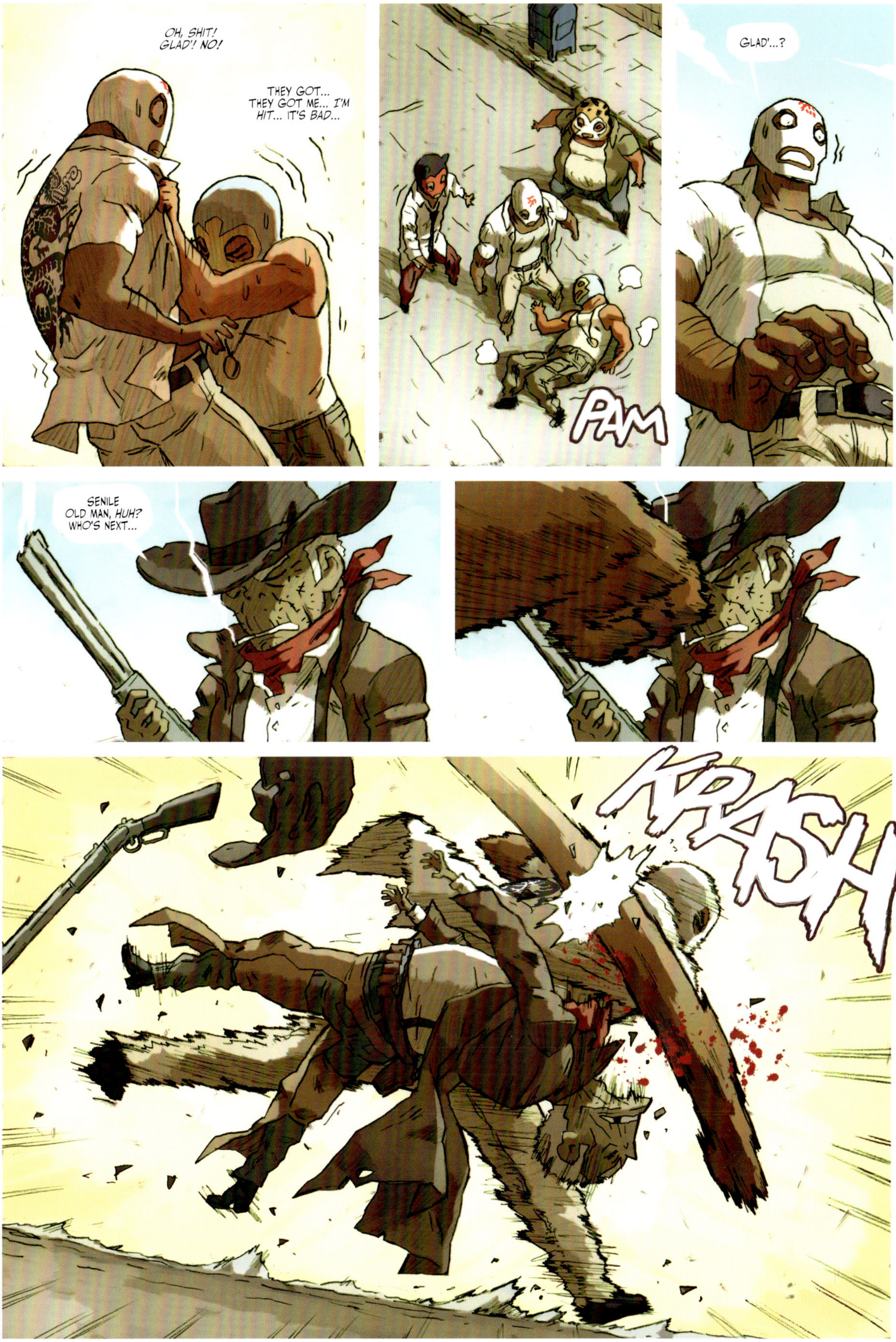
OH, SHIT! GLAD'! NO!
THEY GOT... THEY GOT ME... I'M HIT... IT'S BAD...
PAM
GLAD'...?
SENILE OLD MAN, HUH? WHO'S NEXT...
KRASH

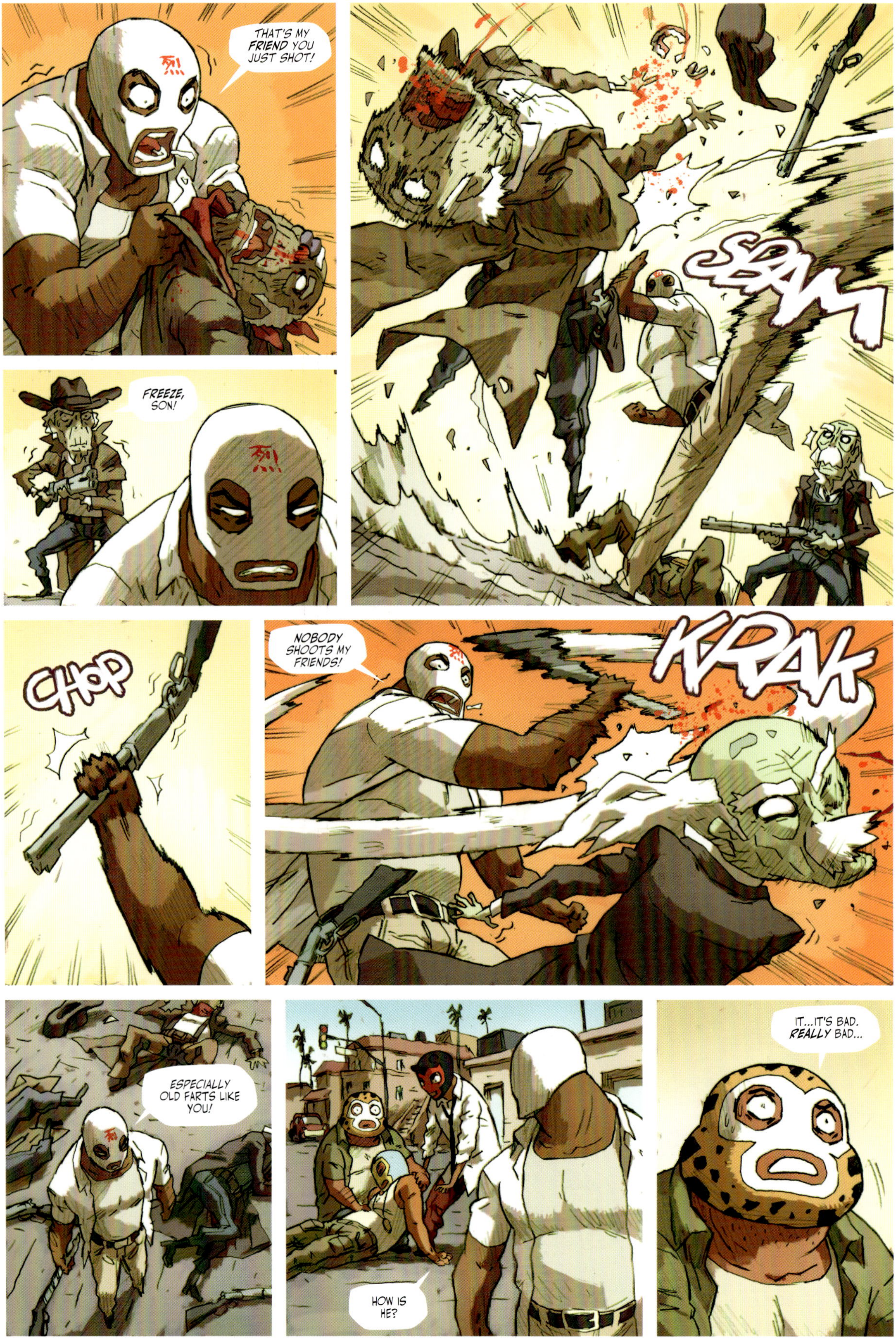
THAT'S MY FRIEND YOU JUST SHOT!
SBAM
FREEZE, SON!
CHOP
NOBODY SHOOTS MY FRIENDS!
KRAK
ESPECIALLY OLD FARTS LIKE YOU!
HOW IS HE?
IT...IT'S BAD. REALLY BAD...

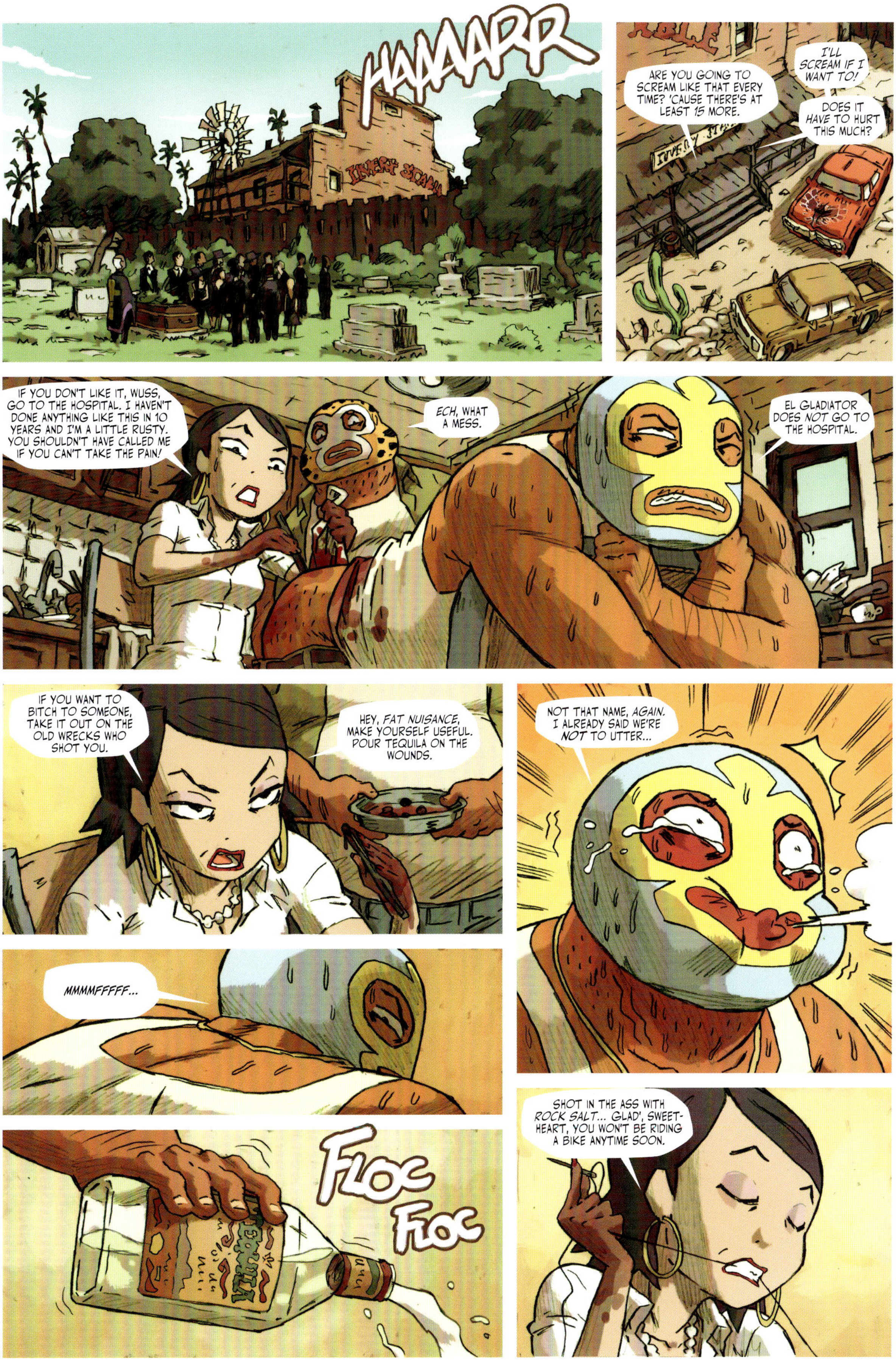
HAAAARR
ARE YOU GOING TO SCREAM LIKE THAT EVERY TIME? 'CAUSE THERE'S AT LEAST 15 MORE.
I'LL SCREAM IF I WANT TO!
DOES IT HAVE TO HURT THIS MUCH?
IF YOU DON'T LIKE IT, WUSS, GO TO THE HOSPITAL. I HAVEN'T DONE ANYTHING LIKE THIS IN 10 YEARS AND I'M A LITTLE RUSTY. YOU SHOULDN'T HAVE CALLED ME IF YOU CAN'T TAKE THE PAIN!
ECH, WHAT A MESS.
EL GLADIATOR DOES *NOT* GO TO THE HOSPITAL.
IF YOU WANT TO BITCH TO SOMEONE, TAKE IT OUT ON THE OLD WRECKS WHO SHOT YOU.
HEY, *FAT NUISANCE*, MAKE YOURSELF USEFUL. POUR TEQUILA ON THE WOUNDS.
MMMMFFFFF...
FLOC FLOC
NOT THAT NAME, *AGAIN*. I ALREADY SAID WE'RE *NOT* TO UTTER...
SHOT IN THE ASS WITH *ROCK SALT*... GLAD', SWEET-HEART, YOU WON'T BE RIDING A BIKE ANYTIME SOON.

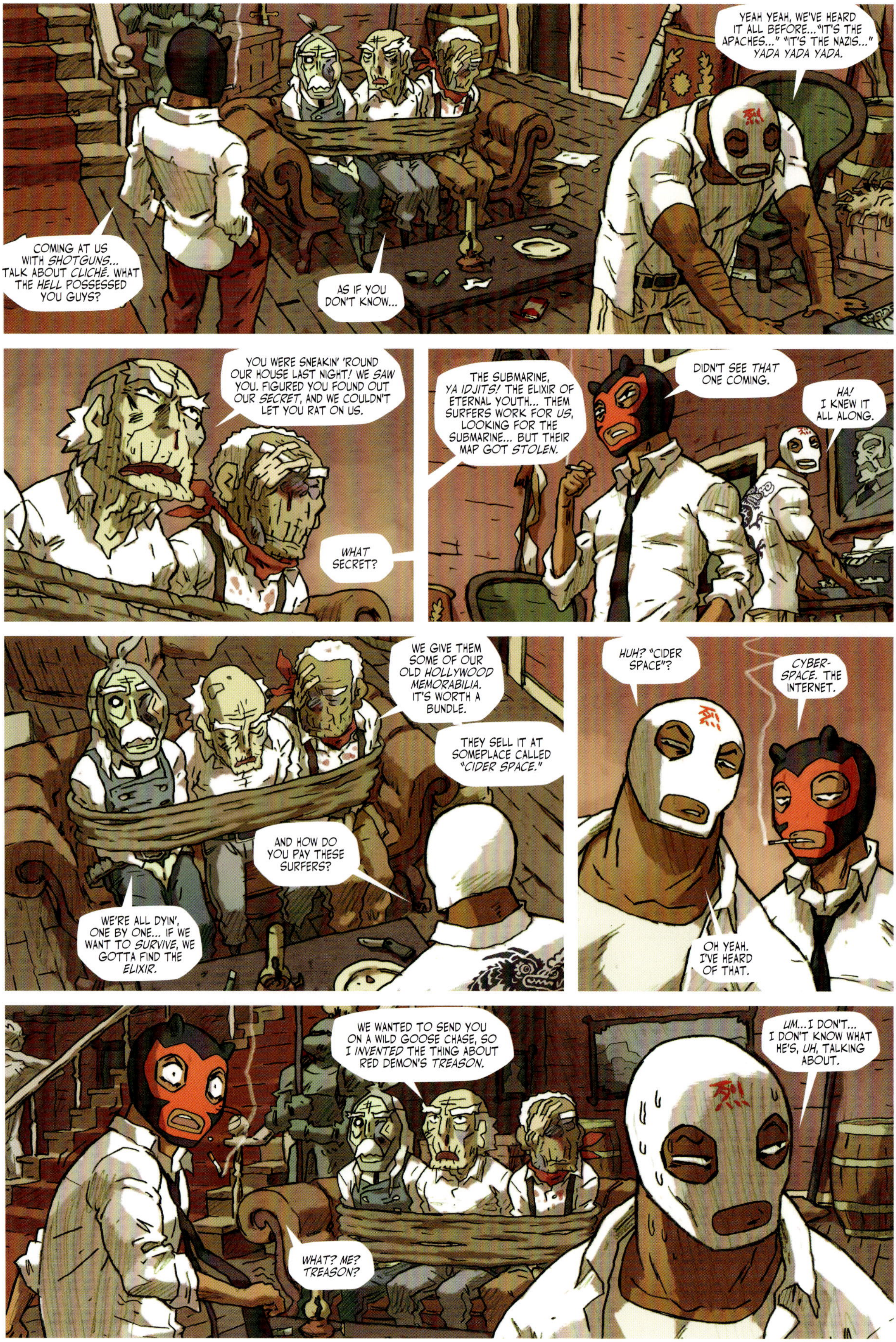
COMING AT US WITH SHOTGUNS... TALK ABOUT CLICHÉ. WHAT THE HELL POSSESSED YOU GUYS?
AS IF YOU DON'T KNOW...
YEAH YEAH, WE'VE HEARD IT ALL BEFORE... "IT'S THE APACHES..." "IT'S THE NAZIS..." YADA YADA YADA.
YOU WERE SNEAKIN' 'ROUND OUR HOUSE LAST NIGHT! WE SAW YOU. FIGURED YOU FOUND OUT OUR SECRET, AND WE COULDN'T LET YOU RAT ON US.
WHAT SECRET?
THE SUBMARINE, YA IDJITS! THE ELIXIR OF ETERNAL YOUTH... THEM SURFERS WORK FOR US, LOOKING FOR THE SUBMARINE... BUT THEIR MAP GOT STOLEN.
DIDN'T SEE THAT ONE COMING.
HA! I KNEW IT ALL ALONG.
WE GIVE THEM SOME OF OUR OLD HOLLYWOOD MEMORABILIA. IT'S WORTH A BUNDLE.
THEY SELL IT AT SOMEPLACE CALLED "CIDER SPACE."
AND HOW DO YOU PAY THESE SURFERS?
WE'RE ALL DYIN', ONE BY ONE... IF WE WANT TO SURVIVE, WE GOTTA FIND THE ELIXIR.
HUH? "CIDER SPACE"?
CYBER-SPACE. THE INTERNET.
OH YEAH. I'VE HEARD OF THAT.
WE WANTED TO SEND YOU ON A WILD GOOSE CHASE, SO I INVENTED THE THING ABOUT RED DEMON'S TREASON.
UM... I DON'T... I DON'T KNOW WHAT HE'S, UH, TALKING ABOUT.
WHAT? ME? TREASON?

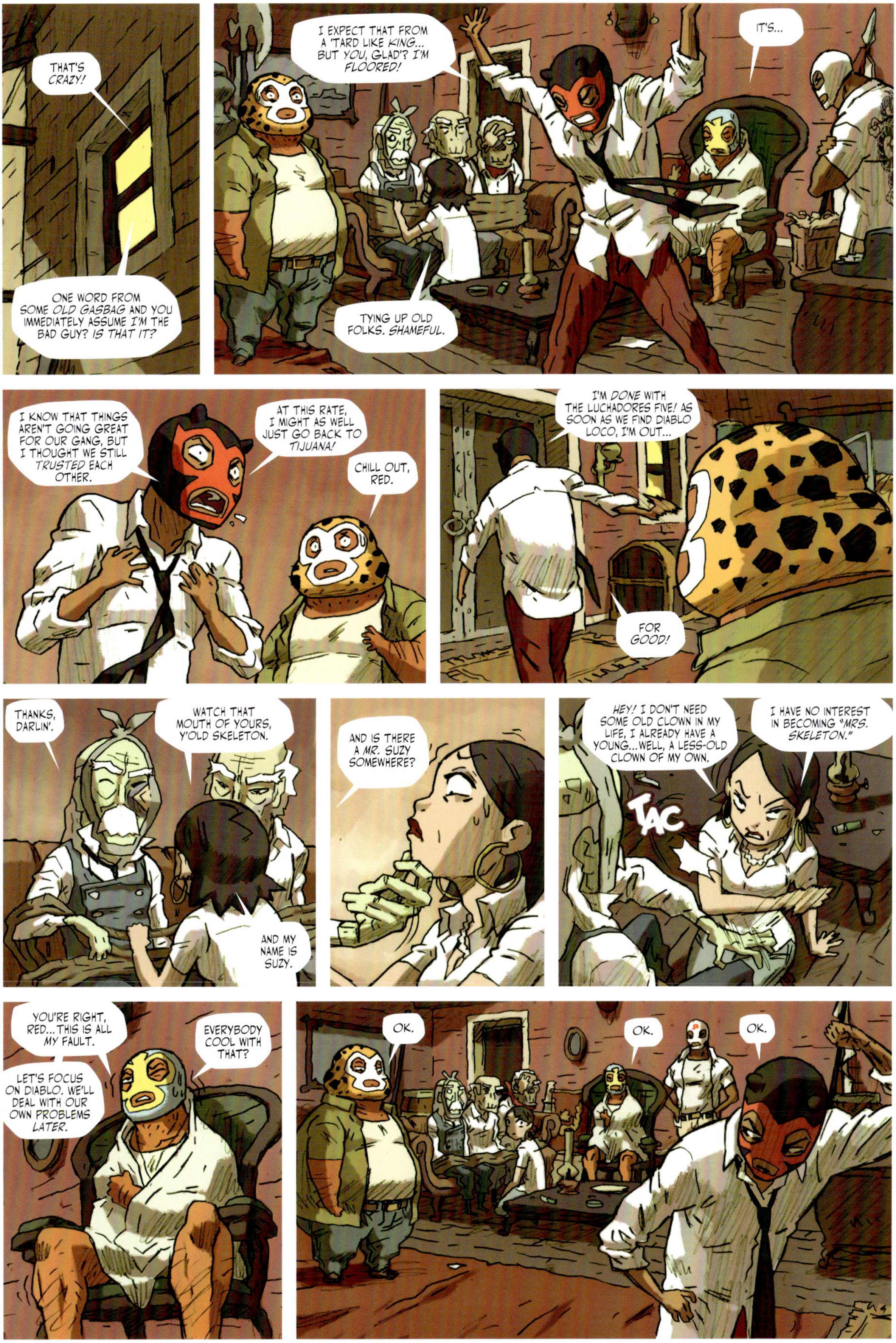
THAT'S CRAZY!
ONE WORD FROM SOME OLD GASBAG AND YOU IMMEDIATELY ASSUME I'M THE BAD GUY? IS THAT IT?
I EXPECT THAT FROM A 'TARD LIKE KING... BUT YOU, GLAD'? I'M FLOORED!
TYING UP OLD FOLKS. SHAMEFUL.
IT'S...
I KNOW THAT THINGS AREN'T GOING GREAT FOR OUR GANG, BUT I THOUGHT WE STILL TRUSTED EACH OTHER.
AT THIS RATE, I MIGHT AS WELL JUST GO BACK TO TIJUANA!
CHILL OUT, RED.
I'M DONE WITH THE LUCHADORES FIVE! AS SOON AS WE FIND DIABLO LOCO, I'M OUT...
FOR GOOD!
THANKS, DARLIN'.
WATCH THAT MOUTH OF YOURS, Y'OLD SKELETON.
AND MY NAME IS SUZY.
AND IS THERE A MR. SUZY SOMEWHERE?
HEY! I DON'T NEED SOME OLD CLOWN IN MY LIFE, I ALREADY HAVE A YOUNG...WELL, A LESS-OLD CLOWN OF MY OWN.
TAC
I HAVE NO INTEREST IN BECOMING "MRS. SKELETON."
YOU'RE RIGHT, RED...THIS IS ALL MY FAULT.
LET'S FOCUS ON DIABLO. WE'LL DEAL WITH OUR OWN PROBLEMS LATER.
EVERYBODY COOL WITH THAT?
OK.
OK.
OK.

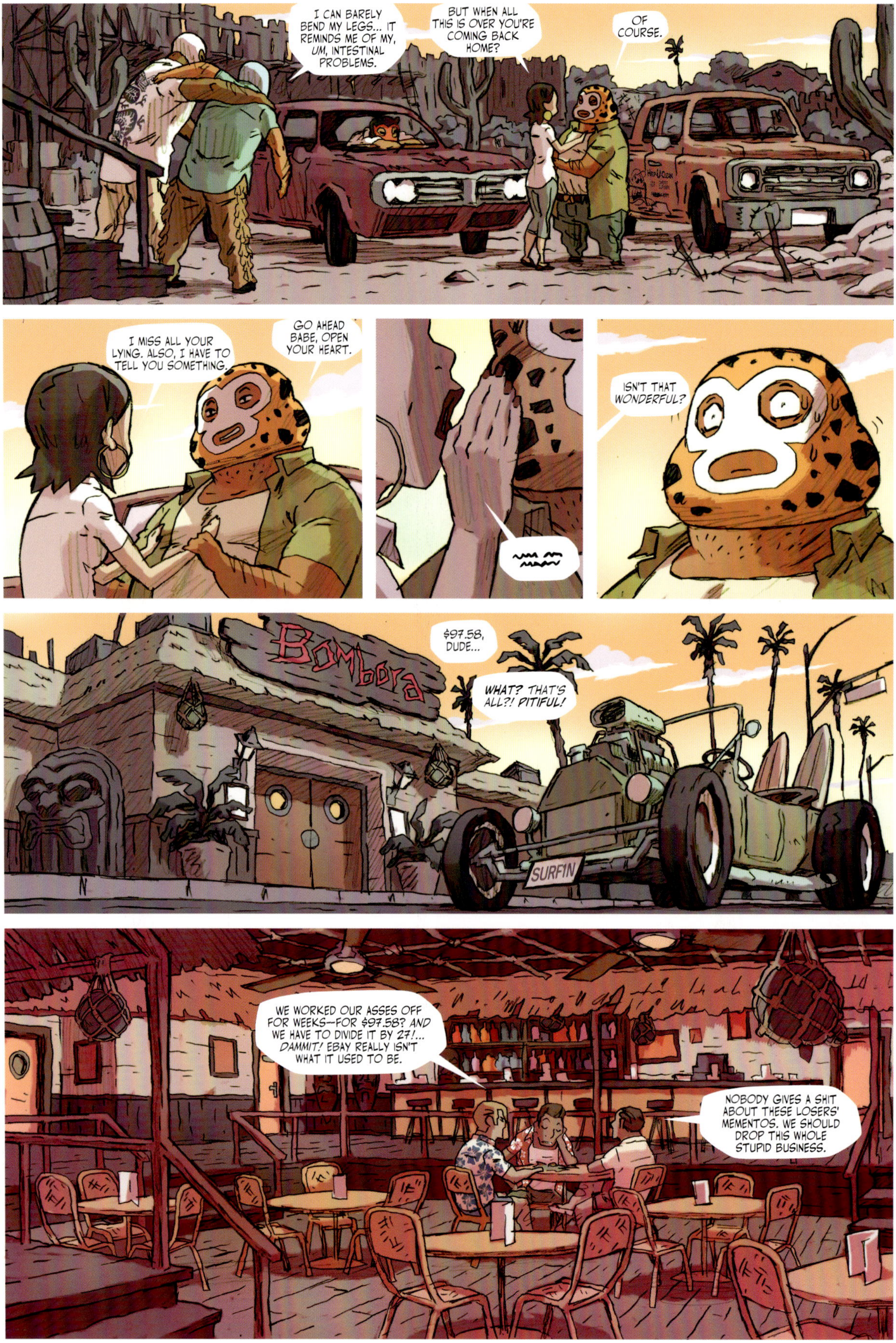
I CAN BARELY BEND MY LEGS... IT REMINDS ME OF MY, UM, INTESTINAL PROBLEMS.
BUT WHEN ALL THIS IS OVER YOU'RE COMING BACK HOME?
OF COURSE.
I MISS ALL YOUR LYING. ALSO, I HAVE TO TELL YOU SOMETHING.
GO AHEAD BABE, OPEN YOUR HEART.
ISN'T THAT WONDERFUL?
Bombora
$97.58, DUDE...
WHAT? THAT'S ALL?! PITIFUL!
SURFIN
WE WORKED OUR ASSES OFF FOR WEEKS—FOR $97.58? AND WE HAVE TO DIVIDE IT BY 27!... DAMMIT! EBAY REALLY ISN'T WHAT IT USED TO BE.
NOBODY GIVES A SHIT ABOUT THESE LOSERS' MEMENTOS. WE SHOULD DROP THIS WHOLE STUPID BUSINESS.

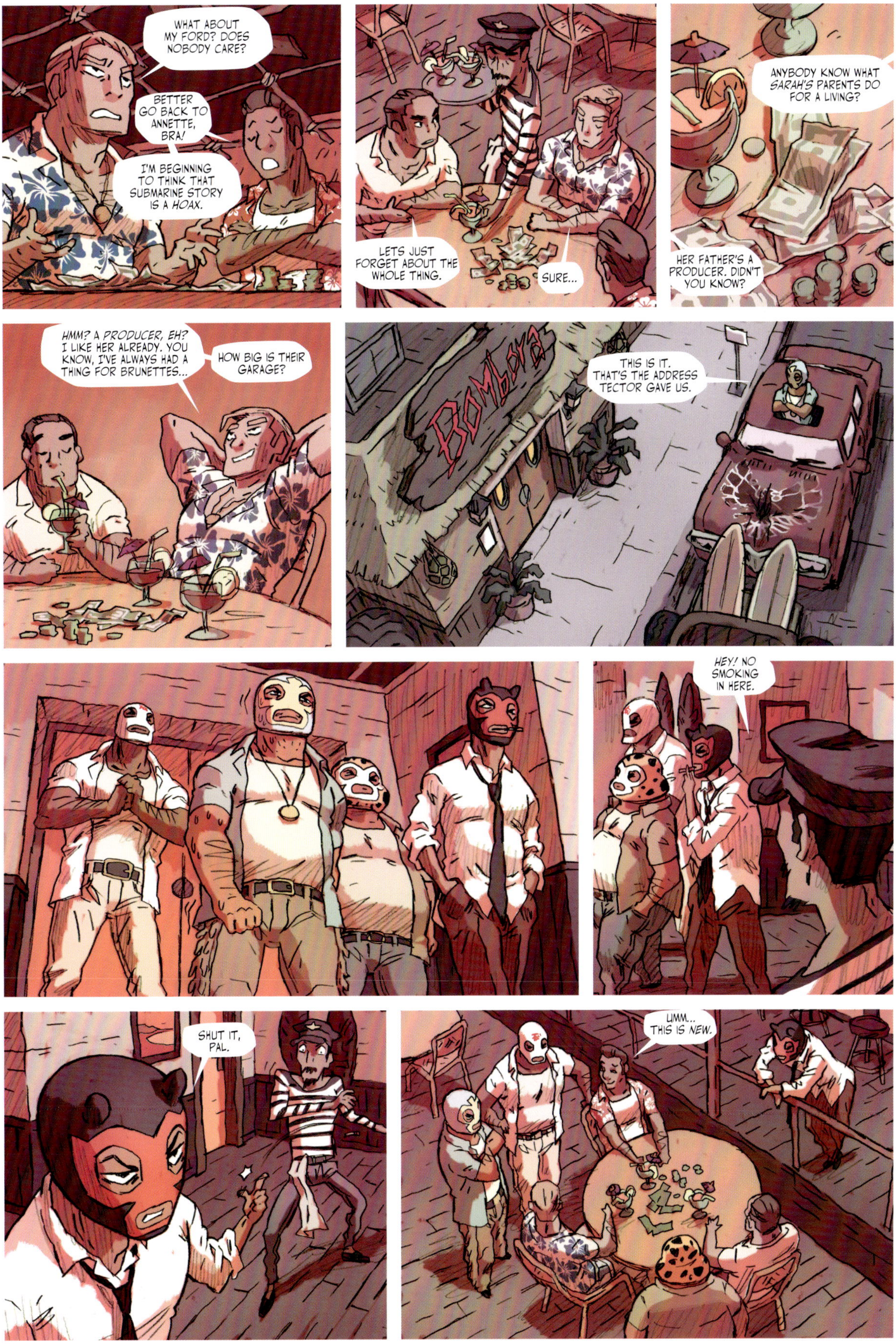
WHAT ABOUT MY FORD? DOES NOBODY CARE?
BETTER GO BACK TO ANNETTE, BRA!
I'M BEGINNING TO THINK THAT SUBMARINE STORY IS A HOAX.
LETS JUST FORGET ABOUT THE WHOLE THING.
SURE...
ANYBODY KNOW WHAT SARAH'S PARENTS DO FOR A LIVING?
HER FATHER'S A PRODUCER. DIDN'T YOU KNOW?
HMM? A PRODUCER, EH? I LIKE HER ALREADY. YOU KNOW, I'VE ALWAYS HAD A THING FOR BRUNETTES...
HOW BIG IS THEIR GARAGE?
Bombora
THIS IS IT. THAT'S THE ADDRESS TECTOR GAVE US.
HEY! NO SMOKING IN HERE.
SHUT IT, PAL.
UMM... THIS IS NEW.

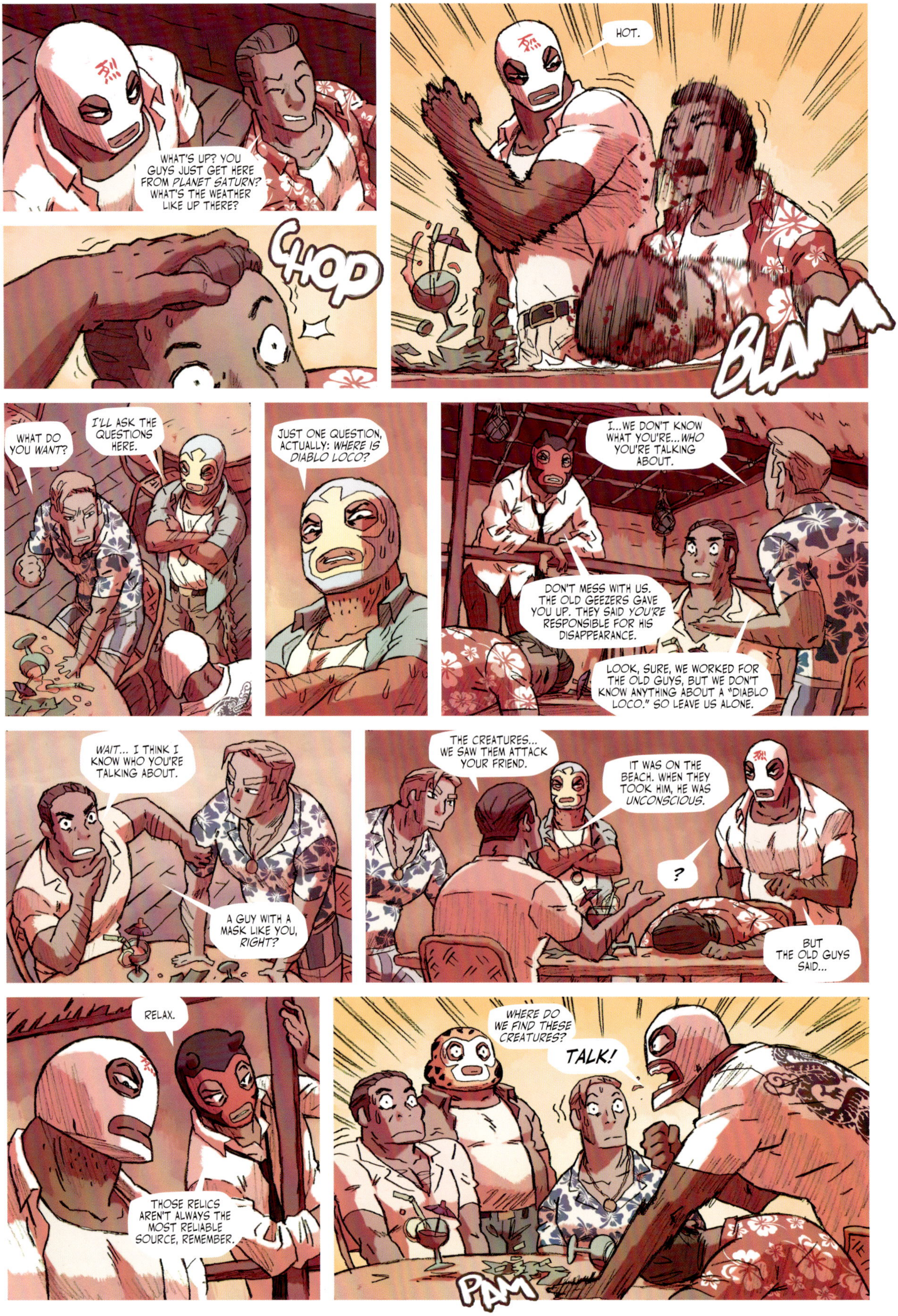
WHAT'S UP? YOU GUYS JUST GET HERE FROM *PLANET SATURN?* WHAT'S THE WEATHER LIKE UP THERE?
CHOP
HOT.
BLAM
WHAT DO YOU WANT?
I'LL ASK THE QUESTIONS HERE.
JUST ONE QUESTION, ACTUALLY: *WHERE IS DIABLO LOCO?*
I...WE DON'T KNOW WHAT YOU'RE...*WHO* YOU'RE TALKING ABOUT.
DON'T MESS WITH US. THE OLD GEEZERS GAVE YOU UP. THEY SAID *YOU'RE* RESPONSIBLE FOR HIS DISAPPEARANCE.
LOOK, SURE, WE WORKED FOR THE OLD GUYS, BUT WE DON'T KNOW ANYTHING ABOUT A "DIABLO LOCO." SO LEAVE US ALONE.
WAIT... I THINK I KNOW WHO YOU'RE TALKING ABOUT.
A GUY WITH A MASK LIKE YOU, *RIGHT?*
THE CREATURES... WE SAW THEM ATTACK YOUR FRIEND.
IT WAS ON THE BEACH. WHEN THEY TOOK HIM, HE WAS *UNCONSCIOUS.*
?
BUT THE OLD GUYS SAID...
RELAX.
THOSE RELICS AREN'T ALWAYS THE MOST RELIABLE SOURCE, REMEMBER.
WHERE DO WE FIND THESE CREATURES?
TALK!
PAM

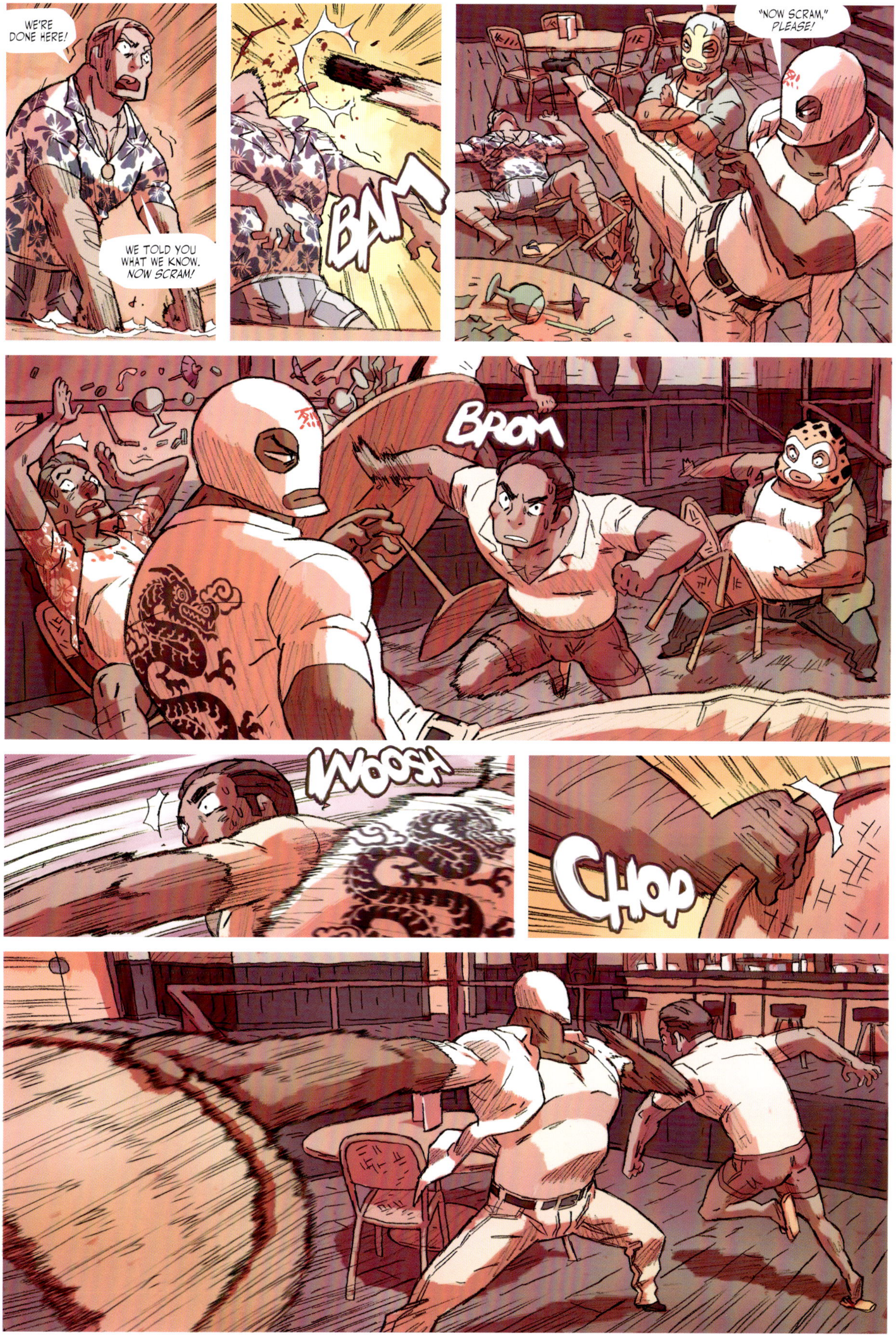
WE'RE DONE HERE!
WE TOLD YOU WHAT WE KNOW. NOW SCRAM!
BAM
"NOW SCRAM," PLEASE!
BROM
WOOSH
CHOP

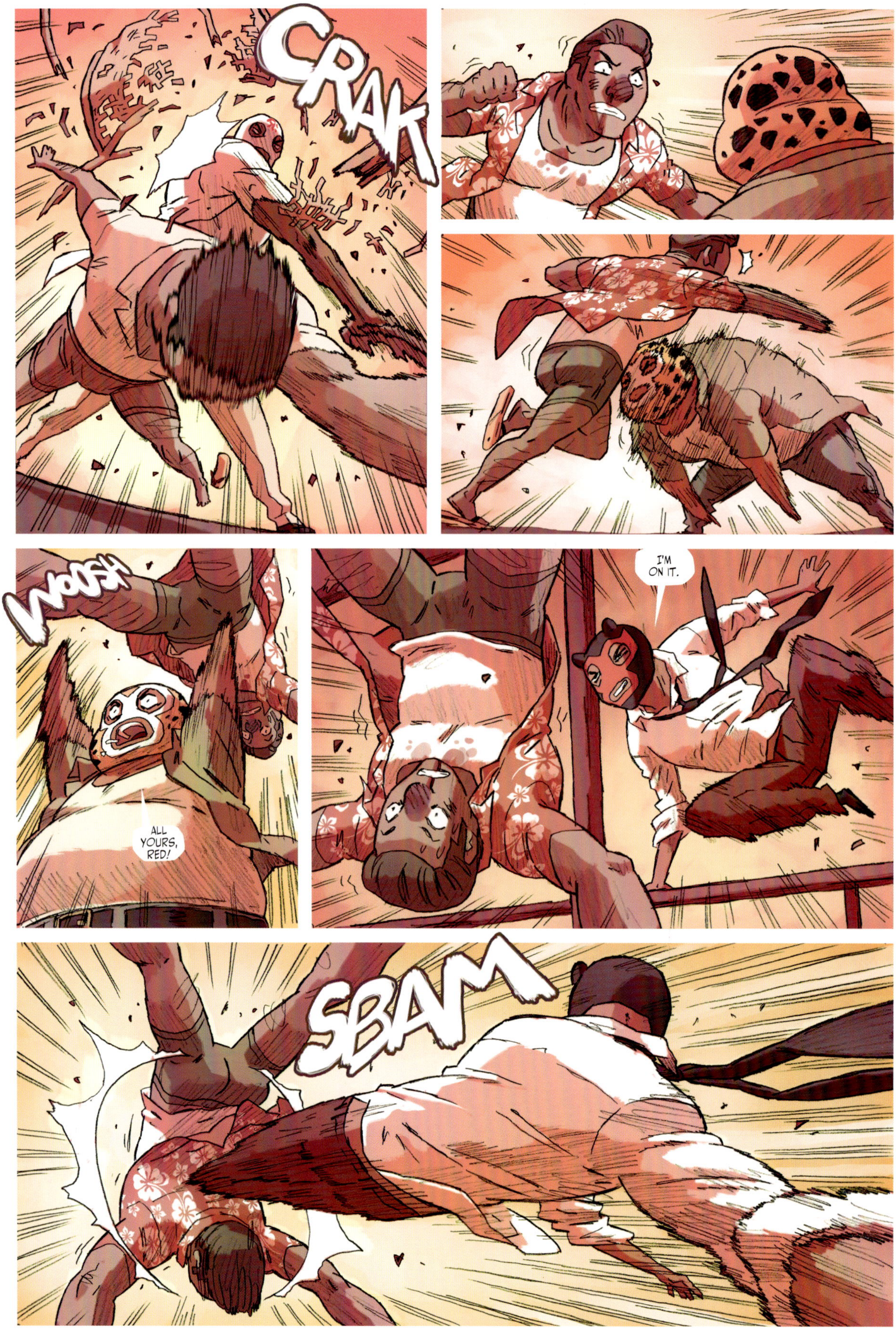
CRAK
WOOSH
ALL YOURS, RED!
I'M ON IT.
SBAM

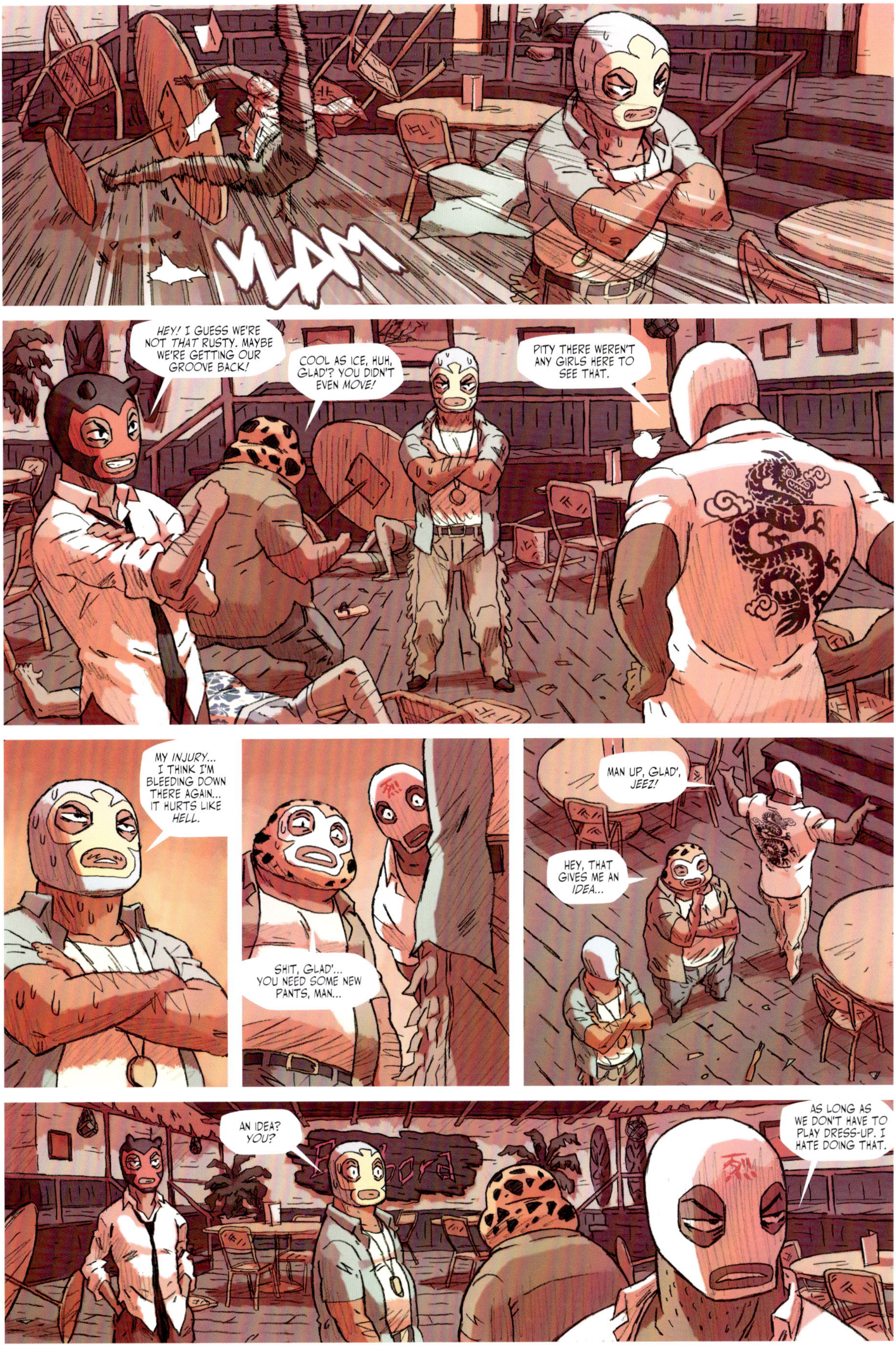
VLAM
HEY! I GUESS WE'RE NOT THAT RUSTY. MAYBE WE'RE GETTING OUR GROOVE BACK!
COOL AS ICE, HUH, GLAD'? YOU DIDN'T EVEN MOVE!
PITY THERE WEREN'T ANY GIRLS HERE TO SEE THAT.
MY INJURY... I THINK I'M BLEEDING DOWN THERE AGAIN... IT HURTS LIKE HELL.
SHIT, GLAD'... YOU NEED SOME NEW PANTS, MAN...
MAN UP, GLAD', JEEZ!
HEY, THAT GIVES ME AN IDEA...
AN IDEA? YOU?
AS LONG AS WE DON'T HAVE TO PLAY DRESS-UP. I HATE DOING THAT.

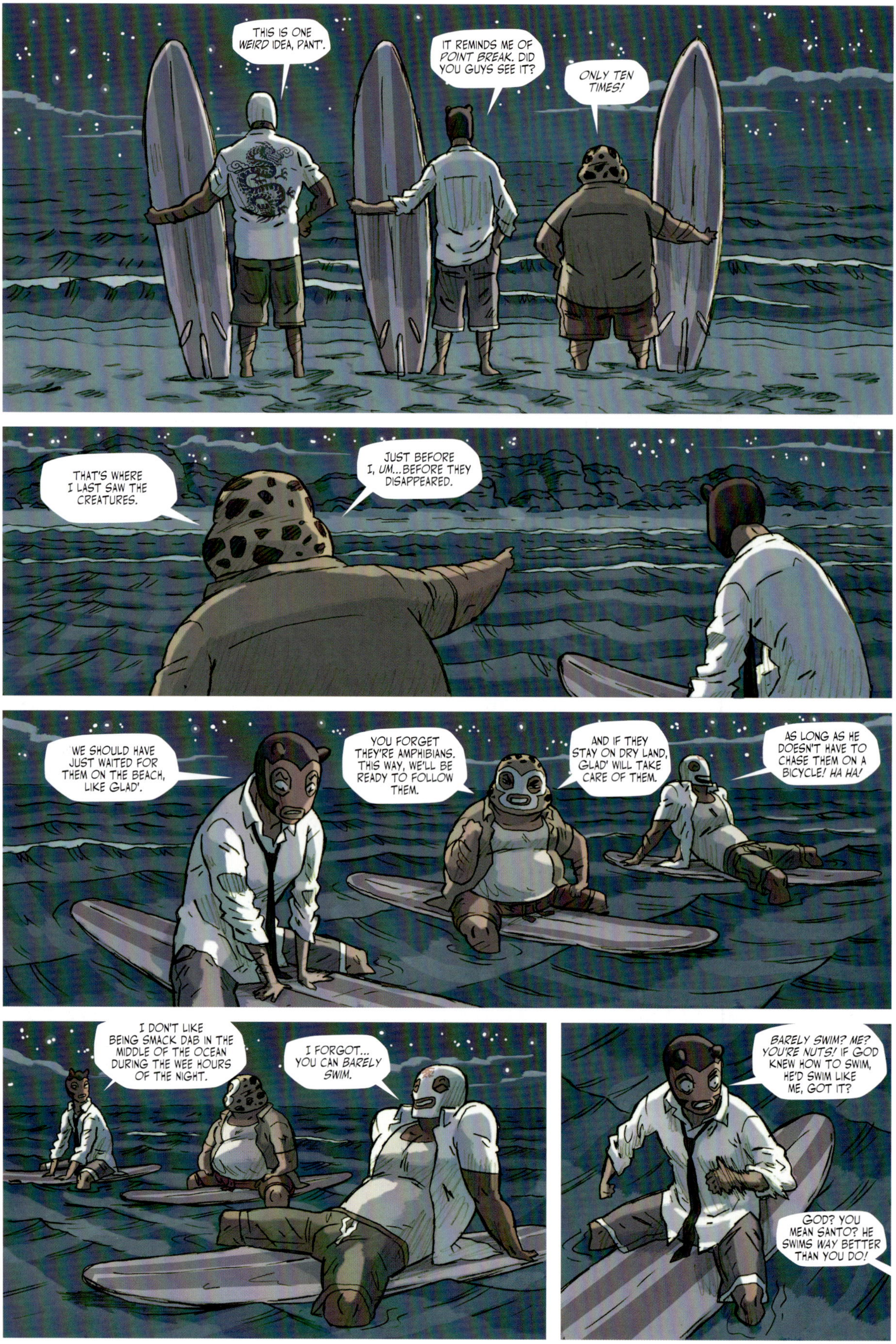
THIS IS ONE WEIRD IDEA, PANT'.
IT REMINDS ME OF POINT BREAK. DID YOU GUYS SEE IT?
ONLY TEN TIMES!
THAT'S WHERE I LAST SAW THE CREATURES.
JUST BEFORE I, UM...BEFORE THEY DISAPPEARED.
WE SHOULD HAVE JUST WAITED FOR THEM ON THE BEACH, LIKE GLAD'.
YOU FORGET THEY'RE AMPHIBIANS. THIS WAY, WE'LL BE READY TO FOLLOW THEM.
AND IF THEY STAY ON DRY LAND, GLAD' WILL TAKE CARE OF THEM.
AS LONG AS HE DOESN'T HAVE TO CHASE THEM ON A BICYCLE! HA HA!
I DON'T LIKE BEING SMACK DAB IN THE MIDDLE OF THE OCEAN DURING THE WEE HOURS OF THE NIGHT.
I FORGOT... YOU CAN BARELY SWIM.
BARELY SWIM? ME? YOU'RE NUTS! IF GOD KNEW HOW TO SWIM, HE'D SWIM LIKE ME, GOT IT?
GOD? YOU MEAN SANTO? HE SWIMS WAY BETTER THAN YOU DO!

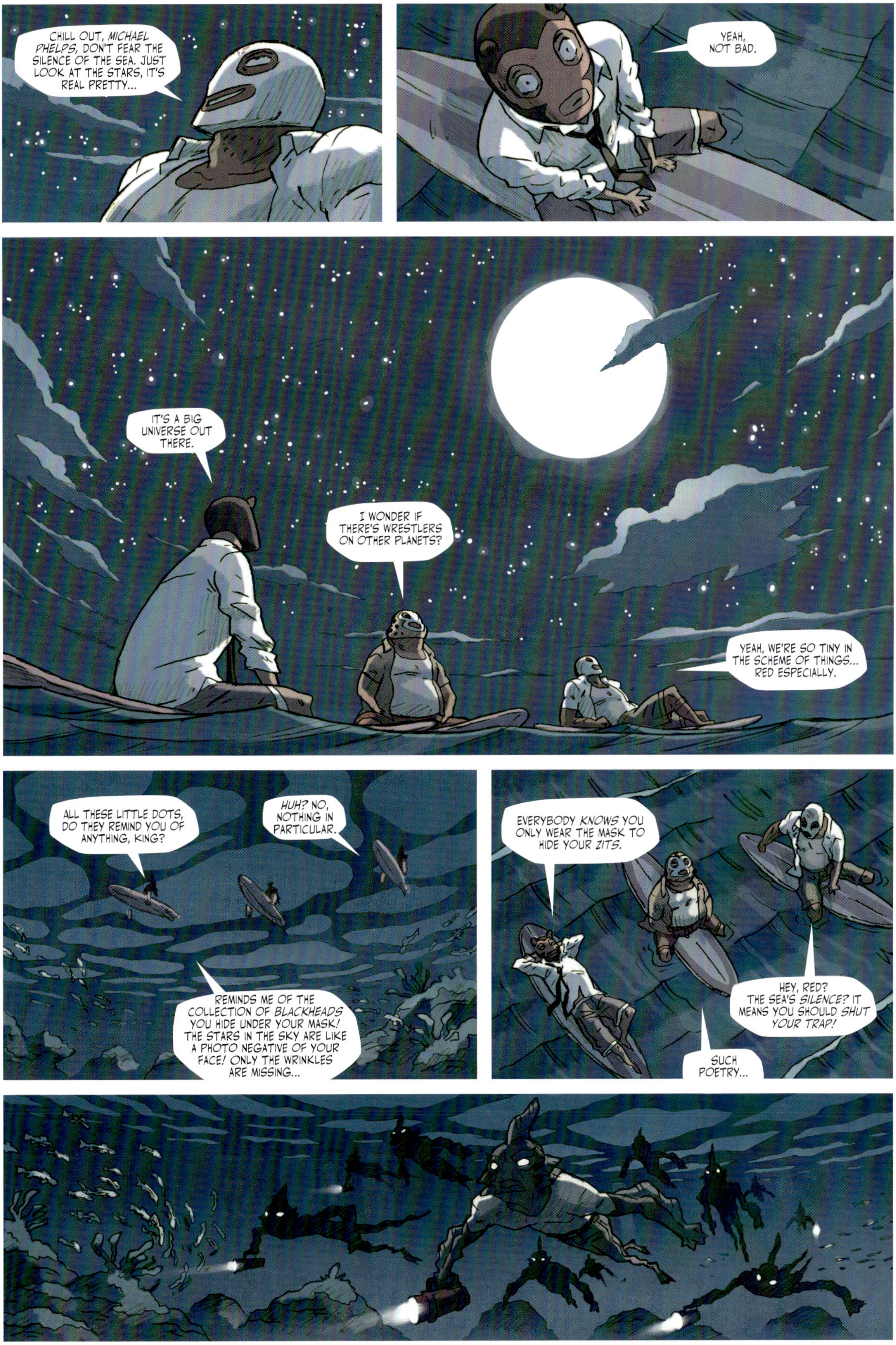
CHILL OUT, MICHAEL PHELPS, DON'T FEAR THE SILENCE OF THE SEA. JUST LOOK AT THE STARS, IT'S REAL PRETTY...
YEAH, NOT BAD.
IT'S A BIG UNIVERSE OUT THERE.
I WONDER IF THERE'S WRESTLERS ON OTHER PLANETS?
YEAH, WE'RE SO TINY IN THE SCHEME OF THINGS... RED ESPECIALLY.
ALL THESE LITTLE DOTS, DO THEY REMIND YOU OF ANYTHING, KING?
HUH? NO, NOTHING IN PARTICULAR.
REMINDS ME OF THE COLLECTION OF BLACKHEADS YOU HIDE UNDER YOUR MASK! THE STARS IN THE SKY ARE LIKE A PHOTO NEGATIVE OF YOUR FACE! ONLY THE WRINKLES ARE MISSING...
EVERYBODY KNOWS YOU ONLY WEAR THE MASK TO HIDE YOUR ZITS.
HEY, RED? THE SEA'S SILENCE? IT MEANS YOU SHOULD SHUT YOUR TRAP!
SUCH POETRY...

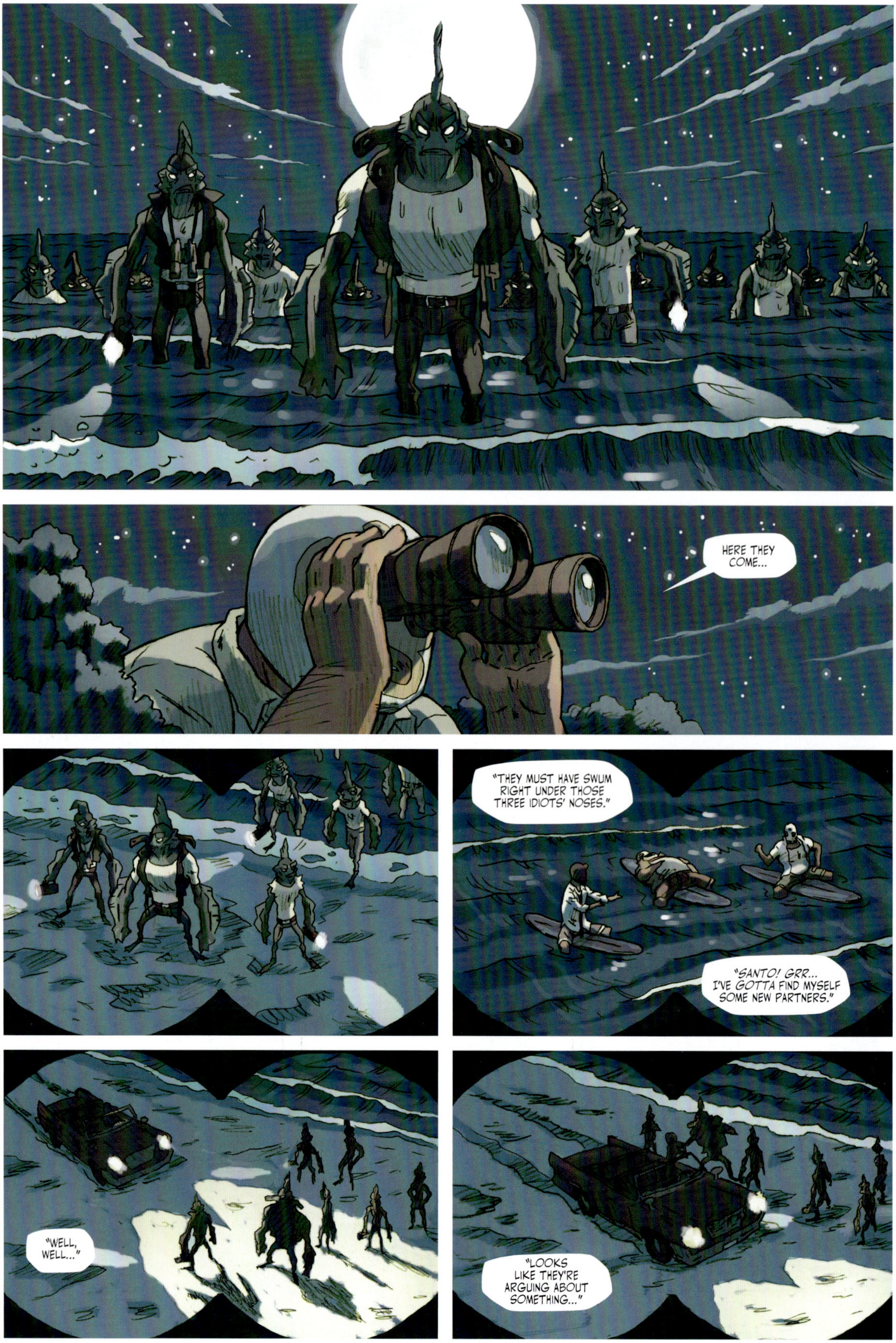
HERE THEY COME...
"THEY MUST HAVE SWUM RIGHT UNDER THOSE THREE IDIOTS' NOSES."
"SANTO! GRR... I'VE GOTTA FIND MYSELF SOME NEW PARTNERS."
"WELL, WELL..."
"LOOKS LIKE THEY'RE ARGUING ABOUT SOMETHING..."

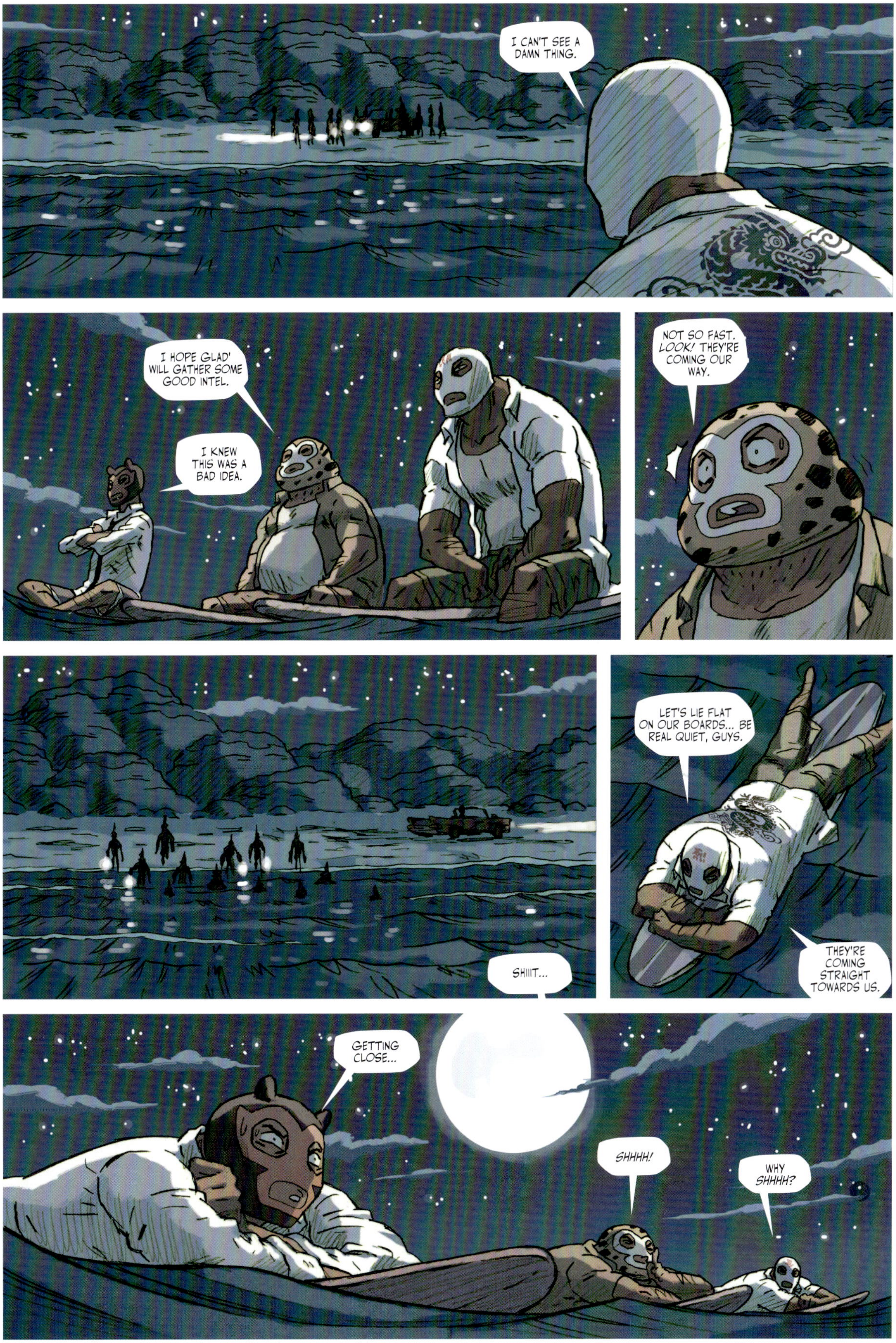
I CAN'T SEE A DAMN THING.
I HOPE GLAD' WILL GATHER SOME GOOD INTEL.
I KNEW THIS WAS A BAD IDEA.
NOT SO FAST. LOOK! THEY'RE COMING OUR WAY.
SHIIIT...
LET'S LIE FLAT ON OUR BOARDS... BE REAL QUIET, GUYS.
THEY'RE COMING STRAIGHT TOWARDS US.
GETTING CLOSE...
SHHHH!
WHY SHHHH?

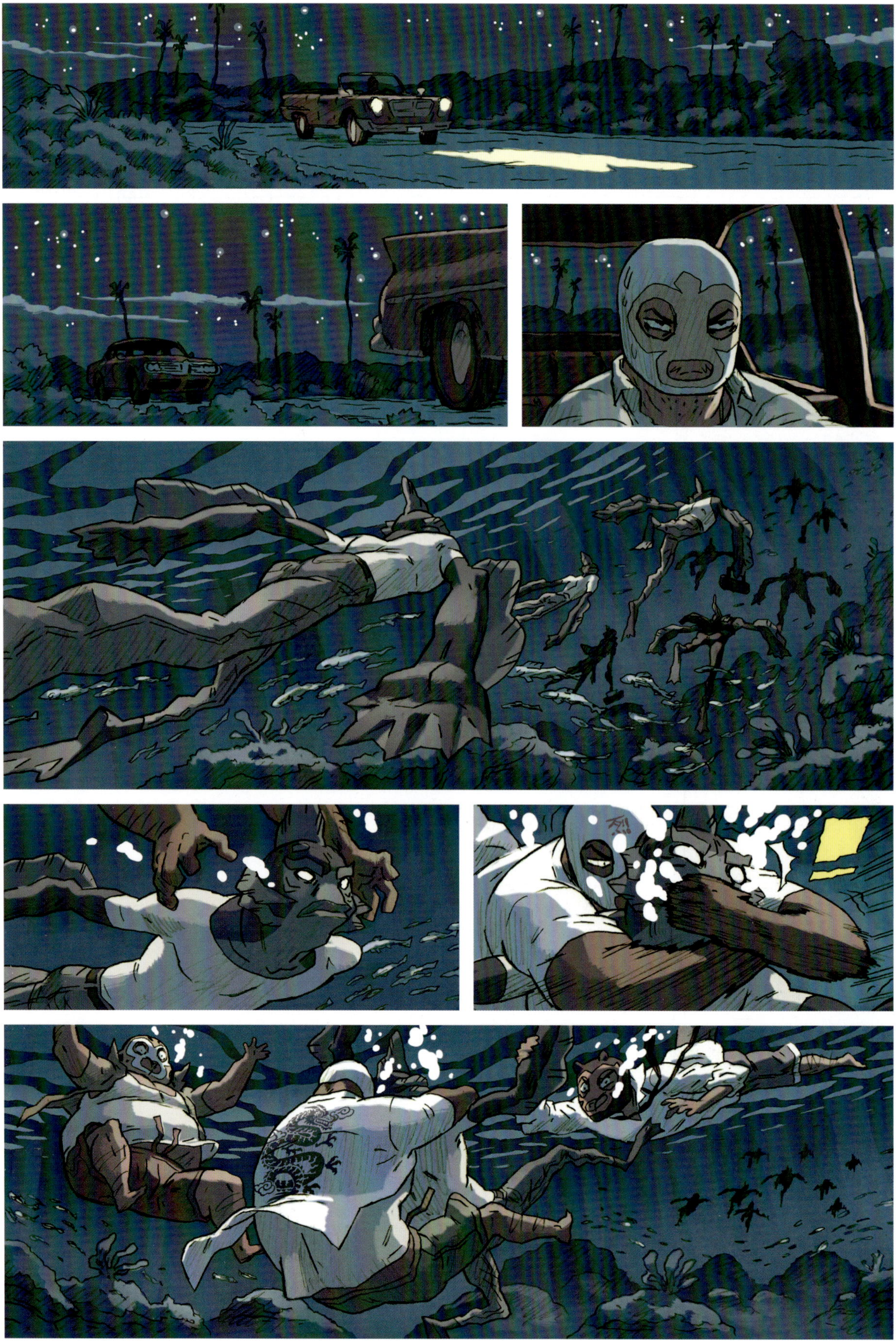

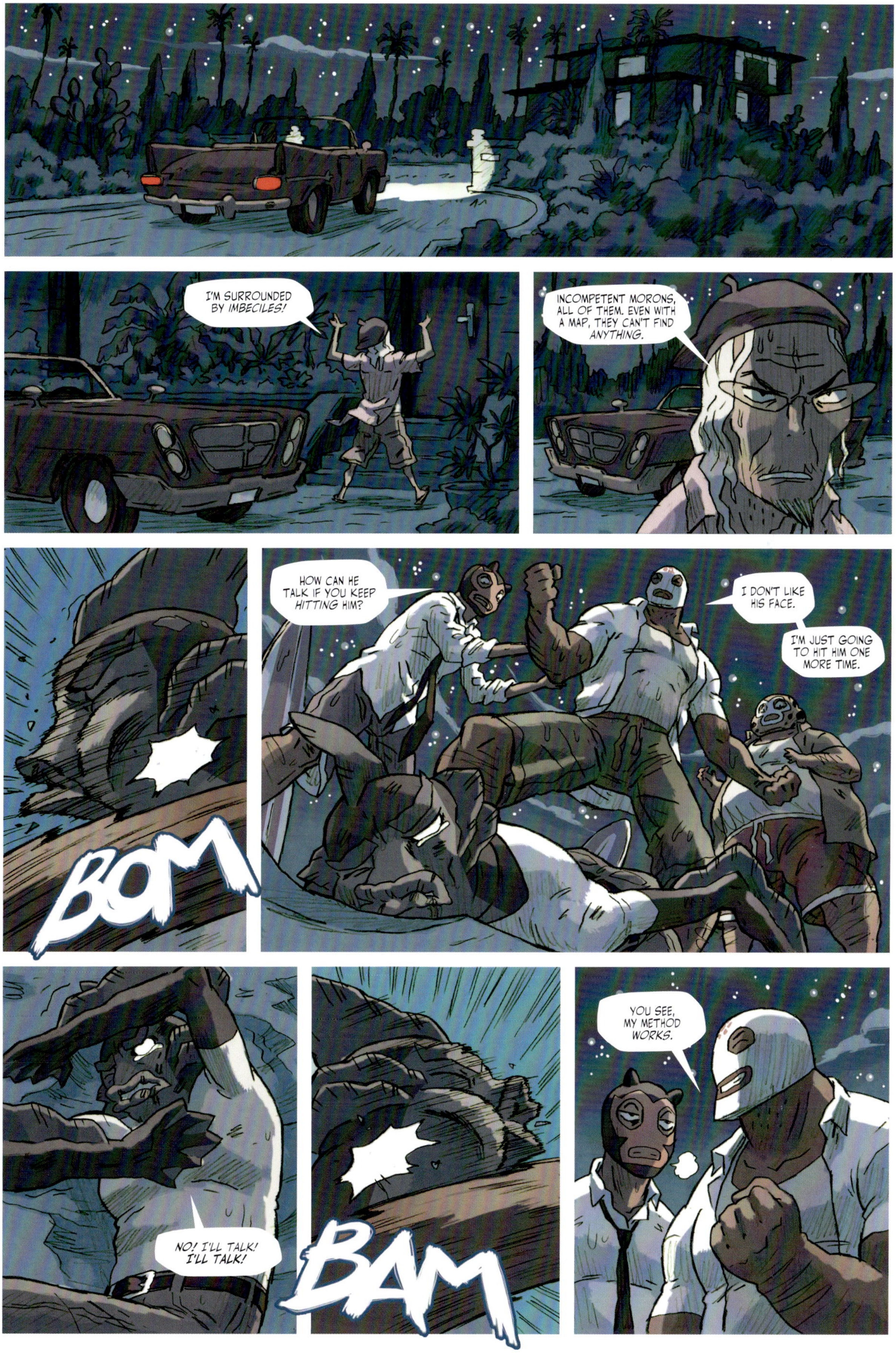
I'M SURROUNDED BY IMBECILES!
INCOMPETENT MORONS, ALL OF THEM. EVEN WITH A MAP, THEY CAN'T FIND ANYTHING.
BOM
HOW CAN HE TALK IF YOU KEEP HITTING HIM?
I DON'T LIKE HIS FACE.
I'M JUST GOING TO HIT HIM ONE MORE TIME.
NO! I'LL TALK! I'LL TALK!
BAM
YOU SEE, MY METHOD WORKS.

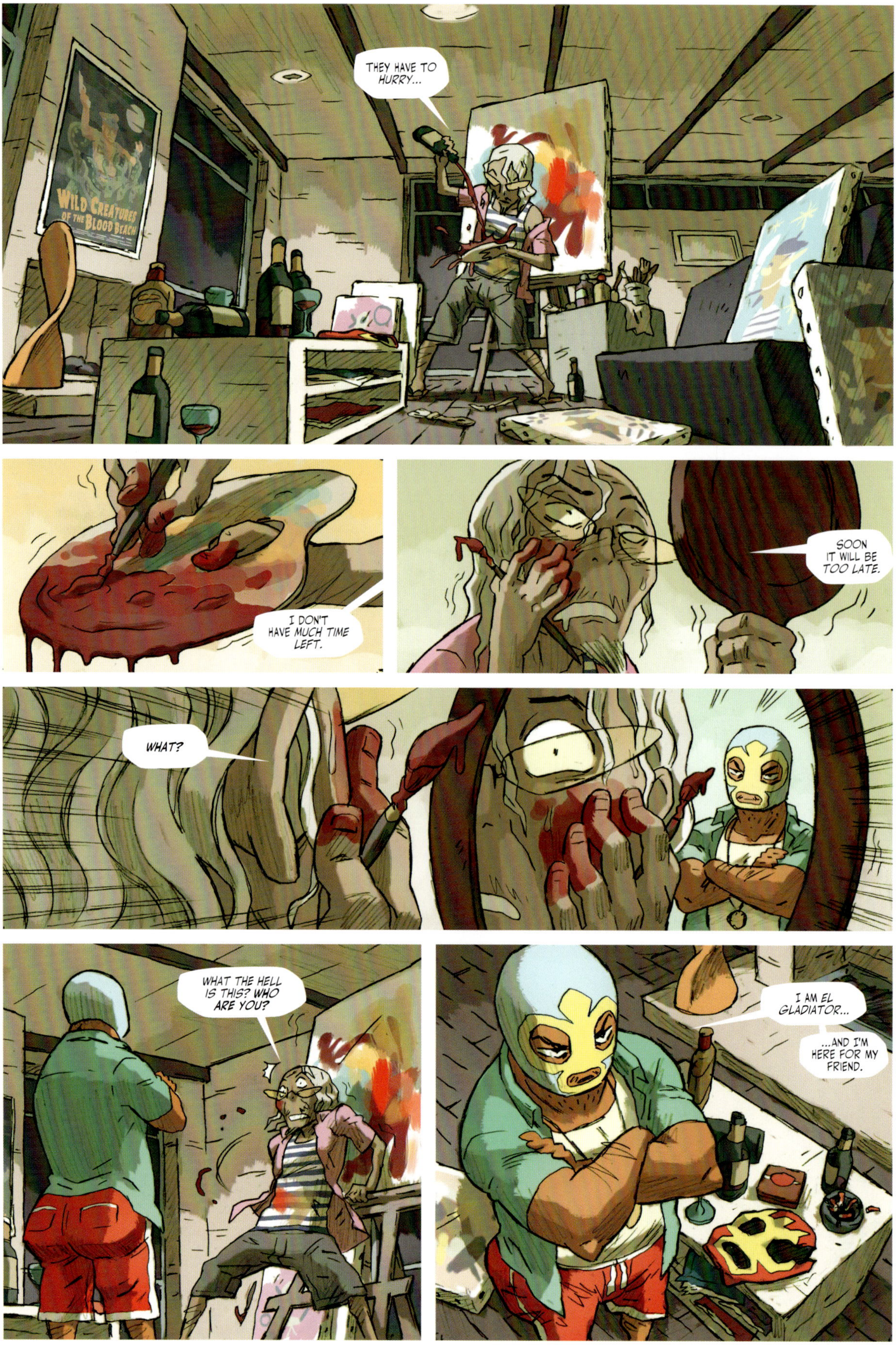
WILD CREATURES OF THE BLOOD BEACH
THEY HAVE TO HURRY...
I DON'T HAVE MUCH TIME LEFT.
SOON IT WILL BE TOO LATE.
WHAT?
WHAT THE HELL IS THIS? WHO ARE YOU?
I AM EL GLADIATOR...
...AND I'M HERE FOR MY FRIEND.

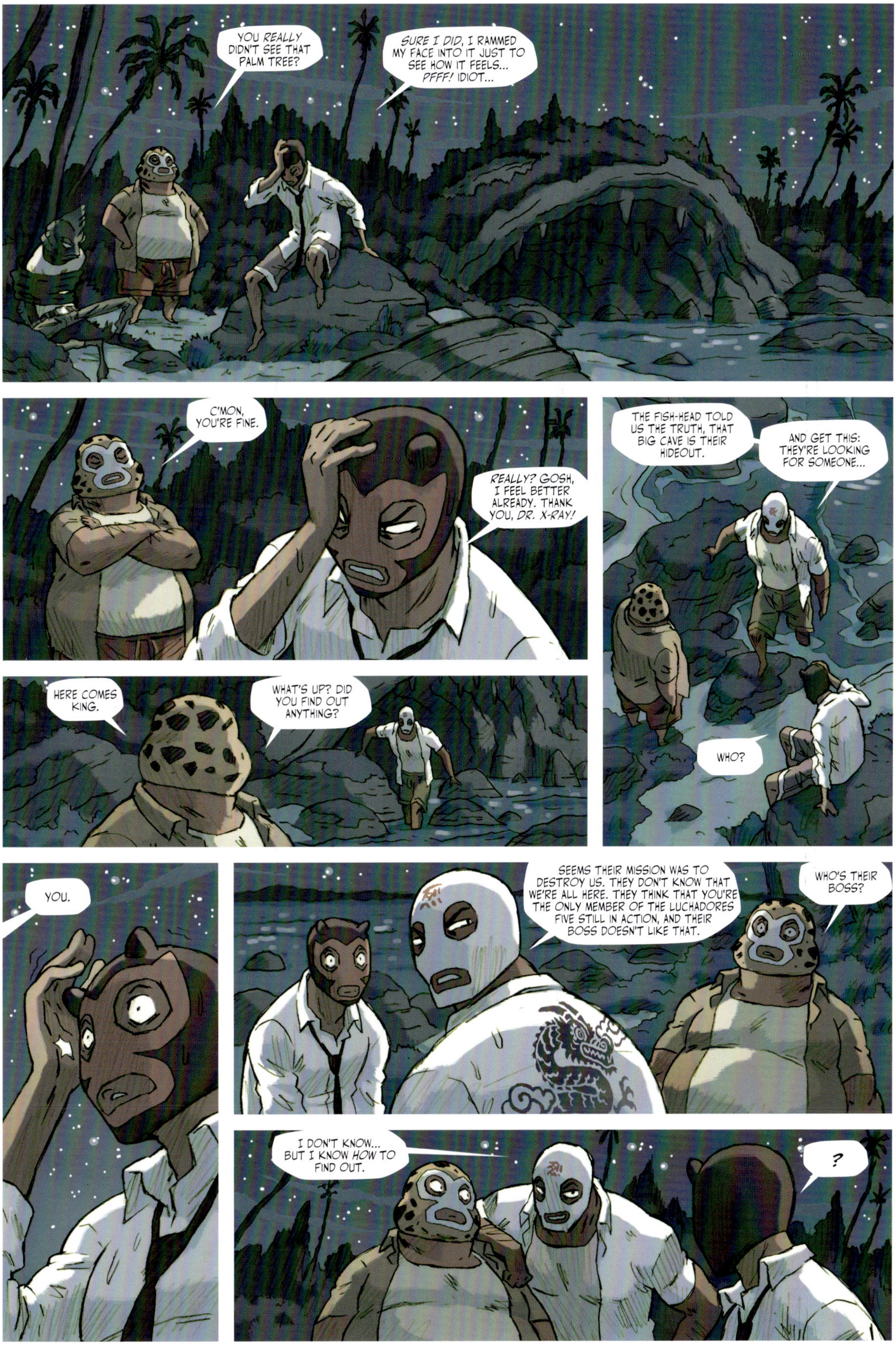
YOU REALLY DIDN'T SEE THAT PALM TREE?
SURE I DID, I RAMMED MY FACE INTO IT JUST TO SEE HOW IT FEELS... PFFF! IDIOT...
C'MON, YOU'RE FINE.
REALLY? GOSH, I FEEL BETTER ALREADY. THANK YOU, DR. X-RAY!
HERE COMES KING.
WHAT'S UP? DID YOU FIND OUT ANYTHING?
THE FISH-HEAD TOLD US THE TRUTH, THAT BIG CAVE IS THEIR HIDEOUT.
AND GET THIS: THEY'RE LOOKING FOR SOMEONE...
WHO?
YOU.
SEEMS THEIR MISSION WAS TO DESTROY US. THEY DON'T KNOW THAT WE'RE ALL HERE. THEY THINK THAT YOU'RE THE ONLY MEMBER OF THE LUCHADORES FIVE STILL IN ACTION, AND THEIR BOSS DOESN'T LIKE THAT.
WHO'S THEIR BOSS?
I DON'T KNOW... BUT I KNOW HOW TO FIND OUT.
?

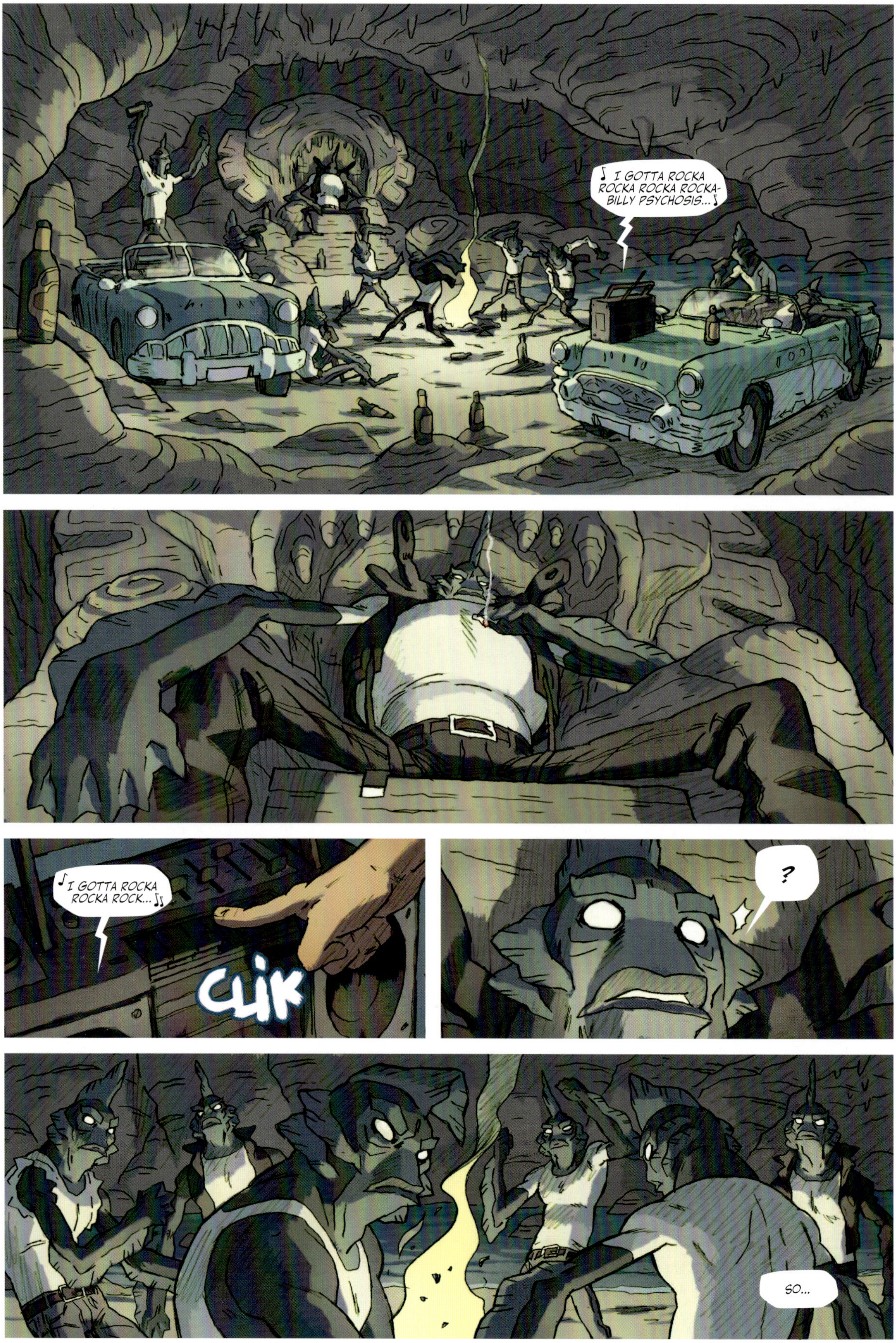
I GOTTA ROCKA ROCKA ROCKA ROCKA-BILLY PSYCHOSIS...
I GOTTA ROCKA ROCKA ROCK...
CLIK
?
SO...

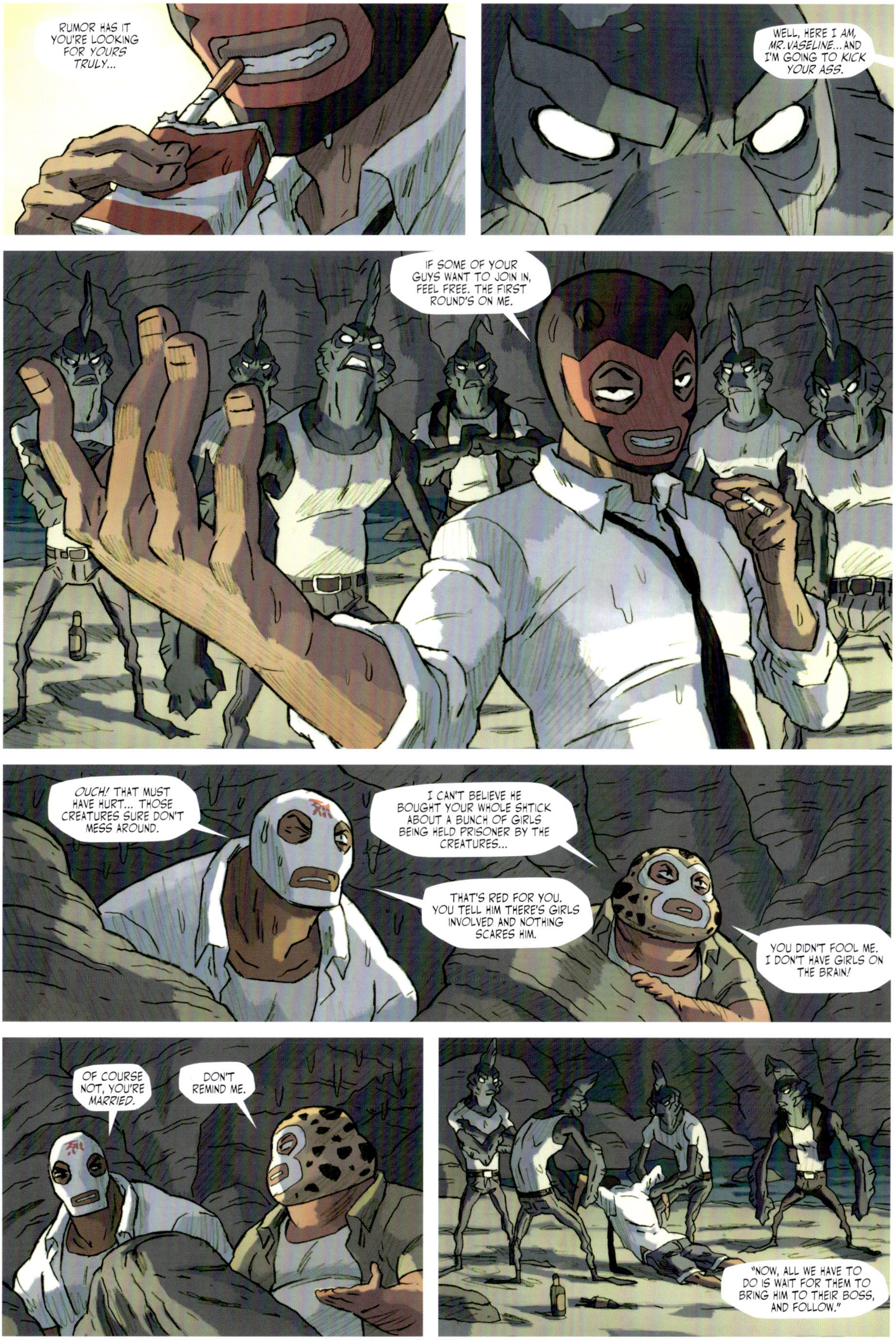
RUMOR HAS IT YOU'RE LOOKING FOR YOURS TRULY...
WELL, HERE I AM, MR.VASELINE... AND I'M GOING TO KICK YOUR ASS.
IF SOME OF YOUR GUYS WANT TO JOIN IN, FEEL FREE. THE FIRST ROUND'S ON ME.
OUCH! THAT MUST HAVE HURT... THOSE CREATURES SURE DON'T MESS AROUND.
I CAN'T BELIEVE HE BOUGHT YOUR WHOLE SHTICK ABOUT A BUNCH OF GIRLS BEING HELD PRISONER BY THE CREATURES...
THAT'S RED FOR YOU. YOU TELL HIM THERE'S GIRLS INVOLVED AND NOTHING SCARES HIM.
YOU DIDN'T FOOL ME. I DON'T HAVE GIRLS ON THE BRAIN!
OF COURSE NOT, YOU'RE MARRIED.
DON'T REMIND ME.
"NOW, ALL WE HAVE TO DO IS WAIT FOR THEM TO BRING HIM TO THEIR BOSS, AND FOLLOW."

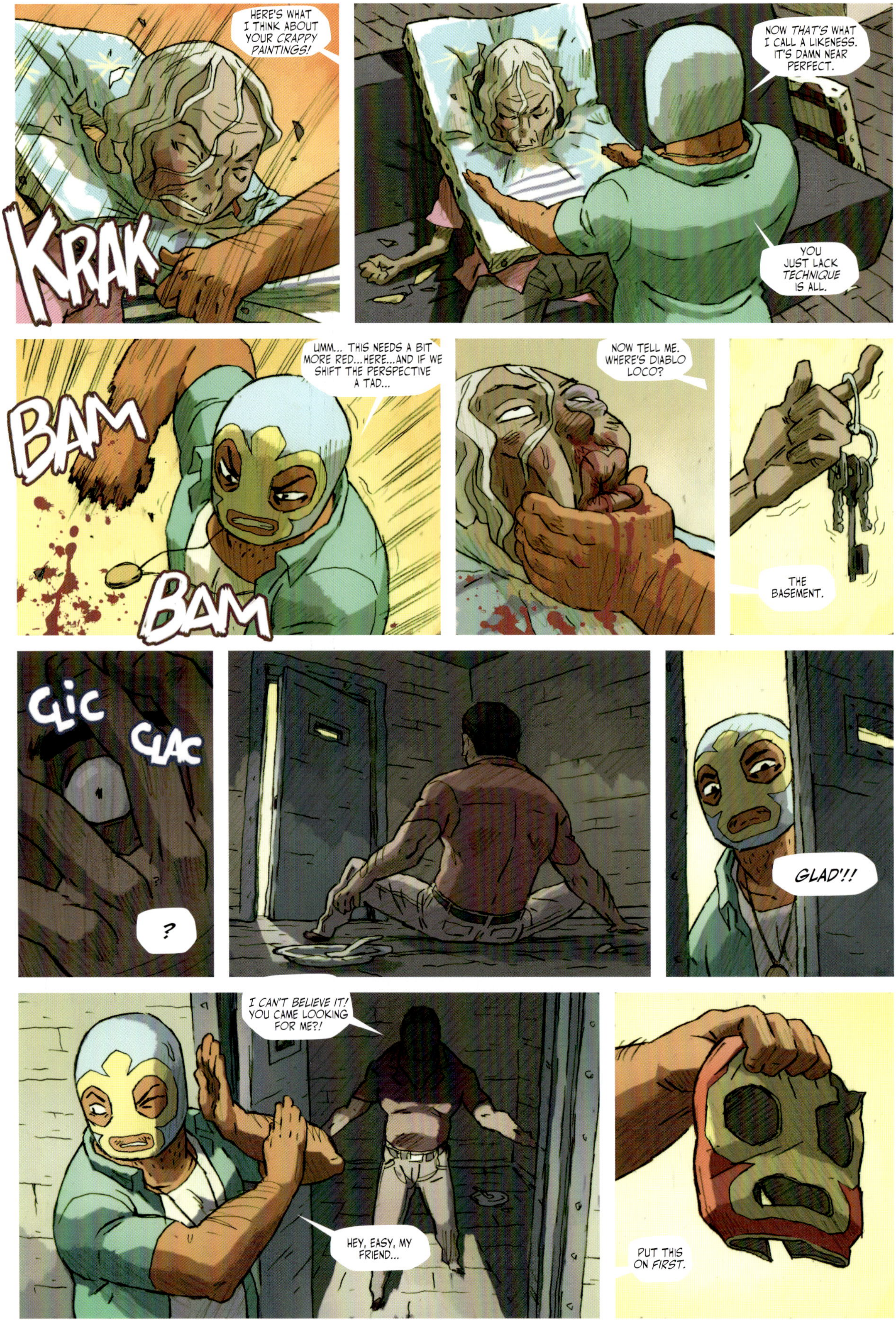
HERE'S WHAT I THINK ABOUT YOUR CRAPPY PAINTINGS!
KRAK
NOW THAT'S WHAT I CALL A LIKENESS. IT'S DAMN NEAR PERFECT.
YOU JUST LACK TECHNIQUE IS ALL.
BAM
UMM... THIS NEEDS A BIT MORE RED...HERE...AND IF WE SHIFT THE PERSPECTIVE A TAD...
BAM
NOW TELL ME. WHERE'S DIABLO LOCO?
THE BASEMENT.
CLIC
CLAC
?
GLAD'!!
I CAN'T BELIEVE IT! YOU CAME LOOKING FOR ME?!
HEY, EASY, MY FRIEND...
PUT THIS ON FIRST.

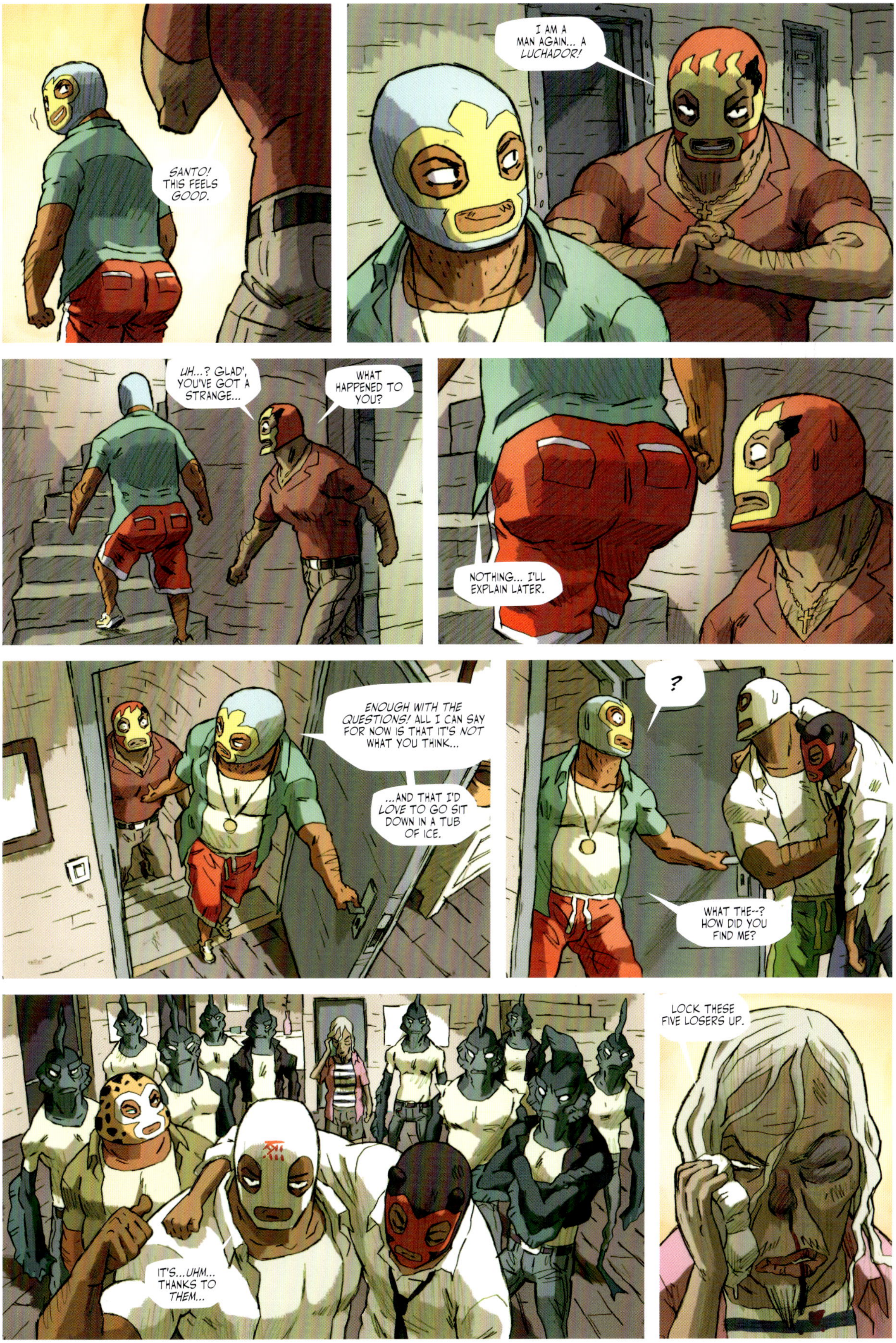
SANTO! THIS FEELS GOOD.
I AM A MAN AGAIN... A LUCHADOR!
UH...? GLAD', YOU'VE GOT A STRANGE...
WHAT HAPPENED TO YOU?
NOTHING... I'LL EXPLAIN LATER.
ENOUGH WITH THE QUESTIONS! ALL I CAN SAY FOR NOW IS THAT IT'S NOT WHAT YOU THINK...
...AND THAT I'D LOVE TO GO SIT DOWN IN A TUB OF ICE.
?
WHAT THE--? HOW DID YOU FIND ME?
IT'S...UHM... THANKS TO THEM...
LOCK THESE FIVE LOSERS UP.

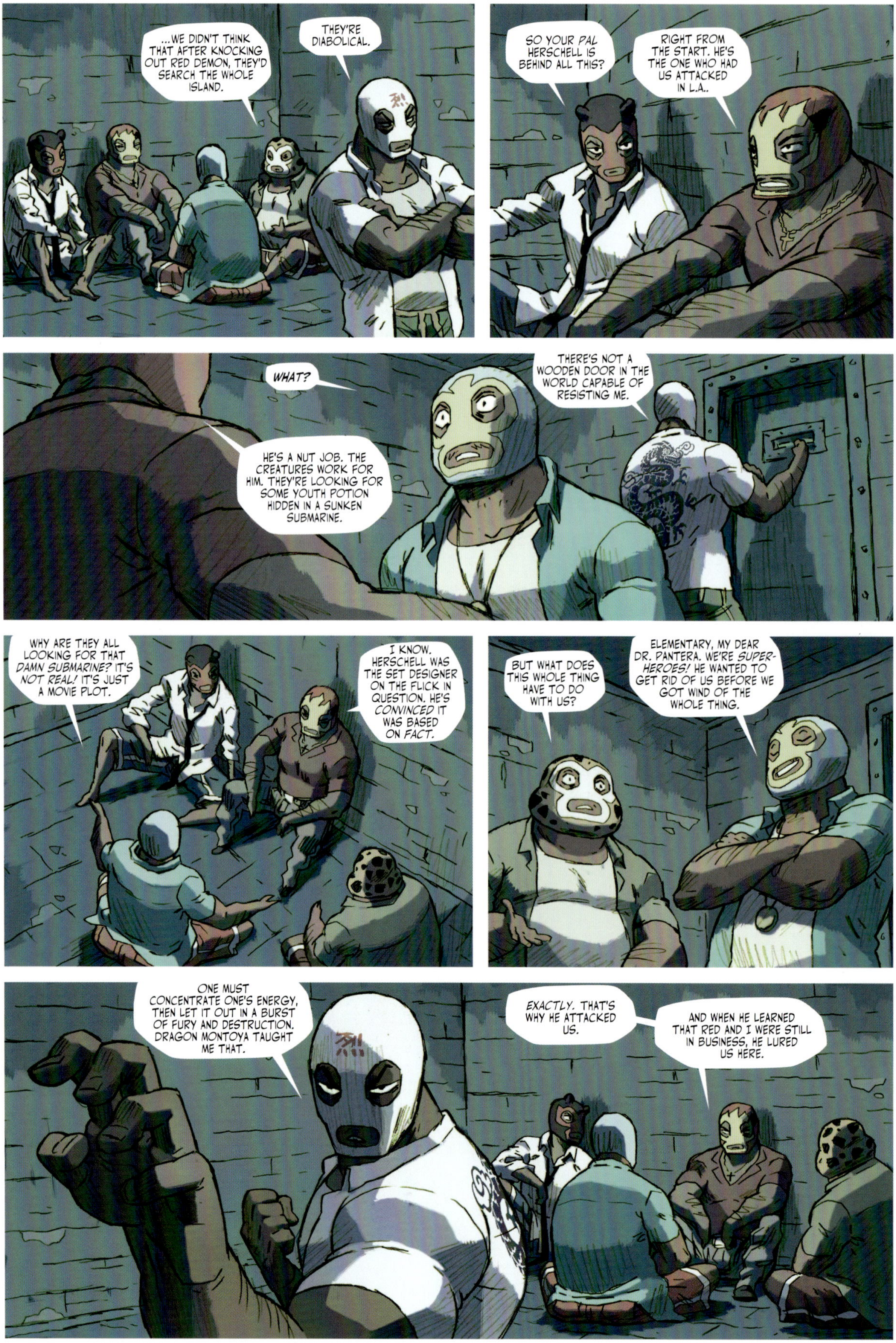
...WE DIDN'T THINK THAT AFTER KNOCKING OUT RED DEMON, THEY'D SEARCH THE WHOLE ISLAND.
THEY'RE DIABOLICAL.
SO YOUR *PAL* HERSCHELL IS BEHIND ALL THIS?
RIGHT FROM THE START. HE'S THE ONE WHO HAD US ATTACKED IN L.A..
WHAT?
HE'S A NUT JOB. THE CREATURES WORK FOR HIM. THEY'RE LOOKING FOR SOME YOUTH POTION HIDDEN IN A SUNKEN SUBMARINE.
THERE'S NOT A WOODEN DOOR IN THE WORLD CAPABLE OF RESISTING ME.
WHY ARE THEY ALL LOOKING FOR THAT *DAMN SUBMARINE?* IT'S *NOT REAL!* IT'S JUST A MOVIE PLOT.
I KNOW. HERSCHELL WAS THE SET DESIGNER ON THE FLICK IN QUESTION. HE'S *CONVINCED* IT WAS BASED ON *FACT*.
BUT WHAT DOES THIS WHOLE THING HAVE TO DO WITH US?
ELEMENTARY, MY DEAR DR. PANTERA. WE'RE *SUPER-HEROES!* HE WANTED TO GET RID OF US BEFORE WE GOT WIND OF THE WHOLE THING.
ONE MUST CONCENTRATE ONE'S ENERGY, THEN LET IT OUT IN A BURST OF FURY AND DESTRUCTION. DRAGON MONTOYA TAUGHT ME THAT.
EXACTLY. THAT'S WHY HE ATTACKED US.
AND WHEN HE LEARNED THAT RED AND I WERE STILL IN BUSINESS, HE LURED US HERE.

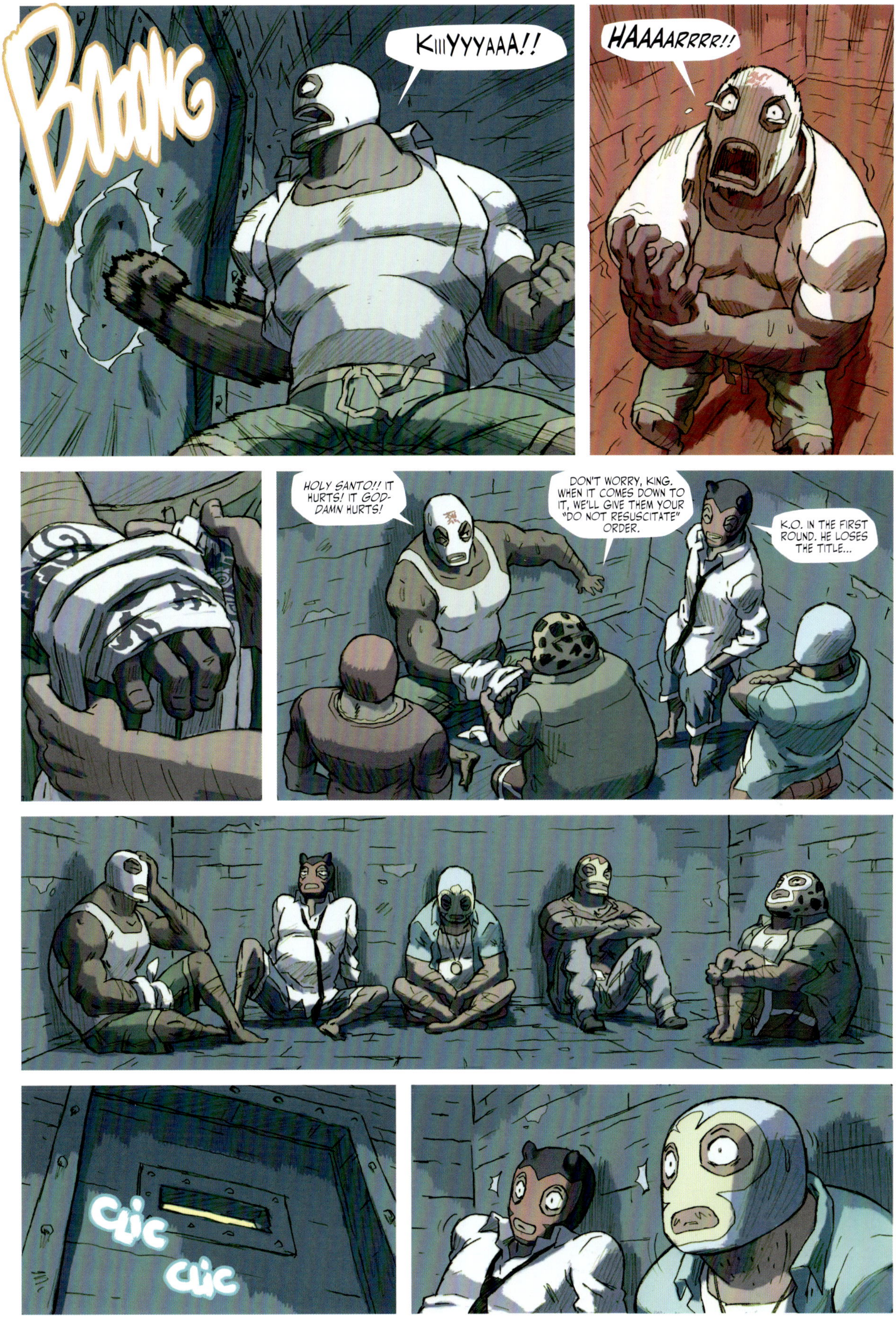
BOOONG
KIIIYYYAAA!!
HAAAARRRR!!
HOLY SANTO!! IT HURTS! IT GOD-DAMN HURTS!
DON'T WORRY, KING. WHEN IT COMES DOWN TO IT, WE'LL GIVE THEM YOUR "DO NOT RESUSCITATE" ORDER.
K.O. IN THE FIRST ROUND. HE LOSES THE TITLE...
CLIC
CLIC

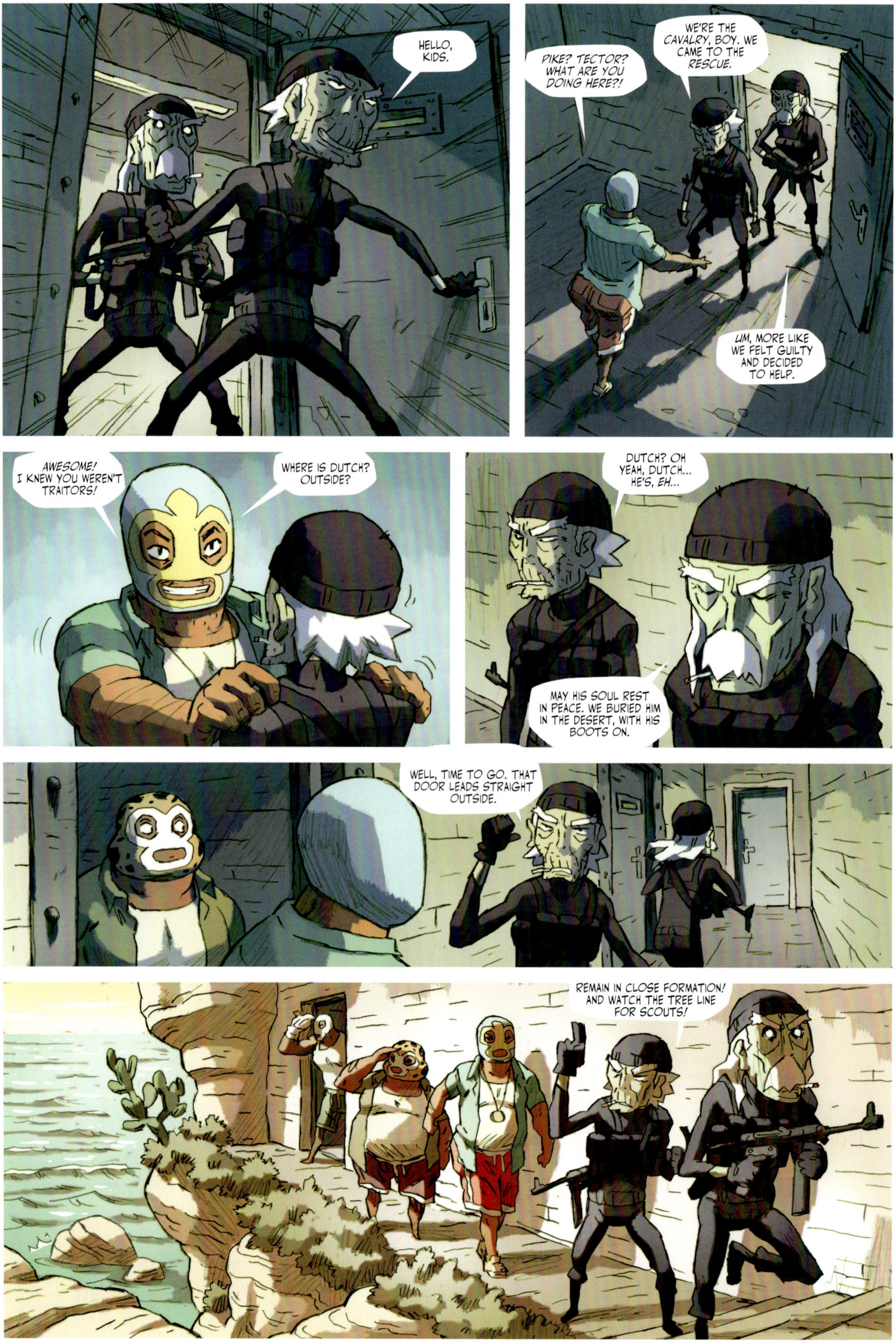
HELLO, KIDS.
PIKE? TECTOR? WHAT ARE YOU DOING HERE?!
WE'RE THE CAVALRY, BOY. WE CAME TO THE RESCUE.
UM, MORE LIKE WE FELT GUILTY AND DECIDED TO HELP.
AWESOME! I KNEW YOU WEREN'T TRAITORS!
WHERE IS DUTCH? OUTSIDE?
DUTCH? OH YEAH, DUTCH... HE'S, EH...
MAY HIS SOUL REST IN PEACE. WE BURIED HIM IN THE DESERT, WITH HIS BOOTS ON.
WELL, TIME TO GO. THAT DOOR LEADS STRAIGHT OUTSIDE.
REMAIN IN CLOSE FORMATION! AND WATCH THE TREE LINE FOR SCOUTS!

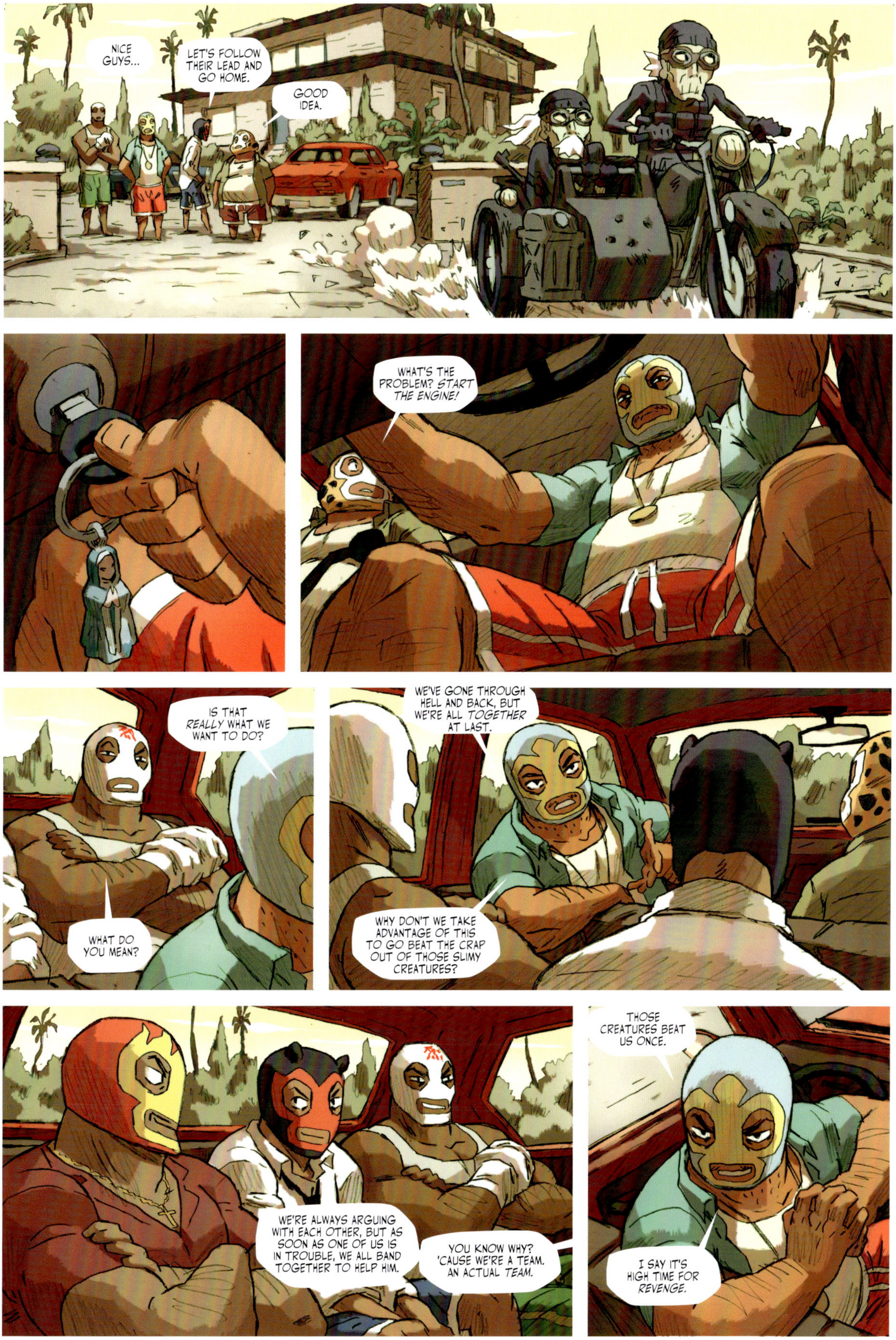
NICE GUYS...
LET'S FOLLOW THEIR LEAD AND GO HOME.
GOOD IDEA.
WHAT'S THE PROBLEM? START THE ENGINE!
IS THAT REALLY WHAT WE WANT TO DO?
WHAT DO YOU MEAN?
WE'VE GONE THROUGH HELL AND BACK, BUT WE'RE ALL TOGETHER AT LAST.
WHY DON'T WE TAKE ADVANTAGE OF THIS TO GO BEAT THE CRAP OUT OF THOSE SLIMY CREATURES?
WE'RE ALWAYS ARGUING WITH EACH OTHER, BUT AS SOON AS ONE OF US IS IN TROUBLE, WE ALL BAND TOGETHER TO HELP HIM.
YOU KNOW WHY? 'CAUSE WE'RE A TEAM. AN ACTUAL TEAM.
THOSE CREATURES BEAT US ONCE.
I SAY IT'S HIGH TIME FOR REVENGE.

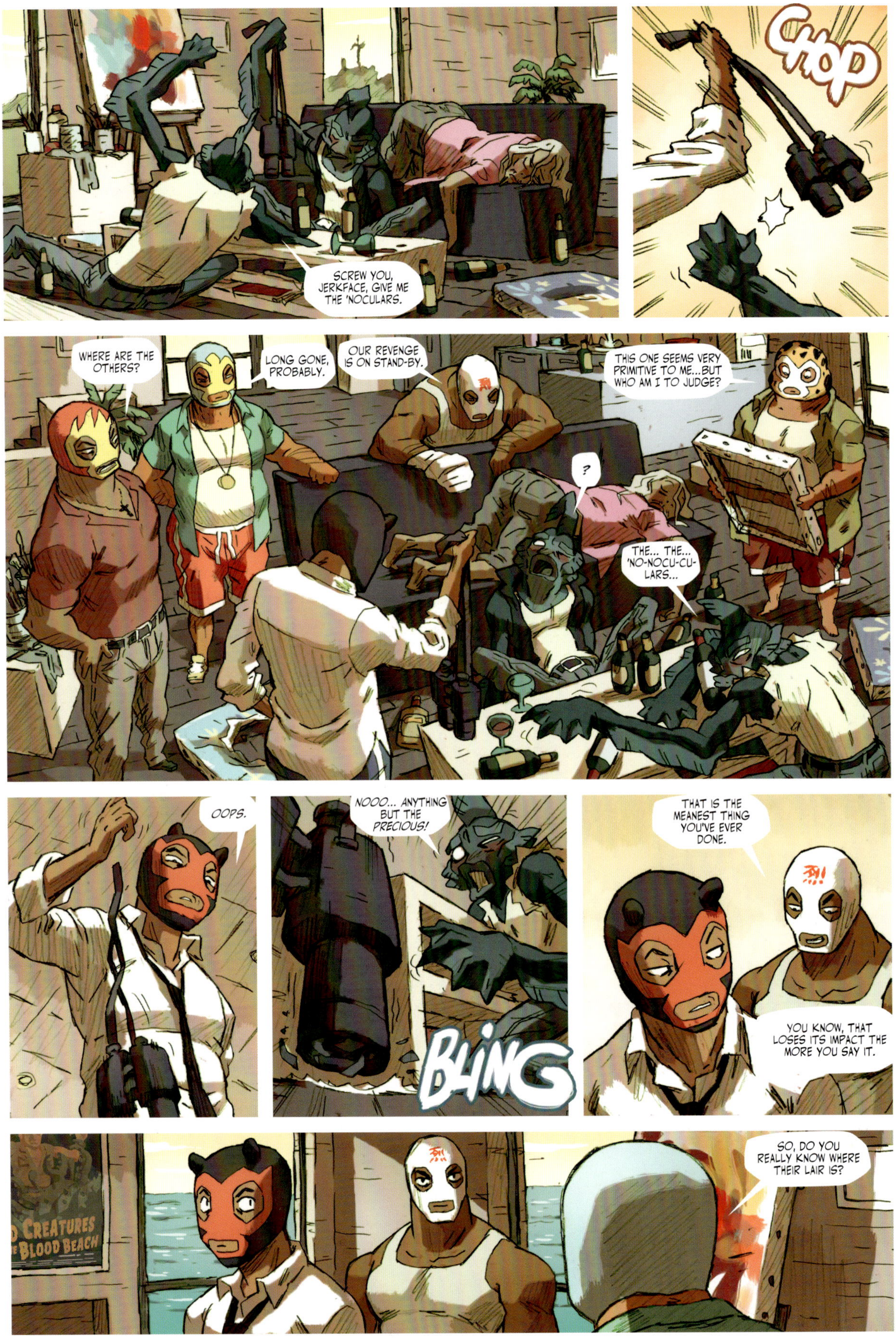

SCREW YOU, JERKFACE, GIVE ME THE 'NOCULARS.
CHOP
WHERE ARE THE OTHERS?
LONG GONE, PROBABLY.
OUR REVENGE IS ON STAND-BY.
THIS ONE SEEMS VERY PRIMITIVE TO ME... BUT WHO AM I TO JUDGE?
?
THE... THE... 'NO-NOCU-CU-LARS...
OOPS.
NOOO... ANYTHING BUT THE PRECIOUS!
BLING
THAT IS THE MEANEST THING YOU'VE EVER DONE.
YOU KNOW, THAT LOSES ITS IMPACT THE MORE YOU SAY IT.
SO, DO YOU REALLY KNOW WHERE THEIR LAIR IS?
CREATURES
BLOOD BEACH

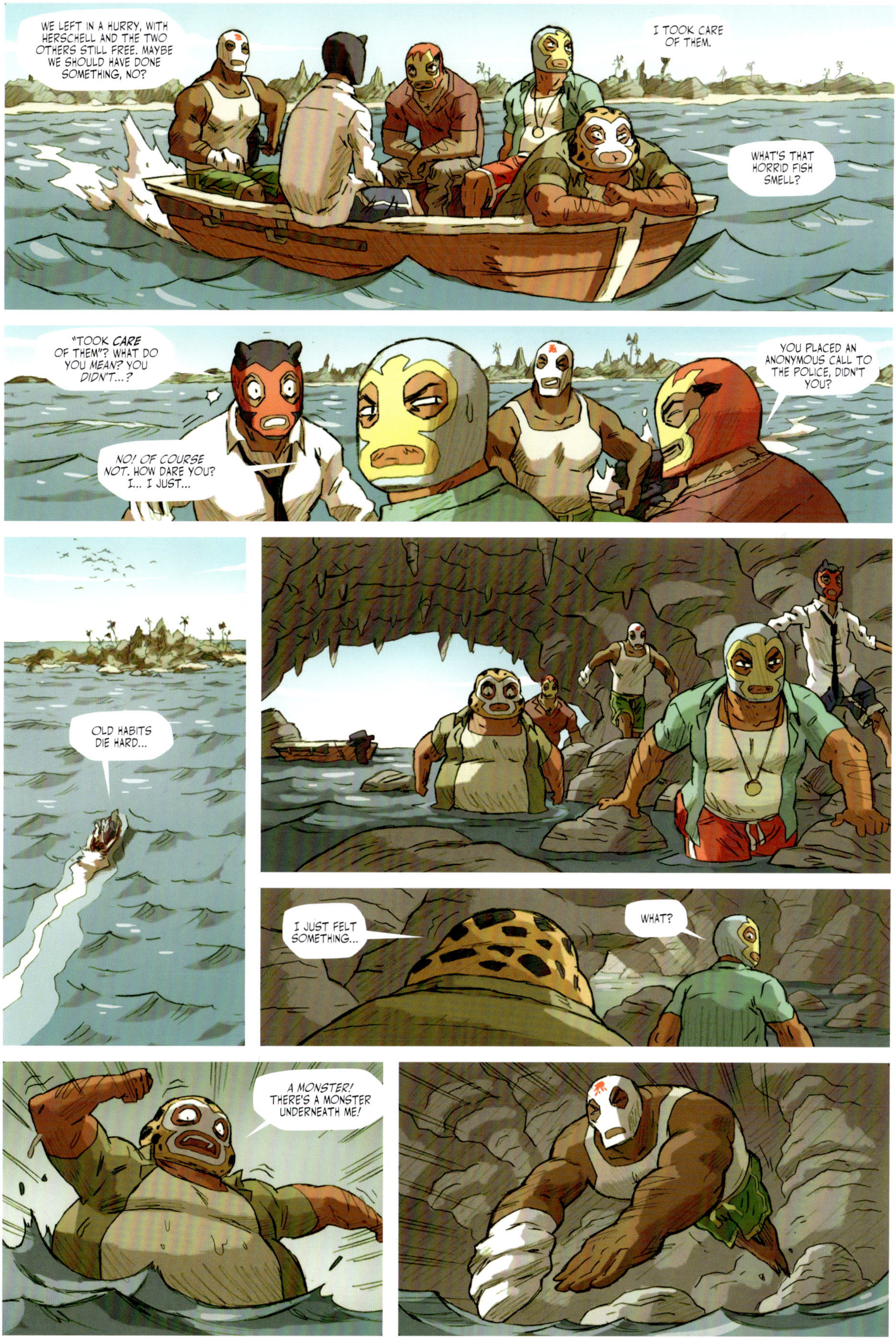
WE LEFT IN A HURRY, WITH HERSCHELL AND THE TWO OTHERS STILL FREE. MAYBE WE SHOULD HAVE DONE SOMETHING, NO?
I TOOK CARE OF THEM.
WHAT'S THAT HORRID FISH SMELL?
"TOOK CARE OF THEM"? WHAT DO YOU MEAN? YOU DIDN'T...?
NO! OF COURSE NOT. HOW DARE YOU? I... I JUST...
YOU PLACED AN ANONYMOUS CALL TO THE POLICE, DIDN'T YOU?
OLD HABITS DIE HARD...
I JUST FELT SOMETHING...
WHAT?
A MONSTER! THERE'S A MONSTER UNDERNEATH ME!

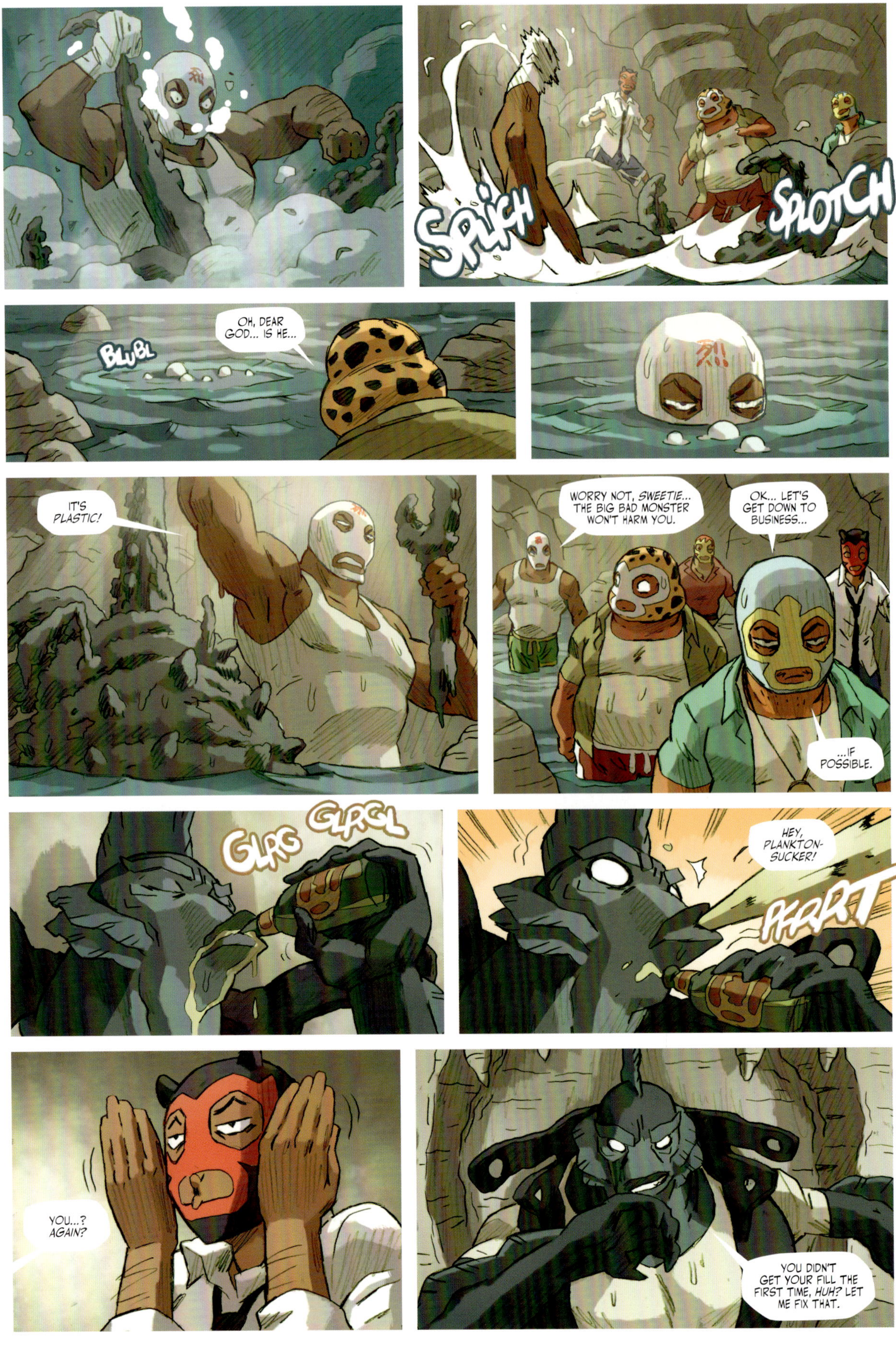
SPLICH
SPLOTCH
BLUBL
OH, DEAR GOD... IS HE...
IT'S PLASTIC!
WORRY NOT, SWEETIE... THE BIG BAD MONSTER WON'T HARM YOU.
OK... LET'S GET DOWN TO BUSINESS...
...IF POSSIBLE.
GLRG GLRGL
HEY, PLANKTON-SUCKER!
PFRRT
YOU...? AGAIN?
YOU DIDN'T GET YOUR FILL THE FIRST TIME, HUH? LET ME FIX THAT.

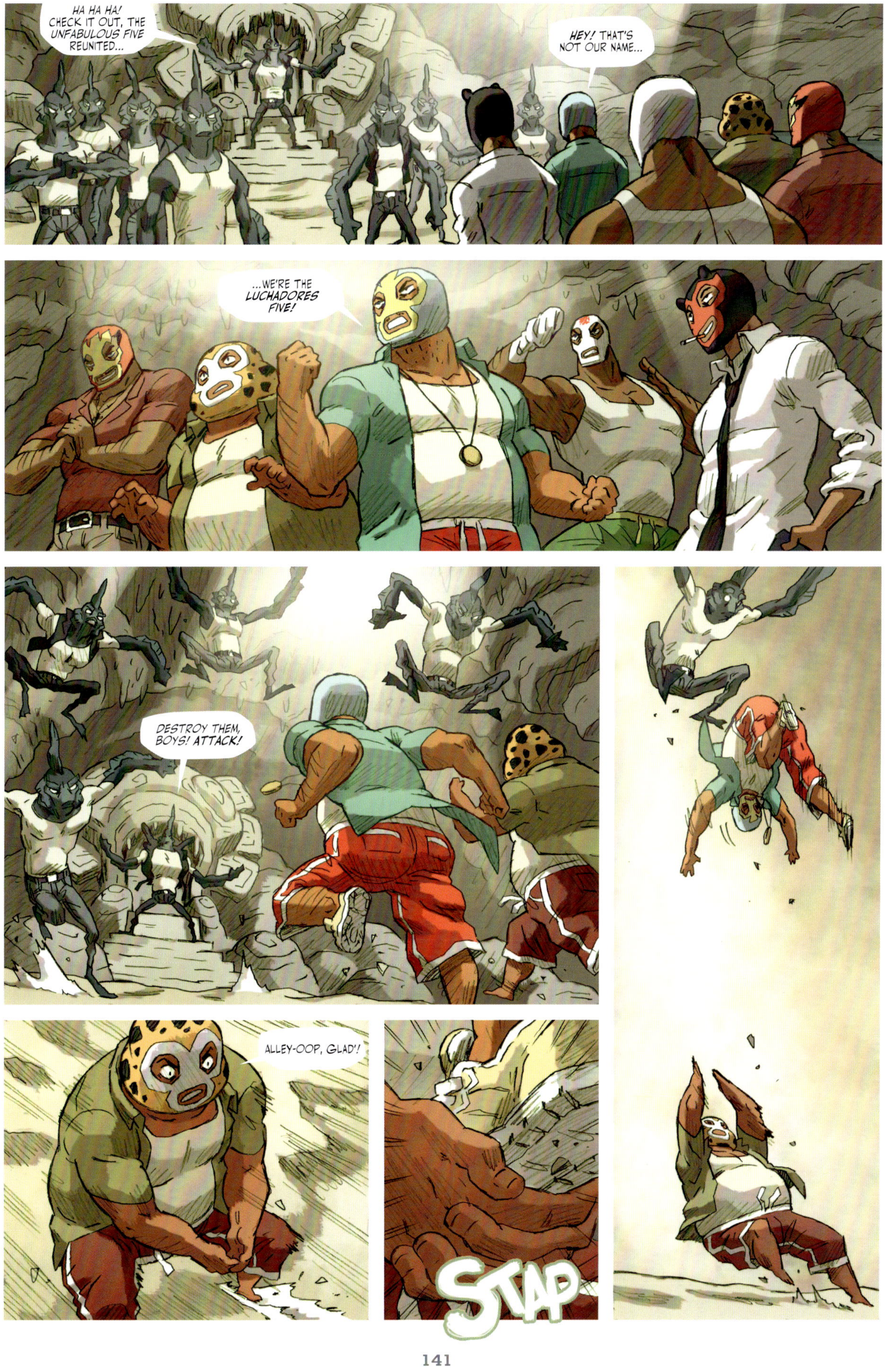
HA HA HA! CHECK IT OUT, THE UNFABULOUS FIVE REUNITED...
HEY! THAT'S NOT OUR NAME...
...WE'RE THE LUCHADORES FIVE!
DESTROY THEM, BOYS! ATTACK!
ALLEY-OOP, GLAD'!
STAP

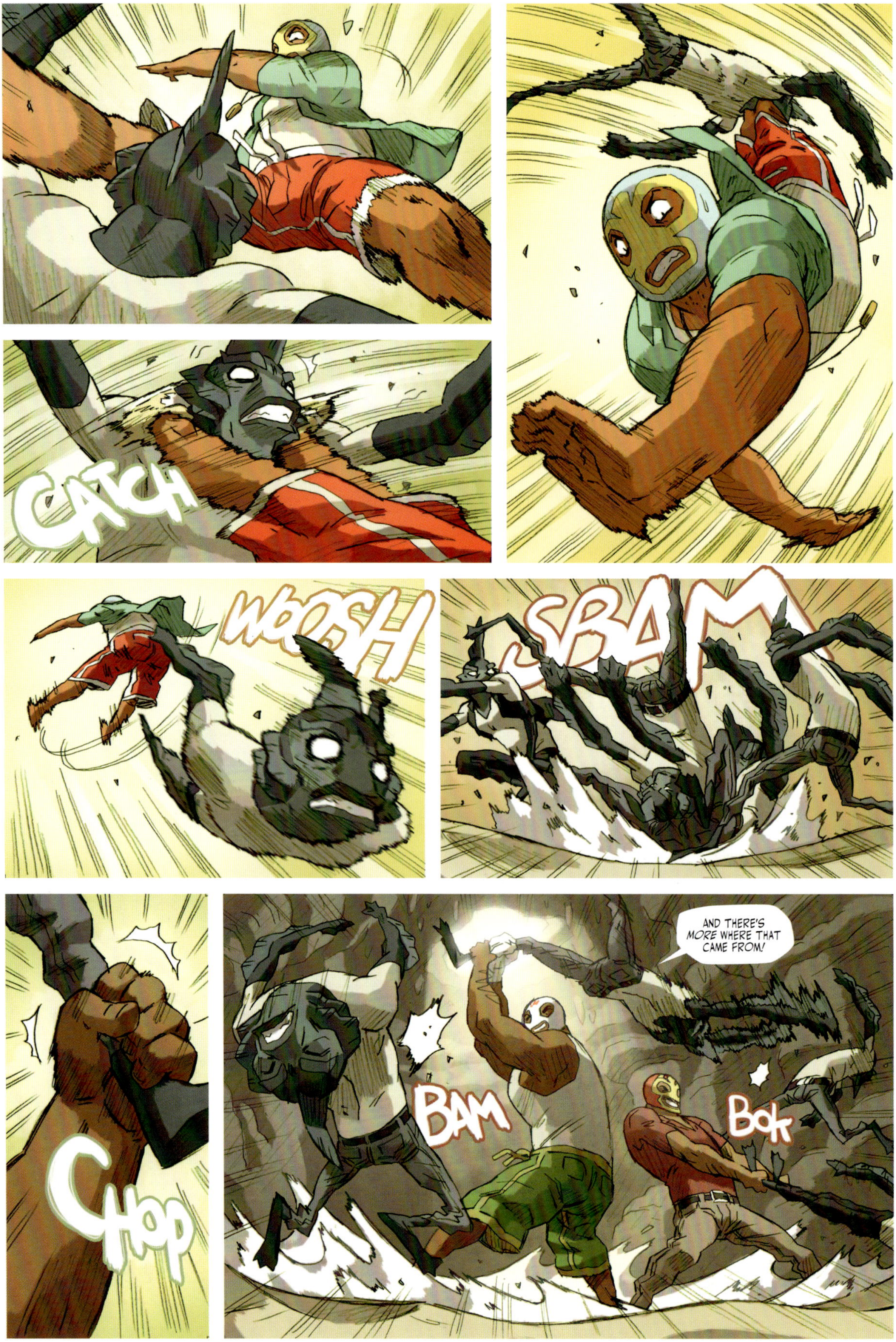
CATCH
WOOSH
SBAM
CHOP
AND THERE'S MORE WHERE THAT CAME FROM!
BAM
BOK

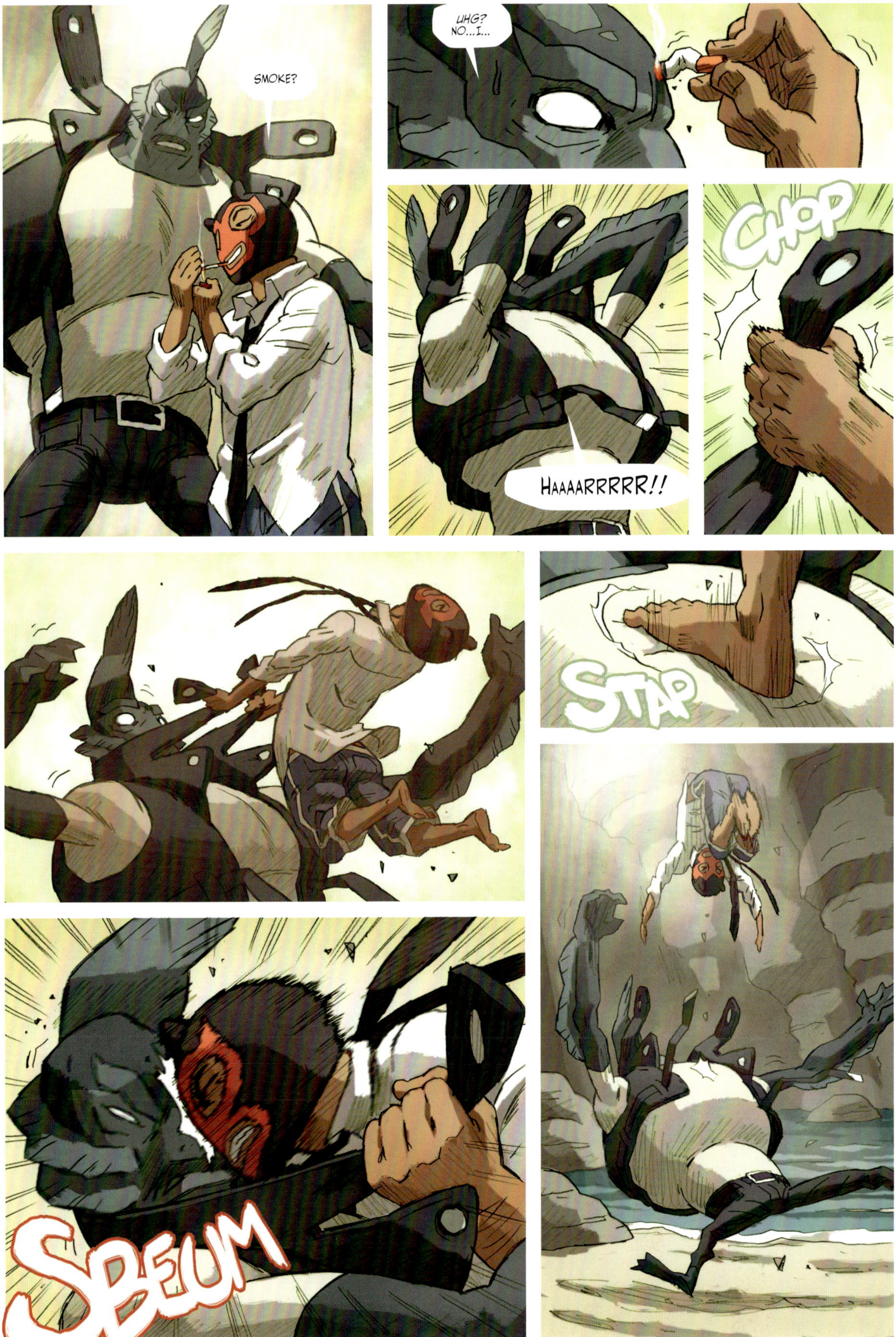
SMOKE?
UHG? NO...I...
HAAAARRRRR!!
CHOP
STAP
SBEUM

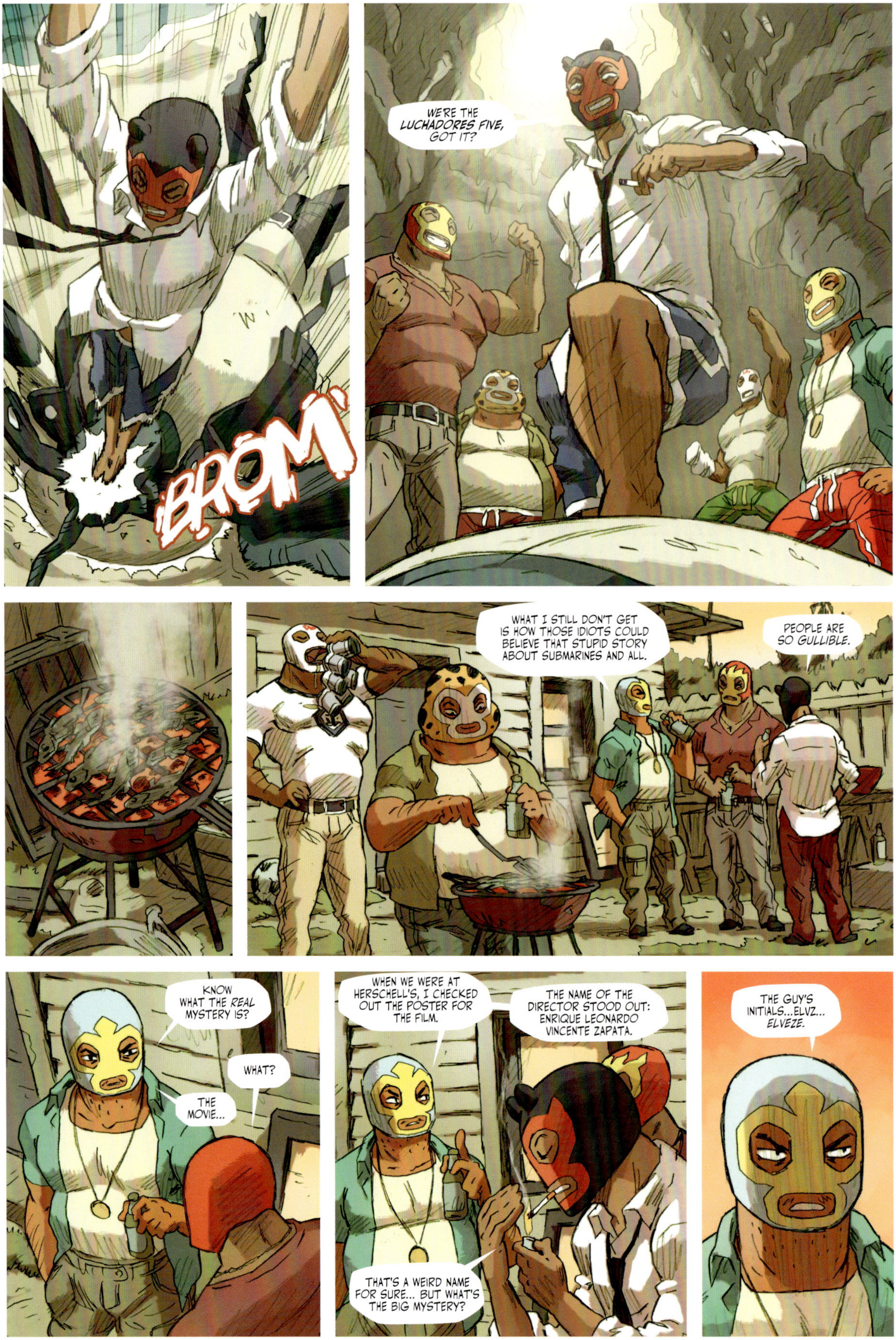
BROM
WE'RE THE *LUCHADORES FIVE*, GOT IT?
WHAT I STILL DON'T GET IS HOW THOSE IDIOTS COULD BELIEVE THAT STUPID STORY ABOUT SUBMARINES AND ALL.
PEOPLE ARE SO GULLIBLE.
KNOW WHAT THE *REAL* MYSTERY IS?
WHAT?
THE MOVIE...
WHEN WE WERE AT HERSCHELL'S, I CHECKED OUT THE POSTER FOR THE FILM.
THE NAME OF THE DIRECTOR STOOD OUT: ENRIQUE LEONARDO VINCENTE ZAPATA.
THAT'S A WEIRD NAME FOR SURE... BUT WHAT'S THE BIG MYSTERY?
THE GUY'S INITIALS...ELVZ... *ELVEZE*.

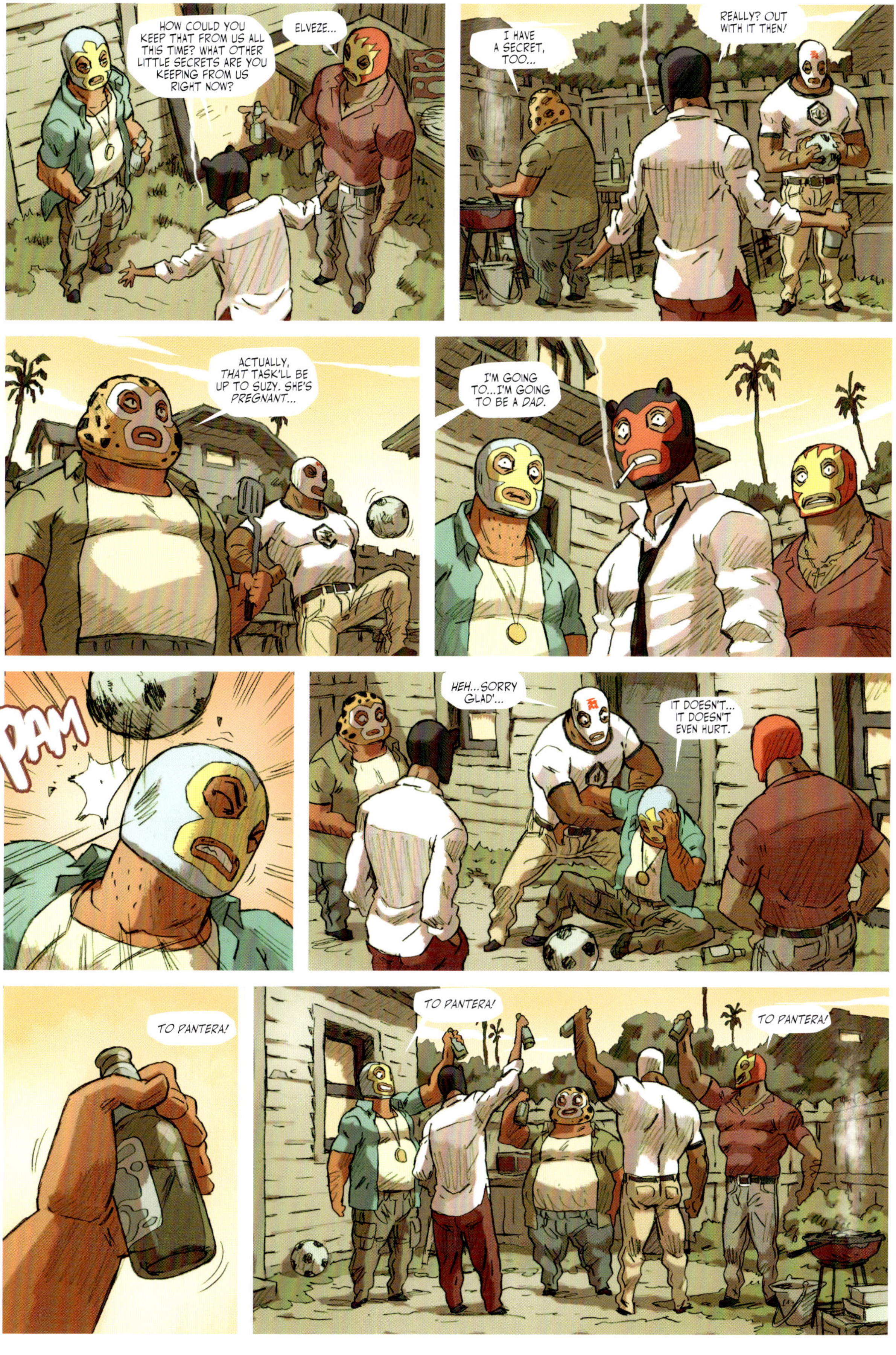
HOW COULD YOU KEEP THAT FROM US ALL THIS TIME? WHAT OTHER LITTLE SECRETS ARE YOU KEEPING FROM US RIGHT NOW?
ELVEZE...
I HAVE A SECRET, TOO...
REALLY? OUT WITH IT THEN!
ACTUALLY, THAT TASK'LL BE UP TO SUZY. SHE'S PREGNANT...
I'M GOING TO...I'M GOING TO BE A DAD.
PAM
HEH...SORRY GLAD'...
IT DOESN'T... IT DOESN'T EVEN HURT.
TO PANTERA!
TO PANTERA!
TO PANTERA!

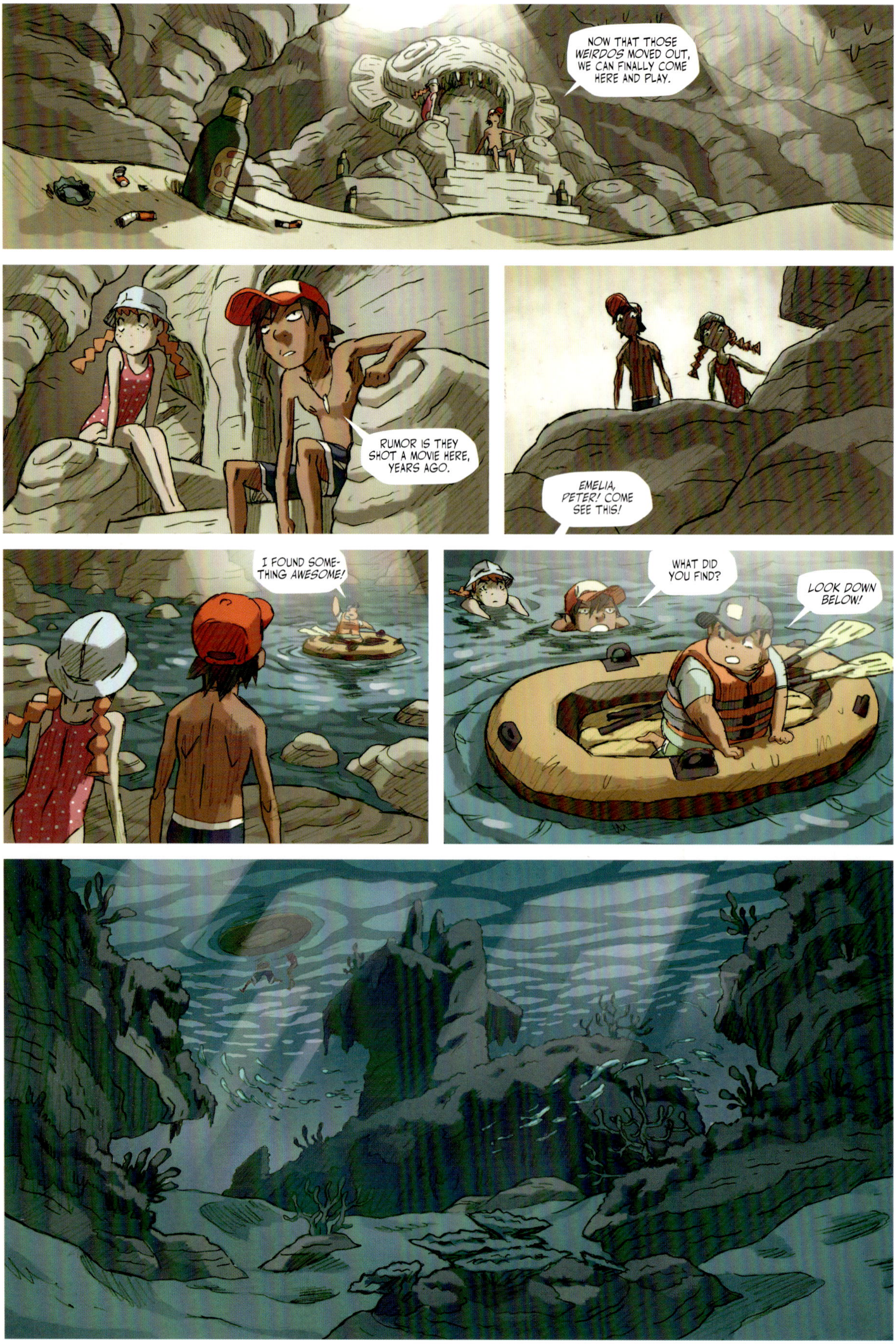
NOW THAT THOSE WEIRDOS MOVED OUT, WE CAN FINALLY COME HERE AND PLAY.
RUMOR IS THEY SHOT A MOVIE HERE, YEARS AGO.
EMELIA, PETER! COME SEE THIS!
I FOUND SOME-THING AWESOME!
WHAT DID YOU FIND?
LOOK DOWN BELOW!

THE END

AFTERWORD

by Philippe Peter

The rich catalog that has been carefully constructed over forty years by Les Humanoïdes Associés (the progenitor of US-based Humanoids) includes several oddities. From audacious projects launched in the cutting-edge monthly comics magazine, *Métal Hurlant*, back in its heyday, to simply daring gambles intended to shake up the established order of the Franco-Belgian publishing world. *Unfabulous Five* (originally called *Luchadores Five* in France) doubtlessly falls into this second category. One needs to be slightly crazy to imagine the burlesque adventures of a gang of equally deluded, but well-meaning, young men, who hide their faces behind wrestlers' masks, believing they are powerful superheroes. This unique group of friends, for whom one cannot help but feel a great tenderness for, bravely stare danger in the face without blinking when crossing paths with dangerous amphibious mutants; howling werewolves; or even "made in France" gangsters, still nostalgic for the past greatness of their beloved Gaul. The creators of *Unfabulous Five* never hold back. And that's what makes this series so impetuous: an abundance of ideas, unequaled audacity, the utter rejection of propriety, and massive amounts of creative energy.

Lucha libre: The trigger

Unfabulous Five was initially the story of "love at first sight": the emotion stirred in the heart of writer Jerry Frissen for the artwork of Bill. Contrary to what his first name would initially suggest, Frissen was born and raised close to Humanoids' own Francophone roots, in neighboring Belgium. He moved to Los Angeles as an adult and has lived there with his wife and children since 2000. Originally known as "Thierry," he changed it to something more Anglophone when Americans proved incapable of pronouncing his first name. Among other early activities, Frissen became *the* graphic designer for Humanoids. In March 2004, he came upon a short story that eventually appeared in *Métal Hurlant* #144, as part of the resurgence of the aforementioned seminal French magazine. The story was entitled *The Fight* (*La Bagarre*) and was told in three succinct color pages by a creator, here both writing and drawing, who went by the sole name of "Bill." It described a friendless child wearing a wrestler's mask who is constantly ready to fight, even with the sweet, young girl who's asked him to play. These three pages had been spotted by a member of Humanoids' editorial team during the 2004 Angoulême International Comics Festival. It was in the show's section entitled "Young Talents," that Bill had been selected. Frissen immediately fell under the charms and casual style of this young 23 year-old artist. It was mainly the tight purple and gold hooded mask worn by the story's young hero that awakened Frissen's gut instincts and reignited his interest in *lucha libre* (Mexican wrestling). Immediately, Jerry decided to write a story for

Bill who shared the same passion. It was also the perfect excuse for the Belgian expat to fulfill a long-held wish to set a story in Los Angeles, his adopted city.

A few days later, Frissen presented the project to Humanoids. It was his first since *The Zombies That Ate the World* (drawn by Guy Davis), a post apocalyptic saga with a dash of cynicism that had served as his calling card in the world of comics. Frissen plunged into this new series, incorporating elements taken from his own urban escapades on the streets of Los Angeles: Latinos in the city's various neighborhoods; the huge and sprawling Southern California freeways; the nocturnal comings and goings of locals; the many dilapidated buildings; crummy bars; and, last but not least, the red Pontiac Firebird that features prominently in the series. An eclectic collection of observations and facts, sometimes insignificant, spiced up the fantastical world of *Unfabulous Five* and, paradoxically, anchored the series in the reality of the daily life of this unique metropolis. Without a set plan—in the sense that *Unfabulous Five* does not have a moral of any kind—Frissen depicted one of the great paradoxes of the City of Angels, where the important Hispanic community—primarily Mexican in origin—lives within the city, while carefully preserving its language, culture and traditional codes. The tensions between them and the other communities are demonstrated throughout, namely through the intervention of a redneck during a brawl between our heroes and a gang of werewolves.

The project takes shape

The first chapter of *Unfabulous Five* appeared in #12 of the American edition of *Métal Hurlant*, in a dense 12 pages. Frissen had already set in place the daring concept of having many secondary characters appear as equally bizarre and deluded as the central protagonists, while being driven by their own inept or obscure goals (such as the werewolves stealing car radios). The idea that anything could happen became the trademark of this eccentric series. The story could easily have remained there, but Frissen revealed his true and "greedy" nature, as he later confessed, by managing to convince Humanoids to launch not one, but five ongoing series that would revolve around the theme of *lucha libre*. However, there was the challenge of finding the ideal artists for this epic wrestling fest. It was at this point that Gobi and Fabien M. climbed into the ring. Bill and Gobi had both attended the *Ecole supérieure des arts décoratifs de Strasbourg*, in eastern France, along with Fabien M. Gobi, who Bill first introduced his tale of Mexican wrestlers to, was immediately enthralled by the universe created by Frissen. Gobi then suggested a parallel series entitled, *Tequila*, the name of one of the former members of the *Unfabulous Five*, kicked out by their leader, El Gladiator. Fabien M. followed in their footsteps with *The Tikitis*, a series that follows the wild adventures of another group of masked do-gooders that reside on a paradisiacal Pacific island. So Frissen found himself with the challenge of writing three series with three young talented artists whose similar styles—a mixture of American comics, Franco-Belgian *bande dessinée*, and Japanese manga—were thoroughly innovative. Little by little, an even more eccentric idea dawned in the imagination of the foursome: a comics magazine totally dedicated to Mexican wrestling. Two years later, this dream became a reality.

Rather than publish the three series separately as traditional albums, the team wanted to offer the public a new reading experience, a total immersion in a wholly original new universe. The idea was initially quite challenging, both financially and logistically, but it eventually saw print as a 48-page anthology, aptly titled *Lucha libre*. Halfway between a magazine and a *Bande dessinée* album, this comics hybrid was published in French in 13 issues between August 2006 and November 2010. Artists Hervé Tanquerelle, Romuald Reutimann (*District 14*), and Witko were enlisted in this adventure alongside Bill, Gobi and Fabien M., all under the leadership of Frissen. The writer took full advantage of the emergence of Skype to organize tele-conferences between the United States and France, where the artists lived. Every three months the Lucha team produced several dozen pages of comics in order to feed their three main stories: *Unfabulous Five*, *Tequila*, and *The Tikitis*. A fourth story, *The Werewolf of Solvang*, began with #10 of the anthology, replacing the completed adventures of the *Unfabulous Five*. The rest of the publication was filled with a series of short stories (*Profesor Furia*, *Los Luchadoritos*, *The Formidables*, and *Los Triplicados*), as well as character bios, pieces on Mexican wrestling and even fake magazine articles, all produced by Frissen. This delicious mixture of offbeat humor, adventure, and crazy combat, all collided at the crossroads of comics, underground films, and pop culture. A stunning and fearless alchemy that has since practically disappeared from France's publishing landscape.

A mad style

The explosive style of Bill's drawings would be the great revelation of *Unfabulous Five*. If the initial pages created by the young artist (Jerry is Bill's senior by 20 years) had already captured Frissen's interest, the prodigy's following work would blow his collaborator's mind. The artist created a palette of characters that were very clearly identifiable by their physical attributes, as well as their distinctive masks. He also judiciously used the urban backgrounds to compliment his characters, good or evil. The settings even occasionally became the main protagonists of the story, such as the crowded streets that are regularly used by the masked superheroes; the sanctuary villa of Elveze; the underwater grotto where the old Z-movie was shot, and even the submarine that is sought by various adversaries. Becoming more assured, Bill's pen was increasingly lively and pointed, adding weight and solidity to the characters, while simultaneously providing a real sense of movement. From Book 2 on, the manga influences were increasingly more visible, notably during the fight scenes where the movements of the adversaries are depicted with assured fluidity. The absence of darker, heavy inking, that would have crowded the pages, gives them instead a sense of lightness. Bill began using a computer, eventually employing a *Cintiq* graphic tablet for his initial roughs before printing them and finalizing his work by hand. It was a technique that he specifically developed while working on *Unfabulous Five* and which he continues to use to this day.

A rare alchemy

While *Unfabulous Five* is very much part of the wider *Lucha libre* brand, the series remains the central focus of this crazy universe, where all genres and pop culture effortlessly fuse together. The 12-page short story published in 2004 became the first chapter in *Unfabulous Five*. This mellifluous mélange of multimedia is best seen in the second episode, which begins with a high angle shot overlooking a Los Angeles traffic jam where the reader discovers a spaceship stuck in the middle of it, with two extraterrestrial twins onboard that bizarrely resemble the Bogdanov brothers (scientists and hosts of a French TV program dedicated to UFOs). Later, the twins are kidnapped by thugs employed by Elveze, who, of course, owes nothing to The King... The next page explains that the cause of the traffic jam is the presence of a smaller, and less aggressive, Godzilla-like creature. Galvanized by the endless possibilities that the characters and the *Lucha libre* project itself offer, Frissen gave himself total creative freedom. The rhythm within the pages remains punchy and frenetic, with numerous plot twists and constantly new angles on iconoclastic characters.

The collaboration between Frissen and Bill will remain, at least in the annals of sequential art, as an ambitious and idiosyncratic adventure to raise the standards of the genre. It testifies as well to that rare and wonderful symbiosis between text and drawings that we know as comic books.

--February 2014